Reinventing the Bush

Inspiring Stories of Young Australians

Reinventing the Bush

Inspiring Stories of Young Australians

Marg Carroll

ABC
Books

First published by ABC Books for the
AUSTRALIAN BROADCASTING CORPORATION
GPO Box 9994 Sydney NSW 2001

First published in February 2008

ISBN 978 0 7333 2141 2

All photography, unless stated otherwise, by Marg Carroll
Poems by Glen Sheppard ('Accepted', 'Elvis Has Left the Building' and
'Topsy Turvey') and James Fitzpatrick ('Plenty', 'Peppercorn Hair' and 'A Breeze')
Artwork by Emily Murphy (*Imperceivable Emotion*)
Cover by Christa Moffitt, Christabella Designs
Internal layout by Agave Creative Group

Dedication

To my dear friend Jan Howe, who dedicated her life to nurturing young talent, and inspired me to have a go at telling the stories of the young. To my mum, Helen Hamilton, whose grit and determination I aspire to, and who believed I could do anything I set my mind to. And to all young Australians.

Life is like a wild tiger
You can either lie down
And let it lay its paw on your head,
Or you can sit on its back and ride it.

Ruth Tearle, *Ride the Wild Tiger,*
(Change Designs Publishing, 2005)

Contents

Introduction

Thirty per cent of young Australians live outside the coastal capitals. You'll find them in cities and smaller communities, on farms and scattered throughout the outback, yet rarely do you hear their voices. The constant babble of bad news about the bush tends to drown out a growing trickle of stories of hope, change and progress. In this book you'll meet nineteen men and women aged from 18 to 35 whose passion is rural Australia and its people. They are inspiring for who they are and what they do and together they present a vivid palette as they reinvent the bush. Their generation is our future.

Picture a tiny child facing pirates as she escaped Saigon on a dilapidated boat, or a young man trapped in his autistic world finding a way to communicate. Imagine how an Aboriginal teenager felt when asked by tribal Elders to lead his people, or the reaction of a young farmer, lying in hospital with a fractured spine, when she was told to forget her work and find a husband to care for her. These defining moments were, respectively, woven into conversations in the Riverland with Lisa Nguyen, over a kitchen table with Glen Sheppard, around a campfire with Murrandoo Yanner and on Deb McLucas's farm. They shed light on what made each person tick and how their characters had been shaped by the precipices and pinnacles of youth.

As I travelled the country gathering material for my first book, *Ordinary People, Extraordinary Lives – Inspiring stories from rural Australia,* and worked in community development in central western New South Wales, I found rapid change in many rural areas. It was confronting and disruptive for some, exciting for others. Many people and communities were caught in prolonged drought, debt and depression. Greater numbers of young people were leaving the bush hoping to find opportunities for education, jobs and adventure. Community leaders lamented the exodus of youthful vigour and talent and the political focus on big cities and big business.

The flow of people to the coast wasn't entirely one way; some were making tree and sea changes, discovering the challenges and joys of the bush. Back home on our farm, dams dried up and crops failed, forcing us to hand feed or sell sheep and cattle. As I pondered the future of rural areas, it seemed bleak – an opportune time to seek inspiration. I wanted to write the personal stories of young people who had promising ideas, tackled challenges, grabbed opportunities and showed the beauty of humanity. I naïvely thought the stories would be short and sweet. After all, how much living can these young people have done?

I was wrong.

The premature death of Jan Howe, a dear friend who nurtured young people's creativity through filmmaking, stirred me to think about making a documentary about young rural Australians. It meant finding people who were articulate and visually engaging for television. The pursuit was like a treasure hunt. Until you meet someone you don't really know what they will be like.

In 2003, documentary maker David Roberts and I set off for four states. We found dynamic people who were galvanised into action by what they saw as the glacial pace of change and crusty attitudes of policy makers or more conservative generations. We filmed Moira O'Brien's innovative management of cattle and land on a remote Territory station. On the Murray, Arron Wood was giving children the skills to teach their peers about river health, and in the Tasmanian highlands seventh-generation farmer Will Bignell was producing wonderful gourmet foods. Mayors Steve Perryman in Mount Gambier and Janie Dickenson in Launceston believed in consulting and involving their communities in decision making. A new breed of young leaders was creating new possibilities and fresh visions. In the end, the documentary wasn't to be, but I was determined to tell these stories.

The young Australians I interviewed opened my eyes, made me laugh and occasionally cry. Aboriginal men and women Trevor Menmuir, Cathy Duncan and the Yanner brothers, Bull and Murrandoo, revealed the imprint of brutality, neglect and ignorance on them and their families. It fuelled their commitment to bring about change in impoverished and dispirited communities. Two people had been uprooted as children and transplanted to Australia: Lisa Nguyen fled from Vietnam and Yasmin Mishare from Iraq as refugees. For them, war was all too familiar. They knew what it meant to leave all you know and love to resettle somewhere safe but completely foreign. Heath Francis and Glen Sheppard, remarkable young men, showed the strength of will – and support – needed to develop abilities when disabilities could have ruled their lives.

Many outback communities battled with levels of ill health, violence and early death akin to the poorest developing country. J Easterby-Wood turned his ingenious mind to revolutionising health promotion in central Australia, while Dr James Fitzpatrick harnessed opportunities for youth in isolated Western Australian communities through a mentoring program, True Blue Dreaming.

In my hometown of Molong, 18-year-olds Emily Murphy and Ellie Middleton highlighted the bonds of friendship and belonging that can form in a small town. Also originally from Molong was Beck Byrne (Carroll), daughter of my husband Bill and me. Sometimes it's tough to be who you are, as Beck and many young people discover in their search for identity. Beck and I ventured into confronting but ultimately liberating territory to tell her story of battling anorexia nervosa.

When I considered what these young people had in common, I realised that many of them had been shaped by experiences of trauma. Despite – or perhaps because of – their experiences, they valued each day, remained undaunted and cultivated their own opportunities. They shared characteristics of strength, courage and resilience, as well as a fierce determination to make a difference in their worlds. I loved their ability to savour life, usually at a clapping pace. The downside was often over-commitment for which some of them paid a price in their health and personal relationships as they aimed high.

All were open-minded learners and great communicators, generous in passing on knowledge. They managed time well, favoured teamwork, service to others and worked like beavers. They set goals driven by values to achieve their visions and ideals. Whatever their education level, these young people picked up the skills they needed from wherever they could and sought innovative solutions to problems. Many had been mentored and in turn mentored younger people. Families played a crucial role in their lives. They shaped their children's values and supported their endeavours. The parallels between Margaret Francis, Heath's mother, and Pam Sheppard, Glen's mother, were powerful as, against steep odds, each helped her son to achieve his potential.

Integral to the stories were Australia's landscapes, whether in the rugged Kimberley or the once-mighty Murray, the red centre or the Gulf – men and women had a deep connection to land and place.

The opportunity to explore a person's life is a precious gift. It was a privilege to have seen something of these nineteen people's lives, heard about their highs and lows and had the opportunity to get to know them. I have learnt much from each one.

Each of them give even staunch pessimists cause to hope. If you are young, may these men and women inspire you to pursue your dreams. If being young is but a distant memory, keep your eyes open for other young people who are shaping our future. They are everywhere – in our communities and workplaces, in our own family. Maybe you can give them a hand, an opportunity and some support or a pat on the back. It all counts.

Marg Carroll

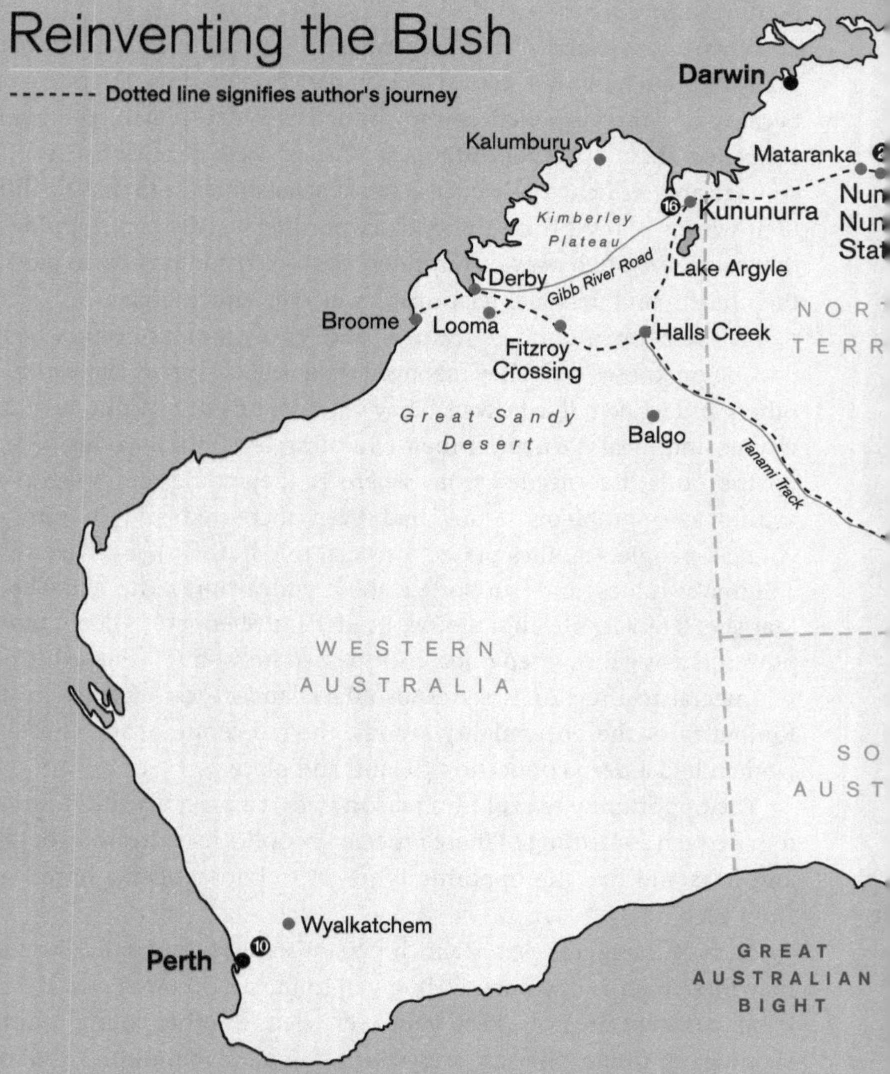

1. Arron Wood, Mildura, VIC
2. Moira O'Brien, Numul Numul Station, Mataranka, NT
3. Glen Sheppard, Nambour, QLD
4. Lisa Huong Nguyen, Berri, SA
5. Will Bignell, Bothwell, TAS
6. J Easterby-Wood, Alice Springs, NT
7. Janie Finlay (Dickenson), Launceston, TAS
8. Murrandoo and Bull Yanner, Burketown, QLD
9. Cathy Duncan, Moree, NSW
10. Dr James Fitzpatrick, Perth, WA
11. Deb McLucas, Middlemount, QLD
12. Mayor Steve Perryman, Mount Gambier, SA
13. Heath Francis, Booral, NSW
14. Emily Murphy and Ellie Middleton, Molong, NSW
15. Yasmin Mishare, Shepparton, VIC
16. Trevor Menmuir, Kununurra, WA
17. Rebecca Byrne (Carroll), Blue Mountains, NSW

GULF OF CARPENTARIA
Borroloola
Cairns
Burketown
8
Lawn Hill
Middlemount
11
Dingo
QUEENSLAND
Nambour
3
Brisbane
Moree
9
Darling River
Tamworth
NEW SOUTH WALES
Gloucester
Booral
13
Molong
14
Blue Mountains
Berri
4
1
Mildura
17
Sydney
Adelaide
Murray River
15
Canberra
VICTORIA
Shepparton
Mount Gambier
12
Melbourne
Port MacDonnell
Launceston
7
TASMANIA
Bothwell
5
Hobart

1 Arron Wood, Peter Garrett and children releasing 1000 yabbies into the Murray, 2003 International River Health conference. **2** Lisa Nguyen, age seven, and her Aunty Loan, Songkhla refugee camp, Thailand, 1980. **3** Glen Sheppard launching his second poetry book, *Elvis Has Left the Building*, Maroochydore, Queensland, 2002. **4** J Easterby-Wood in th gold jacket, accepting the Commonwealth Association for Public Administration and Management award, Singapore, 2005. **5** Will Bignell milking East Friesian sheep at Thorpe Farm, Bothwell, Tasmania, 2004. **6** Annual Inspection Day, Numul Numul Station, 2005: the traditional owners of Num Numul and lessees Moira O'Brien (*front*) and her family.

PART I
New Horizons, New Possibilities

Arron Wood on the banks of the Murray River, 2003

I

The River

Arron Wood, Mildura, Victoria

Dear Murray Darling Basin Commission,
The year is 2007 and I have just been for my annual check-up. I'm sad to report that I am grinding to a halt, especially at my mouth, which needs dredging to stay open. My arteries are clogged by salt and run-off from agriculture and towns. What with those 3500 dams, weirs and sluices, let alone countless irrigation channels that block my flow, my system hasn't had a decent flush in I don't know how long – little wonder my kidneys are packing it in. I've experienced droughts before, but this one is a corker. Blue-green algae are flourishing in my stagnant pools and poisoning the water. I used to be proud of my wetlands, the fish, the bird life, but it's hard to find a Murray cod or a speckled duck now – although the wretched carp seem happy muddying my bottom. My banks are bare and the red gums that shaded me for centuries are dying. My floodplain is also dying – for a drink. Some people think I can go on forever,

providing whatever water they want. They neglect to give any back. I have
to survive too. What will you do?

With concern,

Mrs Murray Darling River

'Here, we live on the driest inhabited continent, yet we are the greatest water
consumers on earth,' Arron Wood said. Arron, a practical and committed
environmentalist, has intelligence, passion and guts and he will need all that and
more to educate us on how to value and conserve our scarcest resource – water.

In October 2003, I flew to Arron's hometown of Mildura on the Murray
River to attend the One Life, One River, Our Future conference so I could find
out what it would take to return our rivers to a healthy state. A series of tents
was set up in the green, shady parkland along the river. It looked as if the circus
had come to town. Hundreds of children, chattering with excitement, crowded
into the main tent to find a seat for dinner. Tables were decorated with boxes
of oranges from this citrus-growing area. Music filled the air. It could have been
a rock concert about to start. Onto the stage stepped a young man with spiked
blond hair, a bouncy walk and impressive biceps. He flashed a smile at the
crowd. You might have picked him as a sportsman, or a television celebrity.

'Hi, everyone, I'm Arron Wood.'

The audience applauded wildly. 'Welcome to Mildura and the launch of
Water Week at our third International River Health conference.' Arron was 27
years old and already had seven years of environmental practice under his belt.

Over the following two days, 650 students and teachers from eighty schools
around Australia and other countries tuned in to listen about the state of the
rivers. There were no adults droning on about which hefty report said what or
flicking through PowerPoint slides: the presenters were 11- to 18-year-olds. At
the heart of One Life, One River, Our Future was an innovative concept dubbed
by students as 'kids teaching kids'.

'When students take responsibility for their own learning and know a topic
well enough to pass it on to their peers,' Arron said, 'it is the highest form of
learning. They decide on a local environmental issue, research it and tailor their
presentations for kids like themselves.'

The students were frank: 'We learn more from our peers because they
understand us. Adults can be long-winded.' These sometimes pint-sized
presenters knew their stuff. They captured audience attention through drama
and storytelling, problem solving and art, scientific experiments and,
occasionally, PowerPoint. Anticipation, genuine interaction and laughter
accompanied the polished performances on myriad topics: protection of native

fish, floodplain management, water quality and reducing community water use. Best of all, a spirit of generosity and fun prevailed: there was no parading of knowledge or put-downs of other students.

These students are the land and water managers of the future and here they were teaching each other to live in harmony with the land instead of battling it. I joined a table of four 10-year-old students and their teacher from Booborowie, a village of 100 people north of Adelaide. One child had never been away from home before; the others had never travelled outside South Australia. They felt like adults, as they registered and received conference packs and name tags, 'Just like Mum wears to work,' one girl remarked.

'Booborowie means waterhole in the local Njadjuri language,' said Rosie Catt, their teacher. In the days of early white settlement, the waterhole was permanent; 150 years later it had run dry. 'The town was using 30,000 kilolitres of Murray water a year – 53 per cent by households and a massive 37 per cent on recreation. In 2002 we became involved in a Goyder Council program to reduce reliance on Murray River water by 20 per cent.'

At the conference the following day, Arron's father Richard, who was employed by Arron as his education coordinator, stood in front of the stage and beckoned students forward. Each spoke for 60 seconds on their school's major environmental issue and how they were dealing with it. One student wobbled in on crutches and three small girls delivered their message as a rap. One Booborowie student walked up to Richard, took a deep breath, then proudly told the audience how children at her school had done water audits at their homes and discussed ways to reduce consumption. The community newsletter produced at the school spread the word among the local community about water-saving ideas and the children received publicity in local newspapers. Gradually, change occurred – all toilets in the school, recreation ground and hall changed to dual flush and the school and hall had rainwater tanks installed to catch run-off. Families took advantage of a $200 council rebate for water-saving devices to install such items as low-pressure shower heads and front-loading washing machines in their homes, and tap timers and dripper systems for their gardens. This student smiled as the audience applauded. The message was clear: if a small school such as Booborowie could trigger change in its community and the effect was multiplied throughout the nation, environmental change was no pipe dream.

Arron and his father recently wrote and self-published *Inspiring Our Next Environmental Leader*, a kids teaching kids resource. In it, Arron compares the fragility of our water resources to the magnitude of human needs. 'A human can survive for only three days without water. On average close to 300 children die every minute from drinking contaminated water. Our world, the blue planet, is approximately 75 per cent water and our own bodies mirror this amount of water.' Arron suggests we take a one-litre bottle of water and imagine it represents all the water on the planet. Then, extract one capful, which represents the 3 per cent of fresh water available; the rest is sea water. But even all of that 3 per cent is not accessible to us because it is locked up in the polar icecaps or deep underground.

Next, we suck up one tiny drop in an eye-dropper. This drop represents all the water our world has for drinking and cooking, washing and toileting, and for crops and animals. 'It is this drop that causes so many arguments between irrigators, farmers and greenies and is likely to be the stuff that wars will be fought over between those countries that share major rivers,' said Arron.

Ticky Fullerton, ABC journalist and author of *Watershed: deciding our water future*, uses the word 'war' for disputes within the country. In a speech she made to the South Australian Parliament, she said that 'The truth is Australia's precious water supply is way over-allocated. State governments in charge of water are stuck in the middle of a war between water users – municipal, irrigators, other farmers and environmental groups'.

The Murray–Darling basin, which covers one-seventh of Australia, is the lifeblood of Queensland's southern region, New South Wales, Victoria, South Australia and the Australian Capital Territory. Only 6 per cent of our rain falls on the basin, yet Australians rely on it for 40 per cent of agriculture and 90 per cent of irrigated agriculture. Added to that, the Murray–Darling river system provides drinking water for 3 million people and supports 30,000 wetlands.

In October 2006, the Murray–Darling basin drought summary statistics based on 115 years of records showed that the basin was gripped by a drought 'more typical of a 1-in-1000-year event than a 1-in-100-year event'. The basin had received only 550 gigalitres of flow in 2006, just over half that of the horrific federation drought of 1902, in which it had 1000 gigalitres (1 gigalitre is 1 billion litres, equivalent to 500 Olympic-sized swimming pools). All aspects of the system were dramatically affected: trees, animals, birds, fish and other aquatic life, agriculture, rural communities – as well as the rivers.

'The inflow that would really make a difference is 3000 gigs; the compromise is 1500,' Arron said. 'The Murray stops flowing at Mildura in dry years. Adelaide then has to be serviced by the Darling River, which joins the Murray below Mildura. Throughout the basin the flow is overwhelmingly regulated by dams and weirs that lose a huge amount through evaporation. Eighty to 90 per cent of the red river gums below Mildura are dead or dying due to rising salt because they are missing out on middle-level floods, which upstream users siphon off.' A note of pessimism crept into his voice as he indicated the skeletons of once magnificent 500-year-old trees across the billabong. 'The scary side is that there were reports of salinity in the Murray River in 1908, 100 years ago, and we're still trying to deal with it. I hope we aren't fighting about these same issues in 20 years. If there are no flushing floods, the only thing that will save the rivers is the return of environmental flows.'

In her book *Watershed*, Ticky Fullerton argued that the water issue is about money and the focus on the basin's 2500 rice growers and 1500 cotton growers deflects blame from successive governments whose policies have promoted unsustainable water use. She identified the nearly $1 billion trade deficit pushing exports such as irrigated agricultural products to increase and states boosting their coffers by selling as much water as possible to the public.

At the time of Arron Wood's first River Health conference in 1999, the environment was just one of many national issues. By 2006, citizens in country towns, on farms and in cities across Australia were discussing water. A litany of problems from the worst drought in a century, disturbing climatic change and severe water shortages made national headlines almost daily. Arron Wood despaired at the lack of political leadership and will to act.

'We don't have time to waste. There is no new source of water on this planet. It is all recycled. A muddy puddle can evaporate and flow back to us as rain. The water our ancestors used is what we use also.'

In the absence of a magical solution to severe climatic problems, including drought, Arron suggests we have to use what water we have more wisely.

'Why not put the large federal budget surplus into something worthwhile for the environment, instead of giving small tax breaks to each citizen?'

He thinks that young people, their minds uncluttered by political considerations, could teach our leaders about conserving the environment.

Arron's touchstone is what he calls 'The River', which gives him his sense of place, of community and of the future.

'I grew up here on the banks of the mighty Murray. I used to wake up to fantastic sights and sounds every day,' he said as he pulled a kayak from the water in front of the family home. Across the billabong glided a black swan and cygnets, a solitary pelican and a medley of ducks. Fish shelter in reed beds along the edge. A flash of azure follows an occasional 'plop', as a kingfisher does what he does best. Kings Billabong, which curves into the Murray, looks pristine.

'When I was a child I used to be able to see my feet in the water here,' Arron said. 'Now you can just see your hand under the surface. Pollution, turbidity and run-off have all played a part. I want every Australian to feel passionate about the environment because I think that is the only way we'll turn around our massive issues.'

He wants to pass on something to be proud of to his children. 'I'd hate to have to say, "Sorry guys, we messed up. It's now up to you to sort it out."

Complacency – you and me not getting off our butts – is as damaging as pollution.'

We sat under the sprawl of a red river gum. Arron looked tired and had a heavy cold. The conference has taken its toll. A quiet paddle on the billabong is rare relaxation in his frenetic lifestyle. His parents, Dianne and Richard, joined us on the lawn. They have strongly influenced their sons, Arron and Liam, to conserve resources and to serve the public good. Richard is a kindly, measured man, Dianne warm and vivacious. She is of Indian origin, but local Barkindji people think she is one of them because of her dark hair and eyes. They also claim Arron, thanks to his mother.

'With Mum a teacher–social worker and Dad as my school principal, I was in trouble from Day 1. I was always in his office in primary school. I probably made some teachers tear their hair out and wonder why they'd chosen teaching.'

Dianne agreed. 'At the age of five, he painted another child's face and was banned from art. Richard was Mildura district arts adviser at the time. The story went around the community like wildfire.'

Arron managed to embarrass his father often in his early years. Richard was concerned about his son so he applied for a job as principal at Irymple South Primary School in Mildura, thinking he would be able to control Arron's education and keep an eye on him. His son had other ideas.

'I decided I could pretty much do what I wanted with Dad as principal,' he recalled, 'although as his son I was supposed to be a good role model.'

'On my first day as principal,' Richard said, 'some older students rushed into my office. "There is a Year 3 boy peeing over the oval fence," they said. Arron's defence when I caught up with him was, "But Dad, it's a long way from the oval to the toilets".'

'I disrupted other students and was always doing silly things, like, in Year 3 I started my dad's car in the school grounds and rammed the bike shed,' Arron said.

'A very naughty boy,' Richard chimed in.

Like many boys who are the bane and the joy of a teacher's life, Arron wasn't good at settling down in the confines of a classroom. He liked to touch and dismantle things to see how they worked. He later found out he was a kinaesthetic learner, one who discovers the world through action, loves sports and games and expresses themself through mime and drama. In their book, Arron and Richard observe that kinaesthetic learners can exhibit so-called behavioural issues because they don't learn well in classrooms dominated by the written word.

Arron's classroom was outdoors. He started a BMX bike gang that roamed the wild bushland around Kings Billabong, spent hours canoeing and fishing in the early morning mists and played football with his mates. David Attenborough was Arron's hero and he aspired to be a wildlife documentary maker. When Arron was in Year 5 and Liam in Year 3, Richard led a teacher exchange to Alaska. Family holidays spent camping in national parks from Alaska to California stimulated Arron's interest in the environment.

Back home at Red Cliffs High School, he entered a darker realm.

'Almost every afternoon for four years two boys used to follow me home from school and beat me up. I tried to befriend them, but it didn't work. I tried to change myself and become quieter. I kept thinking, Why me? I didn't want to go to school. If I hadn't had family support, it might have damaged me more. I kept it to myself, except for telling Mum. It was a secret from Dad because we didn't want him to react protectively. He knows now and was upset he wasn't told. I was taught not to hit back, but I should have dropped them early on. When I have kids, if one of them tells me they're being bullied, I will tell that child, "Defend yourself". Bullies can destroy a child's confidence.'

In 1992, the family accompanied Dianne on a two-year teacher exchange to Montana in the United States. His time there had a big impact on the teenage Arron, who made new friends and was able to enjoy high school. He built himself up, trained with weights and played American football. It is so rough a sport that players wear helmets and padding for protection. By the time he returned to Mildura and Year 12, Arron knew how to defend himself.

'I thumped those guys,' he said with satisfaction. 'It made me aggressive for a while. I used to get into fights after school and at uni. I would still like to tear one of those boy's arms off.'

That's no idle threat, I suspect, and shows the depth of feeling in this otherwise mild-mannered man. The experience has made Arron protective of sensitive children at the River Health conferences.

'I say at the conference outset – "I would like you to show respect for each other". We don't see one kid giving another kid a hard time there.'

Arron went on to study forest science at Melbourne University. His father pinpoints that period as the time when his son's conservation views started to gel. In Arron's final year he won a scholarship to study national park management and environmental communication at Chang Mai University in Thailand. The experience brought home to Arron the necessity for fresh water and clean air and the realisation that these resources cannot be taken for granted as they are in Australia.

'It was the first time I had lived in an Asian country or spent a long period overseas without my parents,' he recalled. 'The smells, humidity and lawlessness were an assault on my senses. I had to finish a 10,000-word thesis in third-world conditions. It was like nothing I had experienced before and it hammered home the reality about other parts of the world after the cocoon that was Melbourne University. I think it is part of our psyche to need to get off the beaten track. To explore and discover new things satisfies early instincts and an innate requirement to challenge ourselves. In modern times we find it so much more difficult to do.'

Arron graduated in 1997, having majored in communications and politics in the water industry.

'I came home for Mum's cooking and decided I wanted to contribute something to my own community.'

The river played a pivotal role in Arron's decision to stay in Mildura; saving the river system soon became his life's purpose.

'I missed its calm and beauty, its permanence,' Arron said. 'I got a job for a few months as environmental officer with Mildura City Council and part-time work as Water Watch coordinator with the Lower Murray Water Authority. Then, I moved to the Mallee Catchment Management Authority as a waterway –floodplain manager.' At 22, he was the youngest waterway manager in the state.

Arron's parents were pleased that he was settled in a government job.

'I sat at the first three managers' meetings and didn't say a word. Gradually, my confidence grew. By 1999 I had become deputy chair of the Waterway Managers group.'

Arron was seeking a way to spread the message about water usage and river care into the community and his father, by then principal of Mildura West Primary School, was looking for a way to give more responsibility for learning back to his students. Richard implemented three-way reporting for parent–teacher interviews so as to involve the students, who would explain to the adults what they had learnt that term and the goals they had set for the following term. Richard instigated greening of the school, which was rundown, had few trees and a major litter problem when he arrived. Over 500 students planted trees and began recycling. The school also adopted man-made Lock Island in the Murray River and began to revegetate it. That's where Arron came in.

'I began working with Dad and a group of dynamic teachers. The kids and I created a nature trail with signs about why floods were important and what they meant. It taught me a lot, because I not only had to source funding, but I also had to draft up signs with students, use a shovel to put the signs in the ground and develop the path.'

For three years in a row the school won the Victorian Rural Pride award in the Keep Australia Beautiful competition for schools. The Lock Island project gave Arron an inkling of something larger than the technical issues he was tackling. He started to wonder how he could bring together his knowledge and skills in a career that would enable him to stay in Mildura and realise his dream of helping the environment. In 1999, in conjunction with his father and Mildura West Primary School, Arron decided to organise a Young People's River Health conference in Mildura.

Arron had to raise $60,000 for the conference. It was uphill work because he was unknown and education was not core business for potential sponsors. The Catchment Management Authority helped with funding, but didn't consider educating kids as core business either, so Arron and Richard worked on the project outside their normal jobs.

'I photocopied loads of stuff after hours at Dad's school and individually packed 1000 mailouts to schools along the Murray,' Arron recalled. 'I didn't know how to manage a website, wasn't sure whether schools would be interested and didn't know if I could get the money. It was a huge leap of faith.'

Richard Wood's belief in and experience of students taking responsibility for their learning was crucial. Arron could see its application to the environment, but to take it a step further and apply student-centred learning to a conference presentation was both radical and confronting for many teachers. It required a shift of power within the classroom or, ideally, in the school. Richard realised how daunting it was for many teachers to hand power to their students to plan and prepare a workshop presentation. In *Inspiring Our Next Environmental Leader*, Richard described how he urged them to try it and reassured them that 'they would find the outcomes and depth of learning far outweigh the disquiet of power-sharing'.

Teachers guided the learning areas, but the students chose their topics. They took the theme of that first conference seriously and, in the process, became mini experts. 'Tell me and I will forget, show me and I may remember, involve me and I will understand.' Arron aimed for a head, heart and hands approach to young people that could combine their passion for environmental issues with the rigour of their minds, and then translate their work into practical action projects. The schools organised mentors in industry and natural resource management to work with students for months before the conference to support and help them get their facts correct.

'We tempered the enthusiasm of the young with the wisdom of older people by connecting them in this relationship,' Arron said. 'Mentoring created a powerful cocktail of students learning from older people and industry linking with schools.'

Two interrelated concepts formed the educational basis. The development of the resilient child, as it was known in the literature, one who is motivated, has high self-esteem, respect for other people and can bounce back from adversity, was introduced alongside the student-centred, or kids teaching kids approach. Children learnt how to cater for the different abilities and learning styles of their peers. Their teachers, with guidance from Richard and Arron, helped students recognise that some of their peers loved words, others numbers; some were creative, others active, and some liked to learn in groups while others were more solitary. To engage all of these learning styles, the students experimented with presentations that tackled hard scientific data through drama, problem-solving scenarios, scientific data collection and analysis, storytelling, poetry and music or a combination of several approaches.

The conference attracted over 300 students and teachers and an array of celebrities.

'Kids were battered around the ears by bad news about the environment,' Arron said. 'We involved celebrities such as botanist David Bellamy, and Ian Kiernan, founder and chair of Clean Up Australia, to make the environment fun and to help identify ways forward.'

'That first conference was a great success, but we were both exhausted,' Richard recalled.

The following year the Murray–Darling Basin Commission (MDBC) was looking at running a student conference in New South Wales. Arron had already started to plan the 2001 River Health conference, so he and Richard spoke to the Commission and they agreed to combine forces. Since then, the MDBC has had conference-naming rights in return for financial support. Arron's workplace would support the conference if it was conducted outside his floodplain management role. He argued that community education was vital to his role, to no avail. During this period he and Damien Heintze, a workmate, used to meet in the pub every Friday after work and hatch plans for sweeping change to save the river system. After eighteen months they felt they had talked long enough and decided to start their own environmental business. They handed in their resignations to the Catchment Management Authority and sold their cars for start-up money.

'We called our business Firestarter and gave ourselves six weeks. It was a bold move.'

'Arron took Dianne and I out of our comfort zones when he said before the 2001 conference that he was starting his own business,' said Richard.

Damien and Arron wanted to concentrate on community education. They knew there was brilliant scientific research being carried out in institutions such as the CSIRO, but the information wasn't getting through to the community. Arron's experience had shown that many people wanted to do the right thing by the environment but felt frustrated and cynical or didn't know how to. At one end of the spectrum, scientific reports complicated the issues; at the other end, governments favoured public meetings, forming taskforces and doing lengthy studies that often went nowhere.

'We wanted to break environmental information into bite-sized chunks and communicate it so people could understand it and not feel overwhelmed. We believed you didn't have to be experts to make small changes.'

Arron was 23 when he instigated the first Young People's River Health conference. By the next conference, two years later, decision makers were beginning to take notice. Leith Boully, chair of the Community Advisory Committee to the Murray–Darling Basin Ministerial Council, described the 2001 conference as 'nothing short of magic'. Arron's initiatives in environmental education saw him awarded Young Australian of the Year for the Environment in 2001.

'What a high,' he exclaimed. 'I started to realise that if you made the right contacts, you didn't have to remain a green campaigner on the outer.'

Something wonderful was happening when students taught each other. They felt a sense of control over what they learnt and how they learnt it. Students were also learning to communicate and relate to one another, their mentors and teachers. A teacher reported a discussion her class of 11- and 12-year-olds had as they prepared their presentation. They anticipated their peers' responses – with accuracy, as it turned out – and countered possible problems. 'We can't have boring worksheets; kids will roll their eyes. We want kids involved in activities. Hands-on is best. We want to include a play to get our message across because kids like seeing other kids act. We need time for kids to discuss and ask questions. When we use a PowerPoint presentation we need to have less writing and more pictures.'

In their workshop the students had all the materials they needed at their fingertips, integrated technology into the presentation, engaged the audience in a hands-on activity, provided reflection time and kept to time.

The learning approach was proving any student's capacity to be a gifted pupil and a leader, provided they had guidance and support. Arron remembers a 10-year-old boy who researched the life cycle of the carp and knew his information inside out.

'I accompanied the boy to a local radio studio for a conference interview. The interviewer provided a comprehensive summary of the conference and then asked the student, "And how is the conference, the food, the workshops?" No question about carp. She thanked him for coming and was about to wrap up when the boy politely said he had a few things to add. He proceeded to tell listeners about his findings on the carp and concluded by thanking his mentor and the interviewer for promoting the conference.' Arron chuckled as he recalled how the interviewer was left speechless. 'This student demonstrated all the hallmarks of a future leader. He allowed the interviewer her agenda, but was not about to surrender his own ground and message. Leadership can be demonstrated by all of us, at any age.'

Arron calls it leadership in practice. Teachers involved in the conferences agreed. One quote from post-event evaluations was, 'The students that we brought along had a brilliant time and what I thought was amazing was that they all came away with a profound confidence in their ability to instigate change'.

Children had shown themselves to be credible agents for change. Some years earlier, a local newspaper had reported that a sewage treatment plant was to be built in Albury and that it would discharge effluent into the Murray. That prompted the school where Richard was principal, Irymple South Primary at Mildura, to form Kids Action on River Environment, or KARE. KARE sent postcards to other schools along the Murray that were downstream from Albury, asking about the state of the river in their location. Four thousand children replied. KARE sent cards to anyone with influence over the river – politicians, newspapers and television stations – and members requested a meeting with Albury City Council to discuss the proposed sewage plant. The students prepared for the meeting by collecting and interpreting data with the help of mentors who understood the situation and honed their questions. As a result of the meeting with Albury Council, its plans changed and council planted trees along the Murray rather than discharging effluent into it. KARE's actions made headlines from Adelaide to Albury. Many KARE members later moved into natural resource management.

Arron invited a high-profile green campaigner to open the 2003 conference. Peter Garrett, then head of the Australian Conservation Foundation, was well known to students through his band, Midnight Oil. With his gangly frame and distinctive, shaven skull, Garrett stood out in the crowd, but what really captured the audience were his words. In clear, punchy language, he outlined the challenge – drought now occurs two out of three years instead of one in 20, as in the past. Tens of thousands of red river gums are dying as a result of salinity. The giant Murray cod is threatened with extinction. Worst of all, there is a lack of leadership.

'Our challenge is to restore flows to the river, so we have a healthy system for future generations to enjoy,' Peter said, 'but our challenge, even greater than the health of the Murray, is to learn to live with nature rather than destroying it. My message to you is to learn about the nature of your country. Learn what needs fixing and become as literate in the natural environment as you are in maths or English.'

Peter and Arron took every opportunity to recommend to policy makers that environmental studies should be part of the core curriculum in every Australian school. For Arron and Richard that campaign is ongoing as they continue to negotiate with education bodies for a central place for the subject and to train environmental educators.

At lunchtime, the students joined Peter and Arron on the banks of the Murray to release 1000 yabbies. Children carried paper cups of water containing the tiny yabbies to the river; some children named their yabbies as they walked along. Arron was everywhere, a cool head, seemingly untiring, as he solved last-minute problems, did a string of interviews, welcomed celebrities, chatted with children and autographed their T-shirts. You only needed to find a cluster of children to find him. The conference was designed to make students feel special – from accommodation at the Grand Hotel, with its gleaming wood, and uniformed staff, to connecting them with influential politicians such as Deputy Prime Minister John Anderson and federal Agriculture Minister Warren Truss.

Workshops showed flair, knowledge and imagination. The River Murray Youth Council, which takes in communities along the river, devised The Water Train: the audience represented water flow from the source of the Darling River to the mouth of the Murray. Along the way, participants joined or dropped off the train as salinity, irrigation, weirs, evaporation and draining of wetlands affected flow. By the river mouth at Goolwa, only two of thirty participants were left. The message was powerful – with its flow removed by farming, industry and communities, the basin is under severe threat.

Later, at a media gathering on a riverboat anchored nearby, Arron's fresh face contrasted with his media savvy and eloquence as he explained the importance of the conference to assembled journalists. Two young sisters, who were cub reporters for their school paper, gathered their courage and questioned Peter Garrett and Arron, who gave them the same considered replies as they did the seasoned reporters. Local, state and national media brought the event to a wider audience. *The Big Arvo* aired it on Channel 7 and the ABC's *Australian Story* dogged Arron's footsteps.

'*Australian Story* came back to see me several times,' Arron said. 'Being a subject was pretty scary. Dad was worried because he had seen stories make or break people. He didn't want our integrity to be zapped overnight by a certain angle. Then nothing happened for eighteen months. My story was seen by some ABC people as too positive.'

At this time, Arron's parents were teaching refugees on Christmas Island. Richard emailed Arron. 'We always ask, What next? It's important to give everything our best shot, but what you do cannot be diminished if the *Australian Story* does not screen. There are other things in life.' The story did go to air, just as the Athens Olympics opened in 2004. Well-known Mildura restaurateur Stefano di Pieri, introduced it as a story about a young man he had once employed in his restaurant who was now tipped by both sides of politics to be one of Australia's next generation of leaders. Despite the ABC's misgivings, 1.6 million Australians tuned in; the story outrated the news and

The Bill. Arron was inundated with emails from viewers who responded: 'Thanks for a positive story – enough of bad news.' And the emails weren't only compliments. People were inspired to do something for the environment.

Arron has been approached by the National Party and the Democrats. He intimated on *Australian Story* that he might think about entering politics in the next 10 years.

'It is impossible not to consider when you're in the environmental game. I'd love to go as an independent. Toeing a party line is not the way I operate. I started my own business to get away from that sort of thing.'

That episode of *Australian Story* opened doors for his business. The ACT chief minister asked Arron to set up a youth forum in Canberra. The publicity also helped offset months of intense self-questioning about where the business was going.

'I had to buy out my partner in early 2004. There wasn't enough money left to pay me,' Arron said. 'I felt like a failure. I despaired that three years had gone for nothing because of debts and difficulties getting sponsors for the 2005 kids' conference. It was going to cost $450,000 to run the event. I was about to chuck Firestarter in – the flame nearly went out – when the Catholic church contacted the Murray–Darling Basin Commission about a school project; MDBC suggested me. We went from a low point to taking on a full-time employee and my brother as a part-time staffer.' Then it turned into a crazy year as Arron mustered strength to kick-start three major campaigns and again wrestled with staff and money issues. The business was at a turning point: he needed to keep it afloat and manage the workload.

By early 2005, Arron was upbeat again. He bought a house, although he was in two minds about being tied down.

'I have an issue with being committed to one place for any extended period,' he said at the time. 'My mates are getting married and having babies, but I'm happy where I am at the moment. At 30, I'm still quite young.'

Arron joked that three successful River Health conferences brought Firestarter to the attention of no less than Pope John-Paul. Catholic Earthwatch, the environmental arm of the church, wanted Arron to introduce kids teaching kids about the environment to the church's schools Australia-wide. It saw the potential to reach 5 million Catholics.

Jobs also flowed in as Arron's reputation as a facilitator spread; however, some jobs were voluntary and didn't help the cashflow. State governments were beginning to recognise water as an issue and Arron facilitated a forum in Sydney for Sydney Water about its plan for a desalination plant. Citizens questioned this direction and raised other options.

'The New South Wales Government wants to proceed with desalination,' Arron said. 'It's a copout, a huge cost to build and maintain and will produce unacceptable levels of greenhouse gases. They haven't seriously examined recycling stormwater and sewage, which are currently pumped out to sea. Consumers will have to pay five times more for desalinated water than for recycled water.'

Arron co-produced a documentary and an accompanying DVD for the Victorian Government, *Our Water Our Future*, which was shown on Channel 7. In it, he delved into the big questions of why we need to save water and whether climate change is really upon us. His communication abilities made him a natural for television: he interviewed individuals and business operators who used effective water-saving measures. A designer recycled grey water onto gardens. A dairy farmer drip irrigated, instead of using spray or flood irrigation, and recycled his farm effluent onto paddocks. A municipal council treated wastewater instead of pumping it out to sea. The documentary reinforced Arron's belief in the capacity of television to reach a mass audience and give people an understanding of and ideas for environmental change.

'The challenge is to market the environment as effectively and forcefully as a commercial company promotes its products, so it becomes something everyone is thinking about.'

A Victorian Women's Trust survey of 75,000 people identified water conservation as the state's hottest issue. The powerful Trust enlisted Arron, along with musician John Butler and other prominent environmentalists, as champions for its Watermark program. Their brief was to promote forums to develop solutions for water and create national momentum on the way people think and act about water. Three thousand participants contributed to Our Watermark, a charter that established national goals and actions anyone could use immediately to monitor, reduce usage and re-use water.

As Arron juggled these projects, his long-held dream to see Mildura become the national environmental education centre received a fillip. The UNESCO-approved initiative of a biosphere was coming to fruition. The Barkindji Biosphere, named after the local Aboriginal tribe, would link water, land and biodiversity management over a vast area. Arron could see it attracting people to Mildura and stimulating environmental awareness, business and jobs for young people in the region.

The Barkindji Biosphere launch was in April 2005 at Mildura, the Catholic Earthwatch launch in June and the first South Australian regional River Health forum in July. The Watermark campaign launch was coming up in September. Landcare groups and schools wanted Arron to do water audits, decision-making bodies such as Sunraysia Area Consultative Committee wanted him on the board, TAFE wanted him to lecture on the environment and Arron had a regular environment program on ABC Radio. With his higher profile came invitations to speak every second day on how to integrate the health and care of the environment into community activities. As well as the major conference in Mildura, Firestarter managed regional events at Narrabri, Broken Hill, Adelaide, Toowoomba and, in 2006, Bendigo and Canberra. All this and a business to run. Success was beginning to catch up with Arron.

The International River Health conferences had grown to such an extent that by 2005 the event reached 1100 children and teachers in the lead-up and throughout the conference. Arron applauded the respect children showed each other and how workshop presenters were becoming more strategic. A team from Warwick State High School in Queensland had reported to the New South Wales parliament on the decline of the Darling River. They tested the water from Warwick, where the river was in a 'fair-to-good' state, to Pooncarie in New South Wales, which they described as 'horrible'. When children from Saint Paul's Primary School in Mildura urged local irrigators to donate unused water entitlements to counter the effect of drought on red river gums along the Murray River, they raised 12.95 megalitres of water. One child told his father he hated the rubbish where they fished. His father, who was on Wentworth Shire Council, took notice and, as a result, the council pulled nine truckloads of rubbish from the Darling River.

Arron's vision of schools across Australia producing the environmental stewards and workforce of the future was becoming reality, but the price personally and financially was high. The cost of running conferences was growing and, although Firestarter encouraged schools to seek financial backing, in the end chasing sponsorship was Arron's job.

'River Health conferences come around every two years and they take all of that two years to organise. We have barely finished one and we are into the next one to source funding. We put in 16-hour days in the build-up to such a huge event. We have the massive return of kids doing things, great media stories, and then – nothing. It's a real downer. I've been physically sick afterwards. It's like a marathon: the build-up, the event, post-victory, and then – what do I do next? You almost question your direction.'

Arron didn't lock in a break after the 2005 conference, but flew straight to a speaking engagement. He invested much time and energy in an eight-part television series on coastal environments for Channel 9 that didn't eventuate. Firestarter went from its best-ever funding year in 2005 to a period of no funding.

'I needed a fortnight away to do nothing so I would feel refreshed, but the lack of finances meant I had to keep working,' Arron said. 'I made our project officer, Cathy, take two weeks holiday, but didn't heed my own advice.'

In his low periods Arron wrestled with his deep desire to make a difference in the field he had chosen, while having to live with the uncertainties of running a small business. The irony did not escape him that he had started his business so he could remain in Mildura, but with success and the travel costs around the country he was forced to relocate to Melbourne.

'I thought about taking a good job in a corporation and not having to worry about running a business. I could just enjoy life, but then I wouldn't have the highs of Firestarter. When I worked for the government, it took six months to do anything, whereas on my own I could decide on something and go ahead. I liked having that control and not having to answer to anyone. I also didn't have to wear a shirt and tie.'

In 2006, Arron received a letter from the United Nations Association of Australia congratulating him on becoming a finalist in the 2006 Outstanding Individual Service to the Environment award.

'It was a real shock, but I felt empty inside,' he said. 'I was facing burnout. For six months, I hadn't wanted to go to work. Day after day jobs fell through and things went wrong. We were so much at the whim of sponsors, always putting ourselves out there. The business I had built up with employees who believed in me looked like folding. I had to borrow money from Mum and Dad. I wasn't sleeping and lost nine kilos. Then I broke up with my long-time girlfriend and realised how quickly you can slip down. One more thing can be the straw that breaks the camel's back.'

After struggling on for months, Arron broke down one day when his mother called him. She was worried and insisted that he see a doctor. He was diagnosed with depression and put on anti-depressants.

'It was pretty hard to accept and took me a long time to realise what was going on,' Arron said. 'I joined the burgeoning ranks of Australians looking for answers. It was certainly the darkest period of my life. I would do anything not to go through that again. A regular break would probably be what I needed to keep me going.'

It was in the middle of this depressive bout that Arron learnt that he had won the UN award.

'I was honoured, but you can't stick an award in the bank.'

Gradually, with the support of family and friends, Arron began to recover and see that something positive could come from his depression.

'It has given me more life experience when I talk to kids about the importance of resilience. Depression affects one in five people at some time in their lives. I hope with every project, speech, school visit and newspaper article that I can convince another person to hang on. Better still, I hope our programs can arm the next generation with skills to deal with good and bad times. People thank me for talking about these issues. But I didn't go to a meditation course as I had planned because I was too busy,' he said ruefully. 'That was a mistake.'

Given the overwhelming nature of environmental issues, it would be little wonder if Arron had felt like a voice crying in the wilderness against multinational corporations, political ignorance and individual apathy. He puts his faith in students such as 12-year-old Kelly Sylvester, a student at Mildura West Primary, who wrote him this letter:

> **I live in Mildura and attended the 2005 International River Health conference. I must say (probably like every other kid that attended) I LOVED IT. My school's presentation of the Barkindji Biosphere has been very successful. All of these things wouldn't have happened without you, so THANK YOU VERY VERY MUCH!!! I consider you my Idol and Biggest role model and one day hope to be as successful in teaching others about the environment as you have been.**

Arron sits on influential boards, such as the Port Phillip and Westernport Catchment Management Authority, and he and Firestarter have reached the finals in many awards. As well as being awarded the 2001 Young Australian of the Year for the Environment and being the youngest finalist in the 2003 and 2005 Prime Minister's Environmentalist of the Year awards, he was 2002, 2003 and 2004 finalist for the Eureka Science Prize, 2003, 2004 and 2005 finalist in the Banksia Awards and 2004 and 2005 finalist and 2006 winner in the United Nations World Environment Day Awards.

'Awards and accolades justify us in sponsors' eyes, so I'm over the moon when we are selected, but we have to be prepared to go to an event and not win.'

Arron tells students that they can achieve great things, but the only true measure of success is whether they feel happy. His aim is to make his business secure so he can take regular breaks.

'We are on the brink of signing this big deal with the Feds, but it doesn't take much for the business to go back down. I need to be careful of my own health.'

By early 2007, Federal Minister for the Environment Malcolm Turnbull agreed to Arron's proposal to guarantee the next two years of regional forums and the 2007 conference and has committed $500,000. Arron is elated. He still has to source another $500,000 in matching sponsorship for the $1 million program, but solid backing will give him some respite from the constant struggle to source sponsorship.

Coming up in 2007 is a string of high-profile events: Melbourne Water Yarra River Youth conference for World Environment Day, Portland–Port Fairy Youth Environmental conference and, for the first time, a New Zealand event – Enviroschools Youth Jam in the North Island. Enviroschools is a non-profit organisation that has significant government support to run sustainability programs in schools. The International River Health conference will be in Canberra instead of Mildura, thanks to strong support from national capital organisations. Arron has invited world environment leaders David Suzuki and Al Gore to speak, part of his strategy to awaken Australians – citizens, industry leaders and politicians – to the importance of the environment. In May, Richard and Arron will fly to New York to pilot a kids teaching kids project with five schools as a precursor to an international kids' conference in the USA in 2008.

In January 2007, he was buoyed to hear that the federal government is committing $10 billion to a 10-point water plan. The Commonwealth wants to assume control of the Murray–Darling system from the states and to deal with wastage and over-allocation of water in the basin. The plan includes $1.5 billion to improve water efficiency on farms and $500 million to boost river flows; there will also be investment in irrigation infrastructure, metering, buying back licences and reducing water usage.

'It should have come 40 years ago, but providing it returns water to the environment the plan is sound,' Arron said. 'It's exactly what I have been advocating since the day I started my first job. It's only common sense for this dry continent.'

Dire predictions from eminent researchers such as 2007 Australian of the Year Professor Tim Flannery and Sir Nicholas Stern, former head of the World Bank, put global warming centre stage. The Stern Report found that 'floods from rising sea levels could displace up to 100 million people; melting glaciers could cause massive water shortages; 40 per cent of all wild species could become extinct and droughts could create tens of millions of climate refugees'.

Business as usual is not an option. In April 2007, the prime minister announced zero irrigation allocations for permanent crops from the Murray–Darling basin after 1 July if good rains have not replenished the flow – emergency planning to deal with a pending disaster.

'The true cause of every environmental issue is that we have not lived as part of the environment,' said Arron. 'To bring about real change, we must understand that we are part of a dynamic system and live on this planet as if we intend to live here forever. Why not an environmental levy from every Australian? It wouldn't differentiate between rural and urban dwellers and would focus awareness on the environment. Because people constantly ask where their levies are going, it could be set up similar to what happens with council rates. We can't simply say that because farmers and industry use 70 per cent of water or resources that they should pay 70 per cent of the burden of repair because city people consume most of the produce and expect cheap, clean and green produce on their tables year round. All Australians could contribute, even if only a nominal fee, so they understand that we're all in this together. The levy would need to be coupled with a carbon tax on polluters, similar to the Swedish user-pays system.

'If we don't have clean air and water, it doesn't matter what our share portfolio or salary is. If interest rates rise 1 per cent, that becomes an issue for most people, but if the temperature rises 1 per cent and polar ice caps melt, the consequences will be catastrophic for the planet.'

This letter from an unknown River Health conference participant gave him hope.

Dear Murray–Darling Basin Commission,

The year is 2020 and I have just gone in for my annual check-up. I am writing to report that thanks to the revegetation program and the fact that I have removed salt and nutrients (surplus to my requirements) from my diet, my doctor is thrilled with my recovery. Threatened species have returned to my flow and I feel wonderful. My lower reaches are grateful for the flow of healthy salt-reduced water. South Australia was dying before. Now I am restored thanks to the vision of the students from the International River Health Conference in 2001.

From Mrs Murray River

Arron says he wants to spend more time on longevity than business. 'I don't want to be on my deathbed saying I should have spent more time with someone.'

Aside from the serious stuff, he loves being active – a run in a city, a workout at the gym, scuba diving or snow skiing. He loves the outdoors, the crisp air, the sound of snow underfoot.

'I like to get away with the family to Marlo at the mouth of the Snowy River. We used to go there in summer when we were growing up. Liam, Dad and I enjoy the fishing. That's where I aim to build an eco-friendly house.'

Arron has been awarded a Churchill Fellowship for 2008 to work with the United Nations in New York and Geneva on implementing environmental programs on a global scale, particularly in developing countries.

'I really want to make an impact in environmental education. I would like kids to look back and say they went to a River Health conference and it changed their lives. Ultimately, I do what I do because I'm damn scared about where we're heading. I'm alarmed about big business getting bigger, our lack of tolerance for others and the weakening family unit. I see the environment as a means of unifying people of different races and religions.'

Although children are only 20 per cent of the population of Australia, Arron believes they are 100 per cent of the future. He sees his life's work as imparting skills, knowledge and optimism about the environment to children so they will be able to deal wisely and confidently with the immense issues the world faces – and maybe teach their parents and grandparents a thing or two along the way.

Postscript

The man who only eighteen months before was deep in depression about his business has hit his straps in 2007. Arron won the prestigious Prime Minister's Environmentalist of the Year Award and the 2007 Melbourne Award for Contribution to the Environment. He has completed the training with Al Gore to become an Al Gore Climate Change Messenger and is now an ambassador for Sustainability Victoria. In October, he and his father Richard released their book *Inspiring the Next Young Environmental Leader, Kids Teaching Kids – Addressing our environmental crisis*.

'Best of all, I've finally locked in to do the Vipassana ten-day meditation course in December 2007.'

Arron and his father, Richard, Murray River, Mildura, 2005

Moira O'Brien and friend, Numul Numul Station, Mataranka, NT, 2003

2

Welding a Family of Bosses

Moira O'Brien, Numul Numul Station,
Mataranka, Northern Territory

It was 6 o'clock on Friday, 1 August 2003. The sun's rays slanted over the horizon. A young woman tiptoed across the breezeway, Moira O'Brien, first up and ready for a long day of cattle work. Bodies began to unfurl from their stretchers on the cool breezeway, except for the persistent snorer, who slept on. He was lucky not to cop a flying boot on my first night at Numul Numul Station. Within minutes, Moira was dressed in faded jeans and a blue shirt and setting out breakfast on the two metre long table, a magnificent slab of African mahogany milled by her father Mike. We downed porridge, coffee and toast and were ready to roll by 7 o'clock.

Moira is the youngest of a family of four – a petite, attractive 26-year-old brunette with a turned-up nose and eyes that sparkle, even at 6.30 in the morning. She enquired how we slept. She can smile – she had several walls between her and the snorer.

The O'Briens moved south to the Roper River from the Top End in 2001. Numul Numul Station is 100 kilometres east of the oasis town of Mataranka and its soothing, hot pools. Moira, her parents Mike and Clair, her brothers Patrick and Felix, and her uncle, Rory, took on the massive job of rejuvenating the 500-square-kilometre cattle station. Dinah, Moira's sister, lives in Darwin. Home is two dongas separated by the breezeway, shipping containers with holes cut in them for doors and windows. The complex might not ever be featured in *House and Garden*, but it serves the purpose and saves precious money for the essentials of a working station.

I first met Moira in Canberra in September 2002 when she was finishing her three-year term on the federal government's Regional Women's Advisory Council. Moira, immaculate in a cream suit, was the youngest member. She was just as capable of advising Deputy Prime Minister John Anderson on young outback women's concerns as mustering cattle at Numul Numul. On an isolated station or at the centre of political influence, the focus and determination of this articulate, poised woman is unchanged.

It was the middle of the Dry season. Red dust billowed around us as Mike and I set off in style in the old Toyota. Mike's Irish forebears would have approved of his dry-as-Territory-dust humour, the luxurious, ginger-grey beard and the tall, battered hat perched on his bald pate. He proudly pointed out the miles of new fencing, gates that swing and repairs to the extensive cattle yards that the family have completed in their two short years here. Rusty-ochre anthills, a metre or so high, stand guard over the land. Stands of silver-leaved gums hem the paddocks of savannah grassland. Mobs of grey or red Brahman cattle shelter in the shade of thornbushes and sweet-scented, yellow-flowering kapok trees.

Moira and Patrick caught us up on their workhorses – the quad bikes. Our first job was to move the cows into the main yards for pregnancy testing. Mike left the truck and we set off. I rode on the bike behind Moira. As we bumped around trees alongside a big mob, Moira told me about her childhood.

The O'Briens lived in north Queensland at Craigs Pocket on the Atherton Tablelands, at the headwaters of the Burdekin River. Their fourth baby was to arrive only 15 months after the third child, Felix, but Clair, Moira's mother, didn't know what date to expect her. Clair and Mike drove the eight-hour journey into Cairns to wait for the birth, only to have the doctors tell them the baby wasn't yet due and send them home. A few days after returning home Clair went into labour. She called the Royal Flying Doctor Service (RFDS) in Cairns on the two-way radio and activated their emergency response by blowing a whistle. A doctor instructed her to puff on Ventolin, an asthma medication, to suppress the contractions. The airstrip on their station was not quite ready, so Mike drove Clair to nearby Valley of Lagoons Station, which had a suitable landing strip. To guide the plane in to land they lit flares in upturned flowerpots along the strip.

'Mum made it to the hospital,' Moira said. 'Dad had to return home to pick up the other three children and drive to Cairns in a small cattle truck. The placenta had to be surgically removed. Mum had blood transfusions and spent three days on a drip. If it were not for the Royal Flying Doctor Service she would have died having me at home.'

Clair has always raised money for the RFDS and the Isolated Children's Parents Association, organisations vital to people in outback areas. Her own childhood on a sugar cane farm near Cairns taught her to be self-sufficient. At the time she and Mike were married, Clair still had to rely on a generator for power and a two-way radio to communicate with the outside world.

'We were connected to town power in 1983, but had no phone until 1989. The whole of north Queensland could hear you when you used the two-way radio.'

For Clair and Mike, their children's education was a top priority. They drove long distances for School of the Air activity days when their children could meet children from other isolated stations and learn to mix. Moira had six years of correspondence education through School of the Air and Primary Correspondence School. At one stage, the children had a turnover of four governesses in six weeks. A governess needed special skills and qualities and it was no simple matter to find someone with the experience and stamina to teach four strong-willed children in three different grades. The person also needed to fit into a big family and be canny enough to know when the children were trying it on. One poor governess was invited to try quinine berries, which parch the mouth.

'We didn't have a good run,' Moira laughed. 'I was eight then. Mum wouldn't sack a governess until the next one was ready to come.'

Clair's mother, who lived out of Cairns, would assist in finding new governesses. After she had interviewed another prospect, she and Clair would discuss the applicant in code because people were listening on the two-way. If the governess was suitable and could start, the code was 'The parts you ordered are ready to pick up'. If the governess couldn't come, it was 'raining cats and dogs in Cairns'.

'Mum and Dad thought academic results were a bit overrated. Their philosophy was just to do your best,' Moira said. 'They valued culture and common sense. Uncle Rory, who was an ex-teacher, encouraged us on the academic side. Mum wouldn't hear of us going to boarding school in Charters

Towers because it was still in the bush. She wanted us to see live theatre and have a wider education; she thought we would become insular if we didn't.'

Moira and Dinah went to St Patrick's, a college in Townsville with 140 boarders. During the holidays, Moira brought home girls from Papua New Guinea who lived too far away to return to their homes each holiday.

'I was a shy teenager. I kept my head down and worked hard. I wasn't outgoing until my early twenties. People think that School of the Air students will lag behind academically, but three of us at St Pat's who were ex-School of the Air were in the top 10 per cent of the state in Year 12.'

Clair and Mike instilled the values of doing a job well and helping others. When Moira was in Year 8, she admired a senior girl who did community service.

'I wanted to emulate her,' Moira recalled. 'I coordinated students to help Amnesty International. We raised funds and collected books for kids in Somalia, or did door-knocks for charities like Red Cross.'

Her efforts were recognised by a Christian Leadership award, created to honour a senior student who finished as dux and head girl the year before Moira and was killed in a car accident.

'Go west, young (wo)man' took on a new meaning in 1993 when three generations of Moira's family moved lock, truckloads of stock and barrel from their well-established north Queensland station to the allure of fresh challenges. The station they bought, Carmor Plains, bordered Kakadu National Park in the Top End of the Territory. Moira was 16.

'Our family cattle stud, Coodardie, had been supplying Brahmans to Territory stations for years. Dad and Uncle Rory saw the potential of tapping into the live export trade to Southeast Asia and made the decision to move,' Moira said. 'If we had stayed in Queensland, I might have worked in a city, like Dinah. As a kid I wanted to be a stud cattle groom. Brahmans are totally a part of me. They have so much personality, affection and intelligence, as well as being useful – a total package really.' She laughed at two cows nearby that were shoving each other. They are handsome but comical creatures with their smooth white coats, floppy rabbit-like ears and wobbling humps and dewlaps.

The move to Carmor Plains changed the direction of the family's lives. Even Moira's grandfather moved with them. A convoy of four road trains did trip after interstate trip until the 3000 cattle had been moved.

Moira was part of a close extended family. 'Uncle Rory and G'pa had lived with us all of our lives. G'pa was no bigger than I am, but a charismatic personality. He had been a dairy farmer. His father, Felix, went goldmining in WA with a mate, Paddy Hannan. Paddy went on to discover the main gold-bearing lode at Kalgoorlie.'

Moira's great-grandfather must have had the luck of the Irish. He made money from gold then moved to Queensland. As he was fencing a block outside Brisbane he struck silver and later donated the mine to University of Queensland at St Lucia in Brisbane.

'I believe it's the only uni with a working mine shaft on its site,' said Moira. 'However, as a result of a run of poor seasons, a massive drought and a devastating fire, the family didn't stay wealthy. Dad and Rory grew up on a dairy farm. They milked the cows by hand before going to school. G'pa was a hard worker. He had wanted to move to the Territory after the war. By the time we moved west in '93 he had dementia. You learn patience and acceptance when you deal with someone who has Alzheimer's disease.'

Unfortunately, some people found it too hard to visit her grandfather in his last decade as his personality changed and he didn't recognise anyone.

Moira said, 'He was still sweet-talking the nurses in the nursing home. He and an old lady would carry a chair outside and place it against the fence so he could climb over. The first nursing home mostly housed people with alcoholic dementia. G'pa would get so frustrated with them. "You lazy buggers," he'd say, and he'd pull them out of bed. "Come on, get up and out to work." He instilled that strong work ethic in all of us.'

After finishing high school, Moira received offers from universities to study applied science or fine arts. She decided to defer for twelve months so she could help her parents establish Carmor Plains, but floodwaters at the station, which held up the mail, meant her deferments were never entered and lapsed. Instead, Moira studied native flora and fauna three days a week at Jabiru TAFE in Kakadu National Park, two hours drive from Carmor Plains. The Lands, Parks and Wildlife Management course helped her understand her new environment. Moira's social life revolved around cattle.

'We never ever went on family holidays, but to cattle shows or friends' places for bull sales.'

The family trek from Queensland to more promising land turned into ten tough years. The move coincided with the collapse of the Asian economic markets in 1998 and plummeting cattle prices. A succession of excessively wet years hit their floodplain property. In a bold move, Clair O'Brien turned a feral pig problem in the wetlands into a small but lucrative business. She was delighted when Kakadu Floodplain Pork, which was vegetarian pigs fattened on wetland plants, sold for more per kilo than cattle did.

'We had three markets for the pigs,' Moira said. 'Germans came for safari hunting, pigs were harvested, dressed on site as game meat and exported to

Germany, and Mum sold her Kakadu Floodplain Pork on the home market.'

Clair's free-range floodplain pigs were captured in traps or from quad bikes with ropes on poles. They were taken to Darwin abattoir to be transformed into gourmet sausages, bacon and ham and sold to classy restaurants in Darwin, Alice Springs and Sydney. Her mother's venture taught Moira about ingenuity and survival in downturns.

In 1996, she became involved in the Top End Cattlemen's Association as its first secretary. Her older male colleagues recognised Moira's potential as a leader. At the 2002 annual general meeting, a weather-beaten cattleman put her name forward as president.

'"We need fresh blood. What about a young bloke?" he said as he looked around the room. "How about Moira?" So I had a new job.' Moira laughed. 'The Territory is ahead of other states in involving women because of our smaller numbers and the kind of people it attracts. I've never considered my age or gender an issue. People take you for who you are and how you behave in different situations.'

Her intelligence, matter-of-fact manner and presence, even at the age of 25, stood her in good stead to work amiably with older men, to seek advice and lead wisely.

Seven years after the move to the Territory, Moira finally made it to university in Darwin, but not to study applied science or fine arts. She did the degree that would most help the family business.

'Nobody wanted to do the farm accounts or the GST,' Moira said. 'I can't say I particularly enjoyed them either, but somebody needed to do the financial side. So I studied business and majored in business law. At the end of the day we are all doing business, whether we are selling shoes or cattle. I wanted to learn from the perspective of city people and it was a good chance to teach them about the bush. It gave me a few extra tools in my toolbox.'

In the first few months Moira found it was difficult to meet fellow students at Darwin University: 'They would rock up to classes and then disappear', and she too was busy three days a week on Carmor Plains. It took her a day to travel to and from Darwin and full-time study was crammed into the other three days.

'I was used to going to places where I knew nobody, so I didn't expect to feel lost or lonely,' Moira said, 'but it wasn't until the first exams that we business students really started to speak to each other. Then I began to make friends.'

She equipped a travelling office and carted the all-important laptop, file boxes and printer around. That way she could keep university and station work separate.

'I learnt to use every bit of time I had.'

Moira maintained a distinction level in her business degree, regularly travelled to Canberra from 2000 to 2002 for the Regional Women's Advisory

Council, chaired the Top End Cattlemen's Association branch and worked full tilt on the station.

Moira described Carmor Plains as special country. Its beauty lay in its wetlands teeming with waterbirds and estuarine crocodiles, and the flora of swamp paperbarks and magenta and white waterlilies. After battling for years with poor cattle prices, the encroaching sea waters, and hungry mosquitoes and mites taking their toll on the breeding cows, the O'Briens decided to move again.

'We looked at many options and as a family decided that these girls here' – she indicated the cows – 'and their bloodlines were the most important thing.'

After much soul searching, they took a radical step and chose to sell their land, keep their cows and lease good cattle country further south. Half of the Territory is Aboriginal-owned; other vast tracts lie in corporate hands or are national parks. It made good sense to family members to free up capital and lease instead of having all their assets tied up in property.

'We successfully tendered for Numul Numul,' Moira said. 'The station had only been unmanaged for three years, yet the deterioration was extensive. We spent more than $150,000 to bring it back into operation. The traditional owner, Sammy Bulabul, had a dream to see it as a working station again but didn't have the resources or skills to make it happen. It was his desire to lease the land to people who would genuinely care for it and not just put on as many cattle as possible and create erosion. The Aboriginal sense of family is strong and they could see three generations of us working together in our family-operated business. It was a good starting point for mutual respect. We moved down here two years ago and the property hasn't looked back since.'

In 2001, the station was one of just three in the Northern Territory leased from Aboriginal people. The O'Briens saw it as an opportunity to pioneer a new kind of partnership between pastoralists and Aborigines.

'Getting the people story right is the key with the lease,' Moira said. 'Each party knows its boundaries. They have their land for the community and we have our leased area. This Numul Numul community has a long history in pastoral development. Drovers came through here on their way to the Kimberley, but it was first opened up as a cattle station called Roper Valley in the 1940s.'

The O'Brien home is only four kilometres away from the community. Numul Numul people come to the homestead if they need help or have generator problems. Felix, Moira's brother, a fitter and machinist by trade, is the generator expert and all-round fixer. Mike regularly drives Sammy Bulabul around to see the progress and discuss future plans.

'We all work together as you do with many things in the bush,' Moira said. 'Getting everything up and running – the infrastructure and even the grasses, has been mind boggling. We've got no regrets. We're happy with the community, they're happy with us. Although it is Aboriginal-owned land, we consider it's our responsibility to look after it and to leave it in better shape than it was. We're hoping we can extend the lease after the five-year contract finishes in November 2006. We'll visit the community this afternoon.'

As co-director of the family business Moira put her business law degree to immediate use by selling and promoting the 3000 head of Coodardie stud Brahman cattle to other stations. She is a lynchpin and without her expertise, the high standards set on Numul Numul Station would be difficult to maintain. Her brothers ask her advice on stock management and her father gives her the chance to try any job.

'My philosophy is, "If you don't have the skills, learn them".' Moira follows her own advice: she developed expertise in the everyday tasks of drafting and branding and in the specialised jobs of pregnancy testing and spaying. She picked up the veterinary skills needed for the station through short courses and onsite demonstrations from mentor and artificial breeding guru, Alf Turner.

We arrived with the mob at the yards. There were no brawny men on horseback wheeling mobs of wild cattle in the red dust to the crack of whips and the thunder of hooves. Moira, Patrick and Mike quietly shifted the mob into the holding yard – no yelling, no stockwhips, no cattle prods. The family has adopted low-stress handling techniques introduced to Australia by American Bud Williams as a method of moving cattle without violence or noise. Moira and the boys stepped slowly backwards and forwards beside the cattle, rather than pushing them from behind. It looked like a strange dance movement. They were manoeuvring within the flight zone of the animals – or, in human terms, their personal space, to shift them.

'When we bring the cattle up the race it's a fluid movement. We don't have to yell or use sticks. It's really effective. Without stress cattle keep their weight. They are priced per kilo so that's really important.'

This technique has clearly been an important breakthrough in stock management as the animals are quickly drafted, turned up the race and shut into a small enclosure for pregnancy testing. These cows are not small, but Moira is. She pulled on a long plastic glove and proceeds to insert her hand up to the armpit in the rectum of a big red cow. She feels about inside the cow for the reproductive tract from which she can estimate the stage of pregnancy or whether the cow is barren.

'We are early adopters of large-scale preg testing as standard practice. It increases fertility. With any cow that isn't in calf, I remove its ovaries in a spaying operation and it goes on a boat for live export.'

Much hinges on Moira's skill and strength. After testing 100 Brahman cows, she looked worn out, but didn't stop for a breather. As well as pregnancy testing cows, the O'Briens semen test the bulls they offer for sale. The aim is to breed top-quality, easy-care, fertile cattle. By 2006, Moira had learnt to collect and process the semen onsite at the station. She tested for fertility and kept some for artificial insemination.

'I warn the bulls to watch out, I'm after more than a drop. Our customers are guaranteed a bull that can work, not just a fancy looking steer that's no good to them.' Right on cue a majestic grey bull with sweeping horns ambled past and looks bewildered when we burst out laughing. 'Buyers soon learn to ask that all bulls be semen tested. Any animal that doesn't meet performance standards is sent straight off to slaughter or to live export on a boat to Indonesia or the Philippines.'

Moira is more likely to be knocked over by a friendly bull saying hello than by a rampaging one. The placid behaviour of the cattle instilled trust: later in the day I stood still behind a totally inadequate tree to photograph 200 bulls as they trotted past.

As the afternoon drew on, we drove into Numul Numul community to meet Sammy Bulabul and his people. A welcoming committee of dozens of lively kids ran to meet Mike and Moira. Sammy strolled over and smiled broadly under his black Akubra. He shook hands with us all then adjourned with Mike to the shady veranda to talk fencing and cattle. Mike, a cat perched on his shoulder, was right at home here. As he removed his hat, the children gawked, fascinated by the white man's bald scalp. The boldest ones sidled over and touched it quickly, as if it might burn them. Mike pretended not to notice as they ran off giggling.

The Numul Numul community takes pride in their community. The grass is mown, gardens watered and verandas swept clean of red dust. The children and some of the women took Moira and me to their favourite place, the sacred billabong. It was a hot day, perfect for splashing in the tree-lined pool. Kids speared little fish with sticks and sang out, vying for Moira's attention to regale her with tales of their hunting exploits. She broke into a song they seemed to know the words of; the kids joined in. The English would be surprised to hear their folksong 'Row, Row, Row Your Boat' ringing out from an outback waterhole. The women filled me in on Aboriginal names for medicinal plants and explained how they harvest waterlily roots.

This community maintains its traditions. As we left, Sammy invited the O'Briens to his grandsons' initiation ceremony, an occasion not to be missed and definitely progress in building mutual respect and getting the people story right.

'We'll witness the young fellas being initiated into manhood,' Moira said on the return trip. Then she remembered that it would be circumcision and laughed. 'Well, hopefully, I don't get to witness it, but can join in the celebrations.'

By the time we returned to the homestead at 6 that evening, I knew how Moira kept her trim figure: we hadn't eaten since breakfast. She must run on fresh air.

Two years later, in July 2005, I returned to Numul Numul with my husband Bill after a long, dusty drive from a campsite north of Borroloola near the Gulf of Carpentaria. We arrived as dusk was falling. We planned to help out as Moira prepared cattle for the Katherine Show two days hence. Moira, Felix and Karine, a French girl from the international organisation Willing Workers on Organic Farms, scurried about feeding the show team of six cows and bulls with a ration of copra meal and boiled barley. Poddy calves clamoured for any available teat on a couple of long-suffering dairy cows.

In 2004, after an eight-year absence from the ring, Moira began to show cattle. Their Coodardie stud took home a respectable array of ribbons and Moira sold three bulls. 'They are now on stud duties with their own happy little harems,' she said. She hoped the Katherine and Darwin shows in 2005 would be just as successful.

We all adjourned to the dongas to wash off the dust. Mike and Rory were home, but Clair had built a townhouse near Mataranka and moved there. Moira directs operations for dinner from what is on hand – vegetables from the perishables supply stashed in the coolroom and a delicious roasted haunch of beef. What else would you have here? Over the mahogany table, family discussion about cattle prices and the show was spirited.

Coodardie is one of the larger Brahman studs in the Territory, and it needed up-to-date promotion, so during the long Wet, Moira had used her creative skills to set up a professional-looking website to boost marketing and sales. After dinner, she opened up her computer in the cramped office and downloaded photos of her prize bulls to show Bill and me. In her voluntary role as secretary of the Katherine branch of the Australian Brahman Breeders Association, Moira also spent countless hours preparing the 2005 Show schedule and chasing up display material for that year's celebration of 40 years of cattle showing at Katherine.

The following morning we rose early to muster cattle for the prospective buyers who were coming to inspect them. Good breeding and performance are only the beginning; Moira has to keep developing markets for Coodardie stud to survive. The O'Briens chose the stock they wanted to keep and the rest are for sale.

A young couple, Suzanne and Brett Gill from Mulalungwi between Katherine and Darwin, arrived with their baby son. They were keen to build a quality herd based on Coodardie blood. Brett, who dispenses with shoes, neatly sidestepped as heavy cows rumbled past his bare feet. One wrong move and a foot would be mincemeat. A burly truckie, Prickles, drove in just as Brett finished choosing 110 cows, pregnant or with calves at foot. We shunted the cattle into a huge road train that had 62 wheels – a lot of punctures to fix in any mishap. Prickles's truck roared off in a swirl of dust.

Late in the afternoon we loaded the family truck with the show bulls, cows and a handsome calf called Giuseppe. The men went ahead to Mataranka in our 4WD while I joined Moira in the cattle truck and made good use of time with my captive subject. She loves community involvement – it's a chance to give something back, to help others and influence decisions. Her idea of community is expansive. It may mean local, state or even national involvement.

'I believe you have no right to complain about an issue unless you are prepared to do something about it. That attitude has been the catalyst for my involvement. When I was 20, I was selected for the inaugural Territory Chief Minister's Roundtable and began to develop more confidence talking to people of my own age. At the same time, I was helping Mum in the Mary River Landcare group and was secretary of the Top End Cattlemen's Association. I like the challenge of being first to do things. From that, I was put up for the Constitutional Convention at Parliament House in Canberra.'

Some people remarked, 'Oh, you're just at home' during those five years when Moira helped her parents on Carmor Plains. They may have been surprised to learn that she was becoming known at state and federal levels as an articulate young woman and was named 1998 Young Achiever of the Year for the Northern Territory.

When the prime minister's invitation to the Constitutional Convention arrived, Moira handed it to her mother. 'No,' said Clair, 'they want a young person Moira. It's for you.'

'I knew nothing about it at all. I thought: What's this letter? Did they just go through the electoral role and pick people?'

Each state and territory had a youth delegate selected by the prime minister and Moira was appointed youth delegate for the Territory. One of the youngest of the 140 delegates, she spoke up for Australia as a republic, but not with a directly elected president.

'To have that, the constitution would need complete change. Each delegate had the opportunity to make a keynote address to the convention and the jam-packed public gallery. The delegates really listened to young people. The first time I spoke was impromptu, in response to a monarchist who said all leased land would revert to the Crown. I said, "My family leases Crown land in the Northern Territory and so would be very interested and concerned if this was true. It is not." I was nervous, but I'd be worried if I didn't get butterflies when I speak. You have to work out where you stand on issues as a person, as a young woman. At the end of the convention a big bunch of flowers arrived – I don't know who sent them – with a note saying, "Thank you for such common sense!"'

Moira, nominated by the Northern Territory Cattlemen's Association, was elected deputy chair of the steering committee for the first National Farmers Federation Young Farmers forum in Canberra in 1999.

'I was offered the chair, but declined it and became deputy. I started to gain self-confidence,' Moira said. 'My confidence seems to go up and down with how clear my skin is. I use skin medications for about two years then my face becomes used to them and I need to try something new. It's vanity I guess and not logical, but that's the truth.'

In 2003, the Northern Territory Cattlemen's Association nominated Moira to represent the territory at the World Congress of Young Farmers in Paris. Along with eleven other young Australian farmers, she joined 600 delegates from 100 countries. They met at Le Louvre, the museum famous more for the *Mona Lisa* and her enigmatic smile than for farming conventions. The USA and the United Kingdom were conspicuous in their absence, ostensibly for diplomatic reasons, although the opening of the congress did coincide with the French speaking out against those countries invading Iraq.

It was an eye-opener to Moira to see the European emphasis on farming as a way of life and as protection of culture and community, rather than as a business. An official congress communiqué, drafted by the French, recommended the continuation of European Union protectionist policies. Moira and other Australians took on their French hosts to argue the need for free trade, not 'fair' trade and to reword the communiqué.

'There was a perception that Australian stations covered huge amounts of land and were owned by big corporations with money and no problems. We would say, "Just because you have 500 square kilometres doesn't mean you're rich in Australia. It means rough country and hard work." What really stood out for me was just how lucky and how advanced on women's rights we are here. A third of farmers are women and we have active and influential women in agriculture organisations.'

Moira believes that complacency is one of the biggest issues that agriculture has to face. When she thinks some media outlets are sensationalising the issues and jeopardising vital markets as with the live export trade, she is quick to enlist support via her extensive email networks.

'Live export is the backbone of our cattle industry. Coodardie stud doesn't export much, but we supply bulls to producers who do.'

In March 2004 Northern Territory Primary Industry and Fisheries Minister Kon Vatskalis affirmed the government's support for the Northern Territory trade in the face of media criticisms.

In a media release issued on 31 March 2004, he said:

Recent adverse media reports surrounding the rejection of 50,000 sheep by Saudi Arabian authorities and contamination of feed for sheep destined for the Middle East have cast this industry in a negative light, but I'm very pleased to report the Territory has a good record, recognising the health and welfare of our live exports. The NT cattle exports are short hauls of only four to 10 days with mortality rates of less than 1 in 1500 animals on vessels travelling to Asia.

The local pastoral industry generates $330 million directly into the Territory's economy. In 2006, 46.5 per cent, or 230,000 head, of Northern Territory cattle were exported live to Southeast Asia. The trade is the major component of commercial vessel movements in and out of the Port of Darwin.

On a visit to the southern Philippines in 1998, I saw lot feeding of northern Australian Brahmans destined for the tables of a growing meat-eating Asian population. The animals, which were fed pineapple peelings, looked sleek and healthy. Slabs of beef crawling with flies were sold in the outdoor markets or served as a delicacy, without the flies, in Filipino restaurants. Indonesia suffered a sharp decline during the Asian economic crisis in 1998, but has since emerged as the major market for Australian live cattle, importing 61 per cent of northern production.

We were all staying overnight at Mike and Clair's Mataranka home. Moira manoeuvred the truck into a clearing near a water trough. Wild barking erupted as the resident dog, Stormont, rushed out to greet Moira's dog, Rosy. The dogs were not the only happy ones. A tall, lean man with olive skin, clearly pleased to see Moira, loped over to help unload and feed the cattle. Her boyfriend, Colin, as reserved as a shy bull, is growing pumpkins here at Mataranka. Usually he lives five hours drive away at Humpty Doo, south of Darwin on a five acre block Moira and Felix bought in 2000. In 2002, when he used to work for Telstra, Colin came to Numul Numul to install a two-way satellite dish.

'Colin asked me out, courted me, then caught me,' said Moira with a laugh. 'Telstra has been taking its dues ever since. We phone each other every night. He is of Italian heritage, a proud and quiet man.'

Clair ushered us into a sprawling house of earthy reds and eucalyptus greens. Through large windows, the groves of stringy bark, coolamon and ironwood blended into the home. The Numul Numul dongas are now referred to as 'the bush camp'.

The following day, Moira travelled on ahead with Mike to unload and wash the show team. Later, when we arrived at Katherine showground, the smells hit us first: hot bodies of cattle and horses, straw and sweat. Then there was the assault on the ears – megaphones, bulls bellowing, people shouting. There were horses, dogs, birds and cattle, sideshows, a rodeo and the annual dose of social life for people from remote stations. We spotted Moira with several damp bulls that were tethered to a long rail. She stroked and calmed them, and then led them back to clean pens. Each fall of manure was quickly raked away: green stains on shiny white coats wouldn't do for these potential kings of the show ring.

The O'Brien camp was bustling as five of us groomed and fed cattle, printed last-minute changes to the show schedule and prepared photos for the fortieth celebrations at the Brahman breeders dinner.

Moira hoped for 'broad ribbons', as she calls the winning blues and reds, but competition was stiff from established Territory studs. She thought she had quality bulls, but Moira was the new kid on the block and the Coodardie cattle are not as fat as many of the others.

'I think it's a total farce to feed up an animal excessively,' she said. 'It hides their faults and makes them a less functional animal. A heifer may never be a good breeder if she gets too fat. I like to be able to exercise them while they are on feed, rather than let them lie down and fatten up. However, it does make it harder for most judges to compare between the animals.'

Moira and Felix looked smart in clean jeans, white shirts and ties and their best Akubras as they led each cow or bull into the ring. The cattle have been combed, brushed and hooves polished to shine in front of the judges. An informed crowd of spectators sat on a stand in the hot sun and did their own judging. Discerning onlookers will see past the good grooming to the good breeding beneath, but the broad ribbons certainly help. Coodardie stud acquits itself well; Coodardie Seamus wins Reserve Senior Champion and there were a bundle of other ribbons. Moira was just as proud of the children who entered cattle they had prepared for judging, a special class she coordinated to encourage the next generation into the industry.

After the judging we relaxed under a shady tree away from the bustle. It was the first break Moira had taken in months. The effort and precise preparation in her dual roles as Brahman Breeders Association secretary and Coodardie studmaster is enormous.

'I take it one step at a time, building an image of our cattle in people's minds. That broad ribbon for Seamus helps build a perception for those who don't trust their own judgement,' Moira said. 'Giuseppe is my pick, a magic little calf. I really appreciated the judge saying you could see the depth of breeding, but he was underdone. He was the second youngest in a big class and was misbehaving. He missed his mum. My older heifer, Zara, behaved herself quite nicely in the judging of me as a stock handler. It's about how smart the whole outfit of animal and person look. I could have done with that new cane, which was first prize.'

Moira's show cane, used to scratch and keep the animal content during judging and to position their feet correctly, broke early in the show. She came second in the class.

'I could never imagine life without animals,' she said reflectively. 'In the future, I'd like to see Coodardie stud achieve what I know it's capable of and to get the recognition it deserves. A lot of hard work needs to happen for that. It's important to me that I'm thought of as a hard worker. Some people work hard, but around in circles. I want us to breed good, quiet cattle and for other people to think that I was good with cattle.'

Moira plans to work more with Aboriginal corporations who are managing their own stations. Traditionally, they've had low-grade bulls and feral cattle mustered in from the scrub. Moira wants to help them improve the quality of their herds through the introduction of top-quality Brahmans.

'I reckon I know where they can get some of those.'

In 2006, she did a course in holistic management (HM).

'We're not out for a quick fix or immediate financial gain at the expense of our environment or family. The crux of HM is its decision-making framework, based on shared values that are developed by all who are involved,' she explained. 'We describe how we want our property, community and whole to be and test everything we do back against our holistic goal – "Healthy hearts, healthy country, healthy cattle". We can make a powerful improvement through it.'

The cattle are now run in large mobs – two of 500, one of 2000 – and moved to different paddocks frequently so no one area becomes over-grazed. Fences, dams and tanks have been erected to accommodate the regular moves.

'We have the same amount of cattle on less than half the country. Now there are fifty-seven paddocks, compared to seven only five years ago. We won't go back to set and constant grazing again. The country looks far better, grows better quality grasses and the cattle have improved.'

Moira was keen to share with others in the cattle community what they learnt on Numul Numul. In October 2006, she was co-presenter in Alice Springs at the Indigenous Cattlemen's workshop on holistic management.

'About thirty cattlemen came along from all over the Territory – educated men, bushmen, women and kids. Numul Numul will host their next workshop in September 2007. We'll run an outdoor classroom, bring in some cattle and talk about bull selection, and look at fencing, weeds and watering while we drive around. We'll have a live exporter and buyer to explain their end of the business.'

Involving others in the cattle industry, particularly young people, was Moira's motivation for a new project with Taminmin High School at Humpty Doo. She entrusted fifteen young bush steers to the agricultural students to quieten, groom and handle in preparation for showing at Freds Pass.

'Humpty Doo is on the doorstep of the live export trade from Darwin, so we wanted to teach the kids about export,' Moira said. 'The show was an absolute highlight with nineteen led animals, over twenty kids, teachers and parents, a newly spayed Rosy and her three puppies – and me. Afterwards we had a mini auction and sold off the steers as lawn mowers to blockies on small lots.'

In the 2007 Katherine Show, these students aged 15 to 19 and trained by Moira, 'cleaned up' blue ribbons with their cattle.

'I felt like a proud aunty,' she laughed.

Despite Moira's track record of firsts as a young woman in a male-dominated industry, she maintained that women were expected to work hard in the Territory and that she wasn't unusual.

'Mum has been my mentor and role model,' she said. 'We've changed roles now and she assists me. Felix and I realised just how much she does now that she's not at the station full time. This Dry season we were saying, "We need a housekeeper". Everybody helps out, but it gets a bit much at times. This year I was everything from bookkeeper, cook and housekeeper to musterer and stud groom – all at the same time. I refuse to lose the jobs I like and just do domestic and administrative duties. We need a couple who can manage outside and inside jobs. It's a nicer atmosphere when the house is clean and there's food on the table.'

I noticed that the last one to bed threw the day's clothes in the washing machine and turned it on overnight. Previously, Moira was up late doing the bookwork at night. Now she or Felix spread the load and share yard work and bookwork. Moira is learning how to use a new gadget that can revolutionise not only performance measuring of cattle, but also the paperwork.

'It's like a giant supermarket bar coder. The cows have a microchip in their gut or an eartag. As they step past the machine, their data automatically come up on my computer. Before, I would have to enter data on the computer back home after weeks out mustering from daybreak to dusk. It was the last thing I wanted to do.'

Her major challenge is not managing cattle, but welding a family of bosses into a team. Moira is an advocate of regular family meetings for open communications.

'When things get tense, it's because we haven't had a meeting for a while,' she said. 'We are all capable people, have strong personalities and could be the boss in our own right, but we need to pull our heads in occasionally. We rotate positions as chair and secretary and use a simple pro forma for agenda and minutes. At times we have called in an outside facilitator, someone everyone can trust to facilitate a difficult meeting – for instance, when my older brother Patrick left the company.'

What stood out about the O'Briens was their range of skills and ability to combine strengths to work together towards common goals. Moira described herself as a more conservative family member, one who is slower to take on new ideas, but adaptable and diplomatic.

'You learn to be a negotiator and peacemaker every day of the week in a big family,' she said. 'Dad's an early adopter, always keen to see how we can do something better or to try a new idea – as long as one of the younger ones learn how to drive it.'

Moira's diplomatic skills were much admired by Cathy McGowan, chair of the Regional Women's Advisory Council.

'She would ask that gem of a question that captured the nub of an idea and moved the discussion on. Moira was a great learner of skills, ideas and ways of working with people and used them in other forums, such as her Young Farmer's Council. One night at a formal dinner in Parliament House, a politician was talking non-stop. I was chairing and tried all my tricks to no avail. I gave Moira the eye, asking for help. She gently and firmly asked him if he would like to join her for dinner. He looked at her bright, keen face and smiled, then shut up and meekly followed her to his seat. The rest of the council members gaped. This guy had been holding forth for over thirty minutes and he did her bidding. We thought she might be so practised through working with her dad and uncle and older men on the NT Cattlemen's Association.'

Since the age of 15, Moira has run a thriving leatherwork business in her spare time. At school she used to keep a pocket stuffed with leather lace and an awl so she could make something while she waited in the lunch queue.

'Artwork and leatherwork are part of me,' she said. 'Dad would take me to get supplies at the saddlery where I had my own account. I made bracelets and plaited rings, including coloured ones in red, yellow and black for the Aboriginal girls and red, yellow and green for the Papuan girls. It was pure profit because they were made out of scraps left over from larger projects, such as belts. Whenever I had a leatherwork or craft stall, everyone was an expert and would tell me how to do it. At first I listened and tried what they were saying, but my work suffered so I said to myself: Hang on, I've had the best whip maker as a teacher, Lindsay Whiteman from Townsville, so I'll just stick to the way I know is best.'

Moira can imagine running an art gallery and exhibiting her leatherwork in the future, but for now her focus is the cattle.

'I'm not indispensable to the place. Nobody is indispensable. It's like osmosis. If one part is removed people might do things differently and something or someone else comes to fill the vacant place.'

Just as I thought Moira was completely wedded to cattle – tending and marketing them or weaving their hides into bracelets – she held out her left hand where she wears a gold ring with hands clasping a heart and a crown above.

'It's an Irish Cladder ring that Mum and Dad gave me for my twenty-first. When the heart's pointing out you're on the lookout; when the heart's pointing in and it's on the left hand, you're settled.' Her ring was pointing in.

Colin was joining her at the Darwin Show the following week.

'He's the man. We're a good balance because we're so different. Shows annoy the hell out of him. There are so many things I want to do, but you can't do them all at once. I want to see Mum's place develop under holistic management and perhaps later Colin and I can be based there to look after the stud cattle. I'd like to have kids. We'll take it in small steps and see what happens.'

In December 2005, Moira was appointed to the inaugural National Council of Young Farmers, a twelve-person advisory body designed to give young people a direct voice to Canberra.

'I felt a strong sense of responsibility going onto this council. As I mature I have a different mindset and higher expectations. I wanted tangible outcomes, on water, for instance. We recommended that the minister call a national Young Water Users forum [which was held in mid-July 2007]. We ran Pathways to Leadership with Senator Sussan Ley, a rural politician, and industry leaders to share ideas on bringing young people up through the ranks of agricultural groups. The industry leaders asked how to get young people to their meetings. We said people our age aren't interested in sitting around talking all day. We want action. Short-term projects to achieve something concrete interests young people more than endless meetings.'

The council teamed up with the Year of the Outback and initiated workshops with 330 young rural Australians across the country seeking their views on important issues. Moira helped launch the report, *Outback Youth in Front*, at the Northern Territory cattlemen's conference in April 2007. Young people wanted to see a one-stop shop for jobs and career information out in the regions, more industry and business focus on employing young people, a greater range of flexible training programs and integrated youth services.

In September 2006, the O'Brien family celebrated Moira's thirtieth birthday and thirty years of running Coodardie stud. The occasion marked a milestone for a family of innovators. The date that had them on tenterhooks, though, was November 2006 when the Numul Numul Station lease came up for renewal. The O'Briens trusted that their care of the land, progress on developing the cattle station and strong family focus, as well as their good relationship with Sammy Bulabul and his community, would help them decide to continue the partnership.

That November the historic roles reversed and the Indigenous owners invited the white family to sit down and sign a continuation of the lease agreement for another five years in front of Sammy Bulabul's house in the Numul Numul community.

'We're happy to live with an Aboriginal corporation in the long term,' Moira said. 'We're conscious that farming isn't merely a lifestyle, it's a business, but it's also our home. It's our future. It's really a statement of who we are.'

Moira's Christmas email showed a photo of her left hand with a diamond and sapphire ring on the third finger.

'Colin proposed on Christmas Eve. Rory was the first to notice the ring on Christmas Day. He had wanted to buy me a sapphire ring years ago and invested in gold shares, but his hot tip fell through. Dad was sitting a metre away at lunch and it all went right over his head. Mum noticed my hand and asked, "What does this mean?"'

Colin lives at Humpty Doo and has set up a cleaning business in nearby Darwin. Moira thinks nothing of commuting six and a half hours between Humpty Doo and Numul Numul. They will marry in September 2008.

In the Territory Moira is making a name for herself and Coodardie stud. Her constant search is for better ways of growing top Brahman cattle, for new markets and forging new ways of working with Indigenous people. It is business and reconciliation rolled into one for this modern woman.

Glen Sheppard with his mother Pam at Sunshine Coast University, 2006

3

Has Elvis Left the Building?

Glen Sheppard, Nambour, Queensland

Queensland's Sunshine Coast was awakening to a balmy October morning in 2002: people briskly walked the beach, workers spilled from apartment buildings, street cafés pumped out the aroma of coffee and bacon. I was on my way to interview a most unusual 23-year-old man and was thinking hard about how to do it. Glen Sheppard was initially diagnosed with severe intellectual and physical disabilities, yet now he surprises people with his communication abilities and emotional depth. Glen uses an alphabet board to communicate because he can speak only two words – 'chips' and 'birthday'. He cannot hold a pen or use a computer, yet he is a published poet. Upon this first meeting, my mind is crowded with more questions than answers and I wish I had asked more before setting out.

Pam, Glen's mother, had sent me one of Glen's poems, 'Accepted', that reveals the pain he feels as an outsider in society and at being unable to express his true self.

The Sheppards live in Nambour, a town nestled into the foothills of the Blackall Ranges. Their house, perched at the top of a steep road, is secluded among tropical palms and bright bougainvillea. A woman with ginger pigtails, freckles and a big grin greeted me at the door.

'Hi, I'm Terri, Glen's support worker.'

She invited me to come in and meet Pam and Glen. Pam has a serene and open face framed by short hair. Seated across the room is a young man with spiked hair; he is wearing long shorts and a blue-striped T-shirt. He looked down as he made little 'Urr, urr' noises and rubbed his fingertips together. I took my cue from the poem and leant over to shake his hand and look him in the eye. His keen sideways glance checked me out, then there was a smile. It looked like I was in with a chance.

Glen eyed the sultana bun I brought for morning tea and tucked into a piece as we settled around the kitchen table. Pam showed me the alphabet, or QWERTY board. It looked like a computer keyboard without a power connection.

'He can't touch type by himself,' Pam said. 'I support Glen's arm as he taps the board and read out or write down what he said. It's called facilitated communication. The emotional and physical support, the touch, seem to sort things out in his mind. It's a controversial tool. Some people doubt that the words come from the disabled person because their arm is supported. We battle for its acceptance because it is Glen's lifeline.'

Who would think such a simple device, its letters and numbers in bright yellow on durable black cardboard, could be so important?

We begin. I asked questions and Pam lightly held Glen's right arm as he answered by tapping out letters to make words. He hit the bottom of the board to signal a word's end. Glen tapped fast and at times with his eyes shut. Pam had to concentrate hard, eyes fixed on the board as she read out his words and sentences. She said he recently did an entire TAFE assignment with his eyes shut. Although on one level this was an exchange between Pam and I, punctuated by Terri's throaty laugh at Glen's responses, the focus was clearly Glen. His presence was perceptive and humorous. As he tapped, he hummed or made 'Mm mm' noises, occasionally splaying both hands like a stop sign, at which times he would stray to his favourite chair to rest, as if on a string. He walked with a swaying motion, head down.

'A comfort bunny,' said Terri. 'He goes straight to the spot where he picks up energies in the room.'

At birth Glen was diagnosed with Down syndrome and rushed to intensive care.

'What's Down syndrome mean?' Pam's husband Bruce asked the doctor.

The doctor told them it would mean health problems, intellectual disability and difficulty with walking for a start. They had three choices, he said: 'You can take him off the oxygen and he might die. You can put him in an institution or you can take him home and love him as you would a regular child.'

'I didn't know how I would cope,' said Pam. 'Bruce was marvellous. He was good at learning new skills, the original do-it-yourself man. He could turn his hand to whatever was needed and said, "We will cope". I was a mess. I didn't stop crying for 24 hours.'

As Glen was being tube fed in hospital, Pam was sent home to care for their three-year-old son Paul. They took Glen home three weeks later. It was then that Pam found out that some of the nurses thought she wouldn't return for him. Down syndrome is a genetic condition that affects one in every 800 to 1000 people, regardless of race, sex or economic level. Instead of inheriting the normal twenty-three pairs of chromosomes with half of them from each parent the baby has an extra chromosome. Thus the code in each cell responsible for inherited characteristics contains forty-seven, not forty-six, chromosomes. This excess genetic material gives the baby a distinctive look, which includes an upward slant to the eyes, a small nose and flat facial profile, poor muscle tone and some level of intellectual disability. On the positive side, children with Down syndrome are highly responsive to their surroundings and, with early intervention, good education and a stimulating home environment can go to school, make friends and work.

Glen was a floppy baby with the characteristic Down syndrome appearance. At this time, the family lived in Melbourne. When he was five weeks old Pam took Glen to an early intervention school for Down syndrome children. Of the eighty children there he was one of the slowest developers. But the school gave Pam hope as she persevered. She read to him and taught him how to roll and clap. Then, just as their family life was beginning to adjust to its newest arrival, Bruce noticed blood in his urine one morning. He was tested that same day and immediately admitted to hospital with acute myeloid leukaemia.

'We were in total shock,' said Pam. 'The doctor said he might live one year or seven. I drove home wondering what we would do. I rang Mum, who came and looked after the boys so I could be at the hospital with Bruce. It was a day-to-day existence. You operate on automatic to protect your own feelings.'

Bruce died when Glen was 17 months old. His death plunged Pam into intense sorrow, feelings of loss and concern about how she would manage to care for Glen and Paul alone. She was trained as a hairdresser, but knew Glen was a full-time job and they would have to exist on a widow's pension. Pam's mother became their backstop.

Glen had intensive schooling for three days a week at the Early Intervention School and Melton Special School. He didn't meet the normal milestones for a growing child, although he crawled eventually at 18 months. His mother was determined he would walk.

'Children with Down syndrome can learn by repetition,' said Pam, 'so I put bricks in his play trolley instead of blocks and made him push it up and down the lounge room until he walked. He was three.'

By then she knew something else was wrong. Glen didn't speak or make eye contact, and he lacked coordination, fine motor skills and alertness. The doctors told Pam that her child showed strong symptoms of autism as well as Down syndrome. At first she found the diagnosis a relief. It explained why her son wasn't developing.

The causes of autism are disputed and debated. Some research suggests genetic causes, some environmental reasons, some immunisation, or even food allergies. Other studies point to a combination of genetic and environmental factors as possible causes. The US Bureau of Statistics noted the disturbing trend that:

> **the incidence of autism has increased 870 per cent in 10 years. Genetics alone cannot explain the rise in autism in industrialised nations. This leaves nutrients and toxins interacting with these genes as the most likely candidates as causal factors for autism. While genetics have not changed, our diet and food chain has changed dramatically in that time and may be responsible for the observed increase in Autism Spectrum Disorder.**

Autism affects the normal functioning of a child's brain, making it hard for the child to communicate and interact. These children may repeatedly flap their hands or rock back and forth, make strange noises, resist changes in routine and possess unusually sensitive sight, hearing, taste, smell and touch. Curiously, autism affects four times as many boys as girls.

In the 1940s, two researchers, Leo Kanner in the USA and Hans Asperger in Germany, were investigating children who exhibited such characteristics. Independently of each other, they both named what they found autism, derived from a Greek word meaning 'the self'. While Kanner's group showed learning disabilities and the behavioural signs of autism, Asperger's patients were at the other end of the spectrum and included children who were academically bright and could talk. In 1981 Dr Lorna Wing coined the term 'Asperger's syndrome' to describe the latter group. What is called high-functioning autism includes people who are highly intelligent and excel at what they do. Some scientists, artists and mathematicians who were famed for their original thinking, such as Albert Einstein and Vincent van Gogh, may have had Asperger's syndrome or high-functioning autism.

There is little written or known about the combination of autism and Down syndrome; in fact, until recently, the two conditions were believed not to coexist. The combination is thought to be relatively rare, with estimates of autism in people with Down syndrome varying between 1 and 10 per cent. According to the Kennedy Krieger Institute in the United States, which has studied thirty children with both conditions, there are commonalities but every child differs in one way or another. Some will have speech, some will not. Some will rely heavily on routine and order, others will be more easygoing.

Having both disorders meant Glen had to live in his own world, without speech, unable to point to pictures or words or to use sign language. He needed constant help with the tasks of everyday living, such as toileting, showering, dressing and eating meals.

When Glen was three, Pam met Stan, whose wife had died of cancer. He had five sons. Pam and Stan fell in love and together built a large house; Pam took on care of the household. Glen was the youngest of seven boys under 15.

'Glen was the axis of our family,' said Pam. 'Stan's boys accepted him and the third eldest, Jason, tried to teach him words and to play ball. The boys would race home to tell me what they did at school and to play with Glen. In 1987, we moved to Nambour where we owned a nursery.'

In 1992, at the age of 20, Jason was killed in a car crash. The family was shattered.

'I was shocked first of all,' Glen tapped out. 'However, then a strange, peaceful feeling overcame me. I had the same thing when Dad and Grandma died.'

It was on the night Jason died that Glen first saw his guardian angel: she had golden hair and brown eyes that sparkled.

'We are a spiritual family and believe in angels, angels of good. The golden angel came to let me know that it wasn't the end for Jason, but the beginning of a life that would go on, surrounded by love. Nothing could hurt his spirit any more. I was confused when she first came, but soon I felt peaceful. I feel tuned into the afterlife. The angel is always with me and gives me strength. She speaks to me when I need advice or comfort and puts kind thoughts in my head to help me in everyday life. Her presence is stronger when I need to have deep thoughts about myself.'

Stan and Pam drifted apart and separated in 1992 when Paul was 16 and Glen 13. Pam and her two boys have been on their own since then.

One Wednesday, when Glen was 16 and in the lowest class at Nambour Special School, a speech therapist called Eddie came into the classroom and introduced the six students to a QWERTY, or communication, board, named for the first six letters on the top row of a keyboard.

'Eddie supported my hand and made my index finger point straight,' Glen tapped. 'He kept asking me questions, but made no comment on each of my replies. I was very animated. I was slow to spell words because I had to find the letters on the alphabet board. I had learnt all the letters and numbers from *Sesame Street* and *Play School*. I had taken in everything, so when it came to spelling I was good at it. Eddie videotaped me as I used the board. Then he spent a sleepless night wondering if he had imagined what he saw. The following day he called Mum and Paul into the school.

'They sat there watching the tape, totally dumbfounded. Then Eddie said to me, "How do you feel to have your mother and brother watching you communicate?" I tapped out "Excited", spelt with the x and the c. Mum said, "Where did you learn the ABC? How do you know how to spell that word?" I slowly answered their questions and I said for the first time, "I love you Mum". It was such a relief to be able to express my thoughts and feelings. Then my arm began to ache. I wasn't used to the movement then.'

Pam took up the story.

'I had to sit down because I was shaking. I was totally blown away by what I was seeing.' She wiped a tear. 'I can hardly talk about it still. For sixteen years we had all treated him like a two- or three-year-old. I would condense everything down to a few words hoping he would understand some of it.'

As his mother described this event Glen made his little 'Umm, umm' noises.

'Glen understood *everything*.' Pam laughed and patted his hand. 'Didn't you?

He heard many stories, maybe some he shouldn't have heard. I took the video home and Paul and I watched it over and over. We still could hardly believe what we were seeing. I went out and ordered four CDs of spelling, tables, songs and how to tell the time. I think I was in shock for a fortnight.'

The noise level from Glen increased and his hands splayed towards the ceiling. He was bursting to say something.

'It was the happiest day of my life,' he grinned as he rapidly tapped letters. 'I knew my world was about to open up. It was like being let out of prison for a crime I didn't commit. I just knew someone would help me to communicate one day. I am so grateful for facilitated communication.'

It was the first step out of silence and Glen was going to make himself heard. I laughed as he described finally being able to tell his mother what he really thought about being taken to Riding for the Disabled every Tuesday.

'The horse stank. I could not believe Mum and my teachers expected me to get on that rotten thing's back. I was frightened, but I used to grin and bear it just to keep them happy. I haven't been on a horse since.

'Over the years, it was hard for my soul to be calm and happy. Mostly, Mum knew what I needed, but at times it was very frustrating. Just because you don't have a voice doesn't mean you don't have feelings and opinions. I found school boring because I had already grasped the concepts, but I couldn't tell anyone. I could speak in my head and see words form on others' lips, dropping sounds, like music to my ears. It brought out behaviour problems. I was grumpy and would grunt and throw food on the floor because I was angry with myself for being stuck in a body that wouldn't do what it should.'

Glen can't remember much about his childhood, though Pam said he was mostly a happy boy.

'I had to be guided by his actions. I was never sure that Glen understood what I was saying to him.'

Only once did she wonder if Glen could actually understand what she said. She told him they would go shopping at 3 o'clock one afternoon and noticed him glance at the clock. When she returned at five to three, he glanced at the clock again and made 'Uhr, uhr' noises. Pam overlooked it at the time. As Glen couldn't point or make eye contact she had no way of knowing, apart from the noises, whether he might have understood.

'And the noises are just part of autism. They drive me insane,' Pam laughed. 'Where we might hear one thing at a time, he can hear three or more sounds at once, which makes him irritable. He will go to the garden and get a special leaf and flick it to calm himself. He loves music, especially John Farnham. He can sit quietly and listen to the same tape for hours. Swimming also relaxes him. He should have been a dolphin. Being around positive people means a lot to him.'

'Mum and I have a good understanding,' tapped Glen.

'Occasionally, he might sneak one past, like telling me that he wants chips when he's already had some.' Pam laughed and gave Glen a hug.

'Bloody hell yes! I must get it from you,' tapping and giving his mother a sidelong glance.

Glen can feel energies when he steps into a room or in the street, or when certain types of people are around him.

'The energies I pick up in the air are very strong at times, sometimes from far away. They seem to gravitate to me. There is no rhyme or reason to them, but the energies have a great influence on my life. Sometimes they can trigger my autism. People are the centre of my universe and they create the strongest energies. They create the likelihood of autism being either calm or crazy.'

Autism is like a brown mist over his mind. Glen describes the autistic effect as all this stuff called information pouring in, but without order or purpose for being there.

'It's the way I feel in my mind when all is fuzzy. My mind just does not clear, like the soup of the day. I was 14 before the soup started to clear and something meatier appeared. The tragic events of my life somehow gave it meaning. I think I needed those stepping stones to teach me more about myself and humanity.'

Glen's mind is affected by noises such as the wind. Gusts can bring him to a standstill and he finds it hard to concentrate when the wind is strong. Sometimes he gets stuck on the white line in the middle of a bitumen road and has to be pulled off.

'We call it white line fever and it's frightening,' Glen tapped. 'My head tells me I have to stay on the line while my body says I have to move off the line.'

'How is the soup today?' I asked.

'Clear.'

Glen said his real education came from watching people, the news on television and what was going on around him. He would read a book or paper if it was left open, but he couldn't turn the page.

'I also learnt from the environment where I grew up, a big extended family with something always going on and someone there to play with me.'

When he was 18, Glen left special school and began three years of numeracy, literacy and art in the disability access course at Nambour TAFE. In 2001, he finished Year 10 in a regular TAFE class at Mooloolaba. Armed with only the TAFE numeracy education, Glen passed Year 10 maths in one year. Many of us struggle to pass maths with nine years of formal education. How did he do it? Pam said the autism has given Glen intelligence, including an uncanny ability to understand maths principles and to square and treble numbers in his head. Glen said he just has a brain.

A TAFE teacher introduced Glen to poetry. At first he read poems, and then he started to write his own. He wrote his first poem, 'The Blues Club', after going out for the first time without his family. The music took him outside his body and he danced with everyone on the floor. Glen's teacher and support workers suggested he compile a book of his poetry. *My Book of Life as Told in Poetry* was self-published by Pam and Glen in 2000.

'I wanted people to see that those of us with disabilities have dreams, feelings and ambitions too. I also wanted to inspire others with a disability,' he said, 'to show them a way to get out of being stuck in their own heads.'

Poetry helps put things in perspective for Glen. He writes about people and feelings, about happy times and sad times.

'Writing has become a way for me to be creative and meet people,' he said.

The alphabet board is his door to the world. Its frustrating side is that Glen needs a person with him who can use the board too and who he can trust.

'My life would be easier if I could write myself, but I cannot hold a pen. I have ideas and they are gone by the time I have someone on the board to write them down. It is hard work for me on the board and for my carers who have to really concentrate, especially when I'm pointing fast.'

Finding and keeping reliable support workers, and training them in facilitated communication, takes an inordinate amount of Pam's time. It is a huge concern for all people with disabilities and their carers. When he turned 18 Glen received only a small funding package for outside support. After having been lumped for so long in groups where he felt like a shepherded animal, Glen was unfamiliar with one-on-one support. He expressed great respect and sympathy for support workers whom he said have to put up with moody behaviour, wiping shitty bums, feeding, showering and dressing clients, all for comparatively little recompense. It's no wonder they often move on to easier full-time jobs. For the person with autism, the result is continual disruption to routine and always having to build up new relationships.

'Trust is a major issue for me. I rely on people so much,' said Glen.

In 1999, Pam had a seizure and was rushed to hospital with a suspected brain tumour. Her grandmother and uncle had died from brain tumours before the age of 50. She was worried about what would become of her sons if she got sick or died. Pam did have a tumour, but it was removed and found to be non-malignant.

'I was extremely worried she might die,' Glen tapped out. 'Worry made my autism bad. I was living away from home with carers while Mum was recuperating and I felt insecure. I thought Paul and Mum had realised how much easier it would be without me, but they reassured me that I was a part of the family and my disability didn't make a difference.'

The doctors expected the tumour to grow back and that it would need to be removed again, but it hasn't grown in the seven years since. Pam recovered by learning Reiki therapy and practising on herself, which calmed her mind. She reduced the pressures in her life by giving up a psychology degree she had started and by visualising the tumour receding, instead of thinking about it as the enemy.

'I've always been a good listener and would go out of my way to support people, but my head wouldn't allow me to any more.'

Pam's illness raised the critical question: Who cares for the carer? Full-time caring for a large family and Glen made it impossible to work at her hairdressing, apart from occasional clients at home. When Pam needed extra help with Glen she applied for and was granted the carer's allowance, but it was pitifully inadequate and still is. Ironically, it took a brain tumour to enable her to access government assistance five days a week for extra support and respite care two nights a week.

'I've saved the government millions of dollars by caring for Glen at home for twenty-three years, but I wouldn't have it any other way.'

Suddenly, Glen was busy tapping on the board.

'Stop! I need lunch!' he tapped, then he spoke: 'Chips?'

It came as a shock to hear him speak. He had two words then: chips was one of them. Glen loves chips. In fact he regards hot chips as the major food group. His mother tries to encourage him to eat less fatty foods, without much success. His love of chips surfaces in the poem 'Topsy Turvy' (selected verses).

> *Topsy turvy it goes*
> *in the upside down world.*
> *Chips are GREAT for you,*
> *and vegetables don't exist*
> *(except potatoes of course).*
> *In fact, mothers would be forcing kids*
> *to eat MORE chips.*
> *There would be no such thing as FAT.*
> *It is a struggle to stop*
> *yourself fading away!*

A morning of talking to me by means of the board has exhausted Glen and Pam. After lunch they relaxed while I talked with Terri.

I first heard about Glen through an organisation Terri helped establish on the Sunshine Coast for intellectually disabled youngsters called Power of Arts: Key to

Inclusion (PAKTI). Glen was part of PAKTI, which also had a talented dance troupe who designed their own performances. Terri had worked in the disability field for twenty years; she met Glen when he was 13.

'I was told he was very disabled,' she said. 'A few years later here he was communicating on the board, eating chips and having a conversation.'

Terri is a passionate advocate for those with intellectual disabilities. She remembered the first time Glen's poetry was read at a public performance.

'What a night. Glen stood on stage at the Maroochy Disability Conference in 2000 while one of his TAFE teachers read his poems 'Mothers' and 'Trapped'. The audience of 150 people were weeping. Then, in 2002 at High Beam, a disability and arts festival in Adelaide, I read Glen's poems on stage with him using the board. A high-profile, disabled performer there said he didn't believe Glen could write such poetry. Later, he was convinced by the answers that Glen gave on the board and his distinctive style of writing.'

Terri said that people with disabilities learn to keep the peace and not to say what's really going on inside them. At a Sunshine Coast forum called Dare to Dream, members of the PAKTI troupe were asked if they had been ostracised.

'Nobody said anything,' she said. 'Finally, one spoke up. "I don't fit." It opened a floodgate. Another said, "I hate the way people ignore me", and a third said, "People treat me like I'm eight years old". They have problems processing information and getting it back out; they need physical support to go places, but they are not stupid. If we don't accept them, we miss out on whole realms. I am the person who has benefited most from this work, more than the people I help. Others will comment on how many resources the disabled need, but I find they give so much. They have such amazing heart qualities.

'The intellectually disabled are portrayed as needy, but on stage you see them differently. The arts involvement is good for building their self-esteem because they are seen as performers, not needy people. Glen is saying, "I'm me". He is incredibly intelligent. He has his foibles, but you can look into his eyes and see the spark. I'm blown away by the artistic achievements and joy of these people who are the most marginalised of the marginalised. They may not be able to communicate verbally, but in visual arts and performing dance and music, they have a freedom of expression. People say they are childlike. Well, we all have an inner child; maybe those with intellectual disabilities have it on the surface.'

Glen has a way of coping with his sadness or anger, just as others do.

'I go into my own world and focus on something moving, or music, or laughter. I love to laugh.'

With that, Glen opened his mouth and, in a deep voice, said, 'Birthday!' This was his second word. We all burst out laughing. The previous day had been his twenty-third birthday.

Not only did my visit coincide with Glen's birthday, but it also coincided with the launch of his second poetry book, *Elvis Has Left the Building*. I walked into Maroochy RSL, where the launch was to take place. Ahead was Pam, smart in black, and Glen in cream shorts and a black shirt, his hair gelled and spiked. Many of Glen's friends, who also have Down syndrome or autism, were there with their relatives. The launch, by the then Queensland Minister for Arts Matt Foley, was a lively occasion, with music from Terri's band, Mettaphor. The minister sat beside Glen and conversed with him in an animated way via Pam and the QWERTY board. Each speaker lauded Glen's achievement, particularly the minister.

'It's about inspiring others, with or without a disability, that they can do something in the community,' he said. 'We assume communication as a right, but in Glen's case communicating is much more complex. When it comes to facilitated communication, I have three left hands. Glen's achievement is far more significant than a book. It is about assisting people to ensure that their dreams become reality.'

Glen took in the praise, a smile on his face. His mother laid a quietening hand on his knee when he threatened to whoop. The foreword, written by Australian Bush Poets Association president Wally Finch, said, 'Glen is a fine example that heroes don't always need extraordinary physical abilities and living proof that the impossible can happen for those with a will.'

As Terri read Glen's title poem, 'Elvis Has Left the Building', there were nods of agreement and enthusiastic applause from an audience who knew so well what he meant.

> *Autism creeps over me like a thick, brown mist,*
> *taking away clear thoughts,*
> *leaving confusion and vacant places in my mind.*
> *I hear people's voices; they sound so far away.*
> *I feel as if I am in some other place.*
> *I fight being trapped in cracks in footpaths,*
> *swirls in carpets, patterns in tiles.*
> *My perception of depth, width and height*
> *is quite distorted.*
> *A break in the footpath appears as an abyss,*
> *so deep I must look like I'm drunk stepping so wide.*
> *When I feel autistic my mind becomes*
> *pebbles of rice swirling around so fast*

People clustered around afterwards to congratulate Glen. His brother Paul sat beside him, beaming at his little brother. Glen had told me Paul was his best friend and support. Paul is sensitive, friendly and clearly loves his brother.

'I grew up with Glen,' he said. 'To me he is a normal brother. Now he has his life and I have mine. He hangs out at my place, we have a drink together and watch movies. I've never felt left out. I always had the attention I needed and feel really proud of Glen's progress.'

Glen smiled at his well-wishers then headed for the real attraction. Over on a table groaning with goodies for the celebration was a huge birthday cake Pam had cooked.

'What's it feel like to have two poetry books under your belt?' I asked the guest of honour.

'Bloody good. I'm proud of myself,' Glen tapped. He reached for a slice of cake.

'What's next for you?'

'I want to have fun, write music and poetry and go to uni. I need lots of physical support, but my brain is good. I want to tell the world about the people in it who are not the regular type of person, but I have a big job ahead. Just to try will be rewarding.'

In 2003, Glen was invited to perform in Brisbane at the Wataboshi Asia–Pacific Music Festival as a result of a PAKTI proposal to the organisers. It was the first time this high-profile festival for performers with a disability was held outside Japan. Glen played a leading role. In an original performance he conceived called *Horse to Water*, Glen and another young man with Down syndrome sat on stage in a pool of light before 150 participants and spontaneously composed lyrics on their boards. Their respective support workers sang the men's words as they tapped them out on the communication boards to the rhythm of a computerised wind instrument played by well-known musician Linsay Pollack. The audience was full of praise for the extraordinary performances of these gifted men and the musician's ability to weave the words into music on the spot.

In 2004, Glen applied to Sunshine Coast University to study for a Bachelor of Arts and Social Science. Here was a challenge for the university. This was its first application from a student who viewed his disabilities as 'special abilities'. Glen used a facilitated communication board, had poor eyesight and depended on his support workers, and wasn't sure he could control his noises in a lecture theatre. His track record was 18 years of special schools, no communication until he was 16 and three years of part-time TAFE, but he convinced the university of his capability. Glen, accompanied by his mother and support worker, Garry, had successful interviews with the Bachelor of Arts coordinator; the dean of the faculty gave the final go-ahead.

Glen's way of learning makes the normal processes of going to lectures, taking notes, researching and preparing assignments on a computer look like kindergarten play. He has to listen to the lectures while his support workers, Adrian, Garry or his mother, take notes. They later read them aloud to Glen, who has to précis each chapter on the communication board.

'He is so keen. In his first subject, Knowledge, Power and Society, he wanted us to keep reading until we couldn't read another word,' Pam said.

Assignments are another story.

'Glen selects the references, then we read paper after paper out loud in a special room at the library so he can pick out what he wants. We might read solidly for a week. Then he processes that vast amount of material in his head and when he's ready to write, it just flows on the board. Adrian records it and I type it up.'

'Secretaries are the best,' Glen joked.

He aimed high. He achieved an overall credit for that first subject, but was disappointed he wasn't one of the few to receive a distinction. Garry, one of Glen's support workers, was a student at the university. He said the lecturer, who knew him, was worried the work submitted might be Garry's, not Glen's, because of the use of facilitated communication. When she marked a speech

Glen prepared on 'Same-sex marriages should be legal in Australia', she was convinced. 'I knew you couldn't write that well,' she told Garry, who laughed when he recounted this story.

'Glen got a distinction,' Garry said. 'Another time he was blowing kisses to this lecturer. She said, "That won't get you extra marks." We used to sit down the front of these lecture theatres filled with 300 students, but Glen hummed and whistled too much so we had to move back a few rows. It's a massive thing for Glen to be accepted at uni. It breaks down barriers and girls come up and talk to him. A young mum of an autistic child came up because she saw us talking on the board and laughing. She was totally amazed at Glen's skills on the board and was going to look into it for her son.'

The smaller tutorials, with only sixteen students, were where Glen could fit in and shine. He earned respect for the answers he gave.

'Glen loves the interaction with other students,' said Pam. 'For the first three weeks of term, the other students listened to his answers through me, then by the fourth week they were coming up and talking to him as a regular person. They tell me what an inspiration he is to them.'

Glen achieved credits in his five subjects. His most challenging exercise was an exam over three days.

'Oh, what an exam,' he said. 'Feelings of anxiety, pressure, stress and anger manifested into sleeplessness, loose bowels and a rundown immune system, which were compounded by getting lost in the depths of autism. Who would believe that I would be attending university after only three years of formal schooling?'

Glen was becoming known as an inspiring speaker. He would sit onstage tapping out his speech while Pam or another carer sat beside him and read from the board or the letters projected onto a large screen. In July 2004, he opened the Sharing the Road Conference in Brisbane for 240 workers in the physical and intellectual disability field.

'It was magical,' Pam said. 'We came out on a high. They loved Glen's speech and lined up for an hour afterwards to talk to him and buy his books. Glen said, "Oh, it's hard to be humble!"'

It was Glen's week as he was presented with Achiever of the Year in the Arts for the Sunshine Coast at a black-tie dinner. He and his family danced until midnight. The master of ceremonies, the ABC's Adam Spencer, told Glen that he had received the most robust applause. They had a photo taken together.

In his quest to improve awareness about disabilities, Glen spread the word wherever he could: through talks at primary schools, to students at TAFE disability courses, in a palliative care centre and on radio, as well as at conferences. In each place, audiences fired questions at him as they marvelled at his intelligence, wit and speed on the board.

I spent time with the Sheppards again in 2005 and I noticed changes in Glen since my last visit. Public accolades and people accepting his worth have given Glen self-confidence and a new maturity. Speech remained difficult, but thanks to intensive speech therapy he could now speak thirteen words – happy birthday to you, chips, Paul, baa (for his mother), the vowel sounds and shit. When someone can't speak, we may attribute, often unreasonably, qualities to them because we don't know what is going on inside their heads. In Glen's case, a lot was going on in his brain and he now had a voice to express it through poetry, presentations and university. Because we live in a verbal world, we tend to rattle on and use a lot of filler words. Every time Glen taps sentences in a swift, rhythmic beat, they have to be succinct and meaningful because of the effort required to communicate via the board.

When we get together at the nearby Eumundi markets, people jostled past coat-hangers of vibrantly coloured clothes, stands crammed with craft goods and all manner of food stalls. Glen was attracted to the sounds of the honky-tonk piano player. He swayed in time to the beat.

Later, Glen filled in a new carer, Christie, on his idiosyncrasies. I noticed how he related to his other support workers according to their personalities. Boisterous Garry brought out the boy in Glen as they joked and pushed each other around. Adrian, a sensitive, young woman with beaded dreadlocks, he took more seriously.

One morning Glen, Pam and I went for a stroll along the beachfront. We came to a bench overlooking the ocean and sat down. We spoke of love and life, subjects close to Glen's heart.

He paused to think, then was off on the board. 'I would love to have a girlfriend to spend time with, but I feel that is impossible as I cannot do what is needed in a relationship. It's bloody hard to find the words when it comes to this subject. I have normal desires and needs, but I need someone who loves me for who I am and is good on the board.'

'Do you discuss this subject of relationships with your mates?'

'Yes, we have the same dreams in that area,' Glen said.

He sounded sad.

The ever-present fear – and often, unfortunately the reality for vulnerable people with a disability, is mistreatment and abuse instead of a genuine loving relationship.

It occupies Pam's mind and she has acted on this neglected issue. In 2005, she wrote to Queensland members of parliament, ministers and Premier Beatty telling them that the guidelines for employing a support worker were not strict enough to safeguard people with a disability. In her letter she said:

> **It has been recorded that 80 per cent of people with a disability are abused and sexually interfered with in some form. Glen and I wish to put to the government that the recommended Blue Card for an employer to employ a support worker is not adequate for the disability field.**

A Bill was put forward to the Queensland Parliament to tighten the provisions of the Blue Card to include a regulation that those 'of any age' with a disability who are under supervision are not to be touched inappropriately, including a regulation that support workers' backgrounds must be thoroughly checked through a national register. A year later, in August 2006, Pam emailed me to say, 'Great news! My submission for adults under supervision of a carer to be better safeguarded was passed as a separate Bill on 1 July. It is not an extension of the Blue Card. All support workers have to fill out the forms. I am happy about that and Glen is over the moon.'

The *Disability Services Act 2006* (Qld) brought changes to strengthen and safeguard the rights of Queenslanders with disabilities. It includes intensive checks of support workers, including criminal history and indepth personal interviews.

A few months later, Glen asked his mother to email me that he felt happier.

'My thick, brown mist is slowly improving and I look forward to one day having a clearer head. I am still humming and that drives Paul and Mum up the wall. I can stop, but sometimes it is hard, especially in the lecture theatre at uni.'

At last Glen was studying creative writing at university and loved the stimulation of genres new to him, such as fiction. He was achieving credits and distinctions in assignments. He had a new support worker, Desley, a university student. Mostly Glen can stay quiet in the lecture theatre, but lets out a 'Yahoo' as he leaves. As part of his assessment in September 2006, Glen had to write the first chapter of a novel. This became the beginning of his third book, 'Me and the Child', a drama about a young woman with a disability who encounters dubious characters, murder and love. By July 2007, he is halfway through and gaining high credits for each chapter.

Glen is a member of Brotherhood of the Wordless, a group of twelve young men and four women who have autism or Down syndrome, cannot speak and use facilitated communication. Together they write poetry, create inspiring stories and have a great time together once a month in Brisbane. In 2005 they presented some poems at the Brisbane Writers Festival and in May 2006 launched a book and a DVD, *Tapping on the Heart of the World*.

'My passion is to have acceptance from people,' said Glen. 'We are all different and our intelligence can be nothing short of astounding. It is important to get the majority of people in the community to understand disability and its many forms. I strive to spread the word in as many places as possible.'

Glen is a remarkable role model and spokesperson for people with disabilities. His wisdom and wit, ability to express deep emotion and communicate thoughts and ideas surpasses that of most people gifted with speech and other abilities that we take for granted. In *Elvis Has Left the Building*, his second book of poetry, Glen drew an analogy with autism's impact on the brain as similar to Elvis leaving the building after a performance. With the revelation that Glen's disabilities are physical not intellectual, and the brilliant development of his potential, maybe Elvis has not left the building after all.

Glen Sheppard, on his facilitated communication board, with support worker Adrian, Nambour, Queensland, 2005

Lisa Huong Nguyen running a 'Taste Australia' promotion in a Bangkok supermarket, Thailand, 2004

4

Places We Never Dreamed Of

Lisa Huong Nguyen, Berri, South Australia

Lisa Huong Nguyen has brought me to her favourite Italian café in the heart of Adelaide. Barely size 6 and only 1.5 metres tall, this dainty woman, in her short, blue and black patterned dress, looked cool during what was a sweltering January in 2006. Earlier that day I had flown over mile after mile of parched, rusty-brown earth in South Australia, broken only along the Murray River by splashes of green gums, irrigated citrus orchards, olive groves and vineyards. The task of developing agricultural exports for this driest state of the driest continent looked like uphill work, yet this is my lunch companion's field of expertise. Food is the focus of her life she told me as we tucked into seafood pasta, salad greens and glasses of cabernet wine.

Lisa is her Australian nickname; Huong is her Vietnamese name. Traditionally, she would write the family first and the given name last: Nguyen Tien Quynh Huong.

Lisa Nguyen grew up in South Vietnam in the 1970s. Author and war correspondent John Pilger, in his 1989 book *Heroes*, described Vietnam as 'a war, not a country'. Lisa's father, Nguyen Tien Hanh, was away fighting with the South Vietnamese army, so her strongest influences were women – her mother, Le Thi Toan, grandmother and four aunties. They were teachers and skilled seamstresses, thrifty, industrious and financially independent women.

'My mother taught,' said Lisa. 'We lived in a Saigon complex built by foreigners for civil servants. Unlike other Vietnamese houses, which were single rooms offering little or no privacy, ours was solid brick with separate bedrooms, kitchen and dining room, and a full bathroom with Western-style toilet and shower. In the 1970s, people didn't want to live there because they thought seven kilometres was too far from the city. It was traditional for a woman to live with her husband and his family, but my mother put down a deposit and paid for this house before the war and my father lived with my mother.'

Over the ten years from 1965, Pilger wrote in *Heroes*, 'the United States dispatched its greatest ever land army to Vietnam, and dropped the greatest tonnage of bombs in the history of warfare, and pursued a military strategy deliberately designed to force millions of people to abandon their homes, and used chemicals in a manner which profoundly changed the environment and genetic order, leaving a once bountiful land petrified. At least 1,300,000 people were killed and many more maimed and otherwise ruined; 58,022 of these were Americans and the rest were Vietnamese.'

Vietnamese estimates put the number killed as much higher at nearly 3 million people and 4 million injuries. As allies of the USA and South Vietnam, 500 Australians were also killed and 2500 wounded in the battle to stop the spread of communism across Southeast Asia.

In 1950, Mao Zedong's Chinese communist legions had marched and fought their way across China until they reached the frontiers of Vietnam. In 1953, the Soviet Union and China both recognised the Democratic Republic of Vietnam under the communist leadership of Ho Chi Minh. Six months later, in 1954, communist North Korean forces surged across the 38th parallel and captured Seoul, capital of neighbouring South Korea. At that time, US President Truman added a new dimension to his country's foreign policy: the containment of communism, which would be expanded from its European focus to include Asia. Official US spokesmen conceived and propounded the domino theory, a warning that if Indochina (Vietnam, Laos and Cambodia) fell to communism, so too would the other countries of Southeast Asia.

Lisa was nearly three years old when Saigon fell on 30 April 1975 and the country was reunited after 117 years of French colonial rule and wars to become the Socialist Republic of Vietnam.

'When the communists took over they said they needed to take my father away for five days for questioning, but he didn't come back for eight years,' she said.

In the aftermath of the war, South Vietnamese families became households of women and children. At one stage, there was not one male living at home in Lisa's family. Two uncles who were soldiers were sent to labour camps and her father, who had been a captain in charge of artillery, was interned in a concentration camp in Hanoi for 're-education'.

According to historian Stanley Karnow, 'The potential victims of a Communist takeover numbered, in addition to 6000 Americans, more than 100,000 Vietnamese formerly employed by American agencies who, with their kin, swelled the total to nearly a million.'

Karnow recorded in his 1983 book, *Vietnam A History: The first complete account of Vietnam at war*, that 400,000 prisoners were sent to re-education camps where they suffered a regime of hard labour and a lack of human rights.

The communists proceeded to shunt South Vietnamese civil servants and army officers, as well as doctors, lawyers, teachers and journalists and other intellectuals into 're-education' centers. The inmates were reported to suffer from malnutrition, malaria, dysentery and other diseases as a result of inadequate food and medical care, and accounts of torture and summary execution abound ... Many were intense nationalists staying to contribute to their nation's reconstruction. Now, their spirit broken, they dream of escape.

Food was extremely scarce as agriculture was downgraded in favour of industry. The main diet of rice and fish was in short supply because the rice harvest was much reduced and fishermen lacked fuel and nets, and even boats, because thousands of refugees were fleeing the country aboard any vessel available. Hosts of children died of starvation. In a Vietnamese cartoon circulating at that time, Moscow rejected the desperate pleas for help from the Vietnamese. 'Tighten your belts', said a portly Moscow, to which skinny Vietnam replied, 'Send belts'.

Lisa's gentle grandmother, Bui Thi Buoi, brought up the two sisters because their mother was teaching far away in the countryside.

'I was separated from my parents for most of my childhood,' Lisa said. 'Children back then were often neglected, but we were doted on by our grandmother and aunties. They were just like our mother. My grandmother always dabbed perfumed oil on our temples and behind our ears after bathing us because she thought it would keep us from getting a chill. My mother's eldest sister was a seamstress and sewed and embroidered our dresses, which were the European style in pink or white. We had to look after our clothes. Mum was fussy about us going outside to play. My other aunty escorted us to the local school where she taught, so I was never scared to go out.'

The years from 1977 to 1980 became even tougher in Vietnam as the economy teetered towards collapse. The US imposed a trade embargo at the end of the war, which isolated Vietnam from the international community. The embargo was finally lifted in 1994. Over 65,000 political executions took place. The fall of Saigon and currency reform brought with it a wave of suicides, estimated by sources inside and outside Vietnam at 30,000. The number relocated to the re-education prison camps on previously uncultivated land swelled to over 1 million people, many of whom died.

The new government confiscated people's assets. Lisa's mother lost everything – her house, her assets and her teaching job. Lisa's aunties also lost their jobs. No one in the family had a job.

'With hyperinflation,' Lisa said, 'at times it seemed as though you needed a suitcase full of money to go shopping. Life was so tough. We were forced to do things that we had never thought we were capable of doing. My mother and aunties started to sell things to raise money to buy food. During this time my mother even sold cigarettes on the streets.'

They sold their furniture, their belongings, even their clothes. Lisa's mother and aunties sewed and embroidered to make ends meet. Everyone was on rations and there was never enough to eat.

'We would wait for my grandmother to return home with rice, salt, meat and oil – just the staples,' Lisa recalled. 'Rice was often mixed with inferior grains. I remember my grandmother and me sitting at the dining table sorting the rice grain by grain from the muck mixed with it. Meat was extremely scarce. When we had some money my grandmother would buy 200 grams of pork to cook a meal for five or more people and us kids. As children we were always given the meat first for a bit of protein. My mother would say, "Save it for our daughters".'

Lisa remembered one day the government received a big batch of butter from the Russians. Her grandmother rushed out to collect a ration, but it had melted and turned rancid.

'We ate it even though it made us feel sick,' said Lisa. 'We missed out on basic nutrition during a crucial growing period. That could explain why I am so petite. It's also where my thrift comes from.'

More than one million Vietnamese, including members of Lisa's family, fled the country after the war, risking everything for freedom. Aunty Phuong, Lisa's oldest aunty, escaped from Vietnam by boat in 1979 and was the first person in the family to settle in South Australia. Her uncle was picked up from a boat in the South China Sea by a US tanker and eventually settled in Texas. Then Lisa left with her younger aunty, Le Thi Loan, and uncle, Le Van Chung. Her mother didn't want both her children to escape at the same time and to perish together if disaster befell them. She staked her only cash on Lisa finding a better life while she remained in Saigon to care for her younger daughter, Ly.

Lisa's Aunty Loan told me how they had to leave Saigon secretly and hide in a house near the Mekong River. Before dawn, they waded through rice fields to a small boat, which navigated the meandering river. There were thirty-eight people below deck, hidden from the eyes of the local police. The boat missed the chance to sail in the dark, so they had to wait all day packed in like sardines and sail the river as if they were selling goods. Eventually, the boat took them to the mouth of the Mekong where the river met the sea. It was here that they boarded a bigger, sturdier boat, which was to take them across the South China Sea to any of the neighbouring countries. The small boat was sunk.

'At sea, the first big boat that we saw in the distance we thought was a freighter,' said Loan, 'but it was pirates. They boarded the boat and separated women to one place, men to another and children to a third spot. They searched everything. I only had a small gold Buddha I had hidden in my clothes, but they found it.'

Lisa was only seven, but she remembers the journey well.

'We endured ten or eleven days across the South China Sea. None of us were used to the ocean and many became seasick. We encountered eleven pirate ships altogether – Thai pirates who took all our jewellery and belongings.'

The pirates also took their food and contaminated their water with petrol. They were looted so many times that by the time they saw land, there was nothing left but a few boards in the boat. Even the engine had been ripped out and taken, leaving a big hole.

'I was extremely dehydrated from fever, malaria and malnutrition,' Lisa recalled. 'My aunty said that if we had been another few days at sea, I would not have made it. Despite being looted, we were one of the lucky boats because the pirates did not rape the women or throw anybody overboard or kill anyone.'

It was hot during the day and cold at night. There wasn't enough food or water, so in the end they drank seawater, which made them vomit.

'When we saw land and had to jump into the sea,' Lisa remembered with a shudder, 'I was absolutely petrified, even though my uncle was there to catch me.'

They had been swept southwest by the tides across the mouth of the Gulf of Thailand to Thailand's northern shore. Their dilapidated boat beached near Songkhla refugee camp. By good luck or coincidence, the aunty who had escaped first and the uncle who had been rescued by a US tanker had already landed at the same camp.

'We were lucky to strike land, otherwise we would have died,' said Loan. 'You don't know what will happen in your life, do you? Of the people who tried to leave Vietnam, one-third were caught by the police, another third died and one-third made it to another country.'

Any war casualty figures need to include the shocking toll of boat people – Pilger estimated perhaps a quarter of a million who fled lie at the bottom of the Gulf of Thailand and the South China Sea, either drowned or murdered by pirates.

Every country in the region prepared an excuse for rejecting the boat people: Malaysia was not a signatory to the United Nations Convention on Refugees and insisted that its brutal policy [of towing boats which landed back to sea] broke no law. Thailand did nothing seriously to discourage the rapacity of its pirate fishermen whose treatment of the boat people seemed at times unbelievable.

In his book *Heroes*, he wrote that 'Since the end of the war, the USA has taken 560,000 refugees, Canada 94,000 and Australia 91,000'.

The United Nations set up refugee centres in countries near Vietnam, such as Thailand and Indonesia. Australia was one of the first countries to give aid to Vietnam through a United Nations humanitarian program.

'I arrived in the Songkhla camp on a baking hot day wearing only a pair of undies,' said Lisa. 'I was so skinny that my uncle didn't recognise me. I had just lost my front teeth and I didn't look good. I had bites all over my body and was malnourished and confused. I remember my uncle lifting me onto his shoulders saying, "Oh my God, I can't believe it". He bought me a pair of thongs to stop my feet from burning. I remember the UN passing out high-protein biscuits and a can of milk. Everyone forced me to drink the milk, but I hated it because it gave me a terrible stomach ache. Years later I found out that I was lactose intolerant.

'We weren't healthy. I wasn't immunised. There were many mosquitoes and some people got malaria.'

The camp had been built in 1978 to house 1000 refugees. By the following year, there were 4674 people there and another 3000 spread along the coast to the north and south waiting to come in. So when Lisa arrived that year, 1979, a total of 7000 people were already crammed in.

Songkhla camp was enclosed by barbed wire. An open shed with a tin roof housed the refugees, who slept on wooden planks raised off the ground. Thin partitions separated one family from the next. While it was an impoverished existence, they considered themselves lucky to be there and sent news back to Saigon that they were safe.

'I spent my days on the beach,' said Lisa, 'a dirty and polluted stretch, but it provided hours of play. I would catch hermit crabs, put them in a plastic bucket and was bewildered the next day when they had all died.'

There were enough people to create a mini economy of swapping and trading among themselves. Many had relatives overseas who sent them money through the United Nations. The Nguyens had no relatives to rely on, so to earn money for food Loan sewed embroidered clothes as she had back home. Other Vietnamese refugees helped her out with needles, thread and material. Every morning the Nguyens, along with other camp residents, were allowed to go out of the camp to buy vegetables, fruit and meat at the nearby market.

'We would cook it at our spot along the tin-roofed rows,' Lisa said. 'We even had a taste of Wrigley's chewing gum from the US. It was a real luxury and could only be afforded as a special treat.

'No one tried to escape because then there would be no chance of your application being processed. We didn't starve and we weren't tortured, but it was hard. I wasn't homesick. I tried to look ahead.'

In a makeshift classroom under a tree American missionaries stationed at the camp taught English to adults and children. Lisa was a tiny, shy child. She was scared of the tall man who tried to enrol her in lessons.

'I had never seen anybody so gigantic with such blue eyes and blond hair. I scooted off. Needless to say, I didn't learn a word of English.'

They applied to the United Nations for refugee status. People could wait for two years for entry into the US because everyone wanted to go there: it was seen as a land of opportunity and most had friends or relatives there. The Australian representative took everyone who applied, but not many of the refugees wanted to go to Australia because they thought it was a rather racist, isolated country with a small Asian community. Lisa believed that was a legacy of the White Australia policy.

In 1980, the Nguyens flew into Adelaide where the older aunty, Phuong, had already settled. They were taken to Pennington hostel, which housed all the Vietnamese refugees. The cluster of semi-circular, corrugated iron Nissen huts was spartan by Australian standards, but good compared to what they had experienced. Outside the louvred windows, Lisa could see a row of Hills hoists with the washing flying in the breeze.

'I had never slept on a soft-mattress bed before,' she recalled. 'The huts were so, so cold in winter and so, so hot in summer. Thailand had been very hot and we arrived in cold weather. We had only a few clothes, and they were unsuitable for Australia. We had vouchers to go down to the op shop and get clothes and blankets. We would keep our radiators on all night. We feared we'd go up in smoke.'

The food was so different they couldn't stomach it – sandwiches, meat and jelly. Asian food, even rice, was hard to obtain back then. Apart from Lisa and her aunty, most of the Vietnamese didn't know how to use flushing toilets because they were used to drop latrines; they also didn't know how to take a bath or shower because they used basins of water and a scoop to pour water over themselves.

'I felt really homesick then,' Lisa said. 'The climate, the food, the people, not being able to communicate – it was all foreign and I had to relearn everything.'

Friendly Australians who wanted to welcome and support the Vietnamese volunteered to meet them. A Scot named David Binnie, who had served in Vietnam, looked after Lisa and her aunts. He and his parents, Margaret and Robert, and sister Anne and her husband Jim treated them kindly and showed them around the city. Never before had Lisa seen so many buildings and such affluence. David patiently explained Australian ways and, eventually, when the two families became good friends, he invited them all to live with his family.

'I started school straight away. The first year was mostly good,' Lisa recalled, 'but something was missing. Everybody else had parents and I didn't. Without my parents I relied on the love, support and friendship of my extended family. My understanding was limited without English. I was the first Asian child at Nailsworth Primary School. I had my very own teacher of English as a second language, so I grasped the language fast. Not having other Vietnamese kids around forced me to learn and to make friends with children of other nationalities, like Greek or Italian kids. They all wanted to teach me English. What motivated me was a desire to communicate and to relate to others.'

Lisa felt as if she were an only child. She had been without her sister in the Thai camp and in Australia and had little chance to interact with her in Vietnam. In 1983, her father was released from the concentration camp, briefly returned home and then escaped on a sailing boat. At the mouth of the Mekong delta, where the river meets the sea, the authorities chased his boat. Luck must have been on his side because the wind was blowing so fiercely that even the motorboats couldn't keep up with his vessel. The boat was the target of many gunshots, but luckily no one was hurt. His boat landed in Indonesia and from there he was taken to Bidong refugee camp. The United Nations approved him for settlement in Australia.

'The night I met my father for the first time since I was three in 1975, I didn't recognise him,' said Lisa. 'It was tense. He hadn't been a father for so long that he didn't know how to treat me. He said, "You must accept me as your father". I thought: How can I? I don't know you because you've never been there. It was strange to feel you have to get to know your own father. He wanted me to live with him, but he had been a career soldier and not used to children. He was a stern and serious man. You couldn't have a laugh with him. My aunties protested because they said he couldn't look after me. I stayed with my aunties because my mother insisted. What would I have done without my aunties? He moved in with some friends. When he visited, I would hear the gate creak open and run and hide. He would be really upset.'

It was difficult for both of them. Lisa's father also had to cope with the transition to a new country and way of life, as well as the pressure of saving enough money to sponsor his wife and other daughter to Australia. Lisa's aunties celebrated Mother's Day and sent photos of Lisa home to her mother every year.

'It took another three years before our family was reunited,' Lisa said.

Once again, sewing was the family's salvation. Aunty Phuong was a specialist in traditional Vietnamese dresses.

'I remember every dress I had because it was special,' said Lisa. 'My aunty would bribe me with embroidered dresses. That's how she had stopped me using a dummy back in Vietnam. I lived in my own fantasy world. There were so many things Australian girls had that I couldn't have because my aunties couldn't understand why I would need them. Sometimes David would give me those things. I think that is why I don't have hang-ups because he was always teaching me about Australian society.'

David worked for the government during the day and as a milkman at night.

'We used to have tons of milk products around. I couldn't eat them because they made me feel sick – the lactose intolerance. My job was to count the milk money every night. I earned $2 a week and started my own coin collection when I was nine. I lived an Australian life and joined in Learn to Swim classes with all the kids in summer, but I didn't like it because of my experience at sea. I would stay with David's mother, Margaret, during the holidays and come back with a brilliant Scottish accent. Aunty Anne and Uncle Jim took me in to their family as if I were their own daughter. I stayed with them in school holidays and Aunty Anne would take me shopping and to see movies at the Goodwood movie theatres. They wanted to adopt me, but I already had parents.'

Over this time, David fell in love with Aunty Loan. In 1983, three years after the family had arrived in Australia with only their clothes, David and Loan married in a friend's garden. Lisa, dressed in traditional clothing made by Aunty Phuong, was a bridesmaid.

'I had been on a school camp and was terribly sunburnt. How typically Australian. I had a peeling nose so the aunties scrubbed my nose until it was red raw.'

Her new Uncle David was her avenue into a strange world. It was he who introduced her to a traditional Australian Christmas dinner with roast turkey, ham, coleslaw and potato salad. He took her to buy a Christmas tree and stuffed one of his knee-high socks with presents for the little girl.

'He was always a joker,' Lisa said. 'He would organise my birthday parties somewhere exciting each year so I didn't feel different from the other girls – at Hungry Jacks or Pizza Hut, fishing for trout in the Adelaide Hills or having fun at a performing act of dancing galahs.'

Aunty Loan had a law degree from Saigon University, but she learnt English and retrained as an interpreter. Later, she worked as a community liaison officer with teachers, Vietnamese students and parents.

In 1986, Lisa's mother and sister arrived in Adelaide.

'I had not seen them for seven years. I couldn't wait for my mother to arrive. It was a happy and emotional time, not anxious like when my father arrived because I had a better recollection of my mum. I look like her. My sister, Nguyen Tien Hoang Ly, was a gifted musician so she was enrolled in a special music school. My father had high expectations that were hard to live up to. He wanted my sister to become a concert pianist and practise every day, but she rebelled and left home when she was 19. I didn't see her for years.'

Lisa's sister is a full-time student finishing her commerce degree and has worked in aged care. Christmas 2005 was the first time Lisa had seen Ly in ten years. During that decade Lisa had learnt to be self-reliant.

'I like to think that out of every bad situation you learn something new. I began to see that being different could be an advantage. I had learnt how to get along with people, how to share what I had. I think this helped me cope in Australia.'

After her work at the South Australian Department of Primary Industries the day we met, Lisa picked me up and headed to the suburb where her immediate family live. Lisa, her parents and her two aunties bought houses within walking distance of each other.

'I want to protect my family and what we have,' Lisa said as she showed me around the neat, two-bedroom house. 'It stems from feeling really fearful of losing what I've worked for. I acted as security for my parents to buy their house in Adelaide. We wanted to buy houses together so we could all be close, as in Vietnam. Only one other family member can drive. We're not under one roof, but near enough and far enough away. My mother comes every day to look after my house when I'm away. We are together, despite my father's experiences of war, the camp and escape when he was shot at many times. My mother stuck with him through all of that.'

The Nguyens have returned to Vietnam several times over the last 25 years. On their first visit, in 1991, they didn't know what to expect.

'We had to bribe our way through Saigon Airport,' Lisa said. 'Western influences were starting to appear. Business had increased and foreign-based Vietnamese were investing in the country through their families. People didn't ride bicycles any more; they wanted scooters.'

Lisa's family, who are Buddhists, visited the neighbourhood temple and paid their respects to parents and grandparents whose ashes were kept there in sealed jars. Lisa found a sense of calm and rest in the temple. Its care was in the hands of monks who prayed for their relations. Families repay them with monthly gifts of fruit and donations so that the monks can take care of the temple.

The family used to own two houses – a tiny house of two rooms in the centre of Saigon, which was stifling in summer and where they shared a communal toilet, and the more spacious apartment in the suburbs that the government confiscated in 1975. Lisa helped her family purchase the apartment back from the government in 2006.

'It was important to me to keep the house in the family,' she said. 'It was home to us all when we were growing up and during the war. Two of my aunties live there now. The breeze from a nearby lake provides respite from the searing noon-day heat. Water is still rationed, especially when there is high usage, and the electricity can be cut off any time without warning.'

Lisa has fond memories of this house where she feels a sense of security and connection with her former homeland.

'My sister and I would sit out on the balcony with our legs dangling over the edge and wait for my grandmother to come home from the markets. We always hoped she would bring us a little sweet or pancake. My aunty would teach my sister and me at home. We had a large dining table with chairs that were far too big for us. We had to sit on at least three dictionaries to reach the table. We were tiny little beings.'

The next day Lisa and I drove along the lower reaches of the Murray where it slowly winds to the sea, then to the fertile Riverland through the dry country I had observed from the plane. There, Lisa had meetings with fruit producers who export to Asia. The success of many horticultural industries in the region has been through the backbreaking labour of itinerant fruit pickers like Lisa's parents. They were willing to work long, hard hours to get established in Australia. They would leave their daughters for the week to travel the two or three hours to work, and return on weekends.

'Back in the 1980s, mainly Vietnamese people picked fruit in the Riverland, so my parents never felt isolated. They were among their own people. Aunty Phuong would come to look after us when our parents were away. It took its toll as they tried to acclimatise, take care of us, learn to live together again and earn money. The sight of the fruit mesmerised my mother. She loved fruit trees. There were so many pictures of my mother in orchards holding oranges and grapes. To see beautiful, *orange* oranges [Vietnamese oranges are green] or almond blossom always made her happy.'

Lisa's parents set up their own market garden nearer to their Adelaide home. They grew greenhouse vegetables in Virginia on the northern Adelaide plains. In the late 1980s when approximately 1000 Greeks, Italians, and Cambodian and Vietnamese boat people worked on 700 hectares on the fringe of the city, Virginia boasted the largest concentration of greenhouse production in Australia.

'There were many migrants doing it tough,' said Lisa, 'making the best of small opportunities. Although their acreages were small, it was intensive work growing carrots, capsicum, green vegetables and tomatoes.'

They sold via agents. Lisa's father was the Vietnamese representative on the Virginia Horticultural Centre board. She had her introduction to horticulture as proxy for her father when he couldn't go to meetings.

'He never wanted me to work in the markets, but to be a doctor or lawyer or dentist. I said to my father that mastering the English language was what would stand me in good stead. It's a huge part of whatever culture you are in to connect with the people. I think my father agrees with me now.'

Lisa enjoys learning new languages. Upon mastering English, she went on to study French and Italian at Adelaide High School. In Year 11, Lisa's family saved up so she could spend three months as an exchange student in northern Italy.

'I went to Livorno, only ten minutes from the Leaning Tower of Pisa and 20 minutes from Florence, to study and live with an Italian family. I loved Florence. I learnt history, poetry and the language.'

After high school, Lisa completed a bachelor of arts for which she took up Spanish, as well as majoring in Italian. She is fluent in English and Vietnamese, although, to her father's disappointment, she can't read and write Vietnamese. Then she completed a bachelor of management in marketing. In 1995, Lisa became the first Asian banking officer to be appointed by National Australia Bank (NAB) in South Australia.

'It was tough being in an area where nobody had been before, but it was also an opportunity. The hard work paid off because I was invited to assist management in expanding the bank's Asian customer base in Adelaide. I received a professional excellence award.'

While at NAB, Lisa had a manager who was her mentor and inspired her to achieve above her own expectations. In turn, Lisa mentored a young aspiring banker.

'I took the initiative to train her because I saw her desire to achieve. My reward came when the girl told me that she had been promoted to branch manager, four levels above her current position. I found it rewarding to mentor and to be mentored.'

She also discovered that being in a niche position was better than being in the mainstream.

'Many Vietnamese people stuck to their community, but I decided early on to play my differences to advantage. My father's nature was to go against the mainstream. He was a bohemian, heavily into Western philosophy, history and literature, which he read in French and English. He taught himself Chinese. He had strong views about politics. When Saigon fell, my mother burnt many of his books, manuscripts, music and any evidence of Western influence because she was scared for the family. He still reads constantly. Like him, I question convention and seek points of difference.'

One such maverick choice was Lisa's decision to go into the field of horticulture. Funded by the Virginia growers and the Horticulture Research and Development Board, she became the first export market development officer in South Australia.

'Back then there was only one marketing officer for horticulture and that was me,' she said. 'I didn't think it would be the place to start marketing, but by thinking out of left field about my career, I gave myself opportunities that only a person with many years of experience would be offered.'

Virginia was a tough place to begin. Lisa was inexperienced in the horticultural industry and a woman among older males from twenty-eight ethnic groups, many of whom didn't readily accept a female perspective. It was a breakthrough for her industry.

'I'm sure that many people did not expect the first person to be young, Asian and female. It made me stick out from the crowd. I accepted the position to practise the marketing concepts that I had learnt at uni. Little did I know that marketing would be the least of my challenges. The most testing one was dealing with some of the farmers who had fixed ideas.'

Farmers were accustomed to producing what they wanted to sell, rather than what the consumer might want. Lisa worked one on one, going into the paddocks to talk with growers. The first words they exchanged would always be about the weather or prices. Growers mainly supplied the local market of Adelaide. Lisa's job was to familiarise them with exporting and expose them to overseas markets. She would invite international customers to meet them in the Virginia region and also take them to the traditional open-air wet markets of

Asia where local farmers sold their fresh produce – stalls of fruit and vegetables, fresh fish and meat. Her constant aim was to boost overseas orders.

'It wasn't a desk job and you couldn't go onto farms in high heels,' she said. 'Farmers whinge a lot. You just have to put up with it. I identified the movers and shakers in the community, handpicked those I could work with and interacted on a business level. I was more of a change agent than a marketing person.'

Lisa had to learn how to develop and put forward her ideas to the almost fifty growers she was working with, especially on how to understand and produce what the Asian consumer wanted. She found the best way to communicate was via the top 20 per cent of growers – 'the A-team' – who grew 80 per cent of the produce and were export ready, and 'the B-team' who wanted to be export ready. Lisa implemented a host of programs to increase farmers' knowledge, trust and confidence to export.

'I worked with the biggest retail chain in Singapore, Fairprice,' Lisa said. 'We were exporting broccoli by air. My research showed the Americans were able to successfully sea freight lettuce to Taiwan, so I implemented sea freight to Singapore. It meant more consistent supply and higher profits because we could lower the freight costs. Both grower and retailer could offer specials because each sea container carried 440 boxes compared to 50 boxes by plane.'

She persuaded several growers to get together to supply a broccoli order that one alone could not meet. It broke down competitive resistance between growers who, despite being from different ethnic groups, were growing similar products.

'Many growers were illiterate, opportunistic and mistrustful,' Lisa said. 'I had to be sensitive to what mattered to them, namely, confidentiality, whether they were crooks or angels. I did the work and was respected. Sometimes I would see things I wasn't meant to see and be privy to confidential business dealings. If it was a choice between confidentiality and getting the job done, I would always go with confidentiality because I needed to be trusted and to be discreet. Fortunately, I had a mentor in Tony Clark whom I could call for advice.'

Tony, the general manager of Mondello Farms, was chairman of Lisa's advisory group. He credited her with being the first outsider to influence the region's producers to look outward.

'It took confidence and ability,' Tony said. 'She was proactive and successful.'

When Lisa began in the area, it was not very progressive. One farmer told Tony how he was on his tractor one day and spotted a tiny yellow speck in the distance walking towards him across the paddock.

'It was Lisa, only 5 feet tall in her yellow anorak and yellow wellies,' Tony recounts. 'She got on the tractor and the farmer had to listen to her. "I couldn't escape," he later told me. "She was determined." That's how she gradually overcame the indifference. She educated the growers who were not receptive to new ways.'

Lisa felt pleased that she could walk onto small farms, talk to people of many nationalities and be accepted.

'My ability to empathise provided me with a link to them and I used my position to introduce different ideas. I enjoyed it because many of the farmers were self-made people like me. I wasn't rich or armed with a Masters in Business Administration.'

Lisa had to paint a picture of what Australia's competitors did well and show growers facts, figures and comparable prices to prove her point. But many producers still believed they produced value while their competitors produced volume.

'Since then, the international market has changed dramatically with the emergence of China as a major player. I predicted that, but farmers would still say, "We produce quality; China produces crap". It took so much energy out of me trying to convince them. I was exhausted. Once I travelled by myself to four countries in three weeks to promote Australian produce. I realised I had to find an easier way of working. One day, my overseas driver said, "Why, Miss, you do this work?"'

Lisa applied for a job with Food South Australia in a similar field of international market development. She was now responsible for larger international projects: the marketing of Australian products in the affluent new markets of Asia and the Middle East and developing new market opportunities for Australian producers and suppliers.

The Australian Pavilion project in Singapore began in 2001. It negotiated for dedicated floor space in Fairprice stores to stock exclusively Australian products. Lisa had already built a relationship with this major Asian store and set about working with the supply chain to enable South Australian companies to put their products on the shelves of the huge retailer. They did in-store promotions, food tastings and cooking demonstrations to introduce new foods. Since 2001, Australian Pavilions has generated more than $7 million in sales from 230 Australian companies nationally. The distributor has started to implement this successful platform model in other countries, such as Malaysia and Thailand.

Lisa's other focus was Dubai on the Persian Gulf, a totally different environment from Asia. Its focus was tourists and food service in super-smart resorts and hotels. Dubai is home to Burj Al Arab, the world's tallest and first seven-star hotel. This monument to extravagance is shaped like the sail of an Arab dhow. The royal suite sets a lucky guest back a cool $15,000 a night – how else could the hotel pay off the helipad on the roof or the computerised waterfalls in the lobby?

'Burj Al Arab was where the federal and state governments organised a gala dinner featuring Australian foods, such as South Australian kingfish, luscious oysters from Port Lincoln and Australian native flavours, such as wattle seed infused icecream, lemon myrtle sorbet and the like. It was opulent, but the $1 million strategy embedded our quality foods in the minds of Dubai's top chefs.'

Since 2004, total sales to Dubai generated more than $7 million for 40 Australia-wide suppliers.

As we neared the Riverland the dusty landscape changed. The Murray snaked its slow course alongside cliffs. In the distance golden ripening wheat stretches away from the river. Huge round bales of hay dot the paddocks. To see the rows of grape vines and citrus orchards it was hard to believe that towns such as Waikerie had an annual rainfall as low as 300 millimetres. Stone fruit and almond orchards are laid out in neat rows. Irrigation and fertile alluvial soil are the keys.

Leroy Sims is Lisa's partner. A leading producer of almonds, citrus and stone fruit, he runs a large property edged by a stunning windbreak of autumn-yellowed poplars. We noticed lemons lying under rows upon rows of trees. The market has collapsed and they are not worth picking, but were left on the trees to drop or rot. It's much the same for wine grapes. When a major wine company did not renew contracts for the 2006 vintage, the grapes were left to wither into bunches of dried fruit on vines. Leroy said that oversupply generated a massive 1.9 billion litres of wine in storage across Australia in January 2006. His family's packing shed is massive, outfitted with conveyor belts, sorting and grading sieves and storage covering a hectare. His father's engineering genius is responsible for the design and manufacture of components. (Late in 2006 Leroy's father was killed in a car accident in China as he was travelling to develop more horticultural opportunities abroad.)

An outdoor café overlooking the river was the perfect place for a late lunch. We relished prawns from the cool Southern Ocean, salad greens with citrus dressing from the Riverland, a fruity Riesling from the Barossa and homemade crusty bread. Lisa said her next promotional event will showcase such quality South Australian products in the Philippines' capital, Manila, where she was organising a dinner followed by a two-week promotion with businesses, trade importers and distributors.

I asked Lisa what she would select as the most delectable South Australian products for a special meal.

'I love seafood,' said Lisa, 'so I would choose Pacific oysters natural, King George whiting from Port Lincoln, Maggie Beer's gourmet products, homemade pork sausages from the Barossa Valley and Angus beef, guaranteed tender, with a little wine.'

If our lunch is anything to go by, the produce on our plates looked as if it could have marketed itself. Lisa sets me straight on that.

'You need persistence and resilience to market primary products because the knockbacks are many. Many producers and processors are unsure about exporting.'

In 2003, Lisa Nguyen was awarded a Centenary of Federation medal by the Governor-General for her services to the business community and to the Virginia horticultural region. People from Virginia and the business community had nominated her.

'In receiving the medal I felt that Australian society valued my contribution in making a difference in a region that was considered difficult. I felt privileged to be in this country and honoured to be recognised for giving something back.'

Lisa now has an opportunity to help more people through work on advisory councils and boards.

'I served for eight months on the advisory council of the Office of Status of Women for the Liberal Government's Honourable Diana Laidlaw. We helped young women gain financial independence, among other issues. My colleagues were wonderful, but I didn't enjoy the first term. It was a bit lofty; too much talk and not enough action. Then Labor was elected and I was appointed by Premier Mike Rann to the Labor equivalent, the Premier's Council for Women, from 2002 for three years. It was dynamic. The women had experience of grassroots issues and the role of government. One of our biggest contributions was to increase the participation of women on boards from 30 per cent to 50 per cent, partly through use of the Premier's Women's Register which was a way of registering women who aspired to boards.'

It is important to Lisa to help others and, in so doing, develop a balanced sense of self and skills beyond normal work. She is motivated by the need to progress in her work and personal relationships. In a speech delivered to students at her former school, Adelaide High, in 2002 she said that success must come from within.

We are the opportunity, and what we become, we have made out of ourselves. Our backgrounds don't determine what we become. We determine what we become. I don't think it is good enough to say that you didn't have the opportunity, or to make excuses. Successful people come from very different backgrounds, education and circumstances. Investing in yourself through lifelong learning is the best investment you

can ever make. Having personal and professional mentors provides you with leadership and support for important decisions. Rely on your family and friends to get you where you want to be.

Back in the early 1980s, Australia opened its doors and hearts to displaced people such as Lisa and put out a welcome mat to enable her family to start a new life of hope, freedom, progress and, ultimately, happiness.

Lisa said, 'As one of the 20 million refugees around the world who have fled their countries amid war and injustice, I consider myself lucky to have survived. It highlights the resilience of human beings to triumph over adversity. Adversity is not always a bad thing because it can bring out the best in people to strive to achieve more. Some people think that the road to success and achievement is easy, but I can say that it's all to do with hard work, especially when you are a migrant or refugee. Having arrived in Australia with nothing, not even my parents, I have had to build and create opportunities for myself from the bottom up.'

One night Lisa was in Hong Kong dining in a plush restaurant high on a hill overlooking the harbour with its glittering lights of myriad ships.

'I was intensely moved as I thought about how I left Vietnam on a boat like those moving lazily below. Now I was on top of the world looking at it from above. I felt how lucky I was to see the world as a million shiny stars and not a million lights of pirate boats on the sea.'

Lisa is a passionate advocate for refugees and especially for the protection of women and children.

'Refugees are not a threat to Australia,' Lisa said. 'Refugees are themselves threatened and they need Australians' urgent help and protection. Refugees are people who could be an asset to the community and nation. In any refugee population, approximately 50 per cent are women and girls. Stripped of the protection of their homes, women and girls are particularly vulnerable to acts of harassment, sexual abuse and indifference. Effective protection involves giving refugee women the right to access asylum based on their own legitimate claims.'

Refugee men continue to be viewed as sole applicants for refugee status, determination and registration, which results in refugee women having limited access to asylum procedures.

'In many instances, women followed men,' Lisa said, 'even against their will, because they were dependent on them. These issues are forced upon women who seek assistance and protection for social, economic and civil rights. The public debate on the issue of Australia's population is an important and timely one that needs positive action.'

She pointed out that former immigrants and refugees have contributed economically and culturally to Australia and its development. She strongly supports intelligent debate and action on refugee issues as a national priority for this century.

'I used to love having my stars read when I visited Vietnam, to have my life mapped out in a few pages for a few dollars. If only life were so simple. You never set out to define your life, or how it should be. It just happens and you may end up in places where you never dreamt you could be.'

Lisa takes heart from the words of psychologist and humanist Viktor Frankl, who endured soul-destroying treatment in the Nazi death camps in the Second World War. In his 1946 book *Man's Search for Meaning*, Frankl wrote:

> **Don't aim at success – the more you aim at it and make it a target, the more you are going to miss it. For success, like happiness, cannot be pursued; it must ensue, and it only does so as the unintended side effect of one's personal dedication to a cause greater than oneself, or as the by-product of one's surrender to a person other than oneself. Happiness must happen, and the same holds for success: you have to let it happen by not caring about it. I want you to listen to what your conscience commands you to do and go on to carry it out to the best of your knowledge. Then you will live to see that in the long-run – success will follow you precisely because you had forgotten to think about it.**

'My family and I are all happy and successful,' she said, 'not because we set out to achieve such goals, but as a consequence of making the best of every situation that came our way. Life means much more to me than my career or job. I'm comfortable enough now to invest time and effort in my personal relationships.'

At the same time, Lisa wants her family and herself to be secure and comfortably off.

'I can identify with the Aussie battler notion,' she said. 'My fear of losing it all and having to start all over again is always with me, but I turn that into a positive to constantly drive myself forward, to keep improving myself. Some may say that I've been unfortunate to experience so much in my youth, but I tend to think that I've been extremely fortunate to experience challenges that have shaped my character.'

Lisa is fascinated by human nature, by the potential in human beings to strive, however they define progress.

'I love to have deep conversations over dinner about people and how they interact, how they end up teasing solutions from the complex web of life.'

The 1980 photograph of Lisa with her Aunty Loan, taken for the United Nations application for entry to life in Australia, is a great source of inspiration to her.

'It's a universal image that encapsulates our years of loss, hope and a new beginning in our adopted homeland. It makes me feel I've come a long way and have been extremely lucky to be where I am now.'

She holds enduring habits of self-reliance. 'It's part of being a refugee and having to rely on yourself. I've had to learn the meaning of sharing and trust. I have had to learn to let myself be taken care of and to give myself permission to receive from others without questioning the validity. My relationship with Leroy has enabled me to peel away layers to reveal emotions that are important and fundamental. I always thought I understood the meaning of big words such as compromise, happiness, endurance, trust and courage, but they take on a fuller meaning when you decide to share your life with another person.'

Lisa Nguyen's story has become part of the Adelaide Migration Museum permanent exhibition, *Immigration and Settlement of South Australia*, from the 1970s to the present. She has donated a few significant belongings for display to help people comprehend the immensity of her journey – the United Nations photo of the seven-year-old Lisa with her Aunty Loan, as well as her tattered undies, the only piece of clothing and her sole possession when the boat landed at Songkhla refugee camp back in 1979, and her prized Australian Centenary Medal.

Will Bignell climbing Rocky Tom, near Hobart, 2004

5

Miller Bignell Esq.

Will Bignell, Bothwell, Tasmania

It was July 2003. In the central highlands of Tasmania the air felt a bit nippy, even at mid-morning. The scene could have been straight out of an old British painting – a backdrop of rounded hills dotted with yellow-flowering prickly gorse against which was set ancient buildings and trees standing stark in their winter dress. A tall, lean man with dark, curly hair prepared a motor glider for take-off from a paddock. This was 20-year-old Will Bignell. He greeted me with a big grin and we climbed into the two-seater. A qualified glider pilot since he was 18, Will did the final safety checks and we fastened seat belts. He warmed up the engine, taxied to the end of the airstrip and called his codename, Whisky Victor Whisky, over the radio to alert any aircraft in the area. We were cleared for take-off, the glider gathered speed down the strip and suddenly we were in the air. Will searched for thermal air currents. At 1500 feet this graceful craft, with its massive 16 metre wingspan, hooked into one. Will cut the engine and we soared towards the wave clouds for which Bothwell is famous.

'The Roaring Forties blow in an uninterrupted flow from the west across the Southern Ocean and hit the mountains only 50 kilometres from here,' Will said. 'That creates the waves as clouds line up at right angles to the wind. They can take a glider up to 30,000 feet – but not today.'

It was exhilarating. Will describes gliding as being like surfing in the sky, stimulating and peaceful at the same time. With the motor off it is quiet, as free as a bird in its swooping flight. Indeed, we had a bird's-eye view of the valley of farms and the historic village of Bothwell, population 400, clustered along the Clyde River and ringed by the hills. Only an hour's drive from Hobart, it is possible to have this glimpse of nineteenth century rural Tasmania. Will pointed out the gracious buildings, fifty-two of which are either classified by or registered with the National Trust, and Ratho built in 1837, now the oldest golf course in the Southern Hemisphere. The rugged landscape could be Scottish, which may explain why Scots flocked to Bothwell in the 1800s, displacing the original inhabitants of the Big River Aboriginal tribe after numerous clashes. After Scottish settlers came exiled Irish nationalist leaders John Martin and John Mitchel, and other colourful characters, including the bushranger Mike Howe. Howe met a sticky end: he was captured and beheaded in 1818, his head then taken to Hobart Town so the reward offered for his capture could be claimed. Artisans such as bootmakers, tanners, farriers and millers settled to service the growing farming area and convicts were assigned to the free settlers.

Beneath us now was the 2400 hectare Thorpe Farm that stretches along the Clyde on the outskirts of Bothwell; its centrepiece is a large, kidney-shaped lake fed by an offshoot of the river. Symmetrical plantings of pines, poplars and willows mark groups of buildings – the original homestead and outhouses, the modern, low-slung home where Will's family lives and, across the lake, an ancient red-brick building that dominates the landscape. Built in 1823, this is the oldest working watermill in Australia.

'The mill is older than Melbourne. It's an awesome link to history,' Will said. Restoring it has captured his imagination, as it did his father John's.

Thorpe Farm was named by Thomas Axford after his wife Martha's village of Aston Upthorpe in England. They came to the central highlands in 1819 to take over a land grant for the farm. Thomas built the mill with convict labour in 1823 and powered it from the Clyde River. Travel around these isolated places had many dangers. In 1865 Thomas was murdered for his mill takings on the Midland Highway at Constitution Hill by Rocky Whelan, a notorious bushranger.

'According to newspaper clippings of the time, his head was bashed in with a rock of immense proportions,' Will said. 'Rocky didn't find the money, which was hidden in Thomas's shoe. Rocky had a week-long killing spree, was captured and hung in Hobart Town a few weeks later.'

A Bignell ancestor, Fred McDowell, who was a neighbour, bought the mill and surrounding 800 acres in the 1890s for between £400 and £500. He operated it over the turn of the century, but by 1917 the advent of faster, cheaper roller mills put the mill out of commercial operation. Later, the axle broke, floods silted up the mill race and it was looted. The old mill lay derelict for decades until Will's father John and his brother Peter started to restore it in the mid-1970s. They replaced the shingle roof and dug the pit out around the waterwheel in a space less than two metres high and wide. Wielding a shovel in such a small space presented quite a challenge to the two metre tall John Bignell.

'Dad is fond of a shovel,' Will laughed. 'Never be afraid of anything with a wooden lever he always tells me. They had to flood the mill and float the new axle in with pulleys, rebuild its housing, reset the gears and replace the teeth to get it up and running again.'

In the early 1980s, drought and rural depression took its toll on farming. Will's great-great-grandfather had once said that the frosts at Bothwell would ruin anything except cabbages and wool, but John Bignell was determined to find viable alternatives. Will's mother, Jill, earned off-farm income, first teaching at the local school, and then developing foreign languages in the state's schools. In 1982, John won a Nuffield Scholarship to study deer enterprises in Europe. He was among the first permitted to farm wild deer that he captured in the central highlands. Deer was a new industry for Australia and from his research John later published a paper in 1993, 'Genetics of Coat Colour in Fallow Deer', which he had presented to the proceedings of the first world forum on fallow deer farming in Mudgee, New South Wales. Thorpe Farm ran 500 fallow deer, from which John produced venison, in addition to 12,000 sheep and 100 cattle. As we flew over the farm, the deer leapt in skittish fashion. John now sells them live to an abattoir. Will pointed out a mob of rat-tailed sheep in the adjoining paddocks, East Friesians, a breed uncommon in Australia. The Bignells imported genetic material from New Zealand to breed Tasmania's first East Friesian sheep, which are ideal for milking.

In 1991 John needed to find other survival options after the federal government removed the reserve price scheme for wool. As prices crashed and recession set in, farmers around Australia had to shoot sheep. While in France researching the deer, John and Jill had visited a young man whom they knew from a student exchange to Bothwell. The Frenchman now milked goats and sold 300 cheeses a week through the farmers' market in Lyons. John saw an opportunity and on his return began milking a few sheep; he taught himself cheesemaking from books and visited specialty cheesemakers. While he could handle thousands of sheep easily, he drew the line at raising and milking cantankerous goats. Instead, he had goat milk delivered by local women who reared and milked their own herds.

John experimented with sheep and goat milk farmhouse cheeses. Every week he would transform 600 litres of goat's milk into cheese and produced five tonnes a year. His ash-coated, aged or surface-ripened Tasmanian highland chevres and Bothwell blue sheep's milk cheeses became sought after in restaurants and specialty markets around Australia. They won top awards.

'I loved travelling around the cheese factories with Dad when he started to make cheese,' Will said. 'I was encouraged to think with a different mindset. Being seventh generation on this bit of dirt brings with it a lot of pressure not to lose it. My goal is to innovate and improve it.'

When he went to Hutchins school in Hobart to board for seven years, the headmaster told him to grab the many opportunities his school offered.

'I took that on board and tried everything from underwater hockey to canoe polo. I started rock climbing then because I was terrified of heights. My reports always said "a bit over-committed".'

When in Year 10, Will entered a national Plan Your Own Enterprise competition. He developed a business plan for Tasmanian Highland Horseradish combining the Thorpe Farm goat cheese and horseradish in a sauce. He won the state award and finished as national runner-up.

As the glider dropped to 1000 feet, we did a circuit over the trees onto the airstrip. The crisp air gave a hint of how chilly these highlands can become. Temperatures drop so low that eggs freeze if left overnight in the nests. The family takes advantage of this unique climate to grow root crops such as horseradish. Will pointed out a nearby furrowed paddock where he was growing the horseradish roots, which he marketed directly to restaurants in Hobart and through distributors to specialty greengrocers in Sydney and Melbourne. Will's younger brother, George, was producing salsify, a Mediterranean root vegetable. Like Will, George studied agricultural science at the University of Tasmania.

Will's latest venture was a new cold-climate crop for Australia – Japanese horseradish, or wasabi. The idea for growing the plant came from local Asian chefs. No Japanese raw fish or sushi rice dish would be complete without this lime-green paste mixed with soy sauce. Wasabi is to Japanese culture what tomato sauce is to the meat pie for Australians. The prized condiment looks as innocuous as mashed avocado, but it is red hot. The Japanese have long believed and are supported by research that says daily consumption of wasabi can improve health and fight off a large number of illnesses, including reducing the growth of different types of cancer cells, reducing the possibility of blood clots and boosting the body's immune system.

'When we delivered venison or cheese, chefs would say, "You have a cold climate and good water supply. Could you grow wasabi?" Dad read up about it and encouraged me to try. Wasabi is temperamental to grow. It needs consistently low temperatures or it gets black rot.'

Will was experimenting with its temperature tolerance. Back at the house he looked in the fridge for milk and instead pulled out a pot plant and put it on the kitchen bench, which was covered with cake tins full of plants.

'Most bachelors have a six-pack in their fridge. I'm trialling wasabi in here because it's warmer than outside where it can be minus 5 overnight.'

Behind the house, a long metal structure covered in green shadecloth was filled with rows of the violet-like plant. The bright green leaves had a sharp taste, but the surprise was the sturdy stem.

'Basically, you stress the plant for its entire life so it stays dwarfed,' Will said. 'If you are lucky, you get this great stem popping out about an inch around. Theoretically, a plant can last indefinitely because it is always producing new shoots. You can also take cuttings or import tissue cultures.'

Will told me that there are two ways of growing wasabi – in soil or in water.

'Come and see the aquatic beds.'

We walked to the lake and picked our way over a screened outlet that stops fish escaping downstream. Will and George built a small fish farm within the lake.

'We both like fly fishing, so we fattened a few brown trout in here and released them into the lake when they were hand size. The cormorants are thriving on them.'

Downstream of the lake, Will pulled back a tarpaulin to reveal his aquatic beds made of Besser blocks and river gravel. In Japan, top-grade wasabi is traditionally grown in crystal clear mountain streams. Farmers build up their beds in the rivers – boulders at the bottom to progressively smaller rocks and gravel at the surface – where they plant the wasabi.

'The way I grow it is basically an adaptation of Japanese methods. Water can accumulate in the spaces of the beds and flow through fast enough to keep disease levels down.'

It takes two years to produce a crop, but if the water warms up or stagnates, the plants strike trouble. Will's first experimental crop had grown and developed thick stems, but summer heat brought on black rot. A few plants struggled on.

'It's horrible stuff, black and slimy.' Will broke into his infectious laugh. 'We worked out that the water temperature has to be 12 degrees maximum to reduce disease. The research is documented in Japanese so my aunt, who is a lecturer in Tokyo, translated it for me.'

After he finished school Will took a year off to work at home. Those twelve months gave him a chance to experience the full weather cycle, learn what he didn't know about the farm and what he wanted to study in future.

'Through experimenting with wasabi I changed my choice of degree at the University of Tasmania from applied agriculture to agricultural science. I have an inquisitive mind and wanted a depth of understanding on pretty complex questions, such as how the plants extract oxygen from the water and use it for growth? How do I improve yields efficiently? Would saturating the water with fertiliser work better than adding it to the plant?'

Due to its difficult growing conditions and lack of availability, wasabi is still a niche crop that is expensive in the marketplace. Aquatic-grown wasabi commands a higher premium than soil-grown because of its superior taste and appearance. According to Will, the Japanese turn up their noses at soil-grown wasabi; only 5 per cent of sushi shops in Japan use fresh wasabi. Potentially, all the leaves can be sold to the salad trade, but the lucrative part of the plant is the stem. Will can expect to make $100 a kilo for an average quality stem and $200 for export quality. There is a significant off-season market in Japan for this fiery little plant, the stem of which, in traditional Japanese preparation, is grated on shark skin.

'Imagine – exporting Tasmanian wasabi to Japan.'

Chefs from stylish restaurants were clamouring for the wasabi leaves and stem because it was so rare in Australia. In a television program in 2002, *Goodbye Meat Pie*, young chefs from around the country got together for a cook-off using Australian-grown produce.

'My wasabi was used in the entrée section. Three scallops were laid on a wasabi leaf, which has a nice heart shape, and drizzled with a seafood sauce. It was absolutely divine. The dish presented well and you could also eat the leaf. We won the entrées. The judges said the clincher was the peppery-flavoured leaf sourced from Tassie.'

Will has been selling the leaves for several years.

'At times, I bang myself on the head and think: What am I doing out here at two in the morning picking wasabi leaves to go on a bus at 5 o'clock when all I want is to go back to bed? But I need to recoup the money I spent on the shadecloth. I was told by Dad, who is my bank manager, to keep this business pretty much at zero credit level.'

We walked around the lake. Deer grazed in front of the old mill. They were pretty creatures with their coats of brown and white, sometimes pure white. They raced past as we approached and every few steps, some jumped completely off the ground. Managing such flighty creatures takes skill and patience – and high fences. Two and a half metre fences stop mass escape to the hills.

Up close the ancient red mill looks imposing; the mill pond, covered in pink water weed, is fed by a channel from the Clyde River, which flows around a contour, through a sluice gate and via a barrier called a 'cat catcher'.

'It stops cats, sticks or whatever else is in the mill pond from fouling up the works,' Will said. 'When it was working, the whole building would rumble. You felt the vibrations of the machinery. You would hear the roar of the water through the wheel and it had this smell that I remember as the grain was ground. I want to get it going so I can relive all of that.'

Through a wooden door was a large, gloomy room into which shone a shaft of light from a window high up on the northern wall. It lit the uneven stone floor, worn by 180 years of footsteps. Pieces of an ancient millstone of pitted quartz imported from France are laid neatly on the floor. A photo display on the wall tracks the years of restorations.

As a boy, Will used to sit in the window of the mill watching his father milling.

'I love this mill – the sounds, the smells and the feel of it. It was so simple the way it worked. I always wanted a Meccano set, but the mill was what I got to play in. Until the early 1990s Dad used to run tours. Then, when he began making cheese in the kitchen and Uncle Peter started to grow strawberry runners to catch the Queensland spring market, they became too busy to run the mill. Its wooden axle shrank and the waterwheel shifted.'

During school holidays, Will kept at his father and uncle to get the mill going.

'"We don't have time," they would say, same old story – "but once you get to Year 11, you can start working on it." As soon as I was 16, I was in here every weekend, bracing up the wheel shaft. It's an awesome thought to preserve history. When I was a boy I was always inventing. I enjoy building things.'

Will had a keen desire to halt the mill's dilapidation, but no proper equipment or tools. In 2000, he contacted the Tasmanian Board of Studies to see if there was any Year 12 subject in which he could incorporate the restoration work. They suggested applied technology. Will used his school workshop to make new parts or precision lathe those parts long-buried in the mud. At the age of 17, he won an achievement award in the 8th National Historic Machinery Rally for the mill restoration.

To mill grain in the traditional way has inherent dangers. Will showed me a large wooden wheel.

'This cog here is the great spur wheel that grinds the grain. It's made from Tasmanian blue gum to reduce the risk of sparks. When you are milling you have all this fine dust in the air. If you get a spark, you risk the whole thing going kaboom and blowing the top off the mill and your head. It's not just a fire, it's an explosion.'

We climbed down narrow, wooden steps to the waterwheel. It smelt of musty wood. The weight of the water falling from above into a series of buckets makes the wheel turn and provides the energy to drive all the cogs in the spur wheel. We had to shout over the roar of the water running through the wheel, even though it wasn't turning.

'This old mill is like a car with a flat tyre. The engine still ticks, the gears are still there – all it needs is work. If I were to work full bore, it would take only two or three months to finish the job. I just don't have two or three months any more. The whole wheel has to be rebuilt out of a timber like King Billy that will survive the test of time. It would cost about $10,000 – out of my price range. I only have $600.'

In the farm granary are Macrocarpa pine logs that have been donated to deck out the inside of the wheel. Will found a man who would mill the timber in large slabs.

'We have millions of machinery bits too. It's like a disorganised library that will take time to order, but with common sense we can put it all together – slowly. Dad always tells us common sense is the least common of senses.'

The restoration had to go on the back burner until Will finished university. Meanwhile, he ran a stoneground flour enterprise from a second mill further around the lake. It dates from the 1850s and was moved to the farm from northeastern Tasmania by his parents. John and Peter obtained a margarine container of rye corn from the Tasmanian Department of Primary Industry and grew it in the vegetable garden. They harvested by hand until they had enough for a couple of acres and eventually a good supply for Thorpe Farm. Will mills flour from the rye corn and wheat grown on the property.

The grain is stored in a granary built on stilts to thwart hungry mice. Milling is an art Will learnt from his father. With a leap from standstill just like one of the deer, Will jumped a metre up into the granary. He lugged out a bag of wheat, poured it into the hopper at the top of the mill and lifted a long lever into gear. A switch started the mill; no water power here. He moved other levers to adjust the grinding stones for coarse or fine flour, watched the dust levels and sniffed the flour, all the while giving a running commentary. A good nose and a good ear are important to this operation.

'If you adjust too fine, the stones start hitting and you get a sulphury smell in the air. If it's too coarse, the grain just cracks or slips through whole. The miller sharpened the stones. He used to chip away as he held the stone with his hand down the hammer. As the steel flaked off it became embedded in his arms. Millers used to have horrific scars on their arms. The expression "Show us your metal" was a badge of expertise. You showed off your arms to better your employment opportunities.'

The sound of grinding and the smell of freshly ground grain pervaded the air. When he had a sack full of flour, Will ladled it into two kilogram cloth bags, stitched them closed with a small sewing machine and stencilled on his label, 'Thorpe Farm Mill, wholegrain flour milled using century old milling techniques'. It is signed under his cheeky title of Miller Bignell Esq.

'How's this for state of the art equipment?' he quipped as he displayed the recycled ladle, stencil and sewing machine. 'We've got a lot of junk around our farm. Other people call it junk; I call it underutilised assets. My flour sieve is made out of a washing machine motor, some old irrigation pipe and a heater extension cord. Minimal capital input.'

Will now markets three to four tonnes of rye and wheat flour a year to bakeries and restaurants. In the 2002 *Goodbye Meat Pie* cook-off, chefs in the mains section used Will's flour to make a pasta dish. Tourists come to his mill for tours, which he took over from his father. Will channels the proceeds back into tools or parts to restore the 1823 mill.

'Busloads of forty people at a time come to look at the water-driven mill and donate a gold coin. I start up this mill to show them the process and I bag up the flour. They love it. Dad and I have albums of customers' bread photos and favourite recipes.'

Will likes to learn about trends and what people might want.

'I've found a lot of opportunities through listening to other people, to chefs in particular, and reading magazines such as *Vogue Entertaining*. Stoneground flour is part of a trend towards healthy eating because it hasn't lost its fibre and the flour isn't bleached. Modern roller mills separate the grain from the husk and you end up with the white fluff in the middle. That part is high in protein and gluten, but has lost all the outer fibre.'

John Bignell cycled past, his tall frame hunched over a pushbike. He was heading for the cheese factory, which is a temperature-controlled room adjacent to the original homestead. We followed him and donned white gumboots and becoming shower caps at the entrance to reduce the risk of contamination. John was adding a culture to a vat of goat's milk to make it curdle for cheesemaking. In a fridge were samples of goat's milk feta in olive oil and a log of creamy goat's milk cheese. Both were smooth and delicious.

It was a year later, July 2004.

Jackman and McRoss is a classy bakery café in Hobart's historic Battery Point and a regular customer of Will's. The bakery sits on a hill, surrounded by a

United Nations of restaurants – Spanish, French, Italian, Indian, Thai and Australian native foods. It was once a sea captain's residence affording a fine view of ships in the harbour. Around the house were the sailors' support services of the red light district. Small stone cottages with English gardens of lavender, white salvia and red roses line the steep, narrow streets. I met Will at the bakery for brunch. A tempting line-up of breads – crusty white and grain-covered, red pepper and basil, olive and rosemary – are displayed alongside blackberry pastries and homemade chocolates. Waitresses scurry to and fro bearing trays of mouth-watering treats. This place is a magnet for those who love good coffee, sugar and carbohydrates. Patrons in chic black leather and mums and dads enticed in by the aromas enjoy the ambience while their dogs are tied to the lamp post outside.

Will joked along with Justin McRoss, the cheery baker. Justin sells a hefty one kilo Bothwell brick made from Will's low-gluten rye flour. A slice is a meal. Sandwiches made from the brick powered me along many a Tasmanian bushwalk in the following week. People of European background particularly like the dark Bothwell brick and rye flour.

'The flour sells for 80 cents a kilo. I can make $150 to $200 a month and do it as a hobby,' Will said. 'Once I finish uni I can grow the business to a commercial size. The key thing to doing all these things and making them tick is managing my time and taking any opportunity I can. When I'm in Melbourne, I might go to a bakery and break the ice – ask who supplies their flour and get a contact number. It's seizing opportunities to network and talk to people. Whenever I'm somewhere I'm always thinking about what else I can be doing. I look around the farm for ideas or around a business for a machine that I can copy. I'm balancing time, using one thing to complement another – but I haven't mastered that by any means.'

The Thorpe Farm venison, cheese, horseradish and salsify, together with Will's wasabi and flour, supply specialty markets.

'With niche markets someone could come in and wipe us out if we're not careful,' Will reflected, 'but for products such as the cheese, horseradish and wasabi, you need some academic knowledge to develop them in a commercially viable way. That is the challenge and the reward. I like seeing the effect on people when they taste something they have never tried before. Now we have to concentrate on producing top foods and establishing a brand that people want. Dad does it to a high degree with the cheese and I find myself doing it more.'

The Bignells are surrounded by innovative farmers who also diversified during hard times and grow tulip bulbs, garlic and opium poppies in this marginal area.

'We're not viewed as being touched by the other side.' Will laughed at the thought. 'With any new venture, we set it up rough – like typical farmers, she'll be right mate. We use secondhand parts, anything lying around the farm. I lie in bed at night thinking about ways to minimise risk. I don't want to fall flat on my face or lose a lot of money that could be spent upgrading the farm. Some people take out a $200,000 loan to start up a new enterprise. I don't have that much courage and I couldn't risk the farm. With the wasabi, I could have spent thousands of dollars on an A-grade shade house, but if the crop flopped I would have fallen flat on my face or lost money. Now I know the wasabi will grow, I have to have the confidence to develop it. It's a big step onto a larger scale, with people watching, with the interest it generates in Australia. I really feel the pressure at times. I'm only 21 – just a boy.'

Will credited his father with nurturing curiosity and diligence in his sons.

'Dad's a freak. The way he works is phenomenal. He has encouraged the hard-working side in us, although he would probably say George and I don't work hard enough.

'If we're late he threatens to dock our pay, but he just makes us work extra hours. I'm a shocking morning person – 8 o'clock is early for me. Dad's father was hard on him and I'll probably be a real Tartar on my kids too. People tend to focus on Dad. He has certainly taught me to take a risk and all the farming stuff, but my desire to educate and communicate comes from Mum. She always supports me. It can get pretty hard when you are doing all this extra stuff and feel an inner responsibility to come home and help while all your mates are off at Coles Bay diving and having fun.'

While the accepted measure of success in an enterprise is its return, Will also views the money as a means to do exciting things such as spending time in the air. Physical and mental challenges are part of his calculated risk taking. With his father he bought a share in the motor glider in which we flew.

'I love my flying, but it's an expensive habit. Just as well I don't smoke or drink much, otherwise I would be broke.'

At the age of 20, Will obtained his pilot's licence in fixed-wing aircraft and trained as a glider instructor.

'I flew the glider in the Gold C, a 300 kilometre task over five hours, in South Australia where I had to make a three kilometre height gain. You prepare the aircraft in 42 degree heat because that's when the thermals are rising. The sense of a journey is powerful. When I was launched, my heart was going at 100 miles an hour. I felt terrified as I went up. The really scary part is when you are 115 k's from your airfield and worrying about what's going to happen if you don't find the next thermal and have to land in a paddock. I flew up to 14 600 feet. It's a mental challenge – very tough.'

What goes up suddenly can also come down swiftly and Tasmania has much rough terrain where a forced landing would be disastrous. Therein lies the adrenaline rush. According to Bothwell glider pilot Graeme Martin, 'People who learn to fly gliders acquire better judgement and control skills than power pilots of a similar number of hours, probably because they are forced to learn to think ahead at an early stage in their training. They have to plan for a forced landing on every single flight'.

Will's other regular escape was rock climbing. 'It mentally pushes you. It's just you against the rock, finding tiny handholds on a vertical face hundreds of feet off the ground. Your life is in your own hands. I've done hard climbs and I've done easy ones that have been mentally scary because they are so easy. You know if you fall off you're bound to clip a ledge and get hurt. Climbers talk about how the easy stuff scares them because the hard climb has you so focused that you don't think about falling. You're too busy thinking how the hell you are going to hold on when it's only a two millimetre handhold or a curving slope. If you squeeze it enough, you can keep some friction.'

Will's hands are big and strong and his wiry build looks well suited to these Spiderman-like activities. He shows me photos of himself, not only clinging to walls, but also hanging upside down as he inches over a ledge at Rocky Tom, a testing climb within sight of Hobart. Will trained to climb the Totem Pole, a 65 metre stack rising vertically from the sea off the Tasman Peninsula. To a non-climber, it looked a good place to avoid – a slippery four-by-four metre column rising to a narrow tip, surrounded by surging seas and buffeted by high winds, accessible only by abseiling from an adjacent cliff on the mainland or swimming to it. The sea-sprayed base has few handholds.

'We swam across to the base of the rock, which was slippery with kelp and pounded by waves,' Will said. 'I went up a metre and got scared because it was so wet. I just had the wrong mindset that day. It's a major commitment that I'll have to do with top climbers. I'll master it one day.'

His energy and exuberance constantly catapulted Will into leadership. He took on the presidency of the university climbing club because nobody else wanted to do it, was building a new climbing wall and organising the ag science annual dinner in his spare time.

In 2004, Will was one of six young Australians selected by the Australian Sheep Industry Cooperative Research Centre for an undergraduate scholarship, which helped him complete the final two years of his degree. He also won the Robert

Menary University Scholarship to encourage enterprise. Will decided to use both scholarships for his honours project of researching genetic variation in Australian sheep meats. He tested the DNA in wool to select the best sheep for specific markets of wool, milk and meat.

'At home we can boost productivity with the high milk-yielding East Friesians, which are prime lamb mothers.'

Will was profiled as one of twelve high achievers in the 2004 edition of *Young Tassie Scientist* magazine. He and the other eleven students, male and female, promoted science as an exciting career and showed high school students that scientists weren't just bespectacled, middle-aged males in starched lab coats. Will was also profiled in the 2004 edition of *Young Einsteins*, the University of Tasmania alumni magazine that was sent to all graduates.

'Suddenly, all the professors and postgraduates knew who I was and expectations rose,' Will said. 'I had done well in 2003 and won the two scholarships. The vice-chancellor said, "You can go anywhere with your career". It put me on a pedestal, where I felt insecure. Two thousand and four went downhill from then on.'

Will's higher profile coincided with bad marks. He claimed he isn't academically brilliant and doesn't trust himself on details. His strengths are in practical work and problem solving, not exams.

'I failed a couple. My lecturers said, "It's not a matter of your not having the knowledge. You don't have exam technique and can't write what you do know."'

Despite studying hard, Will also found his memory failed him on the range of material. He felt he needed to learn exam technique from a mentor who was trained in science.

'I crashed when I had a time limit and couldn't interpret questions properly. At the beginning of the year, my lecturers said I wouldn't pass with first-class honours. I had to get up the guts to see the disability officer at university student services, who suggested an assessment of my learning abilities. It turned out that I had a rare disability, so I was allowed to sit in a different room for exams and answer in dot points. I still had the same time limit, but could stop the clock at the end of questions so I could get up and walk around, and then resume. By the end of the year, instead of failing exams, I passed with distinctions and high Ds. I'm back on track.'

In 2004, Will was one of fifty young people selected from 367 applicants for the National Youth Roundtable in Canberra.

'It really was a cross-section of Australian youth, every nationality you could imagine. It was great to meet all those 16- to 25-year-olds who had achieved something.'

The participants stayed in four-star accommodation for a retreat-like week of intensive group work. They met Governor-General Michael Jeffery and Prime Minister John Howard.

'We all had to do a team project before we reconvened later that year. I joined the environment and rural team to canvass the relationship between the environment and sustainability. Our team looked at logging in the old-growth forest of Tasmania's Styx Valley.'

He interviewed environmental researchers and designers and went to the Global Rescue Station run by the Wilderness Society. People at the base camp were suspicious of Will. They didn't want publicity. Will and his girlfriend climbed a 70 metre long rope to get to the Global Rescue Station platform in one of the oldest trees.

'I was awed by the size of the trees. The forest changes from dark-brown ferns at the base to light-green shapes and patterns in the canopy. It was a bit gusty so we swung as we climbed. I raced up in seven minutes and then had to take ten minutes to recover.'

As their contribution towards a sustainable future, Will and three others in the team put together an educational pack and DVD, *Exploring Environmental Sustainability*. They wanted to teach Years 9 and 10 students how to research an issue and present an informed argument back to a class; however, their own research team, people from rural and urban backgrounds, struggled with conflict on environmental issues such as old-growth forest logging.

'Producing the resource was a major undertaking when members of our team lived in three different states, had no funding and conflicting views. Eventually, we sourced some funding from the Foundation for Young Australians, which took a huge effort. I was given a hard time from uni for taking on so much. In future I'll avoid situations like that.'

As he continued to rush between Hobart and the farm and had trouble saying no to other demands, Will was becoming overcommitted. Relationships suffered.

'I love farming, but relationships play on my mind. Not many of my mates come out to Bothwell during holidays so it can be a bit lonely, although I get to Hobart a few times a week. I broke up with my girlfriend in September. It made me wake up that I couldn't expect too much of a girl or depend on others. I needed some me time. I told the other pilots that I was swearing off women. They said, "Oh yeah" in disbelief. The plane kept me occupied until another shareholder crashed it in November 2004. It was as costly as a woman.'

In 2005, Will was again featured as one of ten young Tasmanian movers and shakers, this time in the Hobart *Mercury*. His appearance had an unexpected benefit.

'At one in the morning, on the day the article appeared in the paper, I received a text message from Amy, a girl I had met before at uni. She was studying midwifery. We started going out together after that.'

In October 2005 Will was finishing his Honours thesis. It was springtime and the winds gusted around the steep slope where the Bignells were building a townhouse. John designed an ambitious split-level building that has prime views over Hobart. We climbed a ladder to the attic where Will lives. John was juggling the construction of the house with managing the farm; the boys were helping with building.

'It stresses Dad. We were both wrung-out this year. I'm sick of flogging a 1970s tractor. I probably sound like Dad when he was the same age although we can see each other's perspective. I want to buy another tractor, but house building is expensive. I like machinery to be good. A pivot irrigator would also be better for cropping than wasteful flood irrigation.'

During 2005, Will had the chance through his wool research scholarship to learn about the marketing end of the industry. The 12,000 sheep on Thorpe Farm are the Bignells' bread and butter, alongside the exotic, high-value, intensive niche products.

'I made the most of an International Wool and Textile conference in Hobart, going to talks and seeing the wool auctions in Launceston. The sellers gave me a go at bidding. The biggest players in the industry were there from Italy, England and China. I established a good working relationship with the biggest exporter to China and we now sell some wool through them. We changed our thinking from producing a commodity to producing a top product and have joined a wool pool, which should bring about 10 per cent higher returns.'

As he was finishing his degree, near-disaster struck Will's Honours project. The ethanol he was using to sterilise a scalpel caught fire in the laboratory and burnt five of his research samples. He said that it didn't ruin his work, it only ruined his reputation.

'The whole building had to be evacuated. I'll never hear the end of it.'

Will was trying to cram a whole semester into 10 weeks. He had much on his mind, frequently found himself distracted and was often on the run. One finger had a row of stitches under a wad of bandages.

'I hurt myself constantly this year. A week ago I reached around to pick up an angle grinder here on the house site. There was no guard on it and the machine came on by mistake. It chopped my finger down to the bone, but missed the tendon. Earlier in the year, I rolled my car – only going 40 k's an hour, luckily, but it was written off. I fell behind at uni and it cost me a lot to buy another car. The following week I climbed Moai, a high sea stack like the Totem Pole. Two weeks after that, I snapped the lateral ligaments in my ankle and ruptured the tendon. I had one exam to go, which I had to sit three weeks later. So there I was with no car, on my back and an ankle that really hurt. I had to swallow strong painkillers for a month.'

As well as this catalogue of accidents, Will developed groin pain and feared testicular cancer. Diagnosed with a varicose vein, he was dreading an operation. But there was some fun in the form of a time-honoured ag science end-of-term sport: weevil racing.

'We use slaters because they are bigger.' Will, the chief supplier, finds slaters under rocks and rotten logs. 'We auction them off under a microscope for the princely sum of between $1 and $5.'

With climbing relegated to the back seat after the ankle and angle-grinding his-finger accidents, Will took up windsurfing; he loves it. The appeal of Tasmania for adventurous people is the variety of activities close to Hobart – climbing, surfing, rafting, flying. Once he had qualified as an instructor, Will and other glider pilots began taking passengers up over Hobart. From the air, he described it as a landscape of blues and greys – the Derwent River spanned by the majestic arc of Tasman Bridge and the rounded bulk of Mt Wellington rising behind Hobart. For added zest he took on aerobatics in a fixed-wing plane, learning how to loop, spin and stall a plane.

With his undergraduate degree almost over, Will considered what he might do next. Opportunities to develop enterprises were on the farm, but research and the student lifestyle had distinct attractions. In December of 2005, Will graduated. He and a mate warmed up with an hour of aerobatics, and then raced back to Hobart to robe in their black academic gowns, mortarboards and bronze-coloured cloaks for the ceremony.

'Three out of five of us got first-class honours. We were pretty stoked. The governor of Tasmania's son was in my year. After the ceremony we lived it up together before dining out with our families. My honours thesis was published as two papers, which my lecturer presented to an international meat conference in Ireland.'

With his father in Hobart building the house most of the week, Will became a full-time farmer in 2006 with responsibility for Thorpe Farm. The year turned into a rollercoaster of decision making as the drought-inducing pattern of El

Niño affected eastern Australia, even the normally verdant isle of Tasmania. Then, towards the end of January, while Will was baling hay for his uncle, the 1970s tractor caught fire.

'My flying training kicked in and kept me calm. I made a plan and did everything I had learnt for a controlled shutdown. I limited the damage to the machine, which burnt to the ground, but managed to save the baler and not start a grass fire. Dad wrote off the fire tanker racing to put the fire out.'

The insurance didn't quite cover the new John Deere tractor Will bought.

'You couldn't wipe the smile off my face for weeks,' Will said. 'I drove the new tractor off the truck in the afternoon and got straight into sowing a crop. I didn't stop until I had 50 hours on the clock. It's the best machine we have ever bought and will boost productivity no end.'

During the week Will worked hard on the farm, trying to adjust to drought and social isolation from his friends.

'Many of the ideas I wanted to implement weren't possible due to lack of money and a tight-looking season ahead. Then, on weekends, I was building the house at the drop of Dad's hat. It was trying on my relationship with Amy, who was working and studying at uni to become a midwife. Dad and I also had our ups and downs. It hit me that I wasn't ready to come home full time yet. Doing a PhD was sounding good.'

In winter, Will and Amy snatched 15 days to tour the south island of New Zealand together in a campervan. They climbed glaciers, crossed snow-covered mountain passes, bungee jumped and skied.

'I tried a few laps down a half pipe, which was rather hair raising and faster than I thought, but I didn't break any bones.'

They also visited a wasabi farm in NZ, reputed to be the best outside Japan.

'Growing the plant in water is very hard to do,' Will said. 'I observed their water management and growing conditions. Back home I built new shade houses and bought 300 tissue-cultured plantlets that a Tasmanian grower had imported from Taiwan.'

Will had high hopes of success with these disease-free plants, planted a new bed in soil behind the house and potted up the rest for the water site.

'In spring, we had around twenty-five pet lambs to look after, including two sets of quintuplets. Two ewes dropped five lambs each, an effort that unfortunately killed the ewes. We managed to mother some of the lambs onto ewes that had lost lambs using the dead skin trick [stretching the dead lamb's skin over the orphan lamb so the ewe will accept the lamb as her own, thereby allowing it to feed from her].'

It was the driest winter in the Tasmanian central highlands for twenty-four years, with no spring break and a long, dry summer on the horizon. Rainfall for the year was 250 millimetres in an area that normally received twice that amount.

'We marked lambs early and turned them onto 200 acres of crop that we had to write off. We sold older sheep for between $1 and $10. By then our flock was halved to 6000, and we were hand feeding. The goats dried off so there was no cheese production for a few months. Our tank water ran out and we were purifying river water for the house.'

To help pay some bills Will decided to grow pink-eye potatoes for the Christmas–New Year market. He rolled out of bed on winter nights to turn the frost-protection sprinklers on the potatoes, which is what saved them. Many poppy crops were frosted and died off up to three times on Bothwell farms.

'By mid-September our irrigation allocation from the Clyde was halved and the Bothwell town reservoir was drying up.'

To top everything off, their farmhand lost his licence for two and a half years due to drink driving. During the dry weather, the house in Hobart had a close encounter with a bushfire, which raced past the back door in a 25 metre wall of flame. Fortunately, the Bignells had cleared a fire break and back-burnt, so the house was unscathed.

John had bought a 1927 Huon pine sloop cheaply and in between house building and farming Will persuaded his sailing mates to teach him how to sail.

'It's a 28 foot yacht with an outboard motor and goes fast,' Will said. 'I learnt all I could about rigging before taking it off its mooring and into the big old Derwent River. I was also learning to snorkel along the coast for abalone and the elusive rock lobster. We would go down 15 metres without tanks, just holding our breath. You have to pop your ears by blowing your nose to equalise the pressure. I set a goal that on the opening day of the crayfish season in November, I was going to catch one. It took me two hours, but I came up victorious with my first cray.'

Will worked on scholarship applications to do his doctorate in 2007, but was in two minds about what he really wanted to do. His confidence ebbed because he wasn't in the select groups for organisations such as Meat and Livestock Australia and Australian Wool Innovation.

'I applied for a heap of scholarships, but could tell I was going to get knocked back.'

His usual optimism might have vanished at the prospect of the varicose vein operation in November.

'I was having tests and felt scared and worried. Amy found it hard to understand my fear of hospitals, tests and operations, but she was a reassuring rock in my life and kept me going throughout the year. She makes me really happy.'

The operation went without a hitch and Will was soon back into work, making silage for stock feed. He drove the new tractor for more than 12 hours a day over four days.

'It was epic. Feeding out the silage gave me a real sense of achievement. Then, during December, my crops failed, except for one puny wheat crop, and we had to keep feeding the sheep. I was having trouble sleeping and felt strung out about what I wanted in life. I got my scholarship results back and only received an Australian postgraduate award from the Uni of Tasmania. I felt like the research industry wasn't interested in what I had to offer, even after getting first-class honours.'

A timely confidence boost came at the end of 2006. Will was awarded a coveted Partnership Award from the university for his contribution to the subject of entrepreneurship and creativity. Will had made his mark by 'inspiring his peers to find excitement in the management and control of risk', the citation read.

His lecturer, Colin Jones, describes Will as 'a rare guy, larger than life. He was in a quiet group, but before the semester finished he had them climbing the 150 metre vertical Organ Pipes at Mt Wellington. He taught them and more significantly – convinced them they could do it. He looks as if he's hell bent on going to an early grave, but he always manages the risk and inspires confidence. Will is a natural leader.'

'The award was pretty big, with only five being given,' Will said, 'including to former premier Michael Field and two of us students.'

Will had his own risk to manage when it came to selling the pink-eye potato crop. 'I really liked potato growing, but all the greengrocers wanted was to screw you on price and find faults to discount your product.'

He persevered with his aquatic wasabi farm, rebuilding and replanting.

'The plants are actually growing. I've mechanised much of the horseradish work and am still milling flour. I'm developing an outlet at Victoria Market in Melbourne – 750 gram bags with a see-through panel and blurb on the mill and myself. I've ventured into more root vegetables – Jerusalem artichokes and Hamburg parsley, which has an edible taproot like a parsnip. George's salsify was used in a dish that won the Lord Mayor's Best Salmon Dish. All of our products are starting to get a good name around Hobart.'

In his spare time, Will was shooting short films about extreme sports for a competition run by a friend.

'I took a mate, Ian Brodie, flying and we filmed aerobatics, which we edited into a five-minute package. His expressions were priceless. In the first manoeuvre of a barrel roll when you turn the plane upside-down, he was looking down at the ground with a huge grin that said it all.'

In January 2007, Ian was moving irrigation pipes on a farm with another worker when they clipped overhead power lines. They were both electrocuted. His friend's death hit Will hard.

'It shocked me. I accepted it was a freak accident, but his death made me slow down and appreciate each day.'

At 24, Will was facing a dilemma of not wanting to leave the farm, but feeling isolated there, missing Amy and wanting to pursue his research.

'I think I need to be married to live there as a full-time farmer and be happy. I hardly flew, climbed or scuba-dived last year when I was home because there was so much work to do.'

Things started to look promising for Will in 2007 when he received scholarships from the University of Tasmania and the Tasmanian Institute of Agricultural Research; he decided to do his PhD. Over three years, he will research genetic markers for carcase quality in five sheep breeds with the aim of selecting top meat producers.

'Sheep are our farm's main source of income. Molecular genetics is a daunting field, but all livestock industries will be using molecular markers in 15 years time. I want to make the most of my unique position. I'm home two days a week as well as fitting in my leisure activities and uni. Amy and I have moved into a unit together just around the corner from Jackman and McRoss in Battery Point.'

In May 2007 Will flew in the Australian Light Aircraft championships in Bundaberg, Queensland, doing competition aerobatics in a fixed-wing aircraft for the first time. Afterwards he wrote an article, 'Close Call', that was selected for publishing in a flight safety magazine. Will had arranged to hire a Cessna 152 Aerobat for the competition because he couldn't afford to fly his club's aerobatic aircraft. He practised on the hired Cessna when he arrived at the event, but felt nervous as he climbed into the cockpit. It was a tight fit for a man two metres tall.

'I completed three manoeuvres and at 4000 feet I entered a one-and-a-quarter spin to the left. The plane entered a lovely spin and I watched for my exit mark out through the roof. As it came around I applied full right rudder, pushed the joystick forward and looked out along the wing to check that the plane was vertical. Due to practice this had become a fluid, automated process. It was at this point that it all started to go wrong.'

Will felt a click near his hip and pressure on his waist and shoulders. His whole body slid forward towards the top of the instrument panel then stopped.

His left knee was near his face. 'I remember looking down the wing and trying to pull the joystick back to exit the manoeuvre, but it was jammed.' Will pushed against the door which opened enough to release him from the instrument panel so he could regain control. The plane was plummeting towards the ground 'dead vertical'. He was able to pull out of the dive just before the wings were likely to fall off because of the speed. Will didn't know what had gone wrong. He adjusted the seat, fixed the harness and decided to finish the sequence. When the plane was flying upside-down again the seat clicked, but stayed in place this time. Will successfully completed the manoeuvres, landed and tried to tell other pilots and the judges what had happened.

'It really hit me then just how close I was to dying. Emotion overwhelmed me and I couldn't talk.' The seat had come adrift from its moorings and catapulted him forward. His tall, slim figure slid out of the safety harness and jammed hard against the instruments immobilising the joystick. Will wrote that he felt fragile for hours after the flight. 'The competition judges and officials were incredibly supportive towards me and I was surprised when I was awarded third place. Upon reflection I am happy with how I handled the situation; I did not panic at any point and I believe exceptional flying training from my instructors and regular participation in extreme sports is the only reason I am alive today.'

Will is a person who lives life to its fullest. He is fired up by being able to capitalise on the unique position of his home at Bothwell. His paddock-to-plate enterprises rely on innovation and Will's ability to take an idea, research and test it in a small way, and then expand as he finds markets. The challenges in flying a glider, scaling a cliff or diving to the depths require the same formidable focus, judgement and nerve he needs for success in the competitive world of niche products.

No visit to Thorpe Farm would be complete without a home-grown meal. Will, his mother and father and I have a hand in its preparation – scrubbing and grating horseradish and salsify roots, picking wasabi leaves, searing venison. John feeds another log into the crackling fire as we sit down at the wooden dining table.

Starters: pecorino merino sheep cheese, delectable white cheese, on thin slivers of Bothwell brick, a coarse, black bread.

Mains: slices of lightly roasted venison, pink in the centre, with a crispy selvage. A bowl of fluffy mashed potato stirred into salsify and laced with traces of sharp horseradish. A green salad of peppery wasabi leaves dressed with a dash of lemon.

Into our glasses Will poured his favourite Tasmanian Stefano Lubiana pinot noir, a vibrant red from the estuary of the Derwent.

'Growing up in an enterprising family is my main influence,' he said, and raised his glass.

A toast to Will and his enterprising family – and to their superb spread. And then, the conversation around the table turned to new horizons, new possibilities.

Will Bignell Esq. with his home-milled flour, Thorpe Farm, Bothwell, Tasmania, 2003

J Easterby-Wood and the Bonya community story, Alice Springs, 2005

6

Start with the Solution

J Easterby-Wood, Alice Springs,
Northern Territory

'When I was growing up, most people thought I would end up in jail.'

The swarthy, bespectacled young man with the gleeful grin looks more like a computer nerd than a career criminal. Thirty-three-year-old J Easterby-Wood throws out sentences like a man with a train to catch. My MP3 recorder runs hot trying to keep up with him.

'I always enjoyed being around and working with people, despite being a loner as a child. I had attention deficit disorder [ADD] and didn't have many friends until my teens, although I was a friendly person. Mostly, my anger and aggression were aimed at myself. I rarely hurt others and I've grown out of it now.' He laughed as I started to back my chair away.

In J's case, the ADD could be triggered by an imbalance of sugars, determined by what he ate or drank. The colour in foods such as carrots and apples would bring on an attack.

'All through primary and high school, even into my university years, I could get slammed on a can of Coke. It would act on my body for days as if I was inebriated.'

At primary school, J would get bored in class as he waited for other students to catch up, and become a nuisance. Another boy would push him off his chair then it would escalate.

'I copped suspensions on a regular basis and was asked to leave five schools. It was always because of less-than-charming behaviour, fighting with other students and the occasional teacher.'

On one occasion J threw a chair at his preschool teacher and broke her arm, an incident he can't remember, but feels enormously guilty about. He would destroy his own belongings – a new schoolbag, toys, clothes – in a fit of aggression.

'My hearing would close down,' J said. 'I could only see black, red or white. I would feel full of rage and punch, kick or destroy. I only destroyed my own belongings because with ADD a lot of the anger isn't focused like anger usually is, but is directed back at one's self – plus the fact that my brothers and sister were experienced enough to make sure none of their toys were ever in harm's way. Afterwards, it was like coming out of a fog. I couldn't remember anything and would feel quite upset. I had superhuman strength when I was in one of those rages, which was frightening to be around.

'I was convinced I was adopted. I look Mediterranean, nothing like the rest of my family, so it was a standing joke that the milkman must have dropped in. My siblings are gifted artists and scientists – I have none of that.'

Attention deficit disorder, or attention deficit hyperactivity disorder (ADHD), is a mental condition that affects 5 per cent of school-age children throughout the world and is estimated to be two to three times more prevalent in boys than in girls. These children are hyperactive and impulsive, with an active intellect; they can also be inattentive. The causes remain unknown, but increasing evidence points to heredity and biological factors rather than oft quoted causes such as food allergies, refined sugar, food preservatives and additives, dysfunctional families, too much television, poor schooling or other environmental factors.

It wasn't until J was 18 or 19 that he could feel the ADD coming on and control it. He used to think ADD was a curse, but changed his mind as he matured.

'It has helped make me who I am today. I know what it's like to be out of control and I can't live like that. I have a lot of energy and enthusiasm and I think differently from other people.'

I was introduced to J Easterby-Wood on a trip through Alice Springs in

August 2005. It was a Sunday, and my husband Bill and I had driven only 300 of the 1200 kilometre Tanami Track to Alice from Halls Creek when the brake line burst as we dodged a pothole. I was keen to hail help from the only two vehicles that passed us on the lonely desert track. The scattered Aboriginal communities were closed to traffic and the midway point of Rabbit Flat roadhouse provided fuel but no emergency repairs.

'We'll be okay, we still have the handbrake,' said Bill, as bull camels trotted over the track and road trains thundered past. This was our taste of the potential for trouble in desert country, devoid of services and communications. I was relieved when we came into phone range near Alice and could ring a friend, Rod Mitchell, who recommended a garage. In the course of our conversation he told me about a young man with whom he was working.

'J Easterby-Wood is his name,' Rod said. 'He is revolutionising how we communicate health messages to Aboriginal people.'

Dr Rod Mitchell was with the Royal Flying Doctor Service in Alice Springs in 2001. Now, as an anaesthetist at Alice Springs hospital, he and J were making an animated DVD together, *Baby Operation Story*, for use in Territory maternity wards and remote clinics.

'We struggle with the issue of Aboriginal people feeling safe in hospital,' said Rod. 'They don't turn up or they check out early or they leave it until they are at death's door with an acute illness such as pneumonia. We provide information for them, but English is not their first language and there is no telephone translation service. With births, it's hard to explain an epidural injection or Caesarian operation and the risks involved.'

Baby Operation Story showed animated female characters in a hospital setting as they described the medical process when a woman had a protracted labour and needed an epidural or a Caesarean. The viewer could choose to hear the dialogue in English or one of four Central Australian Indigenous languages. Rod hoped it would make hospital births less terrifying.

J's office is in Todd Mall, the hub of Alice Springs. His desk is full. Two computers operate side by side and piles of paper and reports are stacked on the floor. Family photos and numerous awards on wooden stands vie for any other nook. J, who manages Interactive Communications and Development for the Northern Territory Department of Health and Community Services, clears a spot for me to sit down. His unit was initially set up in 2003 to improve communications with Aboriginal communities on seemingly intractable problems of alcohol and other substance abuse.

J Easterby-Wood grew up on a mixed farm in South Australia with his older sister Tanya and older brother Wayne. His father was a Vietnam veteran; his parents divorced after J's father returned from the war.

'They had grown apart and both remarried. We kids stayed with Mum so I didn't get to know my father that well then, but these days I have a great relationship with him.'

In 1980, when J was eight, his mother Heather, a nurse, moved to the Northern Territory with her three children and husband George Wood, a former career soldier turned Corrective Service Officer and their son, Shane.

'I grew up with my stepfather. I call him Dad. Our family of six spent two years in a pop-up caravan in Darwin's Malak caravan park because there was not enough housing after the cyclones – Tracy in 1974 and Max in 1979. Darwin was just a big country town where everyone knew everyone. I went to school with kids whose fathers were doctors and politicians. We didn't know our family was poor. Years later I discovered most kids got Christmas presents *and* stuff for school.'

In his school yearbook, J was the one tagged most likely to end up in jail – or to become a successful politician.

'It was Mum who kept me on the straight and narrow. My teachers only saw my behaviour; she saw me. We visited a few psychologists early on in my teens. One said I behaved like I did because of the way my name was spelt. "Give me a break," Mum said. "You should see the way this boy goes off." She would discipline me. I had to write out Bible verses, but my attention span was the size of a newt. Spare the rod, spoil the child applied in our house. My mum and older sister, brother and I came to Christ when I was about 12. George took on three kids who weren't his own, but he never said anything that made us feel we weren't his children. He was a bloke's bloke, ex-military and not accustomed to playing with kids. It made us independent.'

When J was about 16, the ADD induced nausea instead of the violent outbursts. He no longer had to suffer the shame of uncontrollable behaviour. J's youth pastor, whom he tried to emulate, was killed by a drunken driver as he rode his bicycle to work, a tragedy that, combined with his mother's diagnosis of breast cancer, plunged J into depression.

'It seemed like all the good guys went,' he said. 'I felt unglued from the world and lost any motivation. School and a career didn't matter to me.'

He never slept more than four hours and would read to calm himself.

'My grandmother had passed away from breast cancer when my mother was four,' J said. 'I realised that everyone can find excuses for their behaviour, but Mum never used her childhood loss as an excuse, nor let the past interfere with the present. She fought the cancer. She had one breast removed then the other one.'

Heather taught him to love life again.

'Mum was the strongest person I have ever met,' he said. 'She said, "There are two ways to the top. You can claw, scratch and bite your way up, but how long will you stay there? Or you can be a leader and person of vision and take others with you on that journey." She told me to live my life like that. I think it was her guts and determination to make the most of every day and her grace and faith that shaped me into who I am today. I now live each second to its fullest.'

Heather told J that it didn't matter whether he dug ditches or managed McDonald's, as long as he loved what he was doing.

'That is my career goal – to get paid to do what I love.'

J finished school at home, by correspondence, and matriculated. At Darwin University he began an Arts degree and studied history. J wanted to be a maritime archaeologist and work in developing countries, diving and researching. He remembered watching the movie *Raise the Titanic* when he was about 10. It gave him a love of history and archaeology. In the early 1990s, J's mother and stepfather moved first to Queensland and then to Alice Springs, where George Wood became superintendent at Alice Springs prison. J stayed in Darwin during these years and boarded for a time with the Parry family. Suzanne Parry was professor of education studies at the university. Suzanne mentored J and triggered his interest in community development. She and J's history professor, Dr David Carment, challenged him to do his own research and form his own opinions, not just accept what others said. On Suzanne Parry's suggestion J decided to change courses to Indigenous education.

'I was pretty narrow minded then,' J said. 'I thought Indigenous people had it all too easy with handouts and the like and were quite lost. I didn't have much to do with them apart from schoolmates, or hearing about Dad's clients when he was on leave and took me to communities to visit friends working in the sticks. He once told me of this old Aboriginal guy who, every Wet season, would travel out to the jail, get a brick and break a window or something so he could be imprisoned over Christmas and have a three-course meal.'

In 1996 Heather's cancer returned, so he moved to Alice Springs to be with her. J's mother died in 2001 after a sixteen-year battle with breast cancer.

In Alice, J met Anita Spahic, a vivacious woman with a mass of red-brown curls. She was a trainee travel agent at Flight Centre where he also worked while looking after Heather.

'I thought Anita looked like a fairy come to life, straight out of a flower somewhere. As we got to know each other I realised this fairy packed quite a punch. It's hard to believe that so much energy and love can be in such a small frame.'

For her part, Anita fell in love with J's lively personality, his ability to communicate and his compassion.

'He cared about people and loved to help,' she said. 'He was also driven to achieve, as if he had to prove himself. We were married in 1997 and now have two children – Phoenix, who is 5, and Savannah, who is 3. The kids are my bag. J is not the easiest person to live with. I think he still has ADD. He is on the go all the time. Twenty books will last him only a week. He gets bored with everyday things and doesn't think of practicalities. He lives in his head and uses his brain continually and creatively. We are opposites. I remember detail, whereas J empties his brain of unnecessary stuff. J sees the human brain as like a computer hard drive, with temporary files that he clears every 20 days.'

'I don't remember inconsequential details,' he said. 'We were looking at the real estate ads in Alice recently and I saw a house for sale in Kramer Street. I kept thinking, Kramer, Kramer – that sounds familiar. Anita looked at me as if I were mad: "That's our house."'

In 2000, J had taken on the coordination of the Alice Springs unit of alcohol and drug training programs with the Northern Territory Department of Health, as part of a team of six responsible for covering 280,000 square kilometres, one-third of the Territory. This vast southern part of the Territory included small, isolated desert communities that the team could only visit every few months. J helped Indigenous drug and alcohol workers train community members to identify people who were at risk and reduce harm to their family and friends. The team had excellent results in Alice Springs, but the more remote the location, the less successful the training. The team would plan a program and arrive at a community only to find people weren't there. Or there would be twenty participants in the morning and only two by early afternoon.

'Those two only stayed because the Elders told them to,' said J. 'They were usually the hungriest. We used to call it the 20–2 training rule. At first I thought it was me, but it was a common occurrence. Drugs and alcohol were not the sexiest subjects.'

J and his team would use role plays to simulate reality, as they had been taught at university. Half an hour later, participants would be armed and ready to hit each other with nulla nullas (heavy wooden sticks), because the role plays aired unresolved issues of family violence and abuse.

'Another problem was the young kids and teenagers who hum-bugged the adults in class,' J said. 'I had been mucking about with simple animated characters as a hobby, so I set up a computer at the back of the room to distract the kids with them. Months later, when I returned to the same communities, nobody was listening to me rabbit on about drugs and alcohol at the front of the room; they were all down the back playing with these characters. At the same time, we had been told to review training practices because they weren't effective enough. I thought, If you can't beat them, join them.'

J had the idea that the cartoon characters could deliver the training. His thought process began at the goal – people educated and motivated to lead healthy lives. Then he worked backwards to the strategies to accomplish that result. Although computer animation was new technology in 2000, he thought it would catch people's attention and stimulate them to want to learn. J used generic Microsoft characters from the internet. Many outback communities owned computer hardware by then, but people were scared of the technology and had no reason to use it. J knew health promotion posters, such as Cathy Freeman urging people to quit smoking, had had some impact, but after the initial look a poster quickly became another piece of wallpaper. Videos made by city consultants with little knowledge of Aboriginal issues were expensive to produce and used basic material in English, of scant relevance to multilingual, multicultural communities.

From his consultations with Aboriginal people, J realised they had to make training fun, develop resources relevant to their clientele and give ownership to Indigenous people. In 2003, J's unit was funded to do a sexual health project with the Gap Youth Centre in Alice Springs. J wanted to construct the first Indigenous Australian animated character or avatar to represent a real person. Together with a software company, he and some young local Aborigines devised 'Uncle' at the Deadly Mob internet café in the youth centre. Uncle was a walking, talking computer-generated character. In his Akubra hat decorated with crocodile teeth and his red-checked shirt, bare feet and a guitar, he represented a recognisable community leader. The Gap Youth Centre young people then scripted a conversation between Uncle and two young men about sex outside marriage, communicable diseases and using proper protection, such as condoms. It lifted the lid on highly sensitive matters, dispelled ignorance and gave a young person's view.

Opposition to the use of avatars came from J's management.

'One of our Darwin managers sent me an email that I have framed right next to a commendation from the Northern Territory Minister for Health. It said: "J, stop messing about with software. It's not our job."'

Northern Territory Health chief executive officer Robert Griew walked past a colleague's office in Darwin where J was showing Uncle to someone.

'He said, "What's that? What are we doing with it?" I said, "This is Uncle, our first Indigenous character for promoting health. This character is going to be used by the Department of Employment, Education and Training to deliver training because our department doesn't seem interested."'

The CEO immediately invited J into his office. Within ten minutes he had arranged a meeting of executives for the following day to organise how Northern Territory Health could best develop the system J and the kids had created. By the end of that month, a new unit had been set up with the capacity to develop animated stories at a fraction of the cost of video making.

'My responsibility was to find and construct communication technologies to benefit Northern Territory Health,' J said.

Within a few weeks the Pathways to Community Engagement (PCE) program, which was based upon J's experiences, was born. A consortium was developed between Inchain, a Victorian software company, and the Northern Territory Departments of Health and Community Services and Employment, Education and Training. Microsoft launched Uncle in November 2003, only three months after J had been instructed to desist from playing with the software. The young Aboriginal men who had put together the Gap Youth Centre resource received commendation certificates from the then Northern Territory Health Minister, Jane Aagaard, and Microsoft.

'When we began working with them, some of these kids had low levels of literacy and poor self-esteem,' J said. 'They wouldn't read aloud at school because of shame at their lack of skills, but with Pathways to Community Engagement they kept at it. It was fun, engaging and challenging. At the launch, they walked eight feet tall.'

J realised the technology was breaking down cultural barriers when community workers who wouldn't role play, began to work with animated characters. Through characters, which were one step removed from reality, it was possible to broach substance abuse, sexual health and mental health, topics that Indigenous peoples normally could not discuss, and to display emotions people usually kept hidden.

J designed the process of engagement and the software platform and, gradually, PCE developed. The first stage was to find out what communities wanted.

'We could create stand-alone resources, anything from interactive DVDs and CD-ROMs for television, through to printed flipcharts,' J said. 'We designed them with community members, rather than seeking funding to pay outsiders to make a poster or video.'

J could see that every time a community had other people in the middle of the process, information specific to that community would be stifled. But he was concerned that what worked in one small Aboriginal community might not work in another where the problems and dialects were different. This was when he discovered that the lifelike digital characters could be moved to another community and still be relevant, just as a cartoon figure, say, might have universal appeal.

Just then, the talk of technology proved too much for my MP3 recorder and it crashed. J laughed heartily as I hunted in a bag for batteries, and futilely pressed buttons.

'Technology can do that to you,' he sympathised, but he wasn't diverted for long. 'Many Indigenous people can understand spoken, but not written, English so we needed smarter ways of getting health messages across.'

J's next step was to find new ways of looking at literacy. The technology existed that could map from the written text to the spoken word. He demonstrated how on a computer: he typed in dialogue in English, inserted the appropriate sound file of a prerecorded Central Australian language and the character began to speak fluent Walpiri while J read the English translation.

'With this, we can change the language, speed and accent as we go,' he said. 'Technology is the medium, but it is humanised and becomes more personal.'

Using the characters and state-of-the-art voice recognition, text-to-speech and translation technology, J has been able to overcome many of the traditional language and literacy barriers usually associated with resource development. The applications are far-reaching, especially for Indigenous peoples with oral traditions, or where literacy levels are low.

In the final stage of the project, J and his team created fully animated characters. He took digital images of Cathy Freeman and a beer can called Vicki VB to make a resource about safe drinking levels. He clicked onto Vicki VB on his computer and the beer can appeared. Vicki VB wiggled and spoke: 'Have you been drinking so hard your beer can is talking to you? Stop now!'

'People knew a beer can couldn't speak Walpiri or Aranda languages, but they could build their own stories from that point.'

By injecting humour and using respected Aboriginal people to convey the health message, J kept people entertained and more likely to absorb the important information.

'Then we can get some music happening,' he said as he searched a list on his computer, 'and we can create a range of communications. As well as television and online material, we can turn the message into temporary tattoos or T-shirts or armbands.'

It's a clever approach to persistent problems, such as reliance on alcohol or the more recent calamity in some communities of petrol sniffing. Petrol sniffing causes brain damage, long-term disability, even death. Young people wander around sniffing fumes from cans tied around their necks. Petrol sniffing is associated with violence, vandalism and family conflict and is most entrenched in Central Australia, where J is based. According to a Select Committee of the Northern Territory Parliament reported in the Human Rights and Equal Opportunities Commission's *Responding to Petrol Sniffing on the Anangu Pitjantjatjara Lands: A case study*, there were an estimated 350 sniffers in February 2003. In its interim report on issues of alcohol and inhalant abuse and cannabis use, the Select Committee noted that 'Petrol sniffing and other inhalant substance abuse is known to affect up to 30 remote communities in the Northern Territory and surrounding border regions of South Australia and Western Australia'.

Researcher Maggie Brady looked at root causes for substance abuse problems. She maintained it was part of a broader picture of Indigenous disadvantage combined with poverty, racism and frequent bereavement. There were few job prospects in remote communities, especially for those who left school at 15 or 16. Decisions about expenditure of community-managed funds were usually in the hands of male leaders, who would designate funding for ceremonies, funerals and outstation development, but not for youth recreation facilities, even when 50 per cent of the population was aged under 19. Brady maintained that the use of petrol and the style associated with sniffers – listening to heavy metal music and wearing torn denim jeans and necklaces – had become for many young Aborigines a source of power in an otherwise powerless context.

J tackled the issue of petrol sniffing in 2004–05, prior to and during the roll-out of non-sniffable OPAL fuel in Alice Springs. He used PCE with Central Australian communities affected by the devastating practice to help them come up with their own processes to combat it. Young people who had experienced the effects of petrol sniffing first- and second-hand, played character roles and developed the slogan 'Keep the Petrol in the Car, not a Can' for the story.

'It was e-learning to save lives,' said J. 'PCE could deliver the story in local languages. Instead of two or three people turning up for training, we had 200 to 300. We are now running various community projects in partnership with state, territory and federal agencies to prevent substance misuse.'

PCE, and the subsequent software derivative called MARVIN, were economical to develop because they used pre-existing technology and just changed the formats. J used his existing budget. The only equipment he needed in remote areas was a car or a boat with batteries. Face-to-face training was a mere two hours; for more computer-literate people, learning could be achieved from the steps on the MARVIN website.

'We provided digital cameras, sound recorders and interactive training support,' J said. 'Communities achieved a sense of ownership and control over the kinds of health and community messages developed and how they wanted them conveyed. In many places it was the Elders who formally presented the completed educational resource to their community.'

PCE and MARVIN engaged communities and cut across cultural boundaries between men and women, older and younger people and different linguistic groups. Bonya, a small, isolated community four hours east of Alice Springs, was one of J's favourite examples. The community had a shared responsibility agreement (SRA) with the federal government and wanted to show how the SRA had contributed to a healthier, safer, cleaner community. The funding meant infrastructure for Bonya – a new electrical substation, a store that stocked healthy foods, 15 metres of bitumen road that they drove J up and down. In return for the funding, the community ensured good school attendance, removal of litter and car bodies scattered around the streets and regular inspections of town dogs by vets. Bonya people scripted their own story and selected characters such as Uncle to represent Banjo, the community chairman. Members took photos of their community and inserted the images as background. The process of development gave people pride and ownership, and their video had cultural meaning. They made it so well that the video has inspired other communities to do likewise.

'Nobody else could have made a viable video about a tiny community,' said J, 'but we could because we didn't have normal production costs. There were no professional voice-overs, but real people telling real stories.'

Eighty people turned up to the presentation in this remote community of only seventy.

J demonstrated to me how the process worked.

'I need you to speak about anything for ten to fifteen seconds,' he instructed.

It was my ten seconds of fame. 'This story is about J, who is one of the inspiring people in *Reinventing the Bush*, my new book about young rural Australians.'

J ticked boxes on one of his computers and chose an appropriate graphic of a car stuck in a rut as background for our journey to Alice. Then he selected an Indigenous auntie in a brightly patterned dress to speak my sentence and added the music of Big Girl. It took him less than five minutes to make a personalised clip. 'The only other system like this in the world is called Flash. It takes three to four years to learn how to use it and sometimes a month or more to learn how to present a few minutes of the finished product. With PCE, people with no skills can learn quickly and after we've left, keep using it.'

J was working on a raft of animated projects around the country: a national Indigenous governance project, natural resource management projects with the Commonwealth Department of Environment and Heritage, a range of projects from community engagement to employment initiatives for the Commonwealth Department of Employment and Workplace Relations, immigrant resources with Relationships Australia and many others with non-government organisations, as well as the corporate sector. A national renal project with Baxter Healthcare Australia opted for a toolkit of perky-looking avatars. They represented healthy and sick kidneys, blood, even full and empty renal bags that could be used in different mixes of characters to make a range of stories to educate about kidney health.

However, what most satisfied J's idealism was a new initiative he created for business development in Indigenous communities.

'We are training and employing Aboriginal youth to use PCE and MARVIN software to create avatars and animate their Dreamtime stories for television. Over twenty remote communities and/or Indigenous media groups and organisations have signed up with a multimedia cooperative company we established. It will be a self-funding cooperative able to sell the stories in Australia and overseas.'

J's model of engagement is succeeding through the use of storytelling to convey important health promotion and cultural messages, a work team based in the Territory and backing from the world's biggest software company.

'The more I do with technology, the more I realise it's about the people,' he said. 'I have the best team, which I found in different locations. Previously they were under-appreciated; now they are partners in our work. Microsoft is an awesome sponsor. In July 2005, Microsoft demonstrated its global initiatives at a dinner in Los Angeles. It showed PCE and MARVIN as the Australian example of how information technology can benefit humanity.'

By 2006, offers of contracts were coming in to PCE from all over the world. J decided it was time to move beyond traditional bureaucratic processes within government and set up a new consortium made up of Northern Territory government agencies and other partners across Australia. Called the Northern Territory Institute for Community Engagement and Development, or NTICED, it designs and develops animation, communications and community development processes, and is the Territory's first overseas multimedia development agency; J is the partnering director.

'We thought the acronym NTICED was great until we received 4000 emails that mistook the site for a dating agency,' J grinned. Despite this, NTICED retained the acronym.

J was negotiating with the Commonwealth Department of Employment and Workplace Relations for Indigenous cadets to be involved in NTICED and build the technology in various regions of Australia. He found that character-based technology could transform students into teachers who could create their own resources. A number of J's former Indigenous students and trainees are now involved in projects around the globe.

'Because [PCE] overcomes many information and communication challenges we can use it all over the world, especially in countries with significant ethnic and cultural differences and many languages,' J said. 'It enables community members or educators to type their own health messages on a computer or record themselves in their own language, and then see and hear it spoken back by a range of walking, talking computer-generated characters. We're moving into Papua New Guinea, Fiji and Vanuatu, where PCE is ideal because of its low cost and modest infrastructure needs.'

With the new consortium, they can take on the large AusAid and United Nations contracts that were difficult under the previous bureaucratic structure. One of these is an AIDS project in Papua New Guinea. There, people are carrying the HIV infection back to their remote valleys from the townships. Many carriers have low literacy levels and would never learn about the dangers of AIDS in any of the country's 700 different dialects. PCE will enable them to do so.

'We also have a partnership project in West Papua with Sydney's Albion Street Centre, an Australian development partner within the Indonesian AIDS Commission. We have recently signed a memorandum of understanding with Albion Street Centre to work collaboratively on AIDS/STD projects all over the world using the PCE process and MARVIN.'

J thinks PCE can change the way the world looks at the development of training resources. He is branching into avian flu education in Asia.

'We don't have to travel to all these countries. We train people in the agencies, such as Albion Street, who then deliver the programs overseas,' J said.

By mid-2007, J has his most important breakthrough – a deal with Microsoft to take NTICED's MARVIN technology into schools and educational facilities in developing nations around the world.

'One of the key elements of this agreement is the employment of Indigenous trainers and students, trained in MARVIN, to work on projects over the next five years,' J said. 'For example a school in South Africa or Papua New Guinea can contact its local Microsoft office and ask for access to our programs. We then send Indigenous NT staff there with the software to deliver training. This is one of the largest Indigenous information and communications technology employment initiatives and certainly one of the largest software distribution deals ever undertaken by Australia.'

Interest in PCE spread fast. It won twenty-two awards in eighteen months, including four Northern Territory training awards in 2004. In November 2005, J flew to Singapore for the presentation of the Commonwealth Association for Public Administration and Management (CAPAM) awards, the equivalent of the Commonwealth Games in IT circles.

'We were up against the best in the world from 157 countries, some of them multi-billion dollar programs. We thought, "At least we got to Singapore, but we won't win the main award."'

During the day J bought a gaudy, gold silk jacket embroidered with dragons. He was with John Kirwan, the then commissioner of the Northern Territory Public Sector, who bet J $50 that he wouldn't wear the jacket to the awards.

'Anyone who knows me can vouch that when it comes to making a fool of myself, I'm in a class of my own,' J said. 'As the jacket only cost $20, I figured I would come out ahead.'

He wore the jacket, but, as he was telling this story, he suddenly exclaimed, 'I just realised that John never paid up.'

The announcer read out the bronze medal winner, then the silver. The gold medal winner was announced. J was looking around the audience to see who it was. It took him a few moments to realise that it was his program that had just been announced. PCE came equal first for the top award, Innovations in Governance, with India's Gujarat Emergency Earthquake Reconstruction project.

'We felt a bit embarrassed because we'd thrown together a PowerPoint presentation and demonstrated PCE with the judges as characters,' J said. 'It was a first for Australia to win gold. As I walked towards the stage, I was frantically trying to reverse my jacket. Beside the other men in black suits, I looked like a waiter who had sneaked onto the stage.'

On occasions such as this J would automatically have reached for the phone to tell his mother the news.

'She would have been so proud. Dad [George] is incredibly proud. He wants to introduce PCE into the jail system so prisoners can build their stories and tell people back in their communities not to break the law.' A program that J has developed with Queensland Department of Corrections became available from 1 July 2007, and will be accessible interstate for Northern Territory prisons to use.

Winning the CAPAM award marked a milestone in J's career. It positioned PCE as one of 2006's fifteen finalists for the highest public sector award in the world, the United Nations Governance Award. Later in 2005, J and his family flew from a holiday in Tasmania to Sydney for another award dinner. As they drove from the airport into the heart of the city, Anita saw banners everywhere about CeBIT Australia, Australia's leading information and communications technology event and its annual awards night, the Australian Information Industry Association (AIIA) awards.

'I wonder what that is about?' she mused.

'Oh, that's what we're going to,' J remarked casually.

'He hadn't told me anything about the award night,' said Anita. 'I had no dress to wear and two small kids in tow. The event turned out to be 800 people at a gala black-tie dinner. We lasted until 10 o'clock and people complimented us on how well behaved the kids were. After J's program won the AIIA

E-Government and Services award, I asked him to take us back to our hotel because the children were tired.'

Anita resolved she wasn't going to be caught like that again. She would go shopping and buy herself not one, but two glamorous outfits for any future surprises.

J, who was discreetly dressed in black for this award night, arrived back at the dinner in time to hear who had won the main iNspiration award for 'the best of the best'. Federal Minister for Communications, Information Technology and the Arts Senator Helen Coonan made the announcement.

'I nearly died when they called us out as the winners,' he said. 'I showed the award to Anita and she was amazed, "They gave it to you!" Then I rang my brother, who has a Masters degree in computer engineering and really is gifted in information technology and told him I had won Australia's top ICT award. He laughed because he said he wouldn't trust me with his toaster, let alone his computer.'

After a string of mishaps Anita no longer lets her husband near appliances and tools either. The television antenna cost the family over $160 to repair after J pulled it apart to fix it.

Despite his high profile, J is somewhat bemused by all the awards and accolades.

'I get my buzz from creating a commercial product with which others can also achieve their dreams,' he said. 'The night of our first Microsoft launch with the Gap Youth Centre kids was on a par with the CAPAM international award in Singapore.'

J has the air of an absentminded professor. As I lined him up for a photo with life-size cutouts of some of his avatars – Uncle, Auntie, a frill-necked lizard and Sober Bob the Designated Driver – he remembered that he hadn't brushed his hair that day.

In March 2006 I travelled to Canberra to meet J. On the day, our national capital paraded its brilliant autumn russets, reds and yellows. J had a heavy cold and croaked 'Hello' at me, but still managed his trademark grin. Dressed in a pinstriped black suit, purple silk tie and shiny shoes J looked every inch the city businessman. He was here to negotiate with federal bureaucrats on a brilliant idea.

'Aboriginal art and craft, including tourist art has an estimated worth of $300 million per annum,' he explained over coffee and a sandwich. 'The boundaries are blurred nowadays between genuine high-grade Aboriginal art and what is manufactured as tacky tourist art. Asia produces as many didgeridoos and boomerangs as Australia does. It was rumoured that a shipment from China of so-called Aboriginal art was worth $1.8 million.'

Addressing a senate committee hearing in Darwin on the future of Aboriginal art, Territory Arts Minister Marion Scrymgour said the multi-million dollar industry needed to be nurtured, if not protected, to remain sustainable. 'It is the [unethical] shops that are of serious concern. The material they call Aboriginal art is almost exclusively the work of fakers, forgers and fraudsters. Their work hides behind false descriptions and dubious designs.'

Within Australia, Indigenous people in cities are painting certain country or stories or in certain styles that may not be legitimate for them to depict.

'Only a few people in Australia can paint certain Dreaming stories,' J said. 'If a South Australian artist wants to paint a Barramundi Dreaming he or she needs permission from the people of that country.'

As J worked in Arnhemland on the Dreamtime story project, he realised there was no adequate protection of the artworks being produced so prolifically in communities. The industry lacked effective tools to track works of art, dates of production or their value, which made it attractive to potential fraudsters. Some dealers copy Aboriginal art from the internet and create a name for it which they attach to the copy. They then find an Aboriginal person who is willing to be photographed in a suitable location with the copy and sell it as a genuine article that has been created by that person.

'They might pay the Aboriginal person in cash or a used car or even Viagra. There is no transaction document with the fake.'

The Dreamtime story project also alerted J to the need for an authentication and certification system that could verify and safeguard the artwork from exploitation and counterfeiters. He remembered that the car industry had used microdots to stop theft. If a microdot the size of a pinhead could protect cars, why not art?

J handed me a magnifying glass and a phial filled with what look like pepper grindings, but under the magnifier I saw thousands of tiny rectangular silver stickers, each with its own unique markings. Each one can be embedded in individual artworks to identify them, whether they are woven baskets, paintings or artefacts. It can then be read with a simple microscope. J then looked for an additional security system and found that the Broken Hill artist Pro Hart had used biological DNA to tag his art, but it decayed over time. Next, J discovered that the CSIRO, the national science authority, had designed chemical DNA to protect intellectual property and wondered whether this could serve his purpose.

'I found we could use special equipment to spray chemical DNA on the art to back up the dot system. Now we have several levels of anti-counterfeiting security.'

DataDot Technologies Australia, in partnership with the CSIRO, developed the technology. Consumers will pay a $25 fee for tagged works, of which about half will be returned to the artist's community. Once an article has been tagged, the system generates a matching identity number and an image of the article is downloaded onto a central database.

As in the development of digital characters to convey vital health promotion messages, J thought about the solution he wanted and worked backwards towards the problem. He established another new company called IdenteArt to assist Indigenous people to protect the future of Aboriginal art production and to maintain its deserved value worldwide.

'We don't have the luxury of years to establish our system,' J said. 'You always have people trying to beat any system, so we formed the company in partnership with the groups that have the patents and intellectual property rights. In that way, we ensure that counterfeiters cannot readily simulate the technology. The aim of the business is to have 50 or 51 per cent Indigenous stakeholders and investment groups within eighteen months.'

J's primary business, NTICED, became the majority owner in partnership with DataDot Technologies Australia and Indigenous shareholders and stakeholders.

'Our new company has exclusive worldwide rights to the datadot technologies in the field of art, craft and antiquities,' J said.

Indigenous art represented under the IdenteArt system is being made available in 130 galleries that represent over 500 Indigenous artists around Australia and the world. J is also drawing up a document of creation for artists and a gallery transaction document, so that if the artwork is resold, a percentage of the sale returns to the original artist and to the region where the work was created.

The prime movers in the IdenteArt concept are J and deputy director of the company, Scott Wilson, who was formerly with DataDotAM. Their skills and experience complement each other. J focuses on ideas for the company's direction and negotiations with government while Scott puts J's explosion of ideas into practice, does product development and briefs potential clients and investors.

J has met with officers from the Commonwealth Department of Employment and Workplace Relations who have endorsed the IdenteArt business as approved employment and community development activities. The Commonwealth tick of approval opens the way for communities to access federal government funding for training and business development rather than having to use their minimal community financial resources.

All countries with an Indigenous art industry face the same problems of fraudulent replications and exploitation of artists as in Australia. J is interweaving PCE and IdenteArt for Indigenous community good in other countries as well as Australia. In 2007, the two programs – a community animation program hand-in-hand with authenticating local art and craft products – will begin in fourteen First Nations in Canada, Africa and Papua New Guinea.

By October 2006 the Easterby-Wood family had moved from Alice Springs to Canberra, a move that gave J better access to agencies with which he constantly worked and the family more time together. They live in a spacious house looking out towards the Brindabella Mountains and a lake, a far cry from the sandy deserts of Alice Springs. Anita greeted me at the door of their new home. Beside her was three-year-old Savannah, as curly-headed as her mother, and wearing her favourite pink fairy dress. J had returned from Weipa in Cape York the night before and was busy catching up on phone calls in his home office.

'J puts all his energy into whatever he is doing,' Anita said as we took in the view over the lake. 'He has done the legwork to get PCE and IdenteArt going. All these projects have come from the one mind. The move to Canberra is a chance for him to change his work habits and have a decent family life. What's important to us both is being Christians. We believe our lives on Earth are a mere whisper in time. In Alice, when J's mind was overheating with ideas, he would go to church and return a different man, much calmer.'

J joined us for lunch. 'You always wonder if your life is going to make a difference to others in the bigger scheme,' he said. 'The highlight of my career has been to work on PCE with an incredible team of people who have similar goals and visions. PCE and IdenteArt have the potential to impact upon the lives of millions around the world.'

By mid-2007, J was reflecting on the incredible highs and lows of his year.

'Dad [George] was diagnosed with an aggressive lung cancer earlier this year and has been given a short time to live. I try to see him as often as possible. On the work front, the NTICED deal with Microsoft will be really significant in training and employing Indigenous people for international work. IdenteArt was launched in Alice Springs in April and is being trialled to protect sacred sites such as rock paintings. The technology can leave a digital DNA residue in a cave and be used to catch thieves and detect where thefts occurred, all of which was formerly impossible. The technology won a merit award in the security section at the 2007 Australian Information Industry Association awards and we will compete in the Asian–Pacific final. The Greek government is also looking at our technology to authenticate its antiquities.'

The obstacles J Easterby-Wood faced in the Territory were the catalyst that pushed him to devise innovative responses using information and communication technology. J believes that if you are given an opportunity, you have to take it and that you can accomplish anything, no matter where or who you are.

This man is blessed, not cursed as he once thought, with an unusual mind. He likens his way of thinking to the Aboriginal way of looking at time.

'They know that anything in nature or society has happened before, so the answer to any problem is already out there,' he said. 'I link things together in a different way to many people because I know the answer is already there.'

J and Anita Easterby-Wood with Savannah and Phoenix, Canberra, 2007

1 Steve Perryman cray fishing off Port MacDonnell, 2006. **2** Murrandoo Yanner, Gunnamulla homeland, Gulf of Carpentaria, 2002. **3** James Fitzpatrick and his mentee Jack Pink, Wyalchatchem, Western Australia, 2005. **4** Mayor Janie Dickenson (*top right*) at community visioning, Launceston, 2005. **5** Future Farmers Network founder Deb McLucas (*right*) and FFN member Sandy Cole, 2002. **6** Cathy Duncan (*front*) and Aboriginal Employment Strategy staff in Moree cotton fields, 2005.

PART 2
Grassroots Activists

Mayor Janie Dickenson, Launceston, Tasmania, 2005

7

The Designer

Janie Finlay (Dickenson), Launceston, Tasmania

Mayor Janie Dickenson is tall and athletic, a woman who throws herself into caring for her baby and her Canadian partner as well as working 365 days of the year on behalf of her city. In Launceston's smart mayoral chambers which overlook the city's historic core, two playpens full of toys signal a challenge to traditional council boundaries: in 2004, 29-year-old Janie brings her son Zac to work. It is enough to spur some aldermen into action, even trying to overthrow her.

Established in 1806, Launceston takes pride in its history as Australia's third oldest settlement after Sydney and Hobart. Down steep slopes to the river step fine Victorian terraces and mansions, home to long-established citizens who are accustomed to guiding the affairs of this industrious place. That is until 2002 when Janie appeared, giving a voice to the young, artists, surrounding rural dwellers and other citizens who until now had little voice in the affairs of their city. Janie is Launceston born and bred.

'As the only child of parents who both worked, I learnt early on to strive and be self-sufficient, to look after myself in a world of adults.' Helen, Janie's mother, was business manager at her daughter's school, Launceston Church Grammar; Jim, her father, is an architect keen to preserve the city's historic precincts and buildings.

'My parents were both really supportive and drove me hard. I could be stubborn. They encouraged me to explore music, arts and sport. I wasn't much good academically, but won prizes for woodwork and metalwork. I grew up believing I could be whatever I wanted to be. Mum was my role model. She was strong. She would laugh and say, "Go girl!" My parents separated when I was in my early teens and I lived with my mother.'

Janie strove to be the best in whatever she did. Through her high school years, she represented Tasmania in softball; when she was 17 she toured the USA with the Tasmanian Festival Wind Symphony playing the flute and piccolo. From her house high above Launceston, picture windows look out over an attractive, thriving city, a city which, to an ambitious teenager, just didn't shape up.

'I left Launceston in 1993 because I hated it,' Janie said as she settled cross-legged on a small sofa. 'I didn't think it had the opportunities to support me, or to grow my kind of dreams and passions. After finishing school I moved to Hobart.'

At the University of Tasmania in Hobart, Janie studied fine arts and majored in furniture design. Only a couple of women did the course and by the final year, Janie was the only woman among mostly older men.

'If I didn't want to drink beer and play pool, then I wasn't part of it.'

She quickly learnt how to do both, became a mean pool player and graduated top of her class. In her sitting room is a large, leaf-shaped table Janie made at university, a superbly crafted organic form using a striated Tasmanian blackwood veneer. She experimented with other materials, such as moulded acrylic, glass and metal, in her quest to try new and creative forms that conveyed movement and life.

'Lifestyle is important to me. I like things relaxed and casual, comfortable and practical. I made this upholstered sofa using Aussie wool.' She indicated the flowing shape of the tangerine sofa on which she sat.

Janie's dream was to be the best furniture designer in the world, to have a studio among the chic galleries of Greene Street in Soho, New York, and to exhibit in Milan.

'In 1996, when I was 21 I moved to the big smoke, Sydney, to get design experience. I had never been there before and didn't know anyone. I opted out of sport and music and threw myself into designing.'

She got a job at a hotel where she started at four in the morning on the breakfast shift, was in her workshop all day and waitressed at an Italian restaurant at night.

'My life was about attainment and success – in retrospect all the grotty things of life. I found a job as a sales consultant with a furniture manufacturer so I could meet people in the industry – the interior designers, architects, building construction companies, transport agencies and contract furniture makers.'

After six months Janie established her own boutique studio, Aximo Studios in central Sydney, where she designed furniture and interiors. She exhibited in the eastern capital cities and sold work to the USA. She would grab four hours sleep a night and led a rather isolated life.

'In hindsight, I would have burnt out if I had kept up that pace.'

The 22-year-old was on her way as a designer when, in 1996, her mother Helen was diagnosed with cancer. Janie returned to Launceston to care for her mother over the next 10 months. When her mother died, Janie fell into a severe depression that lasted for nine months.

'Mum was my backbone. Through that experience of caring for her and then her death I realised that it was OK to be angry, sad, frightened, happy and confused, and to dream of a better future all at once. I saw a psychologist for a while who helped heaps; I also had some close mates to whom I could talk about anything.'

Janie tried to think about what she would do next. 'Prior to my mother being sick, it was me, me, me. Then, back in Launceston in a caring role, it was mother, father, family, community, people. I'd never been in that world where it was part of me. Going through caring for her full time was about volunteerism and community and support.

'I would trade anything in the world to have my mum back. I miss her heaps, but,' she reflected, 'things happen for a reason. I don't think I could be who I am now without having gone through that. I became a more caring person.'

In her search for direction, Janie left Australia for the USA, where she backpacked down the eastern seaboard and walked New York's Soho galleries that she had dreamt about.

'But I had lost my passion for design, for everything. I was grieving and wanted to open new chapters in my life.'

She returned to Launceston and decided to work as a project manager for the Beacon Foundation, a national youth employment group. It helped young people to develop skills for meaningful employment – young offenders at Ashley Detention Centre outside Launceston and those still at school and at risk of becoming long-term unemployed. One in ten families in Launceston had no experience of employment over three generations. There were huge socioeconomic needs in the community.

'I worked for three and a half years for the Beacon Foundation with students at Launceston secondary college, and six months with Ashley Detention Centre. Ashley served the whole of Tasmania and yet 70 per cent of the young people there were from parts of Launceston.'

Valuable work was being done to integrate young people back into the community, but lack of government funding threatened continuation of the programs. Janie appealed to all levels of government for assistance with youth development programs. When she approached Launceston City Council, the general response was that local government was about infrastructure, not people's needs, and that Janie should go to the state or federal authorities.

'Basically, I got a pat on the head and was told to come back once I knew more about local government. As soon as I heard that I thought, These people are supposed to be leaders in our community and they don't want to understand the needs of young people. What sort of future does our community have if a large percentage of our youth are at risk and not able to develop their potential?'

Council's response fuelled her motivation to act. She met with Alderman Joan Walters to discuss strategies.

Joan suggested Janie stand for council. 'I was one of the youngest and I was nearly 50,' Joan said.

Janie wanted Launceston to be a place where young people had a fair go and didn't have to leave to find opportunities to advance themselves.

'I decided to change priorities from the inside out by standing for local government.'

Janie's inspiration was 97-year-old Dorothy Edwards, the first woman mayor of Launceston City Council in 1956 and one of the first female mayors in Australia. She used to take an eight-week journey by steamer to England for International Council of Women meetings.

At the age of 25, the campaign became the focus of her life as Janie told her story at community gatherings and in conversations as she door-knocked the city and from a stall at the local markets. Over cups of tea and homemade biscuits at members' homes, the influential Launceston Support Group for Women into Local Government assisted Janie with planning strategies.

In November 2000, she received the fourth highest number of primary votes and became the council's youngest ever elected member, half the age of the next youngest councillor. Idealistic and passionate though she was about her platform of youth and community issues, Janie hadn't yet realised what it might be like as an alderman.

'Council was a culture of mostly long-serving older males and it wasn't until the first 30 seconds, when I was being sworn in at the council chamber, that I began to understand. I saw this older alderman coming from the other side of the room and thought, Here comes someone to welcome me into the fold. He didn't even extend his hand to shake my hand, didn't introduce himself or welcome my family and me. Instead he said, "Dickenson, young people should be seen and not heard. Take your place at the table, sit down and shut up." That was like a red rag to a bull for me. Stuff like that energises me.'

At her first meeting Janie knew there was a youth issue on the agenda. Council members wanted to relocate a shelter for young men. Janie thought the shelter should stay where it was, close to the central business district and facilities.

'In the lunch room before the session started, aldermen were trying to burn me up. One man came up to me and said, "I was really worried about you. I heard you were in hospital on Friday." I said, "No, that's not right". He replied, "My mate is a radiographer and he was telling me that you've got a brain tumour. That would explain why you are behaving the way you are. You should settle down and be quiet." It wasn't that long since my mother had been in hospital and died from cancer, but for someone to lie and to try and kick me behind the knees like that ... it shocked me. I knew from Day 1 that there were immature, unprofessional aldermen, so I had to be strong from the start. It's a tough environment.'

There were times at the council table where she was referred to as 'girlie' or 'junior alderman'.

'I came into council with a utopian vision. I bowled in and said what I wanted to say and did things the way that I wanted to. Some aldermen were always at me, against kerbside recycling, for instance, such a big issue that eventually was passed. I kept going because I believed I was on the right track and could achieve positive things.'

In a interview for the ABC's *New Dimensions with George Negus*, Janie told a journalist that she had learnt so much from that rocky first 12 months. 'I wouldn't have developed the skills to deal with what I'm doing – to negotiate and talk to people, or to be confronted in meetings where I'm dismissed as the young female. I can stand up to that confidently now. So you have to thank people for being nasty and making you stronger.'

In what many thought was a brash and naïve statement, which was reported in local media, Janie said she wanted to stand for mayor within two years.

'While I was getting outcomes doing things my way they weren't leadership outcomes, they were just practical things. To change the big picture, I felt I needed to do it from the mayoral position.'

The death of the well-respected mayor John Lees forced an election in February 2002. In a bold move, Janie put her name forward. She campaigned throughout the electorate as she had in 2000, handing out flyers and talking to people outside pubs and movie theatres.

'I received the most amazing feedback when I was out on the streets walking and talking to people. Informal conversations were valuable. People would tell me their concerns and that they didn't know how to bring them up at council. Many felt frustrated because they perceived council did things *to* them rather than *with* them.'

This was only the second popular mayoral election held in Launceston. Previously, aldermen elected the mayor. Against all odds, this disturbing young influence was elected mayor in a previously conservative-voting city. Janie was nearly 1700 votes ahead of the highest tally for any of her seven rivals. She became the youngest female local government leader in Australian history. Janie suddenly had responsibility for the state's largest local government area and an organisation that was one of the largest employers in the region with a $75 million annual budget and 550 full-time staff.

'Launceston is unique in Tasmania because we have such a significant rural hinterland,' Janie said. 'We not only have issues in forestry, agriculture, industry and domestic needs, but also the CBD, shopping centres and suburbs. We have to meet many different needs in our community.'

Janie's campaign to connect with a diversity of people in her community paid off. According to Melbourne's *Age* in 2002, 'The story of Janie Dickenson's conversion and rapid rise said much about how Launceston has changed. But Dickenson will have to fight to stay in her job. She is yet to convince some of the Old Guard in Tasmania's second city that she has a right to carry its flag. When [former mayor] Lee's term expires this year she will have to win another election.'

Janie had an egalitarian view of the mayoral role, much to the annoyance of some aldermen. Her first move after being sworn in was to take off the chain of office. Then she moved down from the mayoral seat above the other aldermen and sat on the same level at their table. She also opened the council to the public.

'Janie doesn't know her place – thank God!' commented Ian Pattie, then a journalist with Launceston's *The Examiner*. The older aldermen didn't like her actions and some were openly hostile. Janie bucked the system by getting the most appropriate person from among the aldermen to represent her at functions rather than automatically appointing the deputy. She tried to overturn seniority seating (in which former mayors and deputies sat nearest to the mayor), but she lost that one. Launceston is proud of its built heritage; Council's business is rates. There were barneys all the time. Aldermen would say, "It's only an old building. Pull it down." Janie supported her father's views.

She would vote against proposed developments on heritage values, which severely irritated some aldermen. Some of them would change their votes, depending on how Janie voted, just to annoy her.'

Local government elections came up nine months later, in November 2002. Despite opposition within the council chambers, Janie was re-elected mayor unopposed. A grassroots politician who believed in openness and consultation, Janie saw the municipality as a living design to be shaped to meet its citizens' needs and values.

'A city needs to be livable, to be walkable and have good public spaces, wide streets, good patterns and rhythms. That's what has guided my decision making in council. The tipping point is to get a lot of people behind initiatives. I love my job because I know it is having an impact.

'I try holding community forums on a number of levels. I cop so much flack over community consultation. Some people won't even try to understand or accept it.'

Janie could see the potential for better interaction if she and the aldermen met informally with constituents over a meal.

'There's nothing like food and drink to informalise a situation and enable people to spend quality time with each other,' Janie said. 'It's really important in understanding people's values.'

So she instigated Politics in the Pub as a way for aldermen to move around city and rural areas to meet and talk with people. Council advertised the venue in advance and Janie and any interested aldermen went to a different local hotel around Launceston each fortnight after the council meeting to have a meal, a drink and maybe a game of pool with the locals.

'Sometimes there's a pubful, other times there are only a few,' she said. 'We used to go into a back room at council after meetings, hide ourselves away and eat crayfish and avocado salad, or some other luscious meal that cost $40 or $50 a head. I thought: Why do we do this – 12 aldermen who don't like each other sitting and yelling at each other after a meeting? Only one business had the catering contract, yet there were many venues around town that served great food. I said, "Why don't we go around and visit different places after our meetings?" I tried to promote Politics in the Pub sessions as a council initiative. The vote went "not to be presented" because aldermen said, "How risky will it be to go out and have a meal in a pub with all those drunken people. You may get attacked!" I found it appalling that they had such lack of respect for people to think that by socialising with them and understanding what they were thinking they would be at risk.'

On one occasion, when Janie and several aldermen went to a hotel for a Politics in the Pub session, she cleaned up the young male patrons at pool then discussed their jobs and interests with them across the bar. Everyone called her Janie.

'It shows I am just an ordinary person who has a life outside being the mayor.'

The first Sunday of every month Janie ran a stall at the local markets and handed out information about council.

'I discover what's going on at the grassroots level. Some people are going to buy their vegies or are just having a day out and may not even know I have a stall there. They see me and say, "Oh – can I talk to you about this?" I see them in an environment where they feel comfortable. That way you get a more honest response that is being offered, not requested.'

One day next to her stall was the Australian Rodent Fanciers Society stall. Janie had never met a rat face to face, but accepted the honour of judging the rodent show.

'I've done some wacky things since becoming mayor,' Janie said, 'but rats! I was surprised to find they were cute, clean and cuddly.'

Her daily routine is punishing – up at 4.30 or 5 to read the papers. Her neighbours might be surprised if they observed her rummaging around in the camellias with a headlamp: she's looking for the newspapers, which are tossed over the fence.

'I can start in the office from 6.30 to 7.00 in the morning, have back-to-back meetings throughout the day and functions to attend at night. In between, I fit in my own planning and thinking time. It's seven days a week and at least 12 hours a day, but is definitely worth it.'

As she drove in the mayoral car with the reporter from *New Dimensions*, Janie indicated her mobile office. 'This back seat's all laid out. I've got signing trays and action needed trays. I spend all day every day with people. I could be at a function with 600 people, or at a community gathering with twenty or thirty people. I'm rarely by myself. At home I can close the door, turn the phone off, just be myself. There are times when I'm go, go, go and live on adrenaline. I love that, but one of the things I've learnt since going through the whole thing with my mother is that you've got to look after yourself.'

Cataract Gorge is Janie's favourite place, a spectacular steep-sided gorge only 10 minutes from the heart of Launceston.

'I walked there as a child, but didn't appreciate how precious it was. When Mum was sick, I would walk there for hours. You can make it your own as a place of solitude, being energetic or watching the turbulence of floods down the gorge. People do white water sports, rafting and hundreds of rock climbs there. For me, it is a place of serenity and recovery. I'm grateful that it's in the centre of this city.'

Through the front door of Janie's house strolled a lean man in a tracksuit. His hair was streaked with bright green. 'Hi,' he said in a soft Canadian accent. This is Derrek, Janie's partner. His appearance triggers a story from Janie. One day in 2002 she was returning to Launceston after speaking at a leadership retreat on Hayman Island.

'I never waste a minute, so while waiting for the plane from Melbourne to Launceston, I sat on the floor of the airport lounge and began working.'

When the departure call was announced, Janie hopped on the plane. A man walked up behind her and introduced himself, even before he sat next to her. He was Derrek Finlay, he said, a Canadian who was heading to the deep black waters of Lake Cethana in central Tasmania for training in deep-sea commercial diving. He told her that, after five stop-overs between Vancouver and Australia, he was jet lagged.

'I introduced myself to Janie and babbled away,' Derrek chimed in. ' "What do you do in Launceston?" "I run the place," she said. I thought, Great, this chick thinks she runs the place.'

'I remember thinking, He's cute,' Janie said. 'It took me the whole 44 minute trip to get the courage to offer him a lift into Launceston. I had a driver, Chris, picking me up, but I was so embarrassed about the lift offer that I didn't talk to Derrek the whole way in.'

'This guy shows up in a big car and picks up my bags,' Derrek recalled. 'Nice guy. I thought he was her boyfriend. She was on the phone the whole way in, but she gave me a card and said to call her for a drink. The guy said they worked at the town hall and to drop in.'

A few days later Derrek was walking past the town hall with his diving colleagues and decided to go in.

'I just asked for Janie – I didn't know her surname. The receptionist said, "You mean the mayor?" I argued with her that Janie couldn't be the mayor. My mates laughed at me when she really was the mayor. I left Janie a note and we went out for drinks that night. The next day she took a day off and suggested a trip to the sea.'

They drove two and a half hours to St Helens on the northeast coast. Five hundred metres from the beach, the car skidded in gravel and rolled.

'It was upside-down with the windshield caved in,' Derrek said. 'I got out, but Janie was so stubborn she wouldn't wait for me to help her. She let herself out of the seat belt and fell on her head. The cops turned up and really gave it to her. Everybody knew who she was, but didn't let on to the media. A cop told us a good dive spot for abalones. It turned out to be the best day of our lives. We went to the pub and played pool, ate seafood on a boat and walked on the beach. The car was written off, so at midnight we had to hitch a lift back in a bread truck. The driver had never seen a human in his truck before and didn't stop talking. I told Janie she tried to kill me on our very first date. We've been together ever since. It may seem as if Janie and I lead two separate lives, but it's one. If I can't come home, she joins me.'

Derrek hit national headlines in May 2003, applauded for his courage and prompt action. He had boarded a plane home to Launceston from Melbourne. The flight had only just taken off when Derrek saw the flight steward pick up a man and they both fell in the aisle next to him. The man had two wooden stakes, which he was stabbing into the back of the steward's head. Derrek tackled both of them in the aisle, disabled the attacker and gave first aid to the flight steward. He applied a compression bandage to hold strips of the steward's scalp in place. The plane had to make an emergency landing back in Melbourne. The incident was later found to be a hijack attempt.

'I was just trying to get home. The steward was the hero,' Derrek said, dismissing any praise for his efforts. His first words to Janie were, 'I'm OK. Love you.'

His background during the 1990s gave Derrek combat skills and a cool head in emergencies. He was in the infantry section of the Canadian military. Later, he was seconded as a United Nations peacekeeper and paramedic in the conflicts between Bosnians and Croats as the former Yugoslavia collapsed, and then between warlords in Somalia.

'I was 19 on my first UN tour in northern Bosnia. As my grandfather used to say – I was young, dumb and full of gum. In the first 24 hours the troop carrier 10 feet ahead of me drove over an anti-tank mine and exploded, killing four soldiers.'

Over the following 18 months with the UN, Derrek came to know the depths of man's inhumanity to man – the mass graves, the terrible smell of rotting, dismembered bodies and sheer brutality. He saw the wrecked lives, the pain and the poverty of the survivors.

'Humans will do anything to survive. If you put Bosnia in Launceston, people would change. The only difference between Bosnians, Croats, Somalis and Australians is that the others were raised holding an AK47 machine gun.'

He and another soldier spent four months on reconnaissance behind enemy lines in the deserts of Somalia dressed like desert people. At one point they had to use all of their SAS-type training to escape a troop of twenty-three Somalis.

'They chased us for a couple of days on foot. We had to run and hide until we made it to some scrub. We fired lots of rounds to scare them off, so they would think we were a big force and not just two men. You couldn't stay in the UN as a peacekeeper for long or you would become a drunk, or go crazy.'

Derrek's training in Tasmania's Lake Cethana became his occupation as he took on the most specialised and potentially dangerous form of diving – saturation diving to install oil pipelines underwater around the world.

'I swore I would never work in oil. Dad worked in the industry in the largest open pit tar sand mine in Canada and was always moving.'

The divers' 'home' is inside a construction bell, under pressure at great depths for many weeks. Their only connection to the outside world is by an 'umbilical cord' and a lock-out hatch system through which food, medicine, even emails can be sent and wastes sent back up. They live under pressure, breathing helium and oxygen in an atmosphere saturated with nitrogen and helium. In 2004, Derrek lived 175 metres under the Gulf of Thailand for more than two months.

'We have everything to survive down there for six to eight weeks, like a space station. The body has to work hard and we lose a lot of weight, although we eat heaps. We're locked out for eight-hour shifts in the water. It's dark and freezing at those depths. We wear baggy denim overalls with a hot water hose attached, which circulates water around our bodies because of the cold. Big gropers, sharks and octopuses are curious and sometimes attack us.'

He thinks at times that he is almost a fish.

Derrek's favourite dives are off the Western Australian coast where the water is clear, the seafloor sandy and colourful fish abound. After working in dangerous jobs, Derrek has little patience with arguing around the council table, even less with mean-spirited behaviour towards Janie.

'In 2004 when I was away diving for 109 days, people were spreading rumours about me leaving Janie. I showed my face at a council meeting at Janie's request, but left halfway through because of aldermen bickering.' He admires Janie's ability to fight for her principles and to turn an issue around. 'She acknowledges, but doesn't bow to, criticism.'

Janie copes by making sure she is well prepared on issues. One of the hottest issues for council in 2003 was the need for a clean, adequate water supply, but this conflicted with the drive for expanded commercial forestry areas. Janie drove me up a rutted, winding dirt road to a ridge near Mt Arthur. The majestic mountain where she bushwalked as a child overlooks the North Esk valley, source of 80 per cent of Launceston's domestic water supply. The once-pristine forested upper catchment lay in the cradle of a ring of mountains. From this vantage point different stages of forestry plantation growth and swathes of bare hilltops scattered with felled trees are visible. The cleared patches looked like mange on a dog's back.

'This is St Pat's catchment,' Janie said, as she pointed across the valley. 'The cleared patches are logging coupes. Most people don't see all this clearing except from the air. All the forestry science said it should be selectively logged and direct seeded back into native vegetation. Instead, the logging operators went in there a few months ago, clear felled it and are putting in windrows to plant *Eucalyptus nitens*. Because that species isn't native to the area, the loggers totally deforest the floor by putting down 1080 poison to kill off the browsing animals and spray to clear the weeds. Council had to be informed that the area was to be clear felled instead of selectively logged, but nobody informed anybody. It wasn't until the day they clear felled and a neighbouring property was flooded by run-off from the bare ground that council knew. The board overseeing the operations also rules whether operations are appropriate, or whether prosecutions should occur. These issues churn me up because I know what I see is not right. It's an aggressive environment and could consume me every hour of every day.'

At that time, Janie saw her next six to twelve months as make or break time.

'The only reason we're here as aldermen is to identify community needs and see how they can be addressed. If aldermen believe they have all the skills and knowledge to decide everything in our community, we will only ever have the minds of twelve at work and not the minds of 65,000.'

Janie believes in balancing the needs of a multitude of groups and interests by talking and working with people and being honest about what council does and why. Not everyone embraces that view. In 2004, council, under Janie's leadership, embarked on Launceston Vision 2020, an intense process of asking citizens how they wanted Launceston to be in the future. 'Unnecessary and complete waste of money', was the view of a number of aldermen.

Janie said, 'It's hard to win over an attitude of "Trust us, we know best. We won't consult because it will take too long, or if we consult we might have to do something we don't want to do. If something goes bad, never mind we can hide it." I believe if you consult you can understand what people need, what their aspirations are, and then you can head in the right direction to meet those needs.'

People wanted to see a commitment to the environment – clean air, clean water – and a vibrant future for young people, respect for the unique heritage, a thriving arts community and Launceston as a magnet for investment and tourists.

As well as giving citizens a voice in local decision making, Janie was involved in a range of organisations that reflected her interests: from Communities for Children and Whitelion youth development to the Metro Tasmania and Tasmanian Symphony Orchestra boards. In 2001, she was elected president of the Tasmanian branch of the Australian Local Government Women's Association and represented Launceston on the state premier's Local Government Council. In 2002, Janie was appointed for three years to the federal government's Regional Women's Advisory Council, which advised the deputy prime minister on issues in regional areas.

'We ran a series of forums on water around the country to feed into the national water policy. One of our initiatives brought Indigenous women together in Alice Springs to discuss their mutual concerns and how to support their communities to help them grow.'

Janie's efforts on behalf of young people and local government were recognised by a Centenary of Federation medal in 2002 and she was selected as a finalist in the 2001 Young Australian of the Year award for Tasmania and the 2003 Telstra Business Women's awards.

There would hardly be one Launceston citizen who didn't know of their mayor, especially after 10 April 2004, when Janie gave birth to Zac. She encountered applause as well as harsh criticism when she opted to take him to work. In a corner of the mayoral chamber were the two playpens where he quietly entertained himself, and in the bathroom, a change table. Zac, an alert child with a winning smile, took a lively interest in the world around him.

'The last two years of combining my roles of mayor, mother and family member have been huge and difficult,' Janie said in October 2005. 'Sometimes others think I rush in. On the contrary, I over-consider. I made a choice not to ask whether I could bring Zac to work because the aldermen would have said no. As a single parent much of the time, I thought I would miss out on his early life. I didn't think he would be a distraction because he was asleep most of the time.'

She later made the choice to move Zac into childcare close to the town hall.

'If I had another baby I would talk it through with council. I think we could come to a good arrangement where all needs and sensitivities were met.'

Taking Zac to work wasn't the only controversial move Janie had made that year. She had previously argued the case for a professional performance appraisal of council's general manager, which resulted in the hiring of a new general manager. She also made the unpopular move to introduce leadership development into council. These changes, despite showing foresight, were viewed as a waste of money by some aldermen.

'There was a real need for culture change within council. I knew we had to do something about the dysfunction and try to build a team. If I'd asked about going ahead, aldermen would have said no, so I worked with the new general manager to organise it. A well-known consultant, Fabian Dattner, did individual audits with aldermen and workshops with us all.'

Janie's mentor, Alderman Joan Walters, had continually encouraged her to give a little on some issues.

'Some meetings were awful,' Joan said. 'Aldermen were constantly arguing and challenging her chairing and Janie would become dogmatic. Fabian Dattner did Myers–Briggs personality profiles with us all. Aldermen were fascinated by their differences and it gave insight into why people acted the way they did. Janie is a visionary who is popular with the electorate, but you can't have disharmony and you always need six other votes for a decision. Janie listened to Fabian's advice about teamwork and after that the interaction around the council table improved.'

From the process, Janie learnt that there was a difference between trail blazing and leadership.

'Initially, I thought I was right and the others were wrong,' she said. 'I now see the role of mayor is to allow all voices at the table to be heard and to take the group decisions forward rather than what you think is the best option.'

Perhaps attitudes were thawing. Janie had four days off work when young Zac had pneumonia and was pleased when aldermen who had never been into her office brought their wives in and asked about her son.

'One alderman, with whom I had no relationship, came and congratulated me after a council meeting.'

A slight thaw in relationships didn't stop a Janie and Goliath struggle ensuing in October 2005 in the lead-up to Launceston City Council elections. Janie's impact as a leader was tested in her run for a second term as mayor. Five years after she burst onto a council she considered took little account of people, her strategies for encouraging participation were paying off. 'When I was in school I didn't know anything about local government. Now I can walk down the street and I'll hear an eight-year-old say "Hey, there's the mayor", or a 15-year-old will approach me and ask what to do about recycling. Or a 60-year-old will stop to talk to me about their issues. Sure it's a small town – 65,000 people – but it's great to have so many people participating. Council is now part of the community – people feel we're approachable. There's a foundation.'

Along the Tamar, on a new boardwalk, people head to fashionable restaurants or a barbecue in the park, walk dogs or play soccer. At a new arts precinct at Inveresk, a crowd gathers for a Vision 2020 event. The city can now play host to international sporting events at York Park, such as the Rugby World Cup between Namibia and Romania and Australian Football League games.

'We're competing against the Noosas, Bendigos and Fremantles of the country, but also Singapore, New Zealand and Japan. What we have in

Launceston is the lifestyle of a beautiful, small city with great opportunities, people who feel positive about themselves and a platform where we can compete in business globally.'

Close to Janie's heart was the fact that numbers at Ashley Detention Centre had fallen from 70 to 30 per cent from Launceston, and business was mentoring young people into jobs.

'I have the best feeling when I walk downtown,' Janie said, 'and see somebody whose path crossed mine at Ashley, and who is now positive and smiling. Young people are also putting themselves forward for local government. In 2000, I was the first young person elected to council. Since then we have had four new members elected.'

The regal red-velvet curtains and comfortable leather seats in the council chambers belied the rough and tumble of this milieu. Mondays continued to be a fortnightly battle as the mayor and aldermen locked horns over important and trivial matters. Janie had become adept at dealing with questions from people in the public gallery. She remained calm and courteous about lack of CBD car parking and council's slow replies to letters.

'Afterwards I can go home and cry,' Janie said. 'I learnt the difference between depression and sadness after my mother died. Tuesdays – did I tell you? I'm learning to fly. I need forty hours and have clocked up six. Wednesdays are Zac and I time. Our lives are about adventure and travel. Derrek's dream is for me to become prime minister and he'll be the PM's partner, or for me to get trained with the Department of Foreign Affairs and Trade and become an ambassador.'

There was only a fortnight to go before the close of voting in the 2005 council election, which was by postal vote. What if she lost?

'I'll face that if I come to it,' Janie said. 'My goal is to get re-elected and support the community to grow. There is still a huge rift between those who have a daily grind to survive and those with the skills to make choices.'

Janie had a princely $2000 in her kitty to fund her election campaign. Derrek was home to support her in the campaign. He looked gaunt and was recovering his equilibrium after a near-miss incident. A few weeks previously, when he was installing pipelines in the Gulf of Thailand 175 metres under water, he had taken over from another diver. Visibility was nil. Derrek heard a loud snap and immediately knew something was amiss. The pipe was at the wrong angle.

'I turned around. A section of pipe weighing 250 tons fell two feet away from me. I would have been completely squished, or trapped there, if my umbilical cord to the bell had been caught underneath that load. It freaked me out a bit.'

Derrek knows about pressure, but chose to keep in the political background.

'Janie will succeed in whatever she does,' he said. 'She is very motivated and knows her own mind. That's what I like about her. She's not a bum. The low points are when she works too hard and we don't see her.'

The next morning Janie's father arrived to mind Zac. This squad of family, friends and supporters is what sustains her.

On 26 October, *The Examiner* ran a front-page story claiming Janie was winning the mayoral vote by 2000 votes. By then, she had 9912 primary votes from the more than 24,000 ballot papers counted. It was a four-way election. Ivan Dean, another contender with the next closest number of votes to Janie, had 7272 votes, but final results depended on the flow of preferences from the other two candidates. The media thought Janie had won and was asking if they could come around to her place.

'I said not until the results are in. I knew it was always a possibility that I might not win, but I felt good about my work and had great community feedback.'

Her scrutineer was confused about the results and told Janie she had either won or lost by 400. It was going to be close.

'It wasn't until the last five minutes when I received a call to say I had lost – by 400 votes. A range of emotions flooded through me. I was devastated. I didn't expect it. The paper took a photo of me with my hand to my eyes when I mentioned that my mum would have been proud of my primary polling.'

Many in the community were outraged that Janie was defeated after she received the most primary votes for mayor. In the race for the six vacant positions as aldermen, Janie secured her position with 6676 votes, a long way in front of other candidates. The next highest vote was 2731.

Janie took a couple of months off to rethink her goals and to give the new mayor a clear run. *The Examiner* reported:

Speculation was rife on what the announcement would be several weeks after an emotional Alderman Dickenson announced she was withdrawing from public life to consider her future. The talk yesterday was that she would announce that she wanted to stand as a candidate for Bass for the Greens in the forthcoming election. Why else would she call the press conference in the park? But other rumours were equally strong. She could leave the Launceston City Council to take up an overseas posting to be closer to husband Derrek. She could be pregnant. But Alderman Dickenson, in her individual style, answered an emphatic no to all of the above. The press

conference was to announce that she had decided to stay on as a council alderman, to see out the term that she had been voted in to do.

'Politics is not necessarily about the outcome,' Janie reflected, 'but about being involved in the process. The new council is more diverse, new people, the Old Guard is moving on. The new mayor is good and reasonable. As an alderman I stick to my guns more and trust my intuition, whereas before I tried to listen to too many and to moderate the outcome.'

The proposed pulp mill in the Tamar Valley was one issue on which Janie now felt braver to stand firm because of the public health and environmental impacts. As mayor, she was attacked when she abstained from voting because of insufficient information.

'Poisonous particles of dioxin in the air and water will affect human and marine life. Even the conservatives seem concerned now, but it's a state parliamentary decision, not council's.'

Joan Walters said that 'Janie put a different face on local government in expanding from the traditional roads, rates and rubbish to the arts, the environment, preservation of heritage and caring about community. She has shown that leaders don't have to be a certain age or experience, and that you can take a community forward when you listen and learn.'

'I think I'm wiser and more generous,' Janie said. 'I learnt to believe in myself and know that I tried my best and that's all I could do. I'm still headstrong, but more organised.'

Janie's advice to those aspiring to enter politics or any public position is that they be who they are and not who people expect them to be.

'You can maintain your integrity even if others are aggressive. You have to know yourself and how to maintain your physical and mental health. It will be peak and trough, peak and trough. I can do seven straight weeks of work, then I read a lot, watch television and eat chocolates.'

When asked about standing for state or the federal government Janie is non-committal.

'I am definitely an independent. Party politics scare me. I know too many local people who are members of a party and believe something, but can't say it because it is not the party line.'

In July 2006, Derrek and Janie married in St Margaret's chapel on top of Edinburgh Castle, Scotland. Derrek has a strong Scottish connection and Janie is uncovering her own Scottish links. Thirty friends and family joined them in the ancient stone chapel and later for a silver-service dinner and Scottish dancing to the lively music of a Scottish country band.

'I felt like a princess. It was a celebration of all that we've done together and our dreams for the future. I'm the luckiest girl in the world to have met Derrek. We sailed off the coast of Turkey on our honeymoon. It was my apprenticeship for our around-the-world sailing adventure in years to come. It's just as well I have good sea legs.'

In her post-mayoral life, Janie tries to achieve similar things for the community as she did when she was mayor. Janie and Derrek are buying an indoor climbing gym as a business and a positive community model where people can be active.

'We are setting up a foundation – the Finlay Foundation. Has a nice ring to it huh? We intend to divert a proportion of our profits from the gym to fund the foundation and support community development projects in Launceston and overseas. I've rekindled a passion for design and successfully completed a couple of fun commissions. One is the interior of a new cellar door on the famous Tamar Valley wine route. The centrepiece is a tasting counter in natural white stone and gloss-finished timber. I also worked on a refit of a hair salon in rich red timbers and glass with old Florentine gilt mirrors. It's in my soul to be creative. Designing – whether of furniture or a city – is about exploring the possibilities and stretching one's capabilities.'

Zac turned three in April 2007. He is a budding surfer, plays the guitar and sings and dances.

'He's go, go, go,' said his mother. 'He looks like his dad and has a lot of spunk. Derrek and I separately thought about adopting our second child from overseas. We don't need to have another child ourselves, but have open hearts and minds to support a child who is struggling in the world and to work wherever that child comes from, probably Colombia.'

When Zac was born, Janie had stitched him a blue patchwork quilt that depicted the globe. At places of significance to the family she sewed treasured pieces of material from that location. Janie told her son, 'This is the world, Zac. Do whatever you want to do, go wherever you want to go, be whatever you want to be.'

The Finlays' dream of sailing a yacht around the world is on their agenda for 2012. 'We want to touch every country on the planet. We want to nurture our kids as children of the world,' said Janie.

The quilt might need to be expanded.

Murrandoo (*left*) and Bull Yanner on Gunnamulla Beach, Gulf of Carpentaria, Queensland, 2003

8

Gulf Warriors

Murrandoo and Bull Yanner, Burketown, Queensland

'Murrandoo was reared at the same place, on the same food, the same tit as the rest of us, but he's special – spiritually, I mean. He has an aura. You can feel it,' said Bull Yanner. 'Even though I am the eldest son, I have given Murrandoo my right to make decisions about our country.'

It's unusual to hear an older brother describe his younger brother thus, but then the Yanners aren't your ordinary Australian family. Bull, aged 35, is referring to his next youngest brother, Murrandoo, who is 33. They are clearly related, Bull the sturdier version, but both well built with olive skin, trimmed moustaches and goatees and a hint of Asian or maybe Mediterranean ancestry – 'liquorice allsorts', Murrandoo calls it.

'After our dad died I realised that I needed to be accepted spiritually, particularly by the Elders,' he said. 'I went through the ancient ceremonies in my great-grandmother's country over the border at Borroloola. It earns respect and I'm a better man for it.'

Up until the age of 20, Murrandoo was educated through the conventional school system, but he wanted to be a traditional man, initiated in 'the rich diploma of Aboriginal law'. Circumcision and ritual scars on his body are marks of pride in his Aboriginality. Jason, as he was previously known, took the tribal name Murrandoo after his uncle, which, in his Gangalidda tongue, means 'waterspout,' describing the strange whirlwinds in the Gulf of Carpentaria.

'Traditional law affects how we treat people, the land and the sea, so we take action to benefit our communities and country and don't sit and whinge like those who have a welfare mentality.'

On Australia Day 1992, Bull also went through traditional law to become a man. Initiation had declined in the lower Gulf over the previous 40 years as lawmen died or missionaries banned the practice of traditional law. Bull was honoured to be the first man initiated in a long time at Robinson River, near Borroloola. Murrandoo invited a respected Borroloola lawman to the lower Gulf to revive the secret ceremonies there and return a sense of identity to young men.

At the time of our first trip to the Gulf in July 2002, our oldest son, Robbie, was working in Burketown as a lawyer for the Carpentaria Land Council, which was coordinated by Murrandoo Yanner. Bill and I had barely pulled up at Burketown in our old yellow 4WD when Robbie announced that we were going fishing with Murrandoo.

We caught up with a 4WD in front that had suddenly stopped in the middle of the Nicholson River crossing out of Burketown. A white man jumped out and sprinted across a grassy patch to grab a bush turkey, which was flapping its wings and standing on one leg. The man quickly turned away and despatched the hapless bird by wringing its neck. His mate joined him. They started plucking the turkey, each holding a wing tip. Robbie introduced the white man as Dave and the beaming Aboriginal man, who proffered a feathery hand, as Murrandoo.

Media grabs usually showed Murrandoo as either a champion for his people or pilloried by police, governments, Century Mine and pastoralists. I was curious to know what Murrandoo was really like. He was only three years older than Robbie, yet since he was 19 had been leader to the 5500 Indigenous peoples scattered over the lower Gulf, an area the size of France.

As we passed Doomadgee, a 1200-strong community, Murrandoo described the need to overturn its almost full unemployment rate, overcrowding due to lack of housing, welfare dependency, alcohol abuse and a frightening suicide rate. He is frequently called by grieving relatives when someone kills themselves. In the summer of 2000, he came to dread the sound of the phone. Eight people, young men mostly, and an eight-year-old boy, committed suicide over this horrific period. Murrandoo invited the sons of murdered South African activist

Steve Biko to Doomadgee. When they came, they expressed shock at conditions more atrocious than in their troubled township of Soweto. Their comments to the media resulted in extra funding for housing in Doomadgee.

'These communities are the way they are because of genocide,' Murrandoo said. 'It was someone's idea to get rid of all the blackfellas, to get them off the good land, throw them in dog boxes and exploit the land around them. Our mob resisted, but our value systems got wiped out. They wonder why, 100 years later, there is so much violence, paedophilia, lack of employment and misery. I believe I can affect the Gulf and make households and communities happier. I've dedicated my life to that.'

In her *Cry for the Dead*, published in 1981, poet Judith Wright told of the Queensland government's 'dispersal of Aborigines in the 1860s and 1870s to open land for pastoral development in the Gulf and Cape York. The Native Police's discreet reports of dispersal really meant that men and women had been shot and tomahawked, all the children killed and the lot left to be eaten by native dogs. The black troopers were mere slaves and automata of murder, unable to leave the service, shot if they deserted.'

In the face of such legacies Murrandoo's task is immense.

The coast 'just down the road' is 250 kilometres away. We drove over dusty, dead-straight roads before we reached white-crusted saltpans pocked by hoofprints. Here, the track vanished. We searched for the best way through the wetlands. Brumbies watched as we skirted pandanus palm and paperbark and dodged fat teardrop-shaped anthills the height of a man. Black kites circled. A billowing, grey cloud signalled the burning of Dry season grasses to bring on a fresh pick irresistible to wallabies and turkeys. Murrandoo looked to the coast. The bush was burning from Mornington Island to Burketown, 200 kilometres of fiery coastline.

It was dusk by the time we reached the beach and the clear blue of the Gulf. Again, the truck in front ground to a halt. This time Murrandoo jumped out. He took a spear and began poking it into the sand at intervals. Leading towards the water's edge were distinctive scrapings in the sand. The first turtle has just laid her eggs on this beach to which she will return with unerring instinct every year until she dies. She has disguised the real nest from predators such as dingoes and spear carriers by making dummy nests. When the spear sank into the sand and came up coated in yellow, Murrandoo knew he had struck gold – egg yolk. He carefully scooped away sand until a nest of 120 eggs was revealed. He removed twenty of the white eggs, which resembled soft-shelled ping pong balls, and covered the nest again.

We set up camp behind the eight mile beach that slopes to the Gulf, a pristine stretch of land and water. Nearby was a midden of alabaster spirals, conch and mussel shells, pearly flat spheres, their innards gouged out by ancestors of the Yanners over the last 2000 years. This is Gunnamulla, home of twelve clan estates in the homeland of the Gangalidda people of the lower Gulf.

Murrandoo boiled the eggs in a billy and cooked the turkey in a camp oven. Later, as the flames lit up the faces of the young men, we celebrated Murrandoo's twenty-ninth birthday with cold beer and the bush tucker feast. The turtle eggs had rich yolks and a watery white. We Carrolls managed one each and Dave three, while Murrandoo munched fourteen.

'One of my early memories is being at Gunnamulla with my brothers and sisters,' he said. 'We learnt bush skills from our father and uncles here – how to find fresh water and turtle eggs and how to live off the sea. The bloke I am named after, old Murrandoo Doomadgee, he used to show us deadly [excellent] stuff like making fire with sticks and how to find mussels in the mud. He was a skilful bush fella with knowledge not just about living off the land, but also law and culture, Dreaming stories of morals and values. He was a great influence in my life.'

Murrandoo and Bull, along with four brothers – Vernon, James, Jagama and TJ – and sisters Shirlene and Justine, are part of a big family. As children they hunted and fished.

'If there was one milestone in my life,' he reflected, 'it was getting out of town and living off the land back here at Gunnamulla where we came from.'

The land was four properties in the hands of an American–British conglomerate of absentee landowners. Bull and Murrandoo's father, Phillip Yanner, known as PY, used to say, 'This is the birthplace of my mother, her father, his father and way back. This is our land and even though it is owned by the other mob, one day we'll get it back.'

'We never did in his lifetime,' Murrandoo reflected, 'but a couple of years later, through the Aboriginal and Torres Strait Islander Commission (ATSIC) land fund and our own money, we owned it proper and legal, not just traditionally. We learnt where our roots were, so that we were not blowing in the breeze like leaves falling off the mother tree.'

To know your history is to know yourself.

The Yanners' great-great-grandfather was born on Gunnamulla beach and died there some time in the mid-1800s, before Europeans came to the lower Gulf. Their great-grandmother, Landillimurra, married a Gangalidda man on the beach. Murrandoo's eldest son is named after his great-grandfather, Old Mangubabijarri, a warrior who resisted white pastoralists. He was known as Gunnamulla George. Landillimurra saw him beheaded in a massacre at Devil Dreaming Point as he defended his country. She fled into Burketown with their small daughters, one of whom later married a Chinese, Kum Sing; the other daughter married Jack Yanner, who was supposedly of Spanish origin. Phillip Yanner was Jack's youngest son, born when his father was in his seventies. Jack was shot in a fight when Phillip was a child. His Aboriginal wife hid Phillip in a pen of goats as the welfare arrived to take the children away. She died when Phillip was young and her sister Maudi took care of the children.

'Granny Maudi brought up thirty-eight kids, including Dad and her sister's other eleven kids, her own kids and another eight or ten she picked up around town who were no relation,' said Murrandoo. 'After I was born we came back to Burketown from Mount Isa because Dad wanted to look after Granny. He moved her from a humpy outside town into a little flat in town. Twenty years later if Dad saw any of those thirty-eight kids at a barbecue – bang, he would knock them on their arse. "You bastards, you never looked after her. She picked you up off the street when nobody wanted you and where were you for her?" I got my values from Dad. He lived what he preached. He never told us what to do, but let us see how he lived.'

Phillip Yanner's influence shaped all of his children. He was a powerful leader, a well-respected man, a fearsome fighter. His fists were important in a frontier that stripped away many vestiges of civilisation and respected basic values such as strength, but his real weapons were his vision and intelligence. He saw a future for his people, one that did not depend upon the colour of their skin.

Burketown was named for one-half of the ill-fated duo who perished on the return expedition from Melbourne to the Gulf in the mid-1870s. The small town boasts a pub, several businesses, a school and preschool and a boiling water bore covered in turkey feathers – a local version of fast food. Gangalidda people call the town Moungibi. Although the population was (and still is) predominantly Aboriginal, businesses, housing and decision making were controlled by a white minority. Phillip Yanner set out to change this.

Land rights were central. Across the border in the Northern Territory the Gurindji people, led by Vincent Lingiari, had sustained a seven-year strike on Wave Hill Station. What began as an issue of workers' rights became an historic step towards Native Title and the reshaping of Aboriginal and non-Aboriginal relations as their demands for return of traditional lands sparked support for Indigenous rights nationally. In 1975, Prime Minister Gough Whitlam returned Wave Hill Station to the Gurindji people, ceremonially pouring soil into the hands of Vincent Lingiari. The following year saw the introduction of the *Commonwealth Land Rights Act (Northern Territory), 1976*, which gave Indigenous Australians freehold title to traditional lands in the Territory and the significant power of veto over mining and development on those lands. In the same year Phillip Yanner founded the Carpentaria Land Council in his quest for change and comparable Indigenous rights in Queensland and the lower Gulf region.

'We learnt the power of the dollar and of businesses where we could employ our own people and be treated with respect,' said Murrandoo. 'We now own one of the biggest businesses in Burketown, Nowland's, which is a store, garage and fuel supplier. It was the first cooperative in the region, which scared some people. Over fifty families, white and black, are equal shareholders – not one or two people or even one family, but 200 individuals. They each hold an equal share, from the biggest families to the drunk in the gutter who hardly contributes but shops there and shows loyalty because he owns part of it. We could have tried for a family or an individual to own that business, but we valued sharing and looking after one another. What's the fun if all your family and mates are still poor and you suddenly become rich and own a speedboat but have no one to go boating with? It's better if everyone owns a tinny and can go out together.

'Dad judged people by the depth of their character, not their colour. He copped no racist talk from us kids. If a big white kid beat us up at school and we swore or said, "White bastard", we would get a quick kick or a clip under the ear.'

Murrandoo and Bull's mother, Irene, and her eleven siblings were Stolen Generation, taken from their mother and separated under official sanction because they were of mixed descent. Irene spent her first 16 years at Croker Island Mission, north of Darwin.

In *Rain Maker*, a 1999 Canadian documentary on Murrandoo, Irene said:

We were called half-breeds and were told we had mud in our veins. We used to make small cuts in our hands and push the blood out to see if this was true. When the white kids cut themselves, I would think; It's the same sort of blood as mine.

'Mum had a hard life,' Murrandoo said. 'Her mother was put in a convent and the government took my mother away, then they took my mother's first son, Craig. Three generations were affected. Craig was born when she was 16 or 17, before she met Dad. We only met him a few years ago because we didn't know where he was. Mum would worry that she wasn't a good mother because she didn't have any role model, but she couldn't have been better. Many stolen children had been fed lies that their families gave them away and didn't love them. This bred suspicion, depression and even suicide in that generation. We still haven't met all of her brothers and sisters. The treatment of my mother and grandmother fuels my anger and drive.'

Murrandoo is incensed that Prime Minister Howard cannot say 'Sorry', despite the 1997 *Bringing Them Home* report, which lifted the tightly sealed lid on the Stolen Generations and galvanised thousands of Australian citizens to support reconciliation.

A year later, in the spring of 2003, on our next trip north, Robbie tracked down Murrandoo. Bull told me that his brother has always been elusive.

'Once Mum sent Murrandoo out for bread and milk and didn't see him for four days. People ask me to find Murrandoo when he is in Townsville. I can't find him in Burketown, so there's *no* chance of finding him in a city.'

Robbie, Bill and I were fortunate to join a family gathering at Gunnamulla. Bull, his sister Justine, her daughter Ashleigh, and Murrandoo, his lovely Papuan wife Rachel and their five children whose names all begin with M – four boys from eight-year-old Mangubabijarri or Mangu, to Murrandoo, Milmarja and Maali and new baby sister, Mayarr – were excited to be camping at Gunnamulla. The Yanners grabbed this chance to visit before the summer Wet when cyclonic storms will churn these waters and the network of streams flowing into the Gulf will flood the lowlands, isolating them from Burketown. Water birds disturbed by our intrusion rise from the mangroves, then settle back to fishing. Waves softly lapped the beach. The pervasive peace recharged our batteries.

The tidal estuary is nature's tuckshop where bigger fish feast on smaller fish and crocodiles snack on schools of mullet or watering wallabies. Bull asked me what sort of fish I felt like. 'Salmon,' I replied as he deftly flicked the bait net over the shallows. The net looked like a lacy white veil, weighted with lead and tricky to throw. Bull pulled it in and found a fish – too big for bait, ideal for breakfast. It was, indeed, a salmon – luck, perhaps, or an example of his understated power in his homeland.

Murrandoo hauled in the crab cage he set the previous night and extracted two big, cranky mud crabs. The men lit a small fire on the beach and placed the fish and crabs on interlacing sticks above the coals. Murrandoo broke a small branch off an overhanging she-oak and handed crab claws to Bill and me on the fresh, green platter. We ate crabmeat sizzling in its juices and delectable salmon with our fingers and silently appreciated the bounty of the sea and the resourcefulness of our hosts. As we finished our breakfast in this place of hard-won battles, the older Yanner boys rounded the bend from the beach, lugging a bag of rubbish they collected.

'We have stopped yahoos coming to Gunnamulla armed with their generators and big Eskies, throwing their rubbish in the bush,' Murrandoo said as he loaded the rubbish into the back of his 4WD. 'We will open the beach with permits to safeguard the environment.'

We women retired to the shade and watched the children play. The little boys chased each other, made and broke sand castles and fished on the beach of their ancestors. Rachel nursed baby Mayarr. She has a quiet dignity and serenity, despite her frequently absent husband and having to raise a houseful of kids. As well as their own five children, she and Murrandoo parent six others from relationships that have broken up: Bull's boys Kyle and Brenton, and the children of Rachel's brother. Rachel and Murrandoo are 'growing them up'.

'My brother and sister's children are like my children,' Murrandoo said. 'That's the way Aboriginal people are. Your cousin is also your brother and their children are your children. You've got as much right as their father has to kick them up the arse and an obligation to feed, support and protect them. Rachel teaches the kids morals and values. I try not to bugger it up when I come home.'

Ashleigh played in the sand nearby. Her mother, Justine, is an intelligent, capable woman who managed the family 'firm' – Carpentaria Land Council – for 15 years and, according to her brothers, was the only person able to contain their fiery natures. I suspected that these strong women were the rocks that anchor the Yanner family.

Murrandoo took up the story we began a year before on this beach. He, Bull and sister Shirlene went to high school as boarders in Charters Towers, north Queensland.

'At boarding school, there were only three or four of us Murris and a lot of rednecks,' Murrandoo recalled. 'They used to make us little kids clean the worst toilets with bloody toothbrushes or mow the oval with a pair of scissors or make you stand with your arms out until they started to drop. Then they hit you with belt buckles. That didn't impress me or reform me or break me. I love what I am. I learnt to hate bullies and not to become one. I had deadly white mates and the education was good. French was fun. I realised that I could learn a foreign language in an Australian school, but not an Aboriginal language.'

PY travelled to Charters Towers for Shirlene's graduation from the girls' school, the first-ever graduation in their family. The girls' school was opposite the boys' school. When Phillip came to pick up the boys, the college said Bull couldn't go because he had been gated for smoking.

'"But we drove 2000 kilometres to take the family to this graduation," Dad said. He came out of the school office and told us to pack our bags. We certainly weren't sad to leave.' Murrandoo smiled. 'We began at another boarding school where there were many more coloured kids and bigger boys from home to look after us.'

Later both Murrandoo and Bull were expelled and sent home. Irene Yanner was in Burketown with the younger children while Phillip was overseeing a road crew on Mornington Island for 12 months.

'Mum put the wind up us and said Dad would sort us out,' Murrandoo said, 'but luckily it was a week or two before we got to Mornington.'

'I wasn't looking forward to that trip either,' said Bull. 'Dad was a hard old man and I copped a good flogging for getting kicked out of school. PY only went to Year 5 and wanted so much more for us kids, but he calmed down and supported what we had done in sticking up for ourselves and others who couldn't defend themselves.'

On Mornington, 1987 was a pivotal year. 'I wasn't going back to school,' said Bull. He was a big boy so his father put him to work. 'I worked during the day at the council office and in the Mornington pub at night for two years, even though I was underage. On weekends I joined a cattle mustering camp.'

He began a relationship and had two sons in his mid-teens. Murrandoo got his studies on track although Mornington lacked educational services. He finished Years 11 and 12 on the mainland in Atherton, where he met Rachel's Papuan family.

'At that time her parents ran the Uniting Church and her father was a director of our college. I was about to be expelled again, but Rachel's father said, "Give him a weekend with me and I'll straighten him out". They were a deadly couple. They fed me up and the night before I went back, they didn't preach to me but said, "You need an education". It really hit home. I behaved then, finished Year 12 and did all right.'

When Murrandoo was 15 he saw an article in which the ABC offered cadetships to train Aboriginal and Islander people as radio journalists.

'I thought that would be deadly. I was just dreaming, but Dad encouraged me. He said, "You can do that". I told a teacher on Mornington about it. For months he would stay behind every afternoon and teach me English and how to use a typewriter and computer.'

Murrandoo applied to the ABC when he was in Year 11, but was too young. He picked relevant subjects and re-applied in Year 12, but again was too young. The following year he began journalism at Southern Cross University in Toowoomba and applied once more – to a third knockback. At uni he lived frugally on steamed vegetables and fruit juice. As he settled in, the larrikin side emerged. One night he prepared for his flatmates a casserole with an unusual taste. 'Add enough tomato sauce to dog food and it disguises the aroma!'

In his second year, Murrandoo succeeded in obtaining an ABC cadetship; he deferred his degree. He was inducted at head office in central Sydney for a month or so and lived with Irene's mother in her pensioner flat. While at the ABC he met Roy and HG and went live on radio Triple J. The ABC sent him to Townsville for a year where he got to know the Aboriginal community and learnt tips useful for later life.

'It was a deadly experience that taught me a heap of stunts like how to get inside a person's mind in an interview,' he said, 'or how to ask loaded questions. Nowadays with journalists I can see such questions coming a mile off and know how to deflect them.'

Rachel and Murrandoo met again in 1990 when her parents moved to Mornington Island so her father could continue his ministry. They married in Burketown in 1998. Murrandoo describes Rachel as the unsung hero of his life. The brothers' carefree youth came to an end in November 1991. As Murrandoo sat in his little flat in Townsville, their mother rang to tell him his father had died suddenly from a heart attack. Phillip Yanner was only 44. It was the biggest funeral ever seen in the lower Gulf.

'He was held in such respect by black and white,' Bull said. 'As the first car arrived at Burketown cemetery, the last one in the cortege left the town six kilometres away.'

Bull, who blamed black politics for the pressures that prematurely killed his father, left and went to Mount Isa for six years. He drove trucks, was a bouncer in rough pubs, worked in the mines and in police liaison. Murrandoo returned to Townsville ABC, but found it hard to settle down.

'I vividly recall one night receiving calls from respected Elders in the Gulf. They wanted me home to do what Dad did,' he said. 'Mum didn't want me to. She had seen Dad's stress and how some didn't value what he achieved until he died. I was well warned.'

But for Murrandoo, the political path had already been set at the age of 19. He returned home to help his mother with the younger boys and 'take up his father's spear' as the elected head of the Carpentaria Land Council.

'In the end we saw Dad's work being ruined by a mob who we felt were wrecking the organisations he set up. The Land Council also had a couple of people who would bend over backwards to do deals with the miners. Dad used to say that there is nothing wrong with power if you use it for good and to protect the weak. If you start using it to look after yourself, or to stand over anyone else, it is no good.'

Murrandoo saw himself as a defender of his people's rights, even though he was young and inexperienced. He now had to draw on all he had gleaned from accompanying his father to meetings. Clarence Walden, his father's old mate who had been ATSIC regional chairman and mayor of Doomadgee, joined him.

'I had the privilege although Dad was gone, of having his number one man. We picked up as a deadly team. I got that mob involved again, but kept them on the straight and narrow as Dad had. I believe in reforming characters. When you've got to chip away at a hard lump of rock to reveal a diamond, you know you are doing well.'

The Carpentaria Land Council (CLC), a Native Title body funded by the Commonwealth, represented the southern Gulf tribes from the Norman River in the east to the Territory border and, from 1999, south to the mineral province around Mount Isa. Murrandoo strove to build a profile for the Gulf and get some control by his people over the rich Gulf resources. Most significantly, he set out to weld the nine tribes into a unified body under the CLC without losing sight of individual tribal goals. The Gulf tribes shared common goals: first, recognition of their land rights, second, protection and preservation of their country and culture, and third, an improved quality of life for poor communities. In an age when some Indigenous leadership structures were characterised by corruption and greed, Murrandoo was paid a salary of $30,000, the same as he was to draw a decade later.

By 1994, the lower Gulf was developing a public image. Lawn Hill gorge, 300 kilometres southwest of Burketown, was the jewel. It is a magic place where one can paddle the green waters between sheer red walls or tumble over the side of a canoe for a spray under Indarri Falls. Along the banks tower white-trunked gums and pandanus palms interspersed with golden-flowering grevillea. The Waanyi traditional owners knew it as Boodjamulla, or Rainbow Serpent Dreaming. According to their beliefs, if the Rainbow Serpent was disturbed in his dwelling place in the gorge there would be big trouble. Trouble came in the form of plans for a huge open-cut mine called Century, not far from Lawn Hill National Park and Riversleigh World Heritage fossil site, that would tap into the largest, purest zinc seam in the world, estimated to be worth $9 billion over its 20-year lifetime. The multinational RTZ-Conzinc Rio Tinto of Australia offered the Waanyi people $100,000 a year to develop Century. Some wanted to accept. Murrandoo argued it would end up the same way the Argyle Mine Agreement had between RTZ-CRA and Kimberley traditional owners.

'Some of them lived in car bodies at Turkey Creek next to the world's largest diamond mine. CRA, which owns Argyle, came here to start Century with the same agreement,' Murrandoo fumed.

Murrandoo cut his political teeth on the battle that ensued over Century during the next eight years. He led determined opposition by the traditional owners to the company, which had government backing to dig a vast hole for the ore. Of great environmental concern was the company's plan to transport the sluiced ore along a 300 kilometre underground slurry line to the Gulf port of Karumba and transfer it to a huge ore carrier moored near fragile aquatic ecosystems.

'We rely on Mother Nature,' Murrandoo said. 'Aboriginal people have lived in harmony with this land for 50,000 years – forever. I have a close spiritual connection with it. That's why I fight for land rights for the dispossessed. It's why I don't support mining.'

In October 1994, 21-year-old Murrandoo first came to national attention when he took 400 Aboriginal people to Lawn Hill National Park to support a land claim under the newly enacted High Court's Mabo decision. Mabo recognised Aboriginal rights to land that they had occupied continuously since white settlement, but in 1994 the court decision was untested. To win a land claim, Aboriginal landowners had to prove their traditional relationship to the land under claim, assisted by extensive research carried out by anthropologists, before a Federal Court judge or Supreme Court of the state. The judge had to be satisfied that the claimants were the traditional owners according to Aboriginal law.

'Clarence Walden and I, the Elders and traditional owners, got a big gang together from Burketown, Doomadgee and Mornington Island, as well as Waanyi people from Gregory Downs,' Murrandoo said. 'We sneaked into Lawn Hill during the night. By the time they woke up, we had taken over the place. We kept the lawns watered and told them to stay out of the way because we were in charge. During that month we ran skirmishes from the national park. We had three carloads of women, children and old traditional owners sitting on a rock at the sacred site of Discovery Hill to stop the mine exploding it. Some people called it stupid, but I saw it as courageous. In the end we won joint management of the National Park for the Waanyi people with Queensland Parks and Wildlife Service. The park changed its name to Boodjamulla. The sit-in forced the mining company to the negotiating table on land rights, business development, training and employment of Gulf people, and environmental protection. The company later blew up Discovery Hill in the course of its mining operations.'

The sit-in lasted four weeks. It alarmed people with the scale of force that could be mustered, seemingly from nowhere, in that sparsely populated land and made Murrandoo a marked man. The police began to pay him undue attention.

'I never had even a speeding ticket until I was 21 and started to get into the action,' he said. 'There had never been any dishonesty, fraud or that sort of stuff. Now there's a list longer than Al Capone's, assault charges through fights with racists out here.'

His family was harassed, including his mother Irene who was arrested.

'She never did anything wrong in her life,' Murrandoo said. 'Mum used to be beefier, but suffered from bulimia when the police raids began.'

In 1995, police raided Murrandoo's house looking for 300 items stolen in Burketown. They found nothing until they opened the freezer and there were two crocodile skins. At that time it was illegal to hunt crocodile, turtle, dugong and bush turkey because they were protected species under Queensland's Fauna Conservation Act. Murrandoo had caught and killed two young crocs, which brought to a head the right of Indigenous peoples to eat bush tucker in their own country. The police charged him, which ensured that the Queensland Police Service's own fishing expedition was successful. Murrandoo fought the case up to the High Court of Australia and won on behalf of all Indigenous peoples.

'We've been eating crocs for a long time,' he said. 'I'd rather be eating them than them me, but I never meant to end up in court. I was just crossing the creek with my cast net to catch bait and these two crocs bailed me up in the middle. It was kill or be killed. When the mud, blood and water had cleared, those two were belly up. I live on crocodile, barramundi, turtle, dugong, goanna, turkey, even beef. We hunt like our ancestors did. The judge said, "Hang on, Mr Yanner, you killed those crocodiles with a gun". I said, "Yeah, you ever jumped on a bastard and wrestled him?"'

When interviewed by the media afterwards, Murrandoo described the High Court decision as 'snappy, with a bite to it'. He then speared a young crocodile to celebrate.

'The government allowed export of emu and 'roo to Texas, but we had to go to extraordinary lengths to eat our traditional food. Bush tucker is my medical food.'

The High Court decision clearing the way to hunt traditional foods, and the purchase of land at Gunnamulla, was a salvation for people from dispirited communities who could now reconnect to their homelands spiritually and return to an age-old lifestyle.

Murrandoo hoped ATSIC might be an avenue for change and was elected a regional commissioner in 2000. Although he applauded the concept of black government with regional and national elections, he became disillusioned and only served one term.

'We're a powerless organisation,' he said at the 2002 Sorry Day at the Sydney Opera House. 'The concept is good, but all that's worth crap when one white bureaucrat in Canberra or regional offices rules the roost. We've got to go back to grassroots, not rely on others because there's nothing so powerful as when you and your mob are empowered.'

The Century dispute was a protracted struggle for Indigenous peoples, many of them old, against the company, state and federal governments, police, ATSIC, media and some Gulf Aborigines who supported the mine. In the end, both Century Mine and the Queensland government respectively offered Gulf people agreements of $60 million and $30 million concurrently over the 20-year life of the mine. The agreements were a mixture of entitlements. They included four cattle stations, training and jobs for Indigenous peoples at the mine, a community development fund and a small amount of cash.

Murrandoo recalled, 'As Clarence Walden, former ATSIC regional commissioner, said in a now famous quote on national television, "$60 million wouldn't feed my dogs". People here were so far behind the eight-ball through historical wrongs – socially, economically, politically and educationally – that $60 million was a drop in the sea. However, it was a far better agreement than the original one that some would have accepted.'

The Gulf Communities Agreement, or GCA, came into effect in September 1997 when Century Mine was purchased by Pasminco from Rio Tinto. Bull Yanner began working at the mine in the same year.

'I have the same beliefs as Murrandoo and our other brothers and sisters,' Bull said. 'We were all taught the same things by Dad; we just do things differently. I made the decision to be involved full time at Century. I believe there are only so many things that you can do or say that have an effect out at the mine site. I thought it better to join them than sit back in town and chip away at them and not really improve things much.'

In 1999, after the Century agreement was struck, opposition shifted to the proposed cyclone mooring buoy. A 5000 tonne barge would be used to transport the lead–zinc slurry out to the exporting mother ship, which lay in deeper waters of the Gulf. Opposition came from scientists, environmentalists, fishers whose livelihood was in jeopardy and islanders, in particular the Bentinck Islanders within whose country, prone as it was to cyclones, the dangerous cargo would be moored. They feared heavy metal spills in the Gulf.

Despite the concerns of the islanders and meetings with the mine's representatives the plan for the bouy went ahead. The Federal Court supported the plan and the orange emergency bouy now bobs off Bentick Island. As it transpired, the islander's fears were well founded: in early 2007 cyclone Nelson hit the Gulf and swamped the 5000 tonne zinc carrier. Crew had to be rescued and the mine later conceded that some zinc may have spilt into the water.

The GCA negotiations attracted much publicity and caused division among Gulf people, who already had their historic feuds and ties. Murrandoo was ostracised, received death threats and his house was burnt down in a spate of arson attacks in Burketown. One of his brothers was nearly run down in an incident that instead claimed the leg of Cape York Land Council boss, Richie Ahmet, who was walking with him at the time.

'Change can happen eventually, if the government and the company stick to their end of the bargain – if they stick to their end of the bargain,' Murrandoo mused in 2002.

Five years after negotiation of the GCA, a review found that the agreement wasn't working. The Waanyi said, 'The GCA was set up to fail, but Century still got its mine', as they were sold short on their agreed entitlements. In Murrandoo's view the company was sticking to the half of the GCA that it liked.

Later in 2002, thirty troop carriers, landcruisers and other assorted 4WDs arrived at the mine gates in darkness. The mine operated 24 hours a day, but the gates were locked overnight; however, the wire fence was pregnable and a 10 yard detour was all that was required. The invasion force was quiet. Murrandoo reassured them that they had just accessed their traditional country. The mob arrived at the site office, politely introduced themselves and proceeded to occupy the mine kitchen and dining hall. The mine had to shut down. Dining tables were neatly stacked, swags unrolled and a good night's sleep was had by all. In the morning, the protest leaders sent a message – 'We need to talk to the mine CEO and Bull Yanner', who was at that time a well-respected senior Indigenous employee.

Negotiations began, instigated by the cost of the shutdown, protesters' judicious use of the media and the discomfort of mine staff, who ate barbecues and takeaway food chartered in from Mount Isa, while the mine's kitchen staff fed the protestors from its pantry. As it wasn't his country, Murrandoo deferred to others such as Brad Foster, a Waanyi man and then CEO of the Carpentaria Land Council. In four days, the sit-in achieved a lot: sacred cultural objects were returned to the Waanyi, millions of dollars in trust money was handed over to the Native Title Group, a process for a more effective review of the Gulf Communities Agreement was negotiated and Bull Yanner ended up in the mine's hierarchy.

It had taken Century Mine and the federal and Queensland governments many wasted years and millions of dollars to reach agreement because of their reluctance to engage with the traditional owners.

The 2002 sit-in at Century Mine showed the anger of people who felt marginalised, even when they were a party to a multi-million dollar contract. It showed the courage and political nous required to lead people in an effective civil action. It also showed the differences in the methods of two brothers cut, as Bull would say in his humorous view of political correctness, from the same non-reflective cloth.

The ushering in of an Aborigine to the lofty position responsible for overseeing the mine's commitments to Aborigines was an unusual move. By 2004, the failed Pasminco group had been resurrected as Zinifex. Bull became superintendent of the Gulf Communities support team, which oversaw the Agreement for Zinifex Century Mine. He and his team were all Murris from lower Gulf communities. His job was to ensure that the relationship between the company and Aboriginal parties was mutually beneficial.

'I'm often in conflict with the mining company and their contractors over their views of what's right with the keeping of traditions and culture,' Bull said. 'If I need advice on cultural issues about the mine, I drive to Doomadgee, Robinson River or Borroloola and speak with the old people about the right way to go about the law.'

The sit-in had laid a new foundation for a more respectful relationship and practical ways to implement a complex legal document. Bull's motives in taking a managerial position were questioned, although not to the face of a man whose build is in keeping with his name. It has been suggested that he and his outspoken brother were in opposite camps. There may be truth in that suggestion, but it is more likely that the Yanners, known for their intelligence as well as their strength, had played another good hand together.

In July 2005, we drove 800 kilometres in one day from Winton to Adels Grove, an oasis near Boodjamulla, where Bull and his vivacious non-Aboriginal wife Mandy live. Mandy worked at Adels Grove and Bull only had to drive 10 kilometres to work at Century Mine. We were to meet Bull in Adels Grove dining area and spotted him standing half a head taller than anyone else among the milling tourists. He took us to his and Mandy's caravan, parked on the edge of Adel's and rustled up a barbecue at the campfire as we yarned over a beer. The campsite with its flower borders and two ferocious dogs, had an air of permanence.

'I got sick of people saying that I shouldn't be superintendent because I'm Gangalidda, not Waanyi. So I live on Waanyi land with my beautiful wife and my pure-bred pit bull, Kostya, and a silly red heeler, Yumbee. Living on country teaches you more about yourself and the environment than you can ever learn by reading books or watching television. I consulted with Waanyi Elders to get their permission and am learning about Waanyi culture, which helps with my job at Century. I don't care what people say about me because I try my hardest to make a decent lifestyle for my people at Century. In the end, I gotta look that old fella in the mirror in the eyes and be happy with what I see.'

The following morning Bull drove us a few kilometres to Riversleigh Station, returned to the traditional owners under the GCA. He was on its management committee. From a vantage point high on the fossil-rich ridge of the Riversleigh World Heritage site, we saw a big mob of cattle resting around a tank on the plain. Since the handover, the place had been restocked with hardy Droughtmaster and Brahman cattle. The station manager trains young Indigenous men from the region as jackaroos. These shy boys showed us their fishing hole behind the quarters, a stretch of shimmering jade overhung by palms.

'These young fellas are the unwanted members of our communities,' Bull said. 'We bring them out here away from the bullshit they have lived with every day of their 17-odd years and show them a different way of behaving to achieve things. Lance and Kylie Hutley take them into their family. They teach them the skills it takes to be a deadly ringer on a cattle station anywhere in Australia. Wherever they end up, the managers will boast that their ringers have come from Riversleigh country up in the Gulf. Not one of them has gone back to the old ways that landed them in trouble. These kids are role models for all those other young people who live the way they did – breaking and entering and hurting their own people. They help change the negative cycle back in our communities. Mate, the Riversleigh ringer program is number one as far as I am concerned.'

The station is adjacent to the mine, so we took the back road past a stream of pristine ponds and waterfalls. In contrast, country closer to the mine was charred by fire. Bull was a familiar face at the gate. After we showed identification, the 4WD was waved through. Onsite, blasting was in operation. When the dust cleared, a huge hole was revealed. Surrounding the hole was a landscape in motion: conveyor belts shifted ore, metal arms stirred slurry ponds, trucks rushed by and staff spilled from temporary buildings. Bull's air-conditioned office was respite from the heat and dust, although he spent more time with workers than retreating to a cool office.

'The mine started in 1997 and so did I, in various jobs,' he said. 'We have 146 Indigenous employees and 30 per cent are women. We make up a quarter of the total workforce, but skill levels in the region block progress. Workers come from the most disadvantaged communities in Australia. We give them skills to interact and develop job paths as tradesmen, truck drivers, cleaners, cooks and engineers. We arrange scholarships and cadetships – for example, two Kaiadilt sisters here from Bentinck Island are on scholarships, one as a doctor, the other one in law and business.'

Lower Gulf people now depend on the mine, but it will cease operations in 2017. Through the GCA, Bull is trying to make communities more sustainable before then by lifting Indigenous skill levels through the mine, on cattle stations and training at tertiary institutions. His best hope is to develop local businesses and regional infrastructure: better roads, medical care and education, with financial support from Century before it closes.

'After Century closes, tourism is an option if we can improve infrastructure and services. Waanyi people could run tours to the mine, Boodjamulla and Riversleigh.'

The Gulf is an exciting place for adventure holidays, bird watching in the wetlands and understanding Aboriginal culture. Bull thought regional development could happen with the emergence of more strong local leaders and more community ownership of businesses such as Nowland's garage. He saw a path to a better future in Gulf communities through mentoring of young Indigenous mine staff to be leaders.

'I have the best job in the world representing my people from the lower Gulf at the mine. If things get too much I ring Murrandoo, who is not only my little brother, but also my mentor and the person I admire most. In my week off once a month, I camp at Gunnamulla to fix myself up spiritually. I spent a month out there in 2006 and went to the places my dad and uncles took me to when I was growing up. It helped clear negative stuff stuck in my head.'

Gunnamulla is also where Murrandoo goes to think and restore his equilibrium. In reports of an outburst or a police charge he is often described by the media as a 'firebrand' or 'an angry man'. He said, 'I hate violence, but I know that if I am truly going to protect my family and friends I need to be strong because there are bad people out there who will hurt you real quick.'

He has been thrown into police cells on several occasions and charged with numerous offences, mostly pub brawls, subsequent assaults and resisting arrest. Since his early twenties, Murrandoo has consistently protested against police treatment of Aboriginal people in custody.

In 2004 Murrandoo found himself incarcerated in Stuart Creek Correctional Centre in Townsville for nine months on an assault charge. He had defended his younger brother against a club bouncer. Murrandoo was already on a suspended sentence from an earlier assault case. He has seen the justice system from inside out and is convinced that in Queensland Aboriginal people are treated differently from other people. If a non-Aboriginal person were in a pub brawl, would he be given nine months in jail?

'Although it was depressing to be in prison away from those you love, you also learn who you can trust and who will look after your interests while you are away. It was my first break from working for others since I was 18 when Dad died, a chance for reflection, to appreciate my wife and kids.'

While in prison, Murrandoo still had a finger on the pulse of Gulf affairs. According to Land Council staff, within 30 minutes of something happening he was on the phone to them. Murrandoo also tried to improve conditions for inmates. He arranged for bush tucker to be sent into the prison via Bull at Century Mine for NAIDOC week, originally called National Aborigines and Islanders Day Observance Committee week celebrations.

'Prisoners had never before been allowed bush tucker. In the kitchen, the men were like kids in a lolly shop with the smell of turtle and dugong cooking, but even better than the feast was being allowed to bring some of our culture into the prison. The best cooks swapped recipes. What they didn't say brought a tear to my eye.'

Murrandoo is unafraid to speak up on violence and alcoholism in communities. He finds funds for legal assistance to Indigenous victims of crime and confronts authority on what he considers to be miscarriages of justice. He has outraged many in white Australia with his outspoken calls for retribution if he thinks the legal system doesn't deliver justice for black and white alike.

In a well-publicised case in 2004, Mulrunji Doomadgee died in police cells on Palm Island.

'We dressed my cousin Mulrunji for burial,' Murrandoo said. 'He had four broken ribs, a ruptured spleen and the liver was split in half, which was not consistent with a young, fit bloke falling on a small concrete step, as the police claimed.'

The initial investigation cleared police of any wrongdoing, which sparked a riot on Palm Island: the police station and courthouse were burnt and thirteen islanders were subsequently arrested. Mulrunji's only son committed suicide after his father's death. Following years of protracted and often emotionally-charged events, including the Queensland premier appointing a former New South Wales Chief Justice to investigate the case, in June 2007, a Supreme Court jury in Townsville heard the defendant's admission that he must have caused Mulrunji's fatal injuries, but that the injuries were accidental. He was acquitted of all charges.

Murrandoo describes himself as a human rights activist. In 1994, neighbouring peoples from three distinct island groups who spoke three different languages – the Lardil, Kaiadilt and Yangkaal – had got together with coastal Gangalidda people and paid a lawyer to lay a united claim to their sea country. Ten years later the Wellesley Island Sea Claim was determined, recognising the traditional rights of these peoples. This was a culmination of Phillip Yanner's work, continued by Murrandoo.

'Native Title is not sovereignty or land rights. It's not what Eddie Mabo wanted. It gets us to the [negotiating] table, rather than fighting for scraps under the table – that's all.'

He saw recognition of sea rights as a step towards Indigenous involvement in the fishing industry, where jobs, training and Indigenous business development could be developed, as had been the case in the Gulf Century Agreement.

'Prawning is a $60 million a year industry that takes bounty out of the Gulf,' Murrandoo said in 2003. 'Not one Murri is employed in the industry. The big fleets don't contribute to local economies. They bring in barges full of tucker and fuel. They don't buy a jerry can of fuel or a can of drink in these dying country towns. Fair enough if they employed locals and bought locally, but they just take the prawns out.'

Murrandoo has a vision of a Gulf Marine Park, along the lines of the Great Barrier Marine Park to stop over-fishing, dumping overboard and killing of protected animals.

'We want the lower Gulf declared as a marine protected area, with agreement on its use negotiated between all stakeholders. We want to manage it as a marine park. For 50,000 years we did a good job. Captain Cook found it in great nick.'

Murrandoo sees a future in which Indigenous peoples are trained as rangers, customs officers, coastal surveillance, fishing inspectors and marine biologists. The capabilities are there. With funding and strong partnerships, his vision could materialise. By March 2007, Moungibi Housing Co-operative, chaired by Murrandoo, had negotiated the cleaning contract at Century Mine. Twenty-one Indigenous people from Mornington Island, Doomadgee and Burketown are now employed as cleaners under the Gulf Communities Agreement.

Murrandoo and Bull Yanner, each in his own way, are warriors on behalf of lower Gulf people. Bull is self-effacing yet confident, passionate in pursuit of Aboriginal rights from within Century Mine. Murrandoo took up his father's spear at the age of 19 after Phillip Yanner died. His belief – 'If it doesn't kill me, it will make me stronger' – has been continually tested in his battles for land, sea and human rights.

'We are working on the one vision to improve the lifestyle of a pretty poor mob,' Murrandoo said. 'If we keep that going through three or four lifespans, not deviating every generation and going, Geez, I'm going to do something completely different, then we can achieve a legacy for our people.'

A bare foot on clean sand, a fishing line in a pristine estuary, the dignity of a job, a future for the children – these are the connections to land and rights worth a fight.

Bull Yanner at Century Mine, Gulf Country, Queensland, 2005

Cathy Duncan at Moree Aboriginal Employment Strategy Office, 2005

9

A Job in the Main Street

Cathy Duncan, Moree,
New South Wales

June 2005. The highway into Moree was a black slick from the first decent rains in many moons. In contrast to the dull day, the Aboriginal Employment Strategy (AES) shopfront in the main street is bright with posters and the AES logo, a cotton ball in the Aboriginal colours of black, red and yellow. It encapsulates an unexpected marriage of interests and needs in this northwestern New South Wales town.

Inside, the receptionist directed me to a meeting room lined with computers where I was to wait for the chief executive officer, Cathy Duncan. An older Aboriginal man with a greying pigtail and a black hat set at a jaunty angle told me that school kids use the computers most afternoons for School to Work training. People came and went through a maze of rooms, answered phones and tidied up. There was an air of anticipation: Noel Pearson, the respected Cape York Indigenous leader, was visiting.

Cathy arrived, somewhat breathless, apologised for being late and hugged me. She was smartly dressed in a black skirt and white shirt with the AES logo embroidered on it. Cathy had dropped her two children at school and driven the 30 kilometres from the village of Biniguy. She introduced everyone in sight, including the pigtailed man, who turned out to be Moree Aboriginal leader, Lyall Munro.

Soon the AES founder, white cotton farmer and businessman Dick Estens, and the Indigenous staff, board members and community people were seated around the room. Cathy welcomed Noel as an honoured guest and inspirational leader. He is a dignified man who chooses his words slowly and thoughtfully, savouring their impact. Noel referred to the 1960s equal wages judgement, which effectively dried up jobs for Aboriginal stockmen on northern cattle stations and precipitated the movement of whole communities from stations into towns and into decades of unemployment in northern Australia. Noel spoke of the need to restore hope and pride in Aboriginal people. Aborigines have the right to jobs just like other Australians, he said. He praised the Moree AES as 'a lighthouse for the rest of us' and said he hoped to set up such a program in Cape York. By July 2007 the program had not yet been introduced, although radical welfare reform in four Cape York communities got underway.

All was progressing smoothly until Lyall rose to speak. He was just warming up when another older man, an Elder, stood up, muttered that Lyall was not a true Elder or representative of Moree Aborigines and walked out. Lyall continued unfazed and Cathy, as the host, handled the interruption with grace and respect for both men and said she hoped the second man would join them for lunch. He did.

Afterwards, we moved into the office Cathy shares with Dick Estens. Their identical black leather chairs are side by side facing identical computers. Percy Duncan, Cathy's husband, joined us. He is tall and lean with a small moustache, a closely shaved head and a big grin. Percy is in charge of security work for the AES and is also a mentor for clients. He answers to the boss, who happens to be his wife.

'How do you cope with that?' I asked.

'It's pretty hard – hectic, I mean. You can't win an argument around here. Too many women.' He caught his wife's eye and they laughed.

Above Cathy's desk, on a large handmade card, was a photo of a cheeky, blue-eyed boy with his two front teeth missing. It said: 'Dear Mum, Happy Mother's Day! Lots of love, Percy xxx.'

Cathy began. She had read my book *Ordinary People, Extraordinary Lives* and anticipated my approach. This effervescent woman had grown in assurance since

I first heard her speak two years before at a regional development conference in Coonamble. She had inspired that audience with her passion and candour about the challenges and joys of finding jobs and a place in mainstream society for Aboriginal people. I was keen to meet this 30-year-old woman with the unusual khaki eyes, pale olive skin and blue-black hair.

'My grandfather was an Indian from Lahore,' Cathy explained, 'but after the partition of India he found his home had become Pakistan. He left on a boat when he was 17 and arrived in Sydney. The boat docked briefly, but my grandfather wasn't allowed ashore. He had a row with the white captain and belted him, then swam ashore because he was worried about the consequences. My grandfather walked the bush selling clothes from a basket on his head. Then he acquired a sulky and became a hawker. Later, he bought a drapery store in Bingara in northwest New South Wales. He met my Nan, Margaret May Griffith, who was a Kamilaroi woman from Walhallow Mission near Tamworth. She had married an Indian man when she was 17, but he died. She married Grandfather and they came to Pallamallawa, a village east of Moree, and had eight kids. Grandfather died when my father, Don Budda-Deen, was only 14. Dad was left as the only son after his brother accidentally shot himself, so he began shearing to help look after his mother.'

In 1957, at a dance in Moree, Don met Cathy's mother, a rock'n'roll dancer of English, Irish and Italian extraction. As she was telling me this, Cathy rang her father to check what happened next.

'Did you look at each other and you asked her for a dance and she fell in love with you?' she asked him. I heard a grunt on the other end of the phone. She giggled and nodded at me. 'Yes, that's right.'

Her parents married and had nine children.

'Mum's mother didn't like Dad because of his colour. Maybe she thought my mother could have done better for herself. I hated her for that. You can't ignore ancestry,' she said suddenly. 'My mother's mother tried to, but just before she died she saw our son Percy, who has her blue eyes. She was stunned. She gave him a box of chocolates for Christmas. It was her first gift to any of us.'

Cathy was the eighth of the nine children. When she was three, the family moved from Pallamallawa into Moree. Her father obtained Aboriginal housing, a source of contention with the white side of the family.

'It was more acceptable to be blue-black Indian or Pakistani back in the 1970s than it was to be an Aborigine.'

All was well when the family lived in the country and Cathy's father was shearing, but trouble began when they moved to town.

'The family had to leave public housing and moved from house to house because it was difficult to keep up with the rent when Dad worked seasonally.'

Cathy left home, sick of fighting with her mother and of her father's drinking.

'I was binge drinking at 12, ran away from home at $15^1/2$ and shacked up with the boyfriend who was $16^1/2$.'

As she divulged this information, Percy, 'the' boyfriend back then, laughed a little apprehensively. Clearly, he was used to Cathy's outspoken ways, but was not sure what she might say next.

'Mum had me lined up for a rich, white prince,' she said, 'so I didn't take Percy to meet her. I escaped from home, but I stayed at school. I didn't want to become a shearer or a shearer's cook. We can all muck up, but we're in charge of our own destiny.'

'We met when Cathy worked at the Kentucky Fried drive-through,' Percy said. He ate a lot of fried chicken. Cathy wondered how he was always there at the same time she was. 'I got hold of her roster,' he laughed.

Cathy believed there were two roads open to her: one was work and family, the other led to a juvenile detention centre. If you didn't have a good education, you didn't get a good job. She lived with Percy's mother, and Debbie, Cathy's older sister, supported her financially. Percy was away shearing and only home on weekends. He urged Cathy to do her homework and finish Year 12. They lived cheaply. An Esky doubled as a fridge and a milk crate as a table.

'Percy's parents are Kamilaroi. He's the fourth generation of his family in Moree. He's strong and proud. In Moree then I had to be the front person if we went somewhere because I'm lighter skinned. Shopkeepers would serve me, not him.'

Three days after finishing her Higher School Certificate, Cathy started work for Percy's mother in her dress shop. In 1991, she began a traineeship in office work and landed a three-month stint at the Commonwealth Employment Service (CES) as an employment officer. She liked helping others; at the end of the three-month period she was offered a job.

'Many clients were Aboriginal people. Girls would say, "Why go to Year 12? I'll have a baby." Twelve months later I would see them pushing a pram past the office. There were no Aboriginal kids going on to Year 12. Whites were starting vigilante groups on black kids. That frightened me. There wasn't much hope and we were self-destructing in Moree.'

The town made the top 10 in New South Wales crime rates. Teachers were accused of manhandling children and calling them black bastards. By her twenties Cathy had developed a hatred of racist attitudes. Some people who came to the CES thought she looked white and would give her their usually low opinion of blacks. It disgusted her to hear such racism and ignorance about her people.

'I wanted to be a tarpot. I revisited my birthplace and bought a house, not exactly at Pallamallawa, but at nearby Biniguy. There were not always good stories of Pallamallawa. I thought it would be like coming to KKKville [the US white supremist group the Ku Klux Klan], but I found out that people are people – good and bad.'

Her anger was tempered over time as she decided colour was secondary to how you related and mixed. Cathy and Percy married in 1998. Their children, Jessica and young Percy, went to school in Pallamallawa.

'In Biniguy we were the Aboriginal family. Children's friendships have no colour,' said Cathy. 'In a school cross-country race once, a man was cheering on another Aboriginal boy because he thought he was my son. Ours was the lighter-skinned, blue-eyed one, but it said something about community acceptance. A white mate of our son's said he wanted to be Aboriginal. I had never heard that before and asked him why. He said, "Because Percy's really special. He knows everything about the bush and how to hunt and fish."'

At the 2003 Coonamble conference, Dick Estens and Cathy Duncan spoke about the Moree AES. Dick, an imposing man who towered above the shy Cathy, told the audience that Moree was notorious for its race riots, crime and segregation. It was dubbed 'the Little Rock of Australia' because of its similarity to the racist town in the US state of Arkansas. The name of Aboriginal activist Charles Perkins was synonymous with the controversial 1965 Freedom Ride that alerted the nation to the parlous living conditions of Aborigines in Moree and other country towns. Perkins, then a university student, fellow Aboriginal student Gary Williams, and the Reverend Ted Noffs of Sydney's Wayside Chapel organised the ride of a busload of thirty white Sydney University students from the Student Action for Aborigines (SAFA) group. When they arrived in Moree and tried to desegregate the Moree swimming pool they were pelted with eggs and rotten fruit. Images of discrimination at all levels, poor housing and unemployment flooded the nightly news, disturbing the digestion of comfortable citizens.

'Aboriginal people were barred from all hotels, not allowed to use public toilets or the swimming pool or to attend functions at the council-owned Memorial Hall,' Dick said. 'It was nothing to have fifty or sixty Aboriginal people rampaging down the main street and by morning seventy or eighty windows would be broken and graffiti scrawled on walls around town. Moree people were sick of talkfests. They demanded more policing and more severe punishments. Police Commissioner Peter Ryan came to town and said he was aware of the problems. A Street Reclaimers Committee formed; it ran for two or three years, then dissolved. People expected government or the police – or someone else – to fix the problem.'

In 1991, Dick was motivated to do something after his house in central Moree was broken into for the tenth time. Instead of imposing harsher penalties, Dick favoured building pride and self-confidence in the Aboriginal community. He thought that Moree needed to fix its own problems and that the answer lay in jobs. In the 1990s the town had a population of 10,000. Of the 7500 non-Aboriginal people, 7 per cent were unemployed compared to 65 per cent of the 2500 Aboriginal people who had been unemployed for most of their lives. The district on its rich, black soil plains generated $1 billion per annum, largely from exporting cotton. Into this situation of great wealth and abject poverty, resentment and violence, Dick inserted a simple plan to find meaningful work for Aboriginal people.

The Aboriginal employment program was a recommendation of the 1991 Royal Commission on Aboriginal Deaths in Custody, but took four years to establish. Dick had three aims: to place Aborigines in jobs, to draw the five mainly family-based factions of the Indigenous community together and build new leadership, and to reward the broader community as the program gained ground. The federal government backed the program with $112,000, and Gwydir Valley Cotton Growers Association, which Dick chaired from 1997 to 2000, contributed $10,000 a year.

'I knew people were talking behind my back,' he said. 'They predicted failure. Nobody in Moree understood my game plan. In fact, it was important that the town didn't know what was happening. It was easier to out-think a community if they didn't know your game plan.'

Dick was seen as that crazy white who wanted to help the blacks. In 1997, he officially began the AES with two Indigenous staff and a steering committee of local citizens. He was also looking for Indigenous leaders. AES had a shaky start because Aborigines didn't register for jobs, having in mind that previous schemes hadn't worked. The AES had to almost haul people off the streets to fill positions. The organisation had no blueprints or success stories to point the way, but Dick persisted.

'Six months into the program we had five Aborigines in jobs. One day all of them went missing,' he said. 'My committee members also disappeared. I thought we'd had it. That was both the worst day of my life and the best. I said to the manager, "Geez mate – it's mentoring. We'd better find them." By 3 o'clock we had four of the five men back on the job. We never did find the fifth one.'

Regular work was unfamiliar territory for these men and the committee of white community leaders put employment of the long-term unemployed in the too hard basket. Dick realised that the AES needed to be more than job placement. It had to build self-esteem in the whole community and target the middle third of the Aboriginal population, not just put anybody into a job. Aboriginal staff mentored clients, many of whom had never had jobs. So AES developed partnerships with the cotton industry and local businesses to boost relationships and job opportunities.

The strategy was beginning to work. By the end of the first year AES had fifty people registered for work and twelve in full-time jobs. It was time for a high-profile launch. Nearly 200 people filled Moree Art Gallery, including fifty Aborigines who gravitated to one end. Three years later by June 2000, the AES had placed people in over 320 positions and 120 were still employed in the longer-term jobs.

While Cathy's energies had been going into job placement through the Commonwealth Employment Service, Dick looked for ways to build harmony and promote reconciliation. The AES introduced the Indigenous music and dance Croc Festival to Moree and mustered Aboriginal and non-Aboriginal people to help organise this showcase for local talent. Dick discerned that football was the modern day corroboree, which could help pull together local factions. He decided to back the local Indigenous team, the Boomerangs, which had been barred from the Rugby League competition over an incident in which the team left the field in 1998. The AES worked through codes of conduct with the club and trained Indigenous security guards to help manage the games.

Thanks to positive media attention from Ray Martin's *Current Affair* team the AES gathered steam. Key people who could influence opinion, such as Lyall Munro, then chair of the ATSIC regional committee, and Vince Tatara, manager of Moree Plains Shire Council, were beginning to accept the employment strategy.

'When Vince turned up, we immediately made progress with Moree Council,' Dick said. 'The AES was able to place six young girls in council jobs. Moree even elected its first Aboriginal shire councillor. I could see community anger beginning to evaporate.'

During the 1990s, Cathy Duncan's initial three months at the Commonwealth Employment Service stretched into eleven years of experience in employing local people. She worked her way up to become district manager for the Department of Education, Science and Training. Cathy was told Dick was headhunting her for the AES.

'I didn't believe that. I didn't know much about Dick,' she said.

Their paths crossed in 2000 after she ran an Education and Employment award program over National Aboriginal Islander Day Observance Committee

Week, NAIDOC. After a successful seven days and nights, Cathy said, 'See, Aboriginal people can do things.'

Dick replied, 'Cathy, I've been waiting for someone like you to lead from the pack.' He advised her not to say the first thing that came into her mind. She was affronted and responded in typically forthright fashion.

'I told him to get stuffed, or words to that effect.' Cathy laughed. 'He's thick-skinned. He retired with an OK. I didn't want to be told how to conduct myself at the age of 27.'

Cathy's daughter Jessica was five. She finished at the Aboriginal preschool and went to a local private school. One day at school Jessica was called a nigger. Cathy decided enough was enough. When Dick invited her to be on the AES board, she gave it serious thought and consulted the Moree Elders who said, 'Why put white people in to solve our problems? We should be doing that ourselves.'

'Dick was chair and the board was all white people,' Cathy said. 'It needed radical changes. The federal funding body said the AES had to be handed over to the Aboriginal community. Dick had privately said that would be over his dead body. He wasn't keen to give it to the older style Indigenous leaders.'

On 9/11 2001, the same day terrorists flew into the twin towers of New York's World Trade Center and the Pentagon in Washington, DC, Cathy was elected chair of the AES board, but she had doubts and thought Dick had picked her because she wasn't from the Mission and was white-skinned. She wondered why he was helping blacks when he could go and live his rich lifestyle. Maybe he was patronising them. Cathy was reluctant to be drawn out of her community or to stand out.

'I didn't see myself as a leader, but I wanted to project the goodness I could see in Aboriginal people in Moree.'

That was the beginning of a partnership between the seemingly conservative cotton farmer and the feisty Kamilaroi woman. Over six years, the AES garnered more than 120 jobs a year to employ 700 Aboriginal people in Moree. By 2003, the town was changing and an Indigenous middle class was emerging.

When Cathy Duncan was elected chair of the board, Dick decided it was time to hand over the AES to the Aboriginal community. It was a big affair, a gathering of sceptics and supporters. There was no huddle of Aboriginal people as there had been at the AES launch: people mixed. Dick's voice choked with emotion as he said what a great privilege it was to work with Moree's Aboriginal community.

'I feel proud of the Aboriginal heritage. The AES has led the way in marketing it as a positive for our town. I'm confident Cathy can do the job as chair.'

Cathy stepped to the microphone and urged people, 'We have to walk together, not only work together, and to respect each other. We have to say hello to each other, not only at official functions where it looks good, but when we are with our families down the street. That's the point of building relationships. My philosophy for life is: Don't walk in front of me, don't walk behind me; walk beside me and be my friend. If we take that to heart, we will make this community grow.'

As she mixed with other board members, Cathy thought about whether she should be developing a more corporate image.

'If you're not level headed, you can get caught up and it will wreck you as a person. Dick told me, "You have to change your vocabulary". I said, No, you just have to get used to me.'

Dick wasn't asking Cathy to mind her Ps and Qs, but to cut out the four-letter words.

'I have respect for Dick,' Cathy said. 'Sometimes I hate his guts and other times I really like him. He probably feels the same about me. It depends on the issue. I have to work out where I stand. Some days I feel an equal and that I am the chair; other days I feel like it is still Dick's show and I am a puppet. I go through doubts: Why me? I don't want to do this. How does this benefit my family and me? There was a lot of stress, but you don't knock back opportunities, because they come for a reason.'

Six months after Cathy took over the chair, an ABC TV documentary, *Message from Moree*, produced by Judy Rymer, recorded her comment to Dick Estens.

'I didn't think that I would be sitting laughing with you and able to have an open and honest conversation. I thought I would keep you at arm's length.'

'Well, if you and I can't have honest communications, then it will take another generation or two,' he responded.

After the screening of *Message from Moree* Cathy experienced racism in reverse.

'Moree can be brutal. Some Aborigines reacted with "She's white, not black". I say, "What percentage of Aboriginal blood do you need to qualify as black?" Many people are of mixed race in Australia. I think of myself as an Aborigine, therefore I am. It's not about your stock, but what is in your heart, how you feel as an individual. If we talk in black and white, we create that colour around ourselves. I have matured and now believe that there are good people out there. Love and friendship don't have colour.'

Some people doubted Cathy's motives for being involved in the AES and accused her of doing it for the money, not the community. Cathy retorted that she had already been doing a damned fine job on a good salary in Aboriginal education and hadn't needed to go to the AES.

'The AES had its detractors and I fell into their sweep. They attacked me and that both hurt and toughened me, but I didn't argue because that's what some people wanted to see. I just kept on getting jobs. If you find someone's granddaughter a job, the whole family can see the benefits.'

Fear of failure was a spur for Cathy and Dick. To be told by doomsayers that they wouldn't be able to work together or make any impact only made them try harder.

'Everyone said, "You can't fix the Aboriginal community, you can't get them to work",' said Dick in *Message from Moree*, 'but we've proved that you can.'

Mentoring has proved a vital element in the success of the AES. Percy Duncan acts as a mentor and AES makes a commitment to do whatever it takes to get people into the right job. The role seems endless. AES discovers the strengths and weaknesses of each client and helps them set realistic work and personal goals to match them with jobs. It also helps clients prepare resumes and develop interview skills, and organises training and transport to and from work. Most importantly, AES supports clients once they are placed in jobs to ensure that there are no workplace issues. In Moree three mentors looked after fifteen to twenty clients each.

'Every AES client has a mentor or employment coordinator,' said Percy. 'I try to help these young fellows who are getting off the straight and narrow to get back on, to give them an opportunity like I've had. I try to get it into their heads that if black and white work together as one, we'll earn new respect.'

Percy mentored Joe Tighe, who finished his panel-beating course in 2005. Joe's mother was on a supporting parent's benefit and they lived in public housing. He left school at 14 to learn a trade.

'Both his school principals said he'd end up in jail,' said Percy. 'He used to curse his mum. The kid was ready to be thrown out of home. I would drive him three and a half hours away to Tamworth TAFE. Now he has his ticket as a tradesman, his own car and has become a respectful young fellow. Other kids respect him and his employer loves him like a son. They've built a really good relationship. They won't let him leave. The crowd turns ugly if you pick on Joe at Moree Panel Works.'

Percy told of how Joe and a workmate were walking home from the panel beaters one afternoon, their clothes splashed with paint, when the police stopped them.

'The coppers didn't believe the boys hadn't been doing graffiti, even though they said where they worked. They gave them a hard time. I went to the police station. I explained they worked at the Panel Works and said, "That's harassment. Give them an apology forthwith." One of the coppers has become Joe's mate.'

Joe was proud of his work and his family was proud of him. Other family members wanted to work as well. Joe credited the AES for his achievements.

Relationships are the key to it. The AES employment coordinators visit businesses and explore what the employer needs. They don't offer government subsidies for positions because that demeans the worker. They aim to build a partnership, which will see AES clients employed over time.

'We actively go and find jobs,' Cathy said. 'We need more sustainable employment down the main street. I say, "Put a black person in your shop or on your farm. It could be the biggest challenge of your life, but you might get the most dedicated employee you'll ever have if you give someone the opportunity." We confront employers and say out loud what they may be thinking. Sometimes we give advice they don't want to hear. Maybe they think blacks are dumb, or will go walkabout. We tell employers the "walkabout syndrome" does not always show a lack of commitment. There may be a family funeral. It may be caused by shame if the client doesn't have enough money for a packed lunch, or proper work trousers, so they don't turn up to work. We can stop that by building a relationship, educating the employer and supporting the client.'

When employers are bemused by staff difficulties, Cathy says to them, 'Go and live in public housing for a day and see what it's like to be in our shoes. The tourist side of Moree just skims the surface. The reality is deeper. We need to ask people why they behave in a certain way.'

The AES convened the first Aboriginal Awards ceremony in 2002 as a way of rewarding students who were achieving – from little kids to apprentices. It showed the younger ones that older students could be good role models and demonstrated to the education system that Aboriginal kids were winners. The large crowd of relatives, teachers and employers whistled and clapped each recipient. Finally, it came to the main award for the employee category.

In *Message from Moree*, a young man called Tyrone Connors, nicknamed Pepe, said he used to be a cheeky little bugger, stoned off his head, calling everyone everything under the sun. Pepe was employed as a farmhand on a cotton farm and said, 'It was pretty choice having money in your pocket when you went home, but for a couple of days I got with the boys. I stuffed up. My boss knew it and I knew it.'

Pepe said he was going to quit. His mentor, Percy, jumped on the tractor with him and told him, 'The boys don't pay your wages. They don't pay your fines. Your employers want you to stay, but you're gone mate if you blow it again.' Pepe didn't quit. He was glad he had someone like Percy to help him. It was Pepe who, three years later, won the Aboriginal Awards Best Employee. His boss looked as pleased as Pepe did.

Cathy found and supported the mentors. But who supported her once she took the monumental step into the position of CEO as well as being chair?

'Dick took us a step further in being able to run our own business. If you are not an Aborigine you can't be one, but we don't understand the business world. I already knew about community, but the business side was pain and heartache. Dick let me make mistakes and fall on my sword. He taught me how to run the company like a business so we would have blackfellas in the traditionally white domains of management and finances. He sat in the office beside me and said, "These things you can do for yourselves". He went with me constantly to see employers, to interview clients. Sometimes he is arrogant and ignorant, but he has the heart of a bear – and he's selfless.'

In 2001, 20 per cent of Indigenous Australians were unemployed – approximately three times higher than the rate for non-Indigenous people. If the 18 per cent of Indigenous people who earned income from Work for the Dole schemes were included in the figures, the unemployment rate would almost double to 38 per cent. Of those who were employed, 60 per cent were in low-skilled jobs. By the 2006 census, the rate of unemployed Indigenous people overall had fallen to 14 per cent, although in regional areas it was 19 per cent. As reported in *Indigenous Health in Australia: The social determinants of health*, a report of the Fred Hollows Foundation, unemployment has severe effects on health, self-esteem and life expectancy.

In 2003, Dick and Cathy expanded the AES into Tamworth, and in 2004, Dubbo. Both towns had high Indigenous unemployment. In the first year in Tamworth, 630 of the Aboriginal population of 2400 registered for work and 151 were placed. The AES was nominated by another business for the Tamworth Chamber of Commerce Best New Business. In the 2005/06 financial year, 1148 had registered and ninety-four had been placed in jobs. It was a similar story when Dubbo City Council approached the AES to open its doors there. Once again, 600 registered and there were over 100 placements in nine months. In 2005/06, 245 registered and 189 were placed in work.

Percy Duncan founded a service within AES to employ and train Aboriginal security guards. He became AES security coordinator in 2004.

'There was too much stereotyping of Aboriginal people around Moree,' Percy said. 'That's why I started the security work. Then the boot was on the other foot in the shops, pubs and clubs that previously wouldn't serve an Aboriginal fella.'

In Moree, the AES had the only all-Indigenous trained security team in Australia. The team of fourteen handled commercial work in town for Moree

Plains Shire Council, Moree Show and the Woolworths store. Of the 700 Woolies stores Australia-wide, the Moree store was the only one where security was subcontracted. Dick received calls of complaint for the first six months from the Woolworths manager, but peer pressure in the community stopped the problems with kids. Woolworths in Moree had been losing over $200,000 a year in theft of its stock. Those losses were more than halved once the AES security guards began.

Cathy described security work as overcoming 'the Lost Warrior syndrome' as it gave Aboriginal men back an important role in society. 'It impacts on families and gives purpose and influence when the men liaise with fathers and Elders. It also reduces the drinking, violence and crime rates and increases pride,' she said. 'When Woolies customers see Aboriginal people providing security and safety, not pinching bags and running off, it has a big impact.'

In Dubbo, the employment and training of community security guards was a vital strategy in 2005 in dealing with the troubled Gordon Estate. The security guards would often find their own sons were the offenders. It gave Aboriginal men a way of caring for the community by diverting kids from trouble and challenged the community security guards to bring the safety message into the home as they modelled a new role of being employed. The 2005/06 *Aboriginal Employment Strategy Annual Report* stated:

> **A major role for the patrols in the Gordon Estate is to provide mentoring to youth. The patrol is never just about 'Policing', but is always about providing needed support to families, youth and the community. In addition, two guards patrol the main streets of Dubbo on foot from Monday to Saturday nights. They break down cultural barriers, give youth a role model, build relationships with mainstream businesses and protect people and property.**

Six months later, in April 2006, I met Cathy in Dubbo at the AES office in the main street. Dick was flying her down from Moree for the day. He had bought a five-seater Cessna to travel between the AES centres. Cathy arrived a little flustered.

'Before we left, he mentioned a crack in the propeller,' she said over a cup of coffee. 'I'm scared of heights and freaked out. "It's not going to come off," he said. Another day we were coming in to land and he decided to cut the engines to see what would happen. He hadn't had time to practise gliding in to land before! Warning lights flashed and signals went beep, beep as we coasted in. I got off with jelly legs. I trust him because he knows what he's doing in planes – but he can't drive.'

While Cathy monitored staff performances and discussed AES expectations individually with staff, I interviewed Dick. I asked about the crack in the plane's propeller.

'I like to take Cathy out of her comfort zone,' he said with a wicked smile.

Dick's drive has guided the AES for nine years. He referred to himself as a conservative cotton farmer, but that was surely a smokescreen for a vision and understanding of human nature far beyond his agricultural interests.

'One never knows where one will end up in life. When I first got going in Aboriginal employment in 1990, I never expected to be working with Aboriginal people.'

He was proud of the enormous impact of the AES. In Moree alone it had placed over 1000 Aboriginal people in employment. In 2003, the AES won the state award in the Prime Minister's Community Business Awards and was one of three national finalists.

The AES works on an empowerment model in which staff members are paid on performance, on the number of jobs they secure and on placing people. There are no upfront dollars.

'Ours is a business, not welfare. We build on our own capacity.'

Staff turnover was a problem, but Dick thought that, overall, it helped to build the community because those staff went on to other jobs. In the Moree office, which had a staff of five, they had employed about forty people over seven or eight years and had a different manager nearly every year. Cathy was a major stabilising factor. Dick was in the process of stepping back and leaving management decisions to her.

'Cathy is able to read people well and lift them up. This company is about people. Most organisations manage down; we manage up. Cathy is brilliant at the human resources side. It was far harder getting her to unwind her own personality because she didn't trust white people. She didn't like herself much either because she wasn't black enough. Cathy had a welfare mentality and wanted to help everyone. If she walked down the street and someone confronted her about something, she would come back and want to change whatever they had criticised, but the next day it might be a different criticism. She had to find self-belief.'

Dick said they talked about issues constantly and Cathy had learnt fast because she was smart.

'If we are to have reconciliation, we have to pull corporate Australia on board. We have school-based training in two of the big banks now: ANZ and the Commonwealth Bank of Australia. Traineeships lead to jobs learning about finance. We will see black faces across the counters in banks, which will break down all sorts of barriers.'

In 2006, twelve Aboriginal students completed the traineeship and went on to full-time employment with a bank or another employer. The AES could boast a

90 per cent success rate for completion of traineeships due to the mentoring support it provided to both the trainee and the host employer. By 2007 Westpac Bank had joined the program, eighty-six Aboriginal students had begun school-based training in Western Australia and Queensland and the program had expanded beyond the three banks to the City of Sydney and Campbelltown City Councils; ANZ has taken the initiative to recruit 300 young Indigenous people by 2009. The AES, which employed forty Indigenous staff, had developed partnerships with other corporate business such as Cotton Australia, Woolworths, Fletchers Meats, Australia Post and Rio Tinto. Dick said that if you took corporate Australia out of the main streets of towns and cities, you would lose 60 to 70 per cent of the jobs. He feels extremely frustrated when bureaucrats seem blind to the success of the AES.

'The amount of horsepower we exert to build a successful company is unbelievable,' Dick said, 'yet we constantly have to prove our worth to the bureaucrats. Any program that has competed with the Job Network gets deliberately shafted.'

Dick contended that there was something like $3 billion of government money going into Aboriginal issues and about two-thirds of that went into non-Indigenous pockets to manage programs which had little commitment to skills transfer.

'That leaves the other third for, say, 400,000 Indigenous people, 60 per cent of whom are on welfare.'

But persistence paid off. In 2005 the Aboriginal Employment Strategy had received a grant of $17 million from the federal government to run the program in Tamworth, Dubbo, Maitland and Moree, as well as expanding into inner and outer Sydney.

'Over 100 Indigenous people have been assisted into jobs in Blacktown [in outer Sydney], with 300 registrations for work since November,' Dick said. 'It's the first time there are Aboriginal businesses in the main streets of these places. People take pride in that.'

Cathy Duncan was clearly a vital element in the AES expansion. Would the company fall apart if she left? Dick considered my question.

'No it wouldn't, but we would have to identify other leaders. There are two terrific managers in the inner Sydney Glebe office. Cathy is the country face of management.'

Cathy soon joined us and the two of them talked at once: it was like watching a tennis match. Then Dick wandered off to talk with staff.

'Sometimes I wish Dick would make all the decisions,' Cathy said, 'but now I'm chief executive officer I can run my own show. We learn how to manage with our heads, not our hearts as an Aborigine does. I used to make decisions from the heart because I care for my community, but I also needed to make mindful decisions. You have to be tough in business.'

Cathy attributes the success of the AES to Aboriginal people doing something for themselves and not waiting for the welfare wagon to rattle into town.

'It's us understanding our own business and respecting the ethos of our own culture, not attacking our weaknesses. We don't dwell on the past, on racism and hatred. We believe it was how it was and we'll only get through it if we build a future.'

Her job of coordinating programs and managing staff in four places is huge.

'Eighty per cent of our staff's lives are after hours in the community, so it's a challenge to keep them on the front foot. Some do fall down so we need to mentor them. We explain that the attitude of "Brother, it's OK if you don't do your part; I'll cover for you" won't do. It's about teamwork and building strengths, but we don't tolerate a bludger. We teach people to take ownership as individuals. For example, AES starts work at 8.30. Staff need to be here then. I have a heartfelt relationship with them, but the bottom line is the good of the organisation.'

When I asked Cathy what was Dick's role now, with a laugh she described him as a big tractor that mowed everything out of the road and allowed them to get on with the job. With his contacts and business savvy, he opened doors to business and government.

'From being on the other side as a former bureaucrat in a federal agency and now being in a non-profit community organisation, I see the naïveté of us Aboriginal people in understanding political structures.'

Expanding the service to Sydney took much negotiation, over six months, by Cathy and Dick with federal bureaucrats, businesses in the top end of town, Lord Mayor Clover Moore, New South Wales politicians, companies such as Woolworths, women's groups in Redfern – the lot, Cathy said – so they would know the issues for Aboriginal people in Sydney. The office is based in Glebe, not the Aboriginal stronghold of Redfern, to bring Indigenous people closer to inner-city businesses where they can get jobs. Cathy was worried that she would have to uproot and move to Sydney to manage the expansion. Instead, she was content to focus on the bush and work with the city managers, Danny Lester and Natalie Ducki.

The organisation had restructured and Cathy moved from being CEO–chair into a position with the rather grand title of Director of Culture and Reputation, in charge of all the country operations. Dick was once again chair and the new AES city manager, Danny Lester, became CEO.

Dubbo AES manager Michael Nolan collected us to go to Dubbo Secondary College where local and many regional Years 10 to 12 students finish their schooling. This city has the highest number of Aboriginal students in Australia and fifty-eight of the 150 are enrolled in vocational education. Cathy was in action as she met with teachers and student advisers from the college and TAFE. They identified a specific problem of transport for Indigenous students from their homes to TAFE. Cathy was also a director on the New South Wales Board of Vocational Education and Training and was able to offer financial assistance to improve transport so the students could pursue career pathways.

As we drove back to the office, she reflected on changes in her time leading the AES. Aboriginal students could now take on bank traineeships and the School to Work computer training program. Many were finishing Year 12. Instead of having babies and existing on Single Parent Benefits, girls could get work and make a conscious choice about whether to have a child. In Moree Woolworths, the manager was asking his Aboriginal AES guards, 'Where have all the kids gone?' Cathy was particularly proud that the AES has taken the audacious move of expanding from the bush into the big smoke.

In 2005/06, as the seven offices gathered momentum, 2500 people had registered for work and 500 were employed as a result of the AES.

'It's not luck when you get a job,' Cathy said, 'It shows that we Aborigines can work and have commitment and dedication. Where previously white people didn't want to mix with Aborigines and we tended to be in menial work, now you can find us in jobs of all kinds around Moree. We can do anything if we are realistic and develop our skills and confidence. AES has become involved with communities and we're determined to stick with it. In future, we need to grow more leaders and staff, to keep the continuity of the founders such as us, but let in new blood. Dick would like to be a pensioner who visits and asks how we are going. I help develop the skills and identity of Aboriginal communities in rural areas. I cop a fair bit of stick, but the AES has made me a better person. I can walk the talk.'

The Duncans chose to live in the quiet of the bush at Biniguy, only a stone's throw from the Gwydir River, so they could camp and fish in their leisure time.

'I use a fancy new rod, while Cathy throws in an old mongrel hand line,' Percy said, 'but she was the one to catch a four pound Murray cod and win third prize in the Pallamallawa fishing competition!'

Cathy described Percy as a good partner who helps and knows how to deal with a dominant woman.

'He fills in for me from Monday to Friday and does everything they say Aboriginal fathers don't do. We don't have evil stuff like infidelities.'

Cathy's children are her joy. After her own childhood of drinking, gambling, violence and lack of pride in being Aboriginal, she fervently hopes their son will escape the drugs and alcohol and their daughter will have a trouble-free life.

'I tell them not to do what I did,' she said. 'I want to be a good mother and wife. I make sure Jessica and I yarn about everything, from aspirations in life to books. Little Percy is always waiting on the steps with a footy when I get home.'

As the AES grew, it began to change. It was the hardest Cathy had ever worked. She was constantly on the move between the centres. With the expansion to Sydney, Cathy felt the AES was losing some of its rural perspective and the ability it had as a smaller operation to get down to the community level. Australia's worst drought in 100 years affected availability of jobs in the bush to the extent that, by the end of 2006, AES had to shed the less viable operations, such as some of the staff in country centres.

'I understood that, but was caught in the middle of it and lost my passion.'

Cathy felt confused by the changes, and vulnerable. She no longer wanted to go to work, felt tired all the time and would burst into tears. Burnout was upon her.

'I didn't like the person I was becoming,' she said in early 2007. Her sister, Debbie likened Cathy's work to a drug and told her to 'pull the AES drip out of your arm and get a life'. Cathy felt the weight of responsibility on her shoulders. Her family was feeling the strain of her being away and she was distracted or asleep on the couch when she was home. Young Percy was playing up at school and Jessica wanted to go to school in Tamworth, two and a half hours away. Percy urged Cathy to leave work.

'Family is so central to Aboriginal people,' Cathy said. 'We had to make a decision, so Percy and I resigned from the AES. I joined it for the kids and I left it for the kids. I wasn't going to let my kids go off the rails because I was too busy saving Aboriginal communities. We were both looking at full-on unemployment and had to trust fate.'

The children and Percy were proud of her. It was a brave move, especially when she had no other job lined up. On the same day Cathy resigned, she saw and successfully applied for a job in Tamworth as an Indigenous Education Solutions broker with the federal government. The position aims to improve links between schools and the community to overcome low literacy rates and absenteeism and to coordinate across government. The Duncans sold their house at Biniguy, moved to Tamworth where they enrolled their children in local schools and Percy got casual work. By July 2007, Cathy was regional manager of Commonwealth education programs for Indigenous students, the children were happily settled into their new schools and Percy was doing casual work with the intention of signing up for the police force or the army.

'It all went so smoothly,' Cathy said in amazement. 'Through the AES, we made a contribution to Indigenous kids looking further ahead than going fishing, having babies and getting the pension. People believe regional Australia is dying. Towns do die on the welfare roundabout, but the AES contributed jobs, opportunities for economic sustainability in country communities and futures for our kids. The biggest thing I learnt about was business and how to market something people didn't want – an Aboriginal jobseeker. I began my career in education and now I'm back. We need to begin at the beginning – educating kids. They are our future.'

Founder of AES Dick Estens and CEO Cathy Duncan, Moree, 2005

James Fitzpatrick with Marcia, True Blue Dreaming photography workshop, Looma, Western Australia, 2006

IO

True Blue Dreaming

Dr James Fitzpatrick, Perth, Western Australia

In 2001, a 27-year-old medical student burst onto Australian television screens when he was named Young Australian of the Year. This unassuming yet eloquent man was warm and funny as he accepted the award for his work in rural health and for his role in establishing the Carnarvon Children's Festival. This festival had been a community response to a spate of youth suicides in that remote area of northwest Western Australia.

'I'm very nervous and my knees are shaking like spaghetti in the wind, but I'm not speechless,' James Fitzpatrick said in his acceptance speech. 'I want all of you to close your eyes. You too, Mr Prime Minister – your security guys can keep their eyes open.'

Then he read a poem that he had penned during an army survival course in the goldfields of the west. It was called 'Plenty'. What follows are some selected verses.

Have you ever gone without?
Not for a day, not for a week;
Have you ever been denied the stuff of life indefinitely?
I haven't. Taps always run water for me, hot or cold.
Food is never far away. Good food, clean food.
I need not catch it, forage for it, disinfect it, queue for it.
I always have shelter. Always a roof. Always warmth.
Sure, the roof may leak, I may get cold, but this is the exception.
I have plenty.

I have freedom.
I can change my life and make as much or as little of it as I desire.
With the gifts of determination and passion I have the power to realise my
dreams.
Many of us do.
If you, unlike me, have been truly without, I salute you.

If you are bound to an existence that you do not desire,
With no hope of realising your dreams,
I pledge to help you.
I do not know you, but I know you are there.
I have plenty. Enough to share.

James's mother, Pam, said, 'There was a palpable silence from the audience for a few long seconds then they clapped and just kept clapping.'

His private pledge of helping those who weren't able to help themselves was now public. This is James Fitzpatrick's story.

James sat on the bank of the Fitzroy River in the Kimberley, a solitary figure in contemplation. Before him the river told its own tale of swirling floods that left debris high in the trees, of crumbling banks and mighty gums with roots exposed, of thirsty wildlife beating tracks to the water's edge. It was September, the last gasp of the 2006 Dry. To snatch some peace, James had to disappear from his working life as a doctor in a Perth hospital and his endless round of community involvements.

The slim, fair-haired 31-year-old in crumpled shirt and shorts climbed the bank back to our camp. The clearing had felt safe enough under a full yellow moon, but now it was pre-dawn. There was the river and there were these orange eyes gleaming in the darkness. Distinctive marks of crocodiles across the sand became visible as the sky brightened. Black whistling kites circled above the remaining sleepers. The chorus of honks, twitters and screeches from the tall grasses and overhanging branches was reaching a crescendo. In the distance, a cow bellowed plaintively.

James came to the community of Looma, three hours east of the coastal town of Broome, to oversee a photography workshop with Aboriginal children. It was part of a mentoring project that he instigated for young people in isolated areas, called True Blue Dreaming. The previous day we drove from Broome across the Fitzroy floodplain into the heart of the Kimberley. The flat, dusty landscape changed as we neared Looma, giving way to rocky red outcrops and perfectly rounded hills covered in lime-green spinifex. Bulbous termite mounds piled one on another like giant chocolate puddings. By the time we reached the first baobab trees, with their bottle shapes and strange upside-down foliage, James was feeling exuberant, but also apprehensive about the weekend ahead.

'I have struggled with whether it's my right to work with Indigenous communities because I'm not Indigenous,' he said. 'I still ask myself. But if I think something needs to be done, I do it.'

The community of 400 people nestled under the serrated ridge of Lizard Rock, Looma in Mangala language. Civic pride and organisation were visible in neat colour-bond houses, trees shading the tarred roads, street lighting and gardens.

Just as Royal Flying Doctor Service founder Reverend John Flynn had a vision of spreading his 'mantle of safety' over the inland for those who were sick, James had a vision of creating a mantle of opportunity for young people in the outback. His aim was to help people younger than himself living in remote areas to realise their ambitions. His plan of a national mentoring scheme was already operating in the south of Western Australia, but he wondered how it would work in this Kimberley community. The health problems of the region eclipse those anywhere else in Western Australia: life expectancy for Indigenous people in the Kimberley is twenty years less than it is for non-Indigenous Australians. Preventable lifestyle and environmental factors, such as poor nutrition, smoking and low standards of living, are closely related to major health problems. Soaring rates of heart disease, Type 2 diabetes, renal disease, lung conditions, sexually transmitted infections, low birth weight babies, alcoholism, violence and suicide are three or four times higher in the Kimberley than for the rest of Western Australia, as was reported in 2004 by the Kimberley Health Service.

James wants to break the cycle of poor health, education and employment, which can spiral into substance abuse and suicide.

'It's hard to break unless we work with youth,' he said. 'Through mentoring we can learn so much about Indigenous culture, while introducing skills and opportunities from mainstream culture that they otherwise could not access. We have to commit to these young people for the long haul so they don't die twenty years younger, or have health prospects many times worse than that of mainstream culture.'

The local clinic in this one community keeps two remote area nurses, two Aboriginal health workers and visiting baby health, women's health and drug and alcohol workers busy. Funerals are a frequent occurrence. People were still reeling from the death of a young woman who hanged herself the previous Christmas. Every evening her relatives held a church service for her in this God-fearing community.

'Up here,' said Ryan Nichols, the Looma clinic nurse on duty for the weekend, 'the third world exists in a first-world country. Resources are not necessarily poor. The ability to service the population may be good, as in our well-equipped clinic, but the number of sick people using the clinic could be better. No single factor stops them coming to the clinic, but shame plays a big role. Here shame is anything that makes you stand out or squirm. To come into the clinic is shameful for some people. Communities are like fishbowls – everyone knows everyone else's business. On the positive side, Looma has strong leadership. It is a dry community and the volunteer wardens are proactive in fining offenders who drink. Three offences and they are referred to the police. The churches are often the glue that binds people. White people like me who work in remote areas are referred to as "missionaries, mercenaries or misfits".'

This is a comment I've heard from black and white people. The echoes of nineteenth century colonialism seemed to endure in some isolated places.

James snatched an hour away from the community to talk to me by a nearby billabong. He pointed out a large croc sliding into the water from its sunny bank. Red Brahman bulls kicked up dust at our intrusion, while three grey brolgas poked through the dirt behind them. A white ibis waded in the shallows to fish for treats in the mud. A spine-chilling bark made us sit up.

'That's a croc marking his territory, James.' I craned around trying to locate it. This was a beautiful, wild spot, but the interview could be short.

Outback places such as Looma are light years from the New South Wales Blue Mountains where James and his two older sisters, Sarah and Kate, grew up. He was far from an A-grade student who followed a clear path straight into medicine. His father, Jim, was a squadron leader in the air force and his mother, Pam, a teacher and librarian.

Pam told me later: 'In primary school, he would have the "ah-ha" response about a year after everyone else. James needed time to grow into his skin. When mothers worry about their kids, I say – just wait. In second class when his marks were well below most other kids in the class, I asked the nun who taught James what was happening. She said by the time he'd mucked around with the kid next to him, laughed at some crazy antic they performed and smiled at the whole class, the rest of the class had finished sums and he still hadn't quite got his books out. He was always in strife, but had fun and loved being with other children.'

James went to boarding school at St Stanislaus in Bathurst when he was 14.

'I felt upset leaving home, but soon I was in my element,' James said. 'I liked the landscape of Mt Panorama and the school farm and loved having mates around 24 hours a day.'

It was a tough regime – a principal who espoused Stannies men and Stannies grit, and priests who administered canings if they were having a bad day. Boys toughened up under the structure and discipline, football training on cold mornings and being knocked about by seniors. When a priest asked the boys to list their goals, James wrote 'to be happy, to make others happy and to reproduce – sir!' At the end of term, when other boys packed their bags, James would just pull a sheet off his bed and throw everything into it. He worked hard, but was no angel. In his final year, James and a mate were suspended.

'We got up at 4 o'clock one morning, nicked pushbikes from a dormitory master and rode to Perthville Girls' School to see some girls we used to write to,' he recalled. 'Stannies was like a low-security prison. You had to break out every so often, but I felt a strong link to it.'

Despite the odd misdemeanour, James finished up as Senior of the Year when he graduated after Year 12.

'I wasn't brilliant, just an all-rounder and well organised by then.'

He liked agriculture, particularly the hands-on side of driving tractors and shearing. He spent holidays at mates' farms, which shaped his decision to study agricultural science at the University of New England (UNE).

'My pastimes at UNE were drinking beer, chasing girls and playing rugby,' he said.

During holidays at home, James was often either drunk or had a hangover. His mother remembered one nocturnal phone call from university.

'James called home at 2 o'clock one morning, probably thinking he was ringing a mate. He said, "Whoo's zis?"' Pam imitated her son's slurry voice. 'I said, "James – this is your mother!" There was dead silence the other end. I wrote to him the next day and said there would be no more Mum-study. His allowance was finished and he had to make his own way through uni.'

She gave him three choices: get a job, go into the army or come home and go to the local university. James joined the Royal Australian Army Reserve for a year to save money so he could return to UNE. The day he checked into the recruiting centre at Kapooka near Wagga Wagga was his nineteenth birthday: he was given nineteen push-ups.

'That year challenged me and I began to grow up,' James said. 'The hard environment of the army could be both invigorating and demoralising. I rose to the rank of corporal, responsible for nine men in an infantry platoon. I was a benevolent dictator. I would push the guys in my unit with physical training and if things were not done, yell or lob empty grenades at them.'

The self-discipline and teamwork convinced James that he could achieve whatever he put his mind to. It also financed his study for a further five years, in return for several weeks of service each year. One day when he was running a cross-country race, he became dehydrated and collapsed from heat stroke. He regained consciousness to find himself lying on an army stretcher with drips attached and fans cooling him. That's when James first thought about doing medicine.

'I wanted to be like the people who cared for me.'

James returned to UNE to study science while applying for medicine for three years without success, a devastating experience.

He enrolled in physiology and psychology. He wasn't encouraged to do medicine. Nobody said, 'Go for it'. Instead it was: 'You're an idiot, you couldn't pass med', or 'You can always be a psychologist if you don't get into med'.

'I got angry and thought, This is what I want to do. I will do medicine.'

James studied and partied hard at UNE, but his heart was elsewhere. He would go to Sydney University library to research science assignments, but read medical books instead; he even bought some doorstopper medical texts. He had to earn money to stay at university, so his father, Jim, helped James build a hotdog vending booth that his son christened Poo's Dogs. James added a personal touch to the fare with messages in tomato sauce or mustard.

'One student wanted "You light up my life" written in cack-yellow hot English mustard on a hotdog for his girlfriend,' he recalled.

According to his sister Kate, 'James is a rare beast, without ego and with a genuine affection for people. He is not judgemental, but accepts people for who they are. He is joyfully unorthodox and unafraid. I remember telling him once that he had no sense of shame. Fortunately, he has progressed from leaping nude onto pub tables to recite poetry and now applies his unconventional qualities to taking his message to the prime minister.'

James was on an army exercise when the faculty of medicine at the University of Western Australia called to say he had an interview. He bought his first tie, flew to Perth and sat the interview in good spirits. At the end, the panel asked if he had any questions.

'What do you think of my tie?' he asked them.

'Loud,' commented the female interviewer.

Apart from the tie – or perhaps because of it; he'll never know – he must have impressed them because he was accepted. James won the UNE physiology award in 1996 and moved to Perth. As well as full-time medicine, he juggled three, sometimes four jobs: tutoring science subjects at college and the Centre for Aboriginal Programs, bar work at the university tavern and part-time Army Reserve. His job as a Boomgate Boy car-park cashier enabled him to study in between vehicles passing through. Here, along with the receipts, he gave out slips of paper bearing inspirational messages.

'I didn't watch telly and didn't waste time. I can't stand letting things pile up.'

James stood for the University Guild Council with a typical undergraduate blurb that said he was 'proficient in seven languages, had read every sacred text from cover to cover – and would install a chairlift from the tavern to lectures'. Students elected him. He doubted whether he did much.

He joined Students and Practitioners Interested iN Rural Practice, Health Education Xcetera (SPINRPHEX), the oldest undergraduate rural health club in Australia.

'They were a great bunch – 300 student members in Western Australia and 5000 across Australia. We worked with government departments, politicians and grassroots members and focused on inequities in rural health. We lobbied to lift services in line with urban centres.'

Involvement in SPINRPHEX built on what James had learnt in the army about leadership and teamwork. In 2000, he became the Western Australia club president and in the following year was elected chairperson of the National Rural Health Network.

In 1999, James received a four-year John Flynn Scholarship, which funded him to do practical work in remote areas during holidays. In 2000, he chose to go to Carnarvon in the northwest. He arrived as a carefree student on his second practical term there. His world soon changed. Two youth suicides and a murder/suicide confronted him with the impact of racism and community dysfunction. Carnarvon was a grieving community. James saw suicide as a potent indicator of a sick society.

'I was standing talking to an Elder at the Aboriginal community on the outskirts of town and two kids were playing in the yard while inside someone was pissed and yelling out. Often children lacked an inspiring role model or mentor.'

James was moved to write a poem called 'Peppercorn Hair'.

Peppercorn hair and black, shiny skin,
Nurtured in dirt and in filth and in sin.
Sin against love and sin against hope,
Sin bred by flagons, sin bred by dope.

The world that you know from the day of your birth
Cages your freedom, as it strips you of worth,
The fabric your family and countrymen weave
Is frayed, torn and soiled. No wonder you grieve,
And curse the white world that won't let you in,
With your peppercorn hair and your shiny, black skin.

He believed that a children's festival was a good way to focus the community on youth, so he joined Gascoyne Public Health unit and mobilised a small army of thirty SPINRPHEX members to organise the first Carnarvon Children's Festival.

'We ran clown workshops, were the musicians and rent-a-crowd, and collected donations of clothes. In the year of the suicides, it made kids feel special and gave them something to do. The festival became a circuit breaker, encouraging people to come together and value their young people. It allowed the community to heal and move on.'

The stunning impact of this now annual festival surprised James.

'It brought black and white together. The purity of children taught adults a little about living in harmony. During and after the festival each year, evaluations showed that crime and underage drinking rates decreased.'

In 2000, James's flatmate nominated him for Young Australian of the Year. He won his section, but not the Western Australia award; however, the panel chose three wildcards. On the strength of his speech at the Western Australia award ceremony, James was one of them. He became one of twenty-one national finalists. He asked his parents what they reckoned his chances were.

'One in twenty-one,' Pam promptly replied.

'That doesn't show much faith,' James said.

'When his name was announced as the overall winner, we nearly collapsed,' Pam recounted. 'He knew he had won, but was not able to let on out of consideration for other finalists. We had plenty of faith in James, but we had no idea beforehand who the other finalists were. The other candidates were so inspiring we realised then what a fantastic job James was doing at Carnarvon and indeed with the whole Rural Health Network.'

Pam described James as an idealist and a romantic who sees the good in other people, though his offbeat sense of humour sometimes got him into strife.

'At dinner after the awards with the prime minister, John Howard, the PM said how difficult it was to remember people's names. James responded, "I know what you mean, Mr Johnstone. I forget names all the time." There was this stony silence, but Mr Howard hadn't actually heard the joke. James apologised and then he had to repeat what he said which made the PM smile.'

Kate described his win as the most incredible adrenaline rush.

'Our table just exploded. James was unperturbed in the presence of celebrities and the prime minister. He was unafraid to say what he thought or to recite poetry. He didn't have a tie with him so before the ceremony we had to hand him a Save the Children Fund tie he kept at home. He also had holes in his shoes. The next day, while attending Australia Day celebrations on a wet lawn in Canberra, James got soggy socks.'

Being named 2001 Young Australian of the Year kicked off a multitude of activities for James, including a visit to Cambodia for the Save the Children Fund (SCF). SCF aimed to rescue more than 20,000 children in Cambodia from child labour and prostitution and to help them into safe houses to learn skills. The trip, which exposed him to the impact of exploitation and poverty in other countries, ignited James's appetite for aid work.

As Young Australian of the Year, James suddenly had a platform. He was a strong voice at influential forums such as the 2001 Centenary of Federation conference of Young People and the Commonwealth Youth Conference. James spoke about inequity in opportunities for youth in rural and outback areas and its impact on their wellbeing, especially their mental health. He had trouble turning down invitations, including one from *Cleo* magazine, which photographed him barely clothed on a beach as one of Australia's fifty most eligible bachelors. To leading questions such as 'Which body part of yours would you most like a woman to wash in the shower?', James replied, 'The dirty parts, I guess. Isn't that what we're there for?'

James wasn't just an eligible bachelor. He also challenged traditional medical views. At a special dinner in the Blue Mountains, doctors dressed in their best were surprised by their guest speaker James who, in his open-necked blue shirt, quoted poetry and spoke of the poverty and ill health in remote Australia.

'It's time that we broke out of the urban-centric, narrow, medical model that has always been applied in rural Australia,' he said. They listened and then questioned him closely.

Some of the medical profession agreed with James. Dr Ray Power, an Irish doctor who lived in Perth at the time and mentored James at the Western

Australia Centre for Remote and Rural Medicine, wrote in *Relating Faith in Public Life: Australian mentoring stories*, (edited by Ruth Prescott and Peter Marshall and published by Openbook Publishers):

> **James likes to push the boundaries, to take risks, to do the right things by people and he is not afraid to make himself vulnerable while he's doing that. He has this approach to life that, if you keep banging on enough doors, some of them will open. He is also very much a doer. He could have 20 projects on the hop at any one time. I admire his charisma and courage. He's committed to rural Australia. Mark my words, that lad is destined for a wonderful career and I'm convinced he will make a huge impact on Australian society while levelling the playing field between the haves and have nots.**

James took the year off university in 2001, the International Year of the Volunteer, to capitalise on his Young Australian of the Year award. He marked the year by touring fifty remote communities with his former army mates, Nigel McNair and Chris Baker, in a Hilux they dubbed 'Old Yella'. They called their odyssey True Blue Dreaming and introduced themselves in their *True Blue Dreaming* report of 2002 as taking off 'With a bagful of dreams and a mountain of hope. To paraphrase Gandhi, we three set about living the change we wanted to see in the world.' They chose to focus on young people, particularly those who lived in the outback. 'These people are not just our future, but vibrant, creative and productive participants in our communities right now.'

The three men started out from James's school, Stannies, at Bathurst and headed north to Mount Isa. They drove 50,000 kilometres around Australia, from Hermannsburg outside Alice Springs to multicultural Broome, from desert communities such as Meekatharra and Kalgoorlie to Ceduna on the Great Australian Bight. They used creative workshops and community forums to draw local people together so that youth could express their concerns, their desires for the future and their strategies to create positive changes.

Substance abuse, violence and crime were festering concerns for the young people. Of the 1395 survey responses the team received, 88 per cent of respondents said they would leave their area at some time for work, study or travel, but 61 per cent of all the kids said they would return. Instead of despairing at the immensity of the problems, James, Nigel and Chris felt hope and optimism for the future as they uncovered a core of commitment and enthusiasm in most communities.

It wasn't all work. James remembered the drive to Cape Leveque north of Broome. Fires burnt either side of the dirt road. 'I tied myself to the roof rack and Chris drove. It was a stupid thing to do, but it was the most liberating experience.'

After James spoke at her school in Karratha, Western Australia, 13-year-old Hailey Mitchell said to him, 'My goal is to be a runner. I will train every chance I get. I can drive a motorbike, car and tractor and I can pull a beer off the tap. I want to be a star.' Hailey's longing echoed that of so many young people in outback communities, who were isolated from opportunity and support. James resolved to do something about it.

A 1995 study by Big Brothers, Big Sisters of America showed that mentoring of young people reduced the start-up rate of illegal drug and alcohol use, school absenteeism and violence. James envisaged mentors as a bridge between rural areas and the cities. He hoped that this newfound support, information and inspiration would better enable young Australians in remote communities to pursue their heartfelt aspirations. After a 12-month pilot period in 2004, his mentoring initiative, True Blue Dreaming (TBD), was funded for four years to the tune of $384,000 by the Commonwealth Department of Families and Community Services and Indigenous Affairs. After driving the project for four years himself, he felt relieved to hand over responsibility to a professional coordinator, Wendy Stewart.

Initially, through TBD James wanted to target two small Western Australian localities: an Aboriginal community in the Kimberley and the wheat-belt town of Wyalkatchem, 196 kilometres northeast of Perth. In Wyalkatchem, the TBD team piloted a process. Wendy and James identified community needs, searched for ways to meet those needs and engage that community through local champions. They aimed to develop young people's skills and confidence and to have fun along the way. The mentors were health and medical students from the University of Western Australia, who helped their mentees set goals for personal and community success.

'We had thirty mentees at the first camp. They were such an impressive bunch, younger than we had anticipated. Many were 10 to 13, a handful 14 to 17, but we responded to the need. Jack Pink, who was 10, wanted to be a doctor. So I said to him, "I'm a doctor – why don't you be my mentee?" He agreed.'

The launch of TBD in Wyalkatchem, which was televised by the ABC with George Negus as host, was a lively occasion. A medley of music, games and speeches drew together children and parents, community leaders and teachers. Jack Pink stood at the microphone and spoke about what it meant to be a mentee; his mentor, James, expressed his thoughts in a poem.

Being a mentor is a big commitment. James spends weekends with Jack and his father, Geoff, whenever he can. 'A young person's view is grounding,' James said. 'Jack inspires me and I've made a new friend.'

Jack returned the compliment. 'James is funny and gives me lots of ideas. I've wanted to be a doctor for a while – four or five months, and James is helping me.'

James took Jack to Fremantle Hospital where he worked at that time to introduce him to the role of a doctor. Dressed in a white doctor's coat and with a stethoscope hanging around his neck, Jack did the rounds of the hospital with James. In the children's ward James introduced him as Dr Pink to Scott, a young patient swathed in bandages.

'How did you have your accident?' Jack asked.

'I was riding my bike downhill, the brakes failed and I fell off,' Scott replied. Jack nodded sympathetically.

James loved taking Jack into the hospital because he could share his medical world with him and introduce the mentoring program to the people in the hospital.

In April 2007, James was shocked to learn that his young mentee Jack Pink was dealing with tragedy. His father, Geoff, was killed in a car accident and Jack had moved to Perth to live with his mother.

'It just does not seem fair,' James said. 'Jack is settling in well with his mother, but the next few weeks will be tough for him as the dust settles and things hit home.'

James's role as friend, supporter and mentor will become even more important to one devastated boy.

In the first 12 months of TBD, Wyalkatchem's young people were selected for prominent forums such as an International Congress in Brisbane and a forum about teenage depression that was conducted on SBS television's *Insight*. One girl, with the encouragement of her TBD mentor, was chosen to attend a National Youth Leadership camp.

In 2004, 11 years after he first made up his mind to study medicine, James graduated as a doctor. He and his girlfriend at that time, Amy, celebrated with a month at Daramsala, the Dalai Lama's home in northern India.

'We immersed ourselves in Tibetan culture,' James said. 'I loved their peaceful, selfless ways. I found it spiritual and comforting to see the Dalai Lama in the flesh and to listen to his practical teachings about Buddhism. It was cold. People would bring us salty, oily tea and fish. It felt like a community should feel.'

In 2005 James began his first job as a doctor, in the Kimberley Population Health Unit. He wanted to work in a bush clinic rather than in Broome, so his boss recommended the remote community of Looma. Once there, James put the idea of helping young people to think about their goals in life to the clinic administrator, Raylene Pindan, and non-Indigenous health sister Sue Lelevere. They suggested James should ask the children themselves, so he walked around the streets and chatted to whoever he met. He found twelve who were interested and took them back to the clinic.

'They soaked up the ideas like sponges,' he said. 'Then I consulted more widely – maybe I should have done that first, but it was spontaneous. I met parents, Elders, teachers and the youth pastor, Jamie, and asked questions about what might work. The kids liked someone taking an interest in their goals and dreams. They loved the movie nights and healthy foods. We made a PowerPoint presentation of their ideas called *A Recipe for Dreams* and presented it to sixty or eighty people who sat on the grass under the stars. For the last session, the kids took us hunting and cooked up a big goanna they caught. Forty-five kids have gone through the program so far.'

The certificate for the goal-setting workshop congratulated the participants on taking the first steps on the long journey towards achieving their goals in life. James added his poem, 'A Breeze' (selected verses).

There's a breeze blowing strong through our country
And it carries the hopes of the young
It carries the tales of a thousand old folk
And a thousand fresh songs not yet sung

And the breeze carries loving and laughter,
And the chatter of children at play
And it whips up a song from the heart of our land
With such force as to take breathe away.

And this breeze, my good friends – you must know it
As it ebbs and flows each time you breathe
You create it yourselves as you live out your lives
And it follows the paths that you weave.

The sensitivities of working in an Aboriginal community are always on James's mind. 'You can do more harm than good. You have to know yourself well and not try and help people because you are needy. The biggest challenge is to build relationships and to really understand what the community wants. It is important to follow the lead of the locals and not to build hopes that later might be dashed.'

Looma is a test of whether mentoring young Aboriginal people can help them transform lack of opportunity into possibility. Cherie Graziotti, who was in final-year medicine and based in Broome, followed up in Looma after James's stay. She mentored the Looma students as a group, gradually building relationships and trust.

'At first they were extremely shy and hesitated when it came to talking about goals and challenges, and the future in general,' Cherie said. 'They would often give the same answer as their friends, or only say a couple of words. After we had a few sessions, grooved to music and learnt dances, chopped up vegies and walked in the bush together, their deeper concerns and thoughts started to emerge. I felt privileged to be someone they talked to. Developing that sense of trust was the highlight of the year for me.'

Cherie remembered one girl who came up to her at a community disco. They sat next to each other for a while, not saying much until the girl disclosed that she was flying to Perth the following day to start high school.

'When I asked how she was feeling, her fear became apparent. She didn't know if there would be a toilet on the plane, or food. She couldn't imagine how the take-off would feel. She didn't know that you don't have to sit completely still for the whole journey. As for Perth itself, she knew few people there and didn't have any warm clothes, despite heading into the middle of winter. I was able to allay some of her fears about the plane, but could understand how challenging the trip was. Predictably, she was back at Looma two weeks later after deciding Perth and a big school were not for her.'

The mentees' first project was to write brief autobiographies. Each week Cherie would show them how to break the task into smaller bites. She had them videoing each other, which built their confidence and gave them new skills. She also wove in lessons about healthy eating and exercise, and sought help from local women to teach students about traditional medicine and bush tucker.

James's next trip to Looma, on which I joined him, was in September 2006. He came straight after a four-month stint as a medical resident at a children's cancer ward. He had been working 76 hour weeks and felt his physical and mental energies ebbing.

'I found that my coping bucket was empty,' he said as we drove to Looma. 'It was draining to see little kids you got to know, who were sick and dying. The parents lived there too. The dynamics were tough. Mum asked me, "Are you sure you're not too soft for this James?" The work was relentless, chaotic, exhausting and bloody hard. I was just exhausted and could only eat, sleep and work. I had two breakdowns where I felt as though I was out of control. I felt depressed and had lost my joy.'

Before James's four months in that job finished, he worked with seniors and colleagues in the unit to ease the stress and improve communications.

'In oncology it's a fine line between life and death. Any lapses in communication and support are dangerous for parents and staff alike. We needed to identify areas for change and to address them.' When he returned to visit the unit just before leaving for Looma, James was not convinced that anything had changed. His trip north was to be a welcome respite.

Back at Looma community, six girls aged from 11 to 13 wanted to learn about photography. They were pleased to see the familiar TBD team of Cherie, James and Wendy, the coordinator, and had a lively curiosity about the photography teacher, Alishia. One girl, Candice, told me she really wanted to write. Only a few months before, Candice would have been too shy to speak to an outsider.

On the green lawn in front of the school, the girls chattered as they clustered around a sheet of butcher's paper and jotted down what they thought was special for young people in Looma: respect for their Elders topped the list, followed by hunting, fishing, dancing and basketball. Some girls lived with their grandparents, others had a parent leave for work elsewhere or pass away. One was rearing her younger twin sisters because her mother was in Derby. Fractured families and responsibilities early in life appeared to be the norm for these girls.

The girls were fascinated by the cameras and quickly picked up the rudiments of digital photography. Their environment was rich in subject matter. Three older women showed them where to find bush tucker: a slow lizard, plump witchetty grubs hiding in tree roots, honey from a native bees' nest. By the time the sun set over Fitzroy River crossing, the girls were setting up tripods to capture the last shimmer of light on the river, a white egret skimming the treetops, or a croc carcase on a sandbank. At dusk they reverted from pro photographers to kids, jumping from overhanging trees into the river, splashing each other and chasing James.

The finale was a barbecue where community members gathered to sup on fresh salmon caught at Broome and brought by a visiting health worker. It was wrapped in foil and cooked over hot coals. The audience sat on the lawn to watch the girls' presentation. Flashed on a screen, their vivid images showed their land and its people, its plants and its animals. Thirteen-year-old Lydia was brave enough to stand up with James and speak about the workshop. Lydia wants to be a doctor and, to that end, hopes to go to high school in Perth. Like all the children in this community, she has to leave the community for high schooling, often far away in Perth or Kalgoorlie.

Students like Lydia who go to boarding schools can get financial support from scholarships offered by schools and Abstudy payments from Centrelink.

'Once the kids turn 14,' Cherie said, 'they are eligible for Abstudy, which also has a boarding supplement for those under 16 years, a school fees allowance and a course cost allowance. The biggest challenges for these kids are not the finances so much, but lack of social support, the transition from remote area to city life and the higher standard of education compared to their own community schooling.'

'We can tell the kids something of the world outside their community,' James said as we drove back to Broome, 'and in turn they can teach us about Aboriginal culture and country. I love the way they think, their focus on family and their humour. We have fun together.'

Despite his overall certainty about mentoring itself, he continually thinks about the best way to proceed.

'Should mentors such as Cherie come into the community from Broome or Perth? It might work better to have someone based closer in Derby, ideally it would be a local who could be in touch with a few communities. Maybe our next move is to support kids who leave Looma and come to high school in Perth. They need help to settle into life in the city. We could do that.'

James's enduring loves are poetry and music. He learnt the saxophone at school, plays the didgeridoo and guitar and bends a mean harmonica.

'I've always written poetry – badly. My first was called 'Unrequited Love', which I sent to the girl and never heard from her again. At the Bush Poets' Breakfast in Broome in 2005 I read a couple of poems and the organisers flew me back in 2006. We spruiked like street performers at the caravan park beforehand, passed around the hat and donated the proceeds to the Royal Flying Doctor Service. Now I have a bush poet as a mentor, a lovely bearded man called Keith "Cobber" Lethbridge.'

James crams more into every 24 hours than most of us do in a week. He brought forty diaries to Broome that span his life from 1997 to 2006. He plans to begin a three-part book in any spare hour he can find. The first part is called *A Mile in My Moccasins* and will contain James's poetry, musings and experiences, the second, *A Mile in Your Moccasins*, a collection of other people's stories, and the third is *A Mile in Our Moccasins*, a tale of hope for the future.

In May 2006, James had the opportunity to reflect on his life while taking part in the Australian Rural Leadership Program. The first session, trekking in the rugged Carr Boyd Ranges of the East Kimberley, held few physical challenges for James, but confronted him emotionally. The hike followed his traumatic period of overwork on the cancer ward, when he had little time off and broke up with his girlfriend.

'I spread myself too thinly. Coupled with the relationship break-up, it was definitely a low,' he said. 'I had to look hard at myself, to sort out my priorities and slow down. I tend to think big, so I try to pare it by half now. One of my stumbling blocks is to commit to strangers more than to those close to me, so at times I neglect family and romantic attachments. Maybe it's so I don't have to admit my flaws – like the Teflon man – and not let family and friends get too close when I'm rundown.'

It's a lonely journey when one shields oneself. James was finding his over-commitment could leave him isolated in his idealism. For more than 15 years, James worked on his schoolboy goals of trying to be happy and to make others happy, but he realised it was better to be true to himself than to try to please others all the time.

James began to speak his mind rather than going along with what other people said. At Looma he knew Christianity was all important to many people.

'I said to one of the parents, "You can act out of love and be a good person whether you have religious faith or maybe have none at all". She accepted that.'

James also began to realise that he expended little energy on himself, so he decided to focus on something he regarded as important, such as becoming a good paediatrician caring for children's health, instead of practising medicine as if it was secondary to his other interests.

'When we began the Australian Rural Leadership Program I felt flat and depressed after the oncology unit work, but I was in a group of rich personalities who worked as a team. One fellow couldn't swim. He was our "lion" when we had to swim through deep pools in caves at night. He wore a life jacket and we dragged him through the water. He just did it. I was also impressed with the way the program switched on lights in participants' heads about Aboriginal culture and the wider community.'

Today's leadership focuses on teamwork. Real leaders can at last show emotions instead of having to present a strong, stoic front at all times.

'The Rural Health Clubs, which I chaired in my uni days, presented an ideal. We believed so much in what we were doing. It's easier if you are passionate and certain about an action. It's harder to take the lead when there are grey areas as at Looma where we have to feel our way. Ultimately, I love leadership because I like to get things done.'

James's respite is sailing. He is now the proud owner of *Platypus 2*, a 20-year-old fibreglass yacht, big enough to sail to Rottnest Island off Fremantle. When he first bought it, James used to swim the 50 metres to its mooring in the Swan River; now he kayaks.

'Buying my little boat was the best thing for me, to be busy while doing nothing. Dad always had a flotilla of leaky boats. *Platypus 2* sleeps two comfortably and four uncomfortably. I catch fish and cook them on a metho stove. I dream of living on a boat and sailing around Australia one day – with my family.'

Family?

'That's the future,' he laughed. 'I want to be the best dad I can be. I used to be focused on finding a partner with qualities similar to mine. It's bullshit though because then you are essentially seeking to fall in love with yourself. Now I really want to find someone I feel good with and can have fun with.'

In 2000, James was galvanised into action on behalf of outback children by his Carnarvon experience and pledged to help those with fewer opportunities to achieve fulfilment in life.

'If I think something is unjust, I don't let it slide. I feel strongly motivated – it's almost a duty to correct that inequality. Society often seems too busy to care for those most in need. The only way forward is to work with children and intervene early to break the cycles.'

James wanted to be involved with people in communities such as those in Looma and Wyalkatchem, as well as to influence the federal government and other decision-making bodies. He is adamant that anyone can achieve their dreams if he can.

'I was an unlikely candidate to become a doctor. Although I was interested and hardworking, I came from a family of non-medicos, went to a rural school where I didn't get ace grades and had to leave uni. My year in the army gave me self-belief and self-discipline.'

As you fly out of Broome stretching below is the turquoise horseshoe of Roebuck Bay, a mecca for migrating birds from the Northern Hemisphere. At low tide the surrounding mudflats form a pattern of branches, waterholes and crusted saltpans. In the Wet, the Crab Creek will cover the plain. The seasons govern the flow of life. Armed with determination, humour and sensitivity, James Fitzpatrick is feeling his way through the seasons of outback life, the constant change and immense challenges.

'Why do I do what I do? Because I love it and because it is the right thing to do. I want to look back later in life when there is equality of opportunity for young people across Australia and think – I'm glad we did something about that.'

James Fitzpatrick, named Young Australian of the Year, 2001

Deb McLucas in a crop of peanuts at Karamarra, Dingo, Queensland, 2005

II

Twenty-first Century Farmers

Deb McLucas, Middlemount, Queensland

The Future Farmers Network (FFN) is the brainchild of Deb McLucas, a 35-year-old Queenslander and former ABC Radio journalist. As a seasoned radio reporter, Deb interviewed many people over the years, some of whom expressed negative views of farmers and farming; others were leaders in agriculture who voiced concern about the shortage of youth in their sector.

I came across Deb and the FFN back in 2003 while browsing the world wide web for inspiring stories of young farmers. I was keen to talk to this woman who had faith in farming beyond drought and debt, was prepared to challenge people's perceptions about agriculture, and the foresight to set up a network for like-minded young farmers.

'I heard derogatory views of farmers such as swilling beer, chasing cows and dodging tax. I also heard industry leaders say they wanted to attract more young people into agriculture, but they didn't act on it.'

In 2000, Deb McLucas left the ABC to marry Rob Bauman, a farmer from Dingo in central Queensland. In July 2005 Deb and Rob's farm, Karamarra, was our destination. My husband Bill and I left the coast and drove 130 kilometres west of Rockhampton into mining and farming country. Dingo sounds like a wild place, not a sleepy country town with a roadhouse, a pub, a primary school, a post office and two sawmills. Karamarra is a further 90 kilometres northeast through miles of dense eucalypt forest. On the way there we passed only the occasional Brahman cow in the middle of the winding dirt road. Just as I was thinking what a hike for a load of groceries, let alone a doctor or schooling, we rounded a corner and before us was a magnificent valley. One huge paddock of yellow and green was scooped from the blue tablelands and edged by the MacKenzie River. Down the middle of the valley an irrigation channel caught the light. A timber house sat on a rise circled by trees laden with oranges and lemons. Behind the house were three shiny John Deere tractors parked at a shed. A whistle escaped from my farming husband's lips – three new tractors.

An attractive, fit-looking woman with cropped blonde hair escaping from under her baseball cap greeted us at the house gate. Propped on her hip was a baby with a fuzz of blonde hair.

'Hi. I'm Deb, this is Hannah. Come and meet Rob and I'll take you down to your accommodation.'

Rob Bauman was tinkering with one of the tractors. He grabbed a rag to wipe off grease and offered a large, square hand. Next to his shed a semi-circle of dongas serve as quarters. Three grey kittens ducked under one of them. That night we dined on a magnificent coral emperor we brought from the coast. Deb presented the fish whole on a platter surrounded by crisp vegetables.

In the morning the valley was shrouded in mist. There was an overnight downpour. The drought that is eating away at much of eastern Australia's productivity and hopes seems to have passed by this oasis.

Deb and Rob rose at dawn, thanks to Hannah. By the time we got up, Rob was back at his tractor and Deb had managed a few hours work on the computer with the help of her offsider.

'Hannah sorts through her dad's pile of papers, brochures and discarded items that he files under his desk,' laughed Deb.

After breakfast Bill joined Rob for men's machinery business while Deb and I settled on the floor with Hannah. The farm may be isolated, but this couple runs a well-oiled business.

Deb's skills as a reporter are immediately evident from her clear, articulate and thoughtful responses. She grew up as the first born of four children on a farm in southern Queensland near Moffatdale.

'My brother Steve and I had a friendly rivalry,' Deb said. 'My second sister Julie acted as mediator. I'm a perfectionist; Steve's laidback, so I sometimes thought he was lazy. He wouldn't bother putting a saddle on his horse – just jumped on.'

The children helped their father move cattle, or ride after a neighbour's rogue steers that preferred the McLucas lucerne to their own paddock. The three older children were close in age; their sister Kate is twelve years younger than Deb. Deb learnt early how to work in a team.

'We had more fun together than playing by ourselves. It was an active, healthy lifestyle so I was never bored. We were part of the workforce and looked after the chooks, dogs and pigs.'

The three older children rode their bikes three kilometres to the one-teacher school at Moffatdale.

'It had about twenty-five kids and usually three in my grade,' Deb said. 'The community was small so you knew everyone. I had responsibility from an early age as a big sister to the younger kids. We kids had to organise the sport, whether it was Red Rover or soccer. We needed everybody to make up a team so there was no such thing as girls' or boys' games. Even at Murgon High School, which had 400 students, girls joined in the touch footy games. Most of us were from smaller schools so we knew how to work together.'

Deb, who loved any sport, was selected for the state team for vigoro, a game similar to cricket. It was a high achievement for a teenager from the bush, but the gun Queensland team had no competitors because no other state fielded a team. Deb loved pony club and rode in gymkhanas and shows.

'Later, I realised what an effort it must have been for our parents. They had to get up in the dark and load horses at 3 o'clock on Sunday mornings. At one stage Mum drove a caravan so we could camp. Pony club and gymkhanas were great social outings where I made lifelong friends.'

When she was 14, Deb started camp drafting, an action-packed sport that replicates cattle mustering. The rider has to cut a beast from the mob, negotiate a cloverleaf-shaped course around trees and urge the animal through a gate, all within a time limit. Naturally, the beast wants to escape back to its mates and frequently succeeds. The sport requires a rapport between horse and rider, quick reflexes and a good understanding of animal behaviour.

'My favourite horse was Rivet, a 15-hand bay with a tremendous heart. She wasn't pretty, a rough old horse who would try anything. I loved the challenge of selecting the right beast, watching the mob to choose one that wasn't highly strung, then bending it around the course. It's a great feeling when you get through the gate and score. About 95 per cent of competitors lose the beast or run out of time before they get to the gate.'

People are now realising from low-stress, animal-handling workshops the importance of the flight zone of a beast. Deb was skilled at judging where to position herself in the flight zone so the animal would do what she wanted. Maybe she had an edge over competitors from her early years of chasing the neighbour's cattle out of the lucerne. In 1987, Deb came third in the 16-years age group for the state camp draft.

Deb remembered about that time, riding with her sister and looking out over their valley.

'We realised for the first time that we would have to leave home to work or study,' she said. 'We had a good life and felt sad at the prospect.'

Nineteen eighty-eight was the bicentennial celebration of white settlement in Australia. Droving '88 selected 300 young people from around the country to work on cattle stations and participate in what was billed as the last great cattle drive. Over four months 1200 head of cattle were moved on the hoof 2000 kilometres from the famous Newcastle Waters Station in the Northern Territory to Longreach in Queensland. During her Year 12 holidays, Deb joined the Droving '88 team and worked as a station hand on Tipperary Station in the Territory, which propelled her into work as a jillaroo on a number of Queensland properties after she left school. Her second job was on a cattle stud where her sister Julie was also working.

'One day at work when I was 18, I was asked to climb a ladder to paint a silo. It felt dangerous because the ladder couldn't be secured. It was just leaning on the silo. While I was up there, another worker was driving a backhoe at the base of the silo and accidentally ran into the ladder. I fell 5 metres to the ground and landed on my head. My sister ran to call the ambulance.'

Deb's spine was fractured from both sides. The broken vertebrae were one millimetre from severing her spinal cord.

'The doctors said I was lucky. They told me I would never ride again and would probably need an operation and a back brace. I was shattered and just cried. My life was cattle and camp drafts – hard, physical work and play. One nurse suggested I would have to find a husband to care for me.'

While she lay on her back for three weeks in hospital, Deb thought about what she wanted to do and where she wanted to be.

'When you are young and fit, you think you are indestructible. I realised after the accident how much I loved the land and refused to contemplate life away from the bush.'

The nurses asked Deb what marks she had achieved at school and what she did.

'When I told them I had finished Year 12 with 900 out of 990 and worked in agriculture, they said, "What a terrible waste of a good brain".'

Deb was incensed. She felt proud to be in agriculture and thought it took more brains to run a farming business than many other ventures. Agriculture was a challenging career and not one for drongos. I'll show them, she thought, and threw herself into recuperating at home, resting and exercising gently to strengthen her back and stomach muscles.

'I tried to stand after a month. It was a big deal when I could go to the kitchen to have a meal instead of eating in bed.'

After six months at home, Deb had improved enough to do light duties on a cattle stud for the next six months. The following year, she found a quiet job that wouldn't inflame her back, as a governess. Two years after fracturing her spine, she decided it was time to test herself as a jillaroo once more. Deb became a senior station hand on Alory Downs, a Territory station between Camooweal and Tennant Creek, and instructed the younger station hands in a stock camp of six led by a head stockman.

'I wanted to prove that I was all right,' she said. 'It was the most taxing physical job – all day in the saddle, and hot, hard work.'

Deb was 20, but the work was also testing for the jillaroos who were younger than her, handling cattle and horses and living out bush with young jackaroos. They had riding accidents and sometimes felt vulnerable or uncomfortable having to listen to the men's sexist jokes. Deb was the only jillaroo who stayed for the nine-month season. She had proved her mental and physical recovery – and her determination. The doctors were amazed that she was riding again and that she didn't need an operation or back brace.

Deb's parents, Russell and Kathy, didn't question her potentially risky return to a stock camp. While Deb was away, they exchanged monthly phone calls. The McLucases had instilled in their children the importance of surrounding themselves with positive people and not blaming circumstances, the government or the weather if something went wrong.

'Some things you can't change,' Deb said, referring to her accident. 'You can only minimise the impact.'

Away from her home community Deb began to realise the value of relationships and good communications. She wanted to share her experiences and skills and decided to study journalism at the University of Southern Queensland in Toowoomba.

'Before uni I hadn't been in an environment where all views were accepted. It encouraged me to challenge opinions and be objective, although I had a natural tendency to sit on the fence and hear all viewpoints before making up my mind.'

In 1996, Deb started work for ABC Radio in Rockhampton. Her first day as a rookie rural reporter was a public holiday. The news was to be relayed from Brisbane.

'I had a nervous start,' Deb recalled, 'and flicked the switch to access the news as I'd been shown, but there was silence. I signalled the breakfast presenter and kept flicking switches, but couldn't find anything. I had to apologise to listeners and introduce a story. I muddled my way through for fifteen minutes. All my friends and family were listening and it was a disaster. I felt so flat. As it turned out, the news team in Brisbane hadn't sent the reel. Rob heard that program and when we met some time later, he told me it wasn't that bad.'

The immediacy and intimacy of radio suited Deb because she could speak to an audience, but have a one-on-one connection to a listener. She loved learning about innovative things that would help her region and trying new things such as an outdoor broadcast from the Rockhampton mall. 'It was about ten minutes walk away from the studio. I arrived fifteen minutes early. The breakfast presenter helping me couldn't get the broadcast lines up, so I rushed back to the studio. Then he called me to say the lines were OK. I had three minutes to sprint back to the mall, but the lines weren't OK.'

Deb did her third sprint in ten minutes, by which time she was late to announce her program; she felt like an Olympic runner being interviewed straight after a race.

'I was so breathless I couldn't talk. I just puffed my way through the first story.'

Deb still meets people who were part of a devoted radio audience. 'So you're the girl who did the *Rural Report,*' they say. 'I used to listen to you every morning.' One such listener was Rob Bauman, who felt he had formed a relationship with Deb McLucas before he ever met her. Rob heard her voice on the ABC every morning and thought Deb was one of the best reporters Rockhampton had ever had.

'I respected her,' Rob said. 'She had the perfect blend of rural expertise and broadcasting skills. I liked the way she asked questions and interviewed people. I had listened to the *Rural Report* for fifteen or twenty years. As I got older, the reporters got younger, but Deb was different. She had spent five years on the land, you could rely on her. Other blokes probably thought that too, but I had to meet her. My chance came at a party, although I was rather drunk. Deb was gorgeous, better in the flesh than on radio.'

'The next day Rob thought of many reasons why he should stay in town,' Deb laughed. 'He said he was smitten before he met me.'

Rob set about redeeming his first impression and two and a half years later proposed. Deb announced their engagement on air. The breakfast presenter who was in another studio thought she was pulling his leg and was speechless for ten seconds. Then the phones and fax machines began to run hot as well-wishers called in. After four years with ABC Radio in Rockhampton, Deb hung up her microphone and moved to Karamarra.

Rob Bauman's ancestors had emigrated from Germany in the 1800s. The first Baumann around Dingo was an earthmoving contractor who cleaned out dams using a horse and scoop. During the Second World War, the family dropped the second 'n' on Bauman to escape being stigmatised as enemy aliens. Rob's parents had owned Karamarra since the late 1960s when they bought it in an auction of Brigalow blocks, a state farm settlement scheme. They managed the farm from another property closer to Dingo until Rob and his younger brother, Sandy, took it over in 1994. Rob lived with his brother on the farm for five years during which time Rob's first marriage ended. Sandy's wife, Elva Cupo, was city born and bred. His family lived in Rockhampton where his wife continued her teaching career and the children attended school while Sandy worked on the farm; he visited them on weekends.

In 2000 the brothers formed a partnership and bought the farm from their parents. The following year they borrowed from the bank against the proceeds of a good wheat crop. The loan enabled them to transform Karamarra from dryland farming and cattle grazing to higher value cropping. Together the men built a network of canals, pumping and pipe equipment to irrigate more than 500 hectares of arable land from a 2600 megalitre dam and the MacKenzie River. The shiny tractors were bought after the development phase to plant and harvest crops, including peanuts, navy beans and wheat.

Even though Deb had grown up on a farm and worked as a jillaroo, it was hard for her to make inroads into the dynamic of two brothers who worked closely together.

'We'd talked before our marriage about what my role might be on the farm,' Deb said. 'Where would I fit in? I wanted to work alongside the men, but Rob was vague. In my family we worked closely together, but at Karamarra I wasn't sure if I was treading on toes and didn't wish to offend anyone or assume anything. Rob and Sandy had a relationship I wasn't part of. I felt like a third wheel and, although after a few years I started to do the books for the business, my role driving tractors and working outside was never acknowledged.'

She was aware that one of the biggest issues determining the success of family farms was how families handled relationships and succession planning. Good businesses often folded through misunderstandings and poor relationships. Deb suggested a family meeting that could be facilitated by a trusted outsider.

'Sandy thought he was being ambushed at first, but it gave us a chance to communicate and cleared the air on issues that were eating away at us. In the end Sandy was so happy that he wanted to have a family meeting every year.'

They all agreed that Deb brought the strengths of her extensive networks, clear thinking and non-judgemental approach to the business. In future, she would do the books and be paid for outdoor farm work.

'We needed to confront potential conflicts within the business and deal with them,' she said. 'At times we have arguments if something is not going well, but we are all friends.'

'Deb brings professionalism to our business in her emails, letters and bookwork,' said Rob. 'She sees all perspectives – negatives and positives – before making up her mind. With her ABC experience she can ask the hard questions, whereas I like to smooth things over and get on with it.'

Deb's life as a reporter had depended on having leads, on knowing who to call for information. Networks were all important and she wanted to replicate that in her new life. She needed something to get her teeth into on Karamarra.

Rapid change was occurring in the rural sector. Agriculture no longer played the dominant role in the Australian economy that it had in the first half of the twentieth century, when wool and other agricultural products accounted for around one-quarter of the nation's output and between 70 and 80 per cent of exports. Farmers in the latter half of the twentieth century had grappled with shifts in consumer demand, changes in government policies, technological advances, emerging environmental concerns and an unrelenting decline in the sector's terms of trade. In response, many people had left the industry; by 2004 farms had become fewer and larger. Two-thirds of production was exported. Exports had become more diverse; there was less reliance on traditional commodities, such as wool, and more on processed products, such as wine, cheese and seafood. Despite agriculture's relative decline in the national economy, it still contributed a substantial $25 billion or 4 per cent of output in 2003–04.

Production and technical issues were important, but Deb could see a much more serious issue for the future – an ageing agricultural workforce.

'There was the likelihood of a void when the current crop of farmers left or died.'

The Australian Productivity Commission's research, *Trends in Agriculture*, published in 2005, showed that in the two decades from 1981 to 2001 the average age of farmers had increased significantly from 44 to 51, and the number of farmers in their twenties had declined by over 60 per cent, trends that were more pronounced in the beef and sheep areas than in dairy and cropping. The report surmised that 'factors contributing to this trend included fewer young people entering farming and low exit rates at traditional retirement age, possibly compounded by the limited interest of young people in taking over the family farm'.

Deb was not convinced by the figures or views about the limited interest of younger people. Based on her ABC experience, she believed there was not a shortage of keen, capable people, but a shortage of opportunities for them to set up a farm or return to rural life. Hence, many would-be farmers were employed elsewhere.

Then, in 2001, Deb attended a grains industry conference.

'A top priority was the future of agriculture. People were concerned about the decline in numbers of young people and how to attract and retain them in the grains industry. At the conference, some of us suggested ideas and plans to address the issue, but nothing came of it.'

Six months later, in 2002, Deb was selected for the national Aglink Youth Leadership program, which is supported by the federal government and the Queensland Rural Training Council.

'We had to have a project.' As Deb sat in the ute waiting for Rob to finish spraying a paddock, she thought about what would really make a difference. Maybe she could do a project to attract youth into the grains industry in central Queensland. 'I was frustrated with industry leaders and their lack of commitment to young people. I wanted action, not words.'

Deb was convinced that a willingness to change and develop, although confronting for many farmers, was vital to success in agriculture.

'I thought young people were more likely to be open to change because the knocks were still ahead of them. We are happy to take on the world when we're young.'

She finally decided to establish the Future Farmers Network (FFN) to expand opportunities for people aged 16 to 35 who wanted a career in agriculture and rural service industries. First, she needed some financial backing.

'I did the rounds of prospective sponsors in established rural organisations, naïvely thinking money would come flowing in for a rural youth network. Everyone was in favour of the idea, but it was hard to get commitment or funding. Rejection left me with a hollow feeling in the pit of my stomach. Perhaps I had jumped the gun and needed to prove myself first. Maybe I should have stuck to my small, original idea in the grains industry,' Deb said somewhat ruefully.

While Deb and I discussed lofty matters, Hannah crawled between us, tugging at microphone cords and practising a wobbly stance against a chair. We had ignored her for too long. What does a girl have to do to get attention around here? She teetered on little feet and took her first steps, then plopped to the floor with a surprised look. Deb and I burst out laughing.

In March 2002, Deb won the $5000 Elaine Brough bursary, awarded each year to an outstanding woman for a project that would benefit rural Queensland.

'It was just enough to get me into trouble,' Deb laughed.

The bursary gave Deb the opportunity to set up focus groups with young people to find out what they needed and how a network could work best. She planned to use the internet, familiar to many young people, as the communication avenue. Word spread fast via e-communication. The bursary helped finance a website and a quarterly newsletter as forums for aspiring and established rural workers to share their success stories and the pitfalls without fear of being judged. The FFN represented a shift from a local rural community to a cyberspace community. This contemporary community could help overcome problems of traditional organisations for which vast distances, changeable weather and busy lives made face-to-face gatherings difficult.

The response was overwhelming. Deb had set a goal of 100 members in the first six months. The FFN reached that target within two months. Operating from her isolated base at Dingo, without any physical presence in other states, Deb saw the network start to blossom far beyond her original concept. Unlike older rural organisations, 96 per cent of FFN members had email addresses, although not everyone was a regular user. Deb found that farmers who worked outdoors had less time and were not as active in discussions as members with desk jobs.

'We had to encourage them to venture into emailing their thoughts and ideas. I was a late convert myself and had never been involved in a discussion group before I started FFN, so I knew how difficult it was.'

Deb was devoting many hours to the FFN as unpaid coordinator, a fact that escaped Rob's notice until just before the launch in August 2002.

'I thought the FFN was a good thing, but didn't realise it was non-profit. I said to Deb, "You do all this for nothing and you've knocked back good paid jobs".'

Only three months after Deb had conceived the idea, the FFN was launched with fanfare in Brisbane by state and federal primary industry ministers, to an enthusiastic audience of 100 young people, industry leaders and media. The slogan 'Young people creating prosperous futures in rural industry' resonated beyond Queensland. Soon Deb formed a management committee to represent members from all states and territories.

What she had tapped into was the positive spirit of young rural Australians who wanted to do something for themselves. Members were sick of the gloom and doom associated with rural Australia and the negative stereotyping. Older members – the 25- to 35-year-olds – had been told by career counsellors that they were wasting their talents and would end up in dead-end jobs if they pursued a rural career. Some members had teachers who thought agriculture was for delinquents and advised the wayward boys to take up the subject.

The FFN was keen to break down the stereotype of drought-ravaged battlers struggling to make ends meet and to provide positive role models, people such as animal nutritionist Cath Marriott, who was awarded Para-Professional of the Year when she studied at Washington State University, and Brett Hills from Mount Gambier in South Australia, who ran Rural Succession Services and helped farming families with succession planning. Annabelle Coppin from Yarrie Station in the East Pilbara of Western Australia had gained first-hand experience of the live export trade by accompanying a boatload of 16,000 head of cattle from Darwin to Jakarta. She was putting her knowledge to use on the family beef property.

Deb met senior students at Rockhampton high schools and told them her own story. Sonya Parker had just completed Year 12 and was interested in agriculture but didn't know where to begin. Deb analysed Sonya's skills and coached her over the phone on how to apply for a job and do a good interview. It was just what the aspiring farmer needed to land her first job with the Australian Agricultural Company in western Queensland.

In less than 10 months the FFN had grown to 200 members. Deb and the management committee were trying to operate a national network on a shoestring. Membership fees had been kept at a level affordable for young people on tight budgets. At the same time, Deb was constantly searching for funding to keep the group afloat. One day she and some FFN members arranged to meet in Dingo with a potential sponsor from Melbourne, who got stuck behind an overturned railway carriage on the road from Rockhampton. The woman rang to cancel the meeting, but Deb persuaded her to meet them in another town.

'I was optimistic because FFN made it to the organisation's shortlist,' Deb said, 'but funding, in the end, didn't transpire because the FFN was deemed not needy enough. It was frustrating and disappointing. There didn't seem to be empathy or a funding avenue to support young rural Australians.'

A survey of members identified career planning and advice as their most important need. Deb well understood this need.

'When I wanted to get into journalism I wrote to *Queensland Country Life* newspaper and asked them what to do. They told me to get a degree or come back when I had some experience. There was no suggestion as to where and how a young girl could gain that experience without actually getting a job in the industry.'

Deb suggested that the FFN's diverse membership share information about jobs and opportunities, and support each other. The federal government provided $4200 to trial such a service via email and phone. Many members rang Deb for career advice, among them the current FFN chair, Joanne Rodney, who wanted to work in education in the cattle industry. Deb put Joanne in touch with a Northern Territory contact and she secured a contract as a project officer with Meat and Livestock Australia in Alice Springs.

What appealed to members of the FFN was its inclusive approach and recognition that agriculture was intrinsically linked to a range of associated industries. It wasn't a government program and had no political or party axe to grind, which nurtured a culture of equality and teamwork.

At the same time Deb was establishing the FFN, she discovered she was pregnant with Hannah. With a baby on the way she and Rob decided to move closer to health services and to family. Sandy was living like a bachelor on the farm while his family were in Rockhampton; he wanted to move and join them.

'In one way we didn't feel isolated because we could connect with people via technology,' Deb said, 'but it was a 230 kilometre round trip for health services in Middlemount where my parents lived and where we played tennis.'

A farm accident brought the issue of isolation to a head, even though Deb kept a medical chest in the house in case of an emergency and there were landing facilities at Karamarra for the Royal Flying Doctor Service or Rescue helicopter.

'Sandy chopped the top off his finger in a pulley at Karamarra and I had to drive him to Middlemount,' Deb said. 'They couldn't help him there so I took him on to Rocky, a 440 k trip.' It was 7 o'clock that evening, nearly twelve hours after the accident, before Sandy had surgery to repair his damaged finger. 'It wasn't a life-threatening situation, but it highlighted that we wouldn't have immediate access to medical help if it was really needed.'

When Rob injured his back he couldn't get to a specialist for three weeks. Hannah was due to have immunisation injections in Middlemount, but a storm damaged the roof of the community health clinic and power failure affected the vaccines. The clinic was closed for six weeks, so Deb had to take her baby on the long haul to Rockhampton.

The opportunity to sell Karamarra arose in 2004. Land values in the MacKenzie Valley had more than doubled since the brothers bought the farm, yet even with compelling reasons for selling, the decision was a big one. The farm remained on the market for six months. Then, in April 2005, Sandy offered his share to Rob and Deb.

'We crunched the numbers and decided we couldn't carry that much debt,' Deb said. 'We decided to lease from Sandy, which enabled him to borrow money and go into his own venture.'

Rob and Deb established a new partnership when they leased Karamarra from the existing partnership of Sandy and Rob. It was Deb's first business venture. Together, they set fresh goals: to profit from and improve the environmental health of the farm. Off-farm income was necessary for their survival so they retained investments in a turf farm and a grain-trading business. Deb was exultant the day their ABN and new trading name, Baumak, came through and the bank approved a loan to buy the farm machinery.

Rob and Deb showed us around the farm that stretches 7 by 10 kilometres across the valley. The vast paddock is fenced around the perimeter. In a continent covered by a thin film of topsoil, this valley is unusual. It has 20 metres of fertile, black silt deposited by the MacKenzie River, which grows sorghum, wheat and chickpeas. Peanuts are also grown on the sandy soils above the floodplain. Flocks of long-legged brolga feed on insects in the sorghum stubble and rose in a beat of grey wings as we passed. Towering above is a centre pivot irrigation system. Three of these multi-wheeled A-frames stretch across the paddock. They creep in a circle with capacity to water over 200 hectares.

'Our goal is to be completely organic,' Rob said as we drove along the irrigation channel to the river. 'We've moved from minimum to zero till in the last five years so we don't disturb the soil. We retain the stubble as mulch instead of burning it.'

He stopped the 4WD. The soil was alive with earthworms and aerating bugs; it smelt sweet and was springy underfoot. Baby Hannah was bursting to crawl around. Deb let her dabble in the soil. Here could be a future farmer in the making.

'We are starting to improve the soil health with biological methods such as the introduction of micro-organisms, which means we don't have to pour on fertilisers,' Deb said. 'These are largely untried on broadacre farms.'

In June 2005, the FFN organised a string of forums across Australia called Future Farmers Week for which it gained funding from the Commonwealth Department of Agriculture, Fisheries and Forestry. At last, a project officer, Bree Robertson, could be employed to share the workload with Deb. From the Atherton Tablelands in Queensland to Launceston in Tasmania, from Alexandria Station in the Northern Territory to Canberra, over 400 young people gathered at fifteen events to contribute to a national Vision Statement. Those who couldn't make it to a forum had a say through teleconferences and email links.

Unfazed by the country being in the worst drought in a century and by perceptions that youth were deserting the bush, participants discussed the future of rural Australia. They homed in on needs for more focus on what markets and consumers wanted rather than what they could produce, for better opportunities and services for young people in rural areas and a need to build respect for rural industries. The Vision Statement, which was sent to ninety stakeholders in organisations across Australia, urged industry and government leaders to mentor young people into positions on boards and for organisations to recognise FFN and build relationships with it. Young people were taking the initiative for long-overdue coordination and cooperation within the rural sector. After the forums, FFN membership grew to 500, 60 per cent of them from Queensland and increasing numbers from other states and territories.

FFN member Oscar Pierce, who worked for the Cattle Council of Australia in 2005, organised the Canberra forum to target industry and services such as banks, as well as government leaders. At the Canberra forum, Federal Minister for Agriculture Warren Truss spoke in support of the FFN. Truss had been president of Rural Youth and understood that young rural people interacted in different ways from their elders. His department set up a Young People in Rural Industries program that offered opportunities for mentoring young leaders, and training programs in leadership, corporate governance and export market development. An interactive national website, Young Australian Rural Network (YARN), was established for sharing information.

Oscar, who had had experience with many state and national agricultural groups, admired the model and strategic thinking behind the FFN.

'Deb McLucas saw a need, found the resources and managed to bring diverse groups of young people together without ruffling the feathers of other farmer groups. The world is changing and farming needs to change. Communication is the key. Many programs and initiatives exist, but often they reinvent the wheel because of a lack of coordination. The FFN didn't set out to be a service provider, but to connect members to existing programs and information. Deb nailed it when she didn't try to displace the old ways of communicating, but added the internet so members could be more aware and involved.'

The FFN is not challenging the politics and established positions of government and industry, but aligning them to work better together. Deb sees this process working through increased corporate membership in the FFN.

'Government primary industry departments and industry groups such as the Grain Growers' Association have joined us,' she explained. 'Since the forums, our feedback is sought on policy such as drought initiatives. It gives young people a say. We encourage organisations to involve youth, to think outside the square and provide opportunities. Awareness of our needs is bringing changed attitudes.'

State farmers' organisations and industry groups are increasingly running their own youth events and training programs. Deb recognised the huge difficulties in overcoming structural barriers to young people entering agriculture. In an environment in which Australia's competitors enjoy average subsidies of 35 per cent in the European Union or 20 per cent in the USA, compared to 5 per cent for Australia according to futurist, Phil Ruthven, it is increasingly difficult for aspiring farmers to get started.

'How can they set up a viable farming business when land costs are so exorbitant?' Deb asked. 'Maybe they can take an alternative approach, such as leasing or share farming instead of buying a piece of dirt. Some take on a highly paid job and save up for a deposit on land. They are innovators who take every opportunity because they have to start from scratch. Others start on smaller blocks and work their way up. Rob and I negotiated with someone outside the family for security with the bank. Through the FFN, members can share stories and connections on structuring a business, training avenues, how to access finance and deal with banks, so they don't take unnecessary risks.'

In January 2006, when Deb learnt that she was expecting another baby, she decided to develop a succession plan to manage her departure from the Future Farmers Network. It had been four and a half years of full-on commitment and the membership had grown to 680; she wanted to encourage others into management but was concerned that if she stepped back the FFN might not have the energy to continue.

'The challenge of leadership is to hand over in a way that is seamless and brings new blood to the organisation.'

Delphine Bentley, a dynamic woman employed by the North Australian Pastoral Company in Brisbane, took over the coordination role from Deb and the challenge of working with young people who were transient and busy forging careers, but who lacked experience. When she left in 2006, Deb felt confident the FFN would continue. It had finally secured major funding of $40,000 from the Federal Department of Agriculture, Fisheries and Forestry, funding that would enable the state and territory directors to meet face-to-face for the first time and to coordinate forums in each location on the question important to agriculture: 'Should I stay or should I go?' The funding also helped update the website, create a members' database and produce communication tools such as the handy *Glovebox Guide* of job and training contacts and services useful to young people. The 'Just for Fun' section directs people to websites for Bachelor and Spinster balls, and to Rural Romeos, should anyone require matchmaking assistance.

Jo Eady, who ran the Aglink Youth Leadership course where Deb first decided to establish the FFN, described Deb as an elder of the organisation. 'She has an incredible heart and has never wavered in her devotion to young people, no matter how busy she has been. Deb knew it wouldn't be easy, but people across Australia wanted to join her and be part of creating the momentum. Now it's an active organisation with volunteers like Deb as key contacts in each state.'

Just one month after Rob and Deb began trading as their own business in 2005 their ideal property came on the market. Deb and Rob, both soil connoisseurs, knew of Bogandilla, and its healthy soil. It was in the heart of cattle country near Middlemount. By reputation, it was one of the best farming blocks in central Queensland and had a history of growing good crops year in, year out.

'We organised to inspect it,' Deb said. 'That was a Monday morning. By 1 o'clock that afternoon we had made an offer.'

After a few days of negotiations, the vendors accepted their offer. Deb and Rob had verbal assurances from their financiers that they could get the money.

'It all seemed too easy,' Deb reflected.

The agent advised them that they would have to sign a contract without a 'subject to finance' clause, which meant they had to be 100 per cent sure of their money.

'That's when the bank started to get difficult and told us they would have an answer tomorrow, or the next day. The agent insisted we sign by the Friday or it would be offered to someone else. We had a good deal and didn't want to lose it in the open market.'

Deb and Rob took a huge risk and signed the contract without official approval on finance from the bank. Rob and Sandy had not sold Karamarra the previous year, so the bank was not confident they now could and refused to provide bridging finance.

'We spent anxious weeks accessing additional security from family and friends to satisfy the bank's requirements,' Deb said. 'It knocked us back a couple of times. Each time we had to regroup and come up with new solutions to their demands.'

The deal went down to the wire.

'At 4.30 on Friday, 30 September 2005, we got the call from our solicitor to say we had officially settled on Bogandilla. What a huge relief.'

To carry two large properties was an enormous commitment, but the couple accepted that Karamarra might not sell. Then, the day after settling on the new property, they had an inspection of Karamarra. Ten days later, Rob and Sandy signed a contract to sell. Within four months, the family's business, geographic and personal circumstances had been upended.

'If you stand still, you get left behind,' Deb observed.

On 28 October 2005, Deb, Rob and Hannah spent their first night in their new abode located in a cattle and coal-rich area on the aptly named Golden Mile Road. The house is a typical wooden Queenslander with a spectacular view of the Peak Range, distinctive conical mountains to the west that stretch for 100 kilometres.

'We are one of only two all-farming properties here. Local people say we are crazy dryland farming, but we haven't looked back. It's like walking on a dry sponge here. You sink in and as you lift your foot, the soil springs up behind you. In our first year we have grown and harvested crops on the 2160 hectares of arable area and had above average yields. The income will make a substantial reduction on our loan, which justifies the risks we took to secure this new venture. We feel in control of our destiny. Every week Rob and I plan and prioritise jobs on a whiteboard. We're organising our own lives instead of responding to demands.'

The property purchase paled into insignificance when Deb found out she was expecting twins.

'Shocked is an understatement,' she laughed. 'If we had been at Karamarra, the family expansion would have been much harder. More frequent trips to the doctor and bouncing over the rough dirt road on a 500 k round trip would have been less than fun.'

Their new home has a bitumen road right to the front door. It is only 30 kilometres to the nearest doctor and hospital and a 420 kilometre round trip to specialist medical care. Laura and Megan Bauman were delivered a minute apart and six weeks early on 7 July 2006 in Mackay hospital. The doctors warned Deb to plan for a four-week stay in the intensive care unit while the babies' lungs developed and they grew strong enough to feed.

'They were just 2220 grams and 2100 grams, a good size for twins at that stage,' Deb said. 'They turned out to be tenacious babies and were only in special care for ten days. We were so proud to drive home with our three beautiful girls. Rob and I can't believe how lucky we are to have a healthy and happy family. It tops off an eventful and productive year for us – in more ways than one!'

The twins look like their sister Hannah – dainty and blonde.

'I get up at four in the morning to either feed the girls or do office work before they wake. Hannah adores the girls, so I can manage three children under the age of two when Rob is outside on the farm.'

It doesn't always work to plan, as Deb emailed me one morning: 'I've fed the girls and am hoping to get an hour in the office before Hannah starts her day. Oops – spoke too soon. Here she comes now.'

'I was better at prioritising when I was at the ABC,' she said. 'I loved my job and regularly did 14 hour days. I was intent on having the latest breaking news story, but was worked into the ground. Now if some things don't get done, they don't get done. What I see as important are our family and exploring an holistic lifestyle. Too many of us are too busy and don't spend enough time with our families and ourselves.'

The access problems have been solved. Rob can go to town to pick up parts and a grocery order at Dysart 30 kilometres away and be home within a couple of hours, compared to most of the day for the trip from Karamarra to Dingo or groceries at Blackwater, a further 50 kilometres.

'I managed to take Hannah to swimming lessons this summer, which would have been impossible at Karamarra,' Deb said. 'My parents are only 40 kilometres away and love to see the girls. To cap it all off we had a fantastic season. Half the farm was sown to sorghum and we harvested wheat and chickpeas in October. We have begun to use brews of mineral-rich compost tea on the sorghum. They ensure that microbes increase and in time we expect the biology in the soil will retard weed growth. We don't have to use residual chemicals, which is a big bonus. The place also has 900 acres of remnant vegetation, home to koalas, possums and birds.'

Deb and Rob believe biological farming is the future for their industry. It is a new way to farm in central Queensland and they have to experiment. There is little science or data available and no manual for implementation.

'It is like creating the ideal vegie patch with compost, mulch, earthworms and nitrogen-fixing plants such as chickpeas, only it's on 2160 hectares instead of a garden bed.'

They learn and read voraciously and rely on their agronomist who has researched and trialled applications with other farmers in the region.

Rob and Deb have envisaged their future in 12 months, five years and then a decade. They constantly review their goals. If all goes according to plan, the family will be off on a holiday to a dream destination before Hannah starts school in 2010 and achieving equity of 80 per cent in their business by 2015. Starting afresh on another farm and having three small daughters doesn't seem to have slowed their stride.

'We have fulfilled many of our dreams with the move,' Deb said. 'We plan to develop Bogandilla into a showcase biological farm, not in the sense of white-painted fences and a fancy house, but to show what is possible if your soil is healthy and alive with earthworms and microbes. We believe the farming methods of the past, particularly the use of chemicals and fertilisers, won't be sustainable in future. We would like to be at the leading edge of biological farming in central Queensland and show you can also be financially viable.'

This couple and other innovators are the new breed of farmer, described by Phil Ruthven in 'Farms of the Future', a *Business Review Weekly* article in August 2005, as 'mostly Generation X people 24 to 44 years of age, who don't want to inherit a family property to be poor all their lives. They see farming and the entire agribusiness chain in a new light. Within a decade or two, expect to see some wealthy farmers again with high incomes, and an overall agribusiness sector that will be ready to take on the world on its own terms.'

In 2002, Deb McLucas set out to have a positive impact on the lives of young people in rural industries and involve them in the FFN.

'Five years later through observation and our anecdotal evidence, we are able to say to rural industries that young people are not leaving the sector in droves and those who do leave are often not pursuing careers elsewhere as their preferred or permanent option. Given the opportunity, they could return.'

The Future Farmers Network didn't collapse when Deb left, but continues to grow and share resources, career and training information, and to be an inspiration to its young members.

The 18-year-old who was told while she lay in hospital with a fractured spine that she would never ride again, and not to waste her good brain on farming, has done more than confound the experts and sceptics. Deb McLucas is showing that agriculture is where she can use all of her intelligence, skills and daring.

'Everyone has a point when they have to decide – will I take the easy or the challenging road? I have chosen the challenging one.'

Postscript

The FFN is continuing to grow and influence young people across the country. More than 400 young people took part in the 'Should I Stay/Should I Go?' forums in 2007 and the findings have been presented to government and industry groups. The main message highlighted the issue of retaining young people in rural industry and that organisations need to be responsive to their needs to ensure they are not discouraged from remaining in the rural sector. However, there is no 'one size fits all' formula.

On the home front, the whole of Bogandilla is planted to wheat, chickpeas and spring sorghum and, with the favourable price outlook, Deb and Rob are quite confident that they will achieve their goal of 80 per cent equity in their business by the end of 2007. This is eight years earlier than they expected.

They have been able to employ a nanny, which has allowed Deb to get out in the paddock with Rob again and to catch up on the bookwork, which was much neglected since Laura and Megan were born. Deb says she is extremely happy with this arrangement – 'although I'm sure Rob is just a little concerned that with a bit more time to myself, there could well be another "project" on the radar for me again soon!'

Deb McLucas and Rob Bauman, with Megan, Hannah and Laura 2006

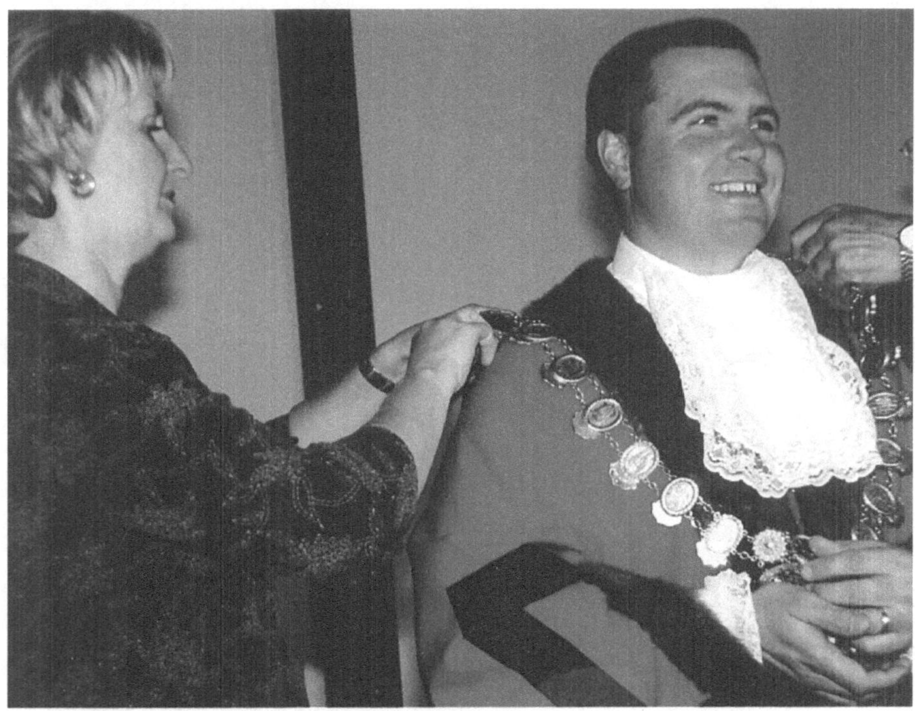

Mayor Steve Perryman being robed up for City Council meeting, Mount Gambier, 2006

12

Fight Fire with Water

Mayor Steve Perryman, Mount Gambier, South Australia

'All please rise for His Worship the Mayor,' the chief executive officer of Mount Gambier City Council solemnly intoned. Steve Perryman entered in full regalia. He wore a bright crimson cloak trimmed in brown fur with a froth of white lace at the neck and a painted Blue Lake medallion on a gold chain. It was hard to reconcile this dignified figure with the cray fisherman of the morning, hard to believe until he took the mickey by welcoming the press gallery: that's me. Steve's mother Cherylynn had told me how she sat in the same gallery for Steve's first council meeting as mayor.

'We were supposed to curtsey, but I cracked up laughing. Here's my baby done up like a Christmas tree. My only advice to him when he became mayor was to think before he spoke because he used to speak quickly. Since then he has matured, is more composed and speaks more slowly.'

In his first council campaign, some people said Steve didn't have enough experience.

'There's no difference between a first-time councillor who is 25 and one who is twice that age,' he pointed out. 'It's the same process of having to learn how things work by being involved. I show that an ordinary person can be well suited to community leadership. I think there is a cultural change. I hear people in the street say, "We're not conservative here. This is a vibrant and progressive place."'

Steve Perryman was proof that young people were politically involved, but their involvement is different to more traditional notions of politics. Steve is an independent thinker who didn't see politics as being synonymous with parties or having to vote along party lines. He is guided by his own conscience.

The Mount Gambier area is rich in resources: lush paddocks dotted with black and white Friesian cattle, neat rows of vineyards, including the renowned Coonawarra area, the green of pine forests and the jagged Limestone Coast where rock lobsters thrive. The region's industries supply 35 per cent of South Australia's agricultural produce. Add to that the tourist magnets – the city's grand historic buildings, the Blue Lake, which mysteriously turns bright sapphire each November, the region's strategic location midway between Adelaide and Melbourne – and Mount Gambier clearly has a lot going for it.

At 3 o'clock that morning, the phone had rung beside my motel bed. 'I'll pick you up in 10,' said an unbelievably bright voice.

I briefly wondered how people begin the day at this hour, but there's no time for navel gazing. First, jump into well-washed clothes borrowed from Steve: blue singlet, T-shirt and sweater, blue woollen beanie, heavy overcoat, thick socks and gumboots – and it is mid-summer. Next, swallow two crumbly ginger tablets left over from a snorkelling expedition long ago and don acupressure wrist bands that assure the wearer they will ease seasickness. Scant ammunition. Last, grab a waterproof bag containing my camera and notebook and then wait on the deserted street wondering what I've forgotten. Just as I'm asking myself why a confirmed landlubber would go cray fishing in the wee hours on a rising sea, Steve Perryman did a U-turn and drove over to the kerb. He flashed an amused glance at my get-up, which came from the same cupboard as his red beanie, blue sweater and white gumboots.

Over the next 36 hours I would see that this nuggetty, boyish-looking fellow was as comfortable in his many hats as he was in his varied garb. After lunch, a tree-planting ceremony called for a sedate suit and tie, which Steve finally discarded for all-in-one blue teddy-bear pjs and furry slippers as he read bedtime stories to his daughters, Baie aged five, Tulle, three, and baby Rori.

But right now we were off to fish for the region's renowned rock lobsters. Port MacDonnell, known as the southern rock lobster capital is 28 kilometres from Mount Gambier. Around the 1880s it was second only to Port Adelaide as the state's busiest port, shipping wheat and wool from the region on clippers to England. Steve's parents, Allan and Cherylynn, live at Port Mac, as it is referred to around here. The Perrymans are sea people and Steve, aged 30, could claim an impeccable fishing heritage. Most cray-fishing boats are father and son businesses, so the expectation that fishermen's sons, and occasionally daughters, would follow their fathers is powerful. But as crays are fished in the warmer months along the Limestone Coast, some men learnt a trade to earn winter income.

'My great-grandfather on Dad's side was a cray fisherman,' Steve told me as we left the well-lit streets of Mount Gambier for the starlit skies of the countryside. 'Most of my uncles and cousins are too. Mum's family also fished. Her grandfather, who always wore a black suit and hat, even on the boat, fished by hand for crays with his five sons. One of his daughters, my grandmother, used to run a fish factory at Carpenter Rocks up the coast from Port Mac. When she died at 48, the family moved to Adelaide and took up prawning. Life would have been a lot different if Nan hadn't died.'

Had she lived, Steve, like many young men around here, might have left high school and started fishing when he turned 15. Steve's first trip to sea, when he was three, was prawning with his father.

'Mum came out too and we spent the night at sea trawling with nets. We kids used to fish and swim from an early age. We were warned of the dangers and learnt to respect the sea. I always bugged Dad to let me go fishing with my grandfather, who was a chain-smoker. The smell of smoke and diesel fumes used to drive me out of the wheelhouse. I would sleep standing wedged behind the wheelhouse and the side of the boat. Those old boats rolled around a lot. I can remember lying on the deck sometimes, wishing I were dead. Even though I was as sick as a dog, as a child I enjoyed being out at sea.'

Steve first worked with his father when he was 14, filling in when the regular deckhand didn't turn up for work. A few years later, he spent several months shark fishing with his father and older brother, Adam, for up to a week in the family's 50 foot Huon pine boat. They would cray fish all summer and in winter fish for shark. It would take three or four hours to pull up the nets. There wasn't much time for sleep between the three shifts in a 24-hour period. The profits didn't reflect all the work. At the end of the week they might only earn $400.

Seawater may have flowed in his veins, but by the time he was a teenager the life of a fisherman no longer enticed Steve.

'I wanted to join the navy and see the world,' he said. 'I went to Grant High School in Mount Gambier because it offered subjects I needed to qualify as a navy officer, but I only knew one boy and the first couple of years were pretty terrible. I didn't have mates then and spent time by myself in the library or computer room.'

He was the only student from Port MacDonnell and was taunted as 'the Port Mac seagull'. These digs made Steve appreciate his Port Mac friends more, but he also recalled that when they finished at school and became fishermen, they dubbed him 'the Professor' because he stayed on until Year 12.

'I didn't enjoy the classroom. If I wasn't away on camp for outdoor education or playing sport, such as cricket or football, I was out taking video footage for media studies.'

As well as being involved in the student representative council, Steve became a peer support for younger students. He believed in seeking opportunities. During his final year he was offered an AFS Exchange student opportunity in Iceland and a place in the Royal Australian Navy. He chose the navy.

'I have one real friend from high school days,' Steve reflected. 'I thought Mount Gambier was a hole, so I enlisted in the navy and spent 18 months training near Melbourne and six months at sea. There were twenty of us submariners who crewed on the HMAS *Kanimbla*. It sailed from the United States home through the Panama Canal. It took twelve hours to get through the canal.'

The new recruits were put in a mess above the boiler room, which made sailing through the tropics even hotter. Steve liked the mateship, the experience at sea and opportunity to travel, but began to see his home from a fresh perspective.

'I hated being in Sydney, walking down the street not knowing anyone,' he recalled. 'What I like about country towns is knowing people, knowing you can go into a shop and recognise someone. I went from thinking that Mount Gambier was a dump and there were far better places to go and better things to do to taking a 180 degree turn and coming back.'

Steve returned home to fish with his father. He met Jaime Childs, a lively, dark-haired girl, through her brother Matt, who was his school friend.

'Jaime and I didn't go out together until I left school,' said Steve. 'She was three years younger. I always thought she was a bit of a hottie. She thought I was all right too, even when I was fat and hairy after I came back from the navy. Her mother predicted she would marry me.'

We reached Port Mac. A full moon split the cobalt sky as it rode across hills of cloud and lit the quiet fishing town. Allan and Adam joined us and loaded styrofoam boxes of tucker from a big shed: bait for the crays, salad rolls for us. The boys told me a dead horse made good bait in the old days, but nowadays it was simpler to buy frozen bream or salmon. As they hooked a dinghy onto the family truck, the talk was about the cold front from the west that would come in over the next six hours. A string of lights guided us along the jetty to the old timber wharf. Allan backed the dinghy into the water and we all piled in. It was a quick trip to the 50 foot family boat, called the *Aquatrice*. She was a graceful craft, long and white. Not so graceful was my heavy-footed clambering up and over the side from the rocking dinghy. A 15 to 20 knot wind stirred up foaming waves along the bow of the *Aquatrice* as Allan navigated through the breakwater.

October 1 is the start of the cray-fishing season in South Australia. After five months off, cashflow is vital. Boats around here fish close to the port early in the season because of the chill in southern waters; by Christmas they are fishing in deeper waters up to 20 nautical miles from port. It was January and we were heading 14 nautical miles west of Port Mac.

Allan was skipper. His sons napped in the cabin as he steered on the hour-long trip to the most distant cray pots. How, in this endless ocean, do they find their own pots? Allan pointed to the day's line-up plotted on the computer using the global positioning system. He explained how he used an echo sounder, which maps the sea floor to find a good bottom for the cray pots. They set up to a half a nautical mile of pots in groups of five, each with three floats. Two white and one red float mark the Perryman cray pots. The echo sounder showed that coral reefs grew on the seabed, pastel-coloured, rather than highly decorative like those in the Great Barrier Reef.

Once at our destination, the skipper manoeuvred the boat so the pot wouldn't snag on the coral as it was winched in. The pots, large, circular wire traps baited with tasty slabs of salmon and fish heads, were dropped onto the seafloor 20 to 55 fathoms (40 to 110 metres) below. The crays crawl along the bottom with their tails flat, grazing on coral and their favourite food – sea urchins. Because they swim backwards they can't see where they are going. They stray into pots, attracted by decaying bait and are jerked to the surface in the pot, hauled overboard and tweaked by their feelers into a plastic crate. After seven years of munching coral, molluscs and small crustaceans, the crays can reach around 9.85 centimetres long, the legal catching size. Any crayfish full of eggs, or smaller than the minimum size, survives to munch another day. The morning's haul includes whole pots of juniors, which the brothers quickly toss back into the sea.

The crays are beautiful, their red shells polished like ancient Chinese ceramics. The spiky head and body, propelled by a flapping tail pleated with overlapping fins, protect a soft underbelly tinged with delicate pinks and purples. Humans savour the tail meat and legs, called spiders, but unfortunately for crays, their underbelly is also a delicacy for predators such as octopuses and leatherjackets.

Adam hoists a healthy octopus from a pot onto the deck. It crawls, humpback fashion, on its eight long tentacles back towards the railing and freedom. Crays are easy prey for the parrot-beaked octopus when they are captive in a pot.

'The octopus injects poison and sucks out the guts from under the soft tail,' said Steve. He caught the culprit and cut off its head. 'A stressed cray may throw off its legs. We put the cray in sick bay, a separate tank with a lot of water circulating, for extra oxygen, but often the flesh turns to mush. We take the octopuses to a Greek friend in Port Mac for pickling.'

Allan steered the boat and pulled levers to wind in the pots while his sons hauled them over the side, exchanged fresh bait for the putrid remainders and sorted the crays, and then decided on the next day's drop, 50 to 100 metres away. In deeper water the tides vary, so the skipper must judge how far to travel forward before tipping off a pot. Pots can get tangled in shipping. One was picked up 40 nautical miles from Port Mac, towed there by a ship.

The brothers are deft and have good sea legs. They didn't grip the handrails or stagger with the swell, as I did. Adam sported a wild mop of gold-tipped hair and Steve favoured a number two buzz cut. To add variety to their work, they swapped jobs every other day. Later I asked Steve how they get on working together.

'It used to be bad,' he told me. 'Adam and I have come to fisticuffs when an argument has snowballed. He's quickly stirred; I'm easier-going. I understand that people are as they are. Only once did I have to show him I was his physical equal. He sprayed me with a hose and threw a punch, so I wrestled him to the deck and pulled his hand behind his back. I'm a calm guy, but when pushed over the line – watch out. I said, "Just because you're my big brother doesn't mean you can shove me about".'

Allan is flexible with the roster. During the season he gives Steve days off to do council work. Allan is not a big talker. There are eighty pots to pull in and tip out – eighty times to say 'Righto', as he steers the boat to the chosen spot. That's about it. I had seen a less taciturn side the previous day when driving with Allan and Cherylynn from Adelaide.

Allan said fishing was all he'd ever done.

'After more than 35 years, I'm getting a liking for it now,' he said. 'You are your own boss and something different happens every day. One night the moonlight was on a dead flat sea. There were dolphins in front of the boat, blue and iridescent in the water. Twenty or thirty cut through the water. The water peeled off them. The boat was going 20 knots, but they effortlessly kept up. Some days there are miles of dolphins on a mission. Other days they hang about the boat.'

Cherylynn told me that Allan was actually allergic to crustaceans: he can never enjoy the fruits of his labour. At the slightest taste of cooked cray or prawns, his airways swell and he can't breathe.

Shadows of other boats materialised as the sky brightened. Fishermen pulled in pots or waved briefly as they cruised by. The sea surged like a huge creature gleaming ice-green in the pure early light, deepening to forest-green fathoms below. The swell left hollows in the water into which the boat swooped, riding up the other side only to slide into another trench. I soon learnt that a dodgy stomach didn't improve in the cabin with its warm close air or when the boat idled at the cray pots, pitching from side to side. When the smell wafted from the thawing bait, it was time to move. I found the best spot on the rails, facing into the fresh wind like a dog sniffing the breeze on the back of a truck. The men turned away and occupied themselves when I went pale-green. The sun peered over the horizon, its blush staining red across the sky. Gales are forecast for the next day.

> *Red sky at night, fishermen's delight*
> *Red sky in the morning, fishermen's warning.*

Mother Nature blessed these cool waters with abundant fish, all manner of sea birds, seahorses, brown fur seals, fairy penguins, huge turtles, dolphins and whales. A white albatross was sighted following a boat, a sign of good luck Steve told me. It used its impressive wingspan to swoop on stray fish tossed overboard. The life of the ocean felt like a different world, carrying on its business oblivious to man.

'At times birds land on the boat,' said Steve. 'They have no fear so you can pick them up. When we had the old boat and the engine was quieter, we were pulling up a pot and about 50 yards off saw a colossal whale. We thought it was a blue whale by the sheer size of her. She dwarfed our 50 foot boat. Then she was 10 to 15 yards off. By the third pot she was just a few yards away. She put her huge eye out of the water for 10 or 15 seconds and slipped underwater again. We pulled the next pot and up she came with her baby which was only 20 feet long. It was a totally exhilarating experience.'

The boys left the eightieth and last pot to me. After a few tries, I managed to hook the floats and winch the pot up the side of the boat. Then it was time to lift out a big cray that was trying just as hard to grab me. I reached for its tail too close to the grasping pincers, instead of behind the head.

'No, not like that,' Steve yelled as I quickly dropped it.

I was just congratulating myself on finishing the job when the boat lurched over a wave and I nosedived towards the cray tank and landed on the only metal sheet in sight. It wasn't much use groaning; the crays had their own worries. It was a lucky day though: in this season the proportion of bigger fish has been between 3 and 8 per cent of the catch; today it was 25 per cent. One whopper weighed 2.85 kilograms. It could fetch $114.

Clean, Green is an industry program developed to ensure sustainability and high quality for this valuable export. At Port Mac these crays are emptied into saltwater tanks where they stay for two or three days to purge the contents of their stomachs. They are then chilled into a coma to be flown in foam boxes packed with icepacks to China and Japan. In the right conditions, they can live up to 56 hours. Sixty boats generate $40 million per annum from this port. The town's population of 800 is mostly fishing families – fishermen as well as mechanics, electricians, truckies and fish factory employees. The industry is traditionally a male culture. No women work the boats, but they fill other important roles in the factory and as business managers, bookkeepers and buyers.

After stocks were over-fished in the 1960s and 1970s, the cray fishing industry brought in a reduction of pots, licence buyback and quota management to ensure sustainability. Stocks rose again. In the late 1990s prices were generally good and remained so until the end of the 2003 season when the severe acute respiratory syndrome or SARS virus hit and Asians stopped eating crayfish at restaurants. Prices dived from $38 per kilo to $30.50. Like other primary industries that depend on exports, cray fishing suffers from fluctuating supply and demand, variable weather and being price takers at the end of the market chain. In the 2006 season, prices over $35 per kilo are good, under $30 unviable.

'Our quota per pot goes on licence, 14 tonnes per season,' Steve explained. 'We have to get our quota by the end of May, so we try to catch 60 per cent by Christmas, although the worst weather is from October to December. Then we can take the foot off the throttle a bit. You need forty pots to fish; if you have less, you can share-fish. The most fish we've caught in a day is 280 kilos. Further west where there are fewer boats, they can catch 500 to 600 kilos a day. While the business can gross $500,000 in seven months, it's a big investment. It's mostly family businesses because to start fishing you need around $2 million to buy a boat, the equipment and quota for forty pots, which is around $40,000 per pot. You require a large deposit or security for the banks and as licences are renewable annually, it's a high risk for them to lend $2 million.'

The Australian industry exports around 4000 tonnes of the prized rock lobster annually, 90 per cent of the harvest going to Asia. This is valued at almost $200 million and injects $0.5 billion into regional economies annually.

Steve said the industry acknowledged that it needed better marketing of Southern Rock Lobster.

'Exporters need to pack the fish better so that they can send it longer distances to the US and European markets. Then, up to 30 per cent of the catch could go elsewhere and provide competition to the Chinese market. It can be fickle because the Chinese control the market,' he said. 'South Australia, Victoria and Tasmania together only comprise 3 per cent of the world supply of crays. It's a niche market.'

In 2006, a delegation of fishermen and exporters went with an Austrade representative to a seafood expo in Germany and much effort has gone into building markets particularly in the United States.

'Tasmanian, Victorian and South Australian industry leaders are working to provide year-round supply to the premium restaurant trade. Cooperation is needed between the states because fisheries in different states vary in their opening and closing seasons. Clients in these top markets demand that the product be available on their menu permanently and don't take kindly to putting lobster on the menu only to have to remove it because they can't source the ingredients. Trial consignments were sent to a few of these high-end restaurants free of charge for chefs to experiment. They judged Southern Rock lobster as at least equivalent, if not better in texture and taste than what they normally used.'

In a year of rough weather and inactive crays, the Perrymans met their 2006 quota on the last day of May.

Back home in Mount Gambier at 11.30, Steve was besieged by Baie and Tulle. Jaime hitched baby Rori on her hip and greeted him more sedately. In green slacks and a white shirt, she looked immaculate, as did the older girls in their matching red summer outfits and hair neatly braided down their backs. I learnt that this wasn't just a special occasion image; it was normal to see them smartly dressed. Steve looked a bit whacked, but rallied to hear the latest from his excited daughters. He's a good sport and let Baie and Tulle make up his stubbly face: they painstakingly applied fetching red lipstick and blue eye shadow and curled his eyelashes. Gales of giggles greeted the results. At lunchtime Steve whipped up a salad of lobster, fresh from the sea, blended with a smooth, creamy dressing and served in the half shells. Lightly boiled in salty water then dunked in icy water, it tasted sublime – a salty, yet sweet crunch to the white meat.

On my visit early in 2006, Jaime was home schooling Baie; Tulle joined in. There are home schooling organisations all over Australia and the Perrymans mix with forty families in their region who home school. At the Perrymans', the kitchen is the schoolroom. Jaime believed that home is the best place to train a young child.

'If the child is good at something, then you can focus on that strength. At high school I thought, Do I really have to know woodwork? School hindered development of my confidence. I never put up my hand because I didn't want to be seen as too smart, or wrong.'

The girls were bright sparks, full of questions and quick to put on a dance show. Baie sat at her well-organised desk, spelling and colouring in maths exercises. Meanwhile, Tulle turned on the computer. She played counting games with total confidence while she gave her father a running commentary. Rori crawled around the floor, itching to join in.

'Neither of us enjoyed school,' Steve explained. 'One bad teacher can crush your self-esteem. We think it is putting your children, the most precious part of your life, in the hands of a stranger for seven hours a day five days a week.'

Jaime said, 'I doubted our decision for a while. We had tried kindergarten for Baie, but found it more hassle than it was worth. I would catch myself yelling, "Hurry up, we'll be late". It's more enjoyable to be home. We started when Baie was three. She learnt simple motor skills. Steve's mother, who works at St Martin's Lutheran College, helped us.'

By the middle of 2006, the situation had changed; Baie started school at St Martin's because her friends also began school.

'She is enjoying the structured program,' said Steve, 'and Jaime tops it up at home. Home schooling has put her ahead. She is ready for Year 1 instead of a year in Reception.'

Jaime's ability to turn her hand to whatever was needed began young. Before she and Steve had children, Jaime worked at three jobs: as a receptionist during the day and two waitressing jobs at night. She bought her own home with a loan by the age of 20. Her overriding goal in life is to be a good parent and nurture the girls' potential.

'I find it hard to let go of our children, but Baie is really happy at school. Tulle and Rori will also go to school.'

Making gourmet lobster salad and looking good in eye shadow are not Steve's only claims to fame. After leaving the navy, he was heavily involved in the South East Regional Youth Council, funded by the South East Local Government Association. The youth council was a leader in raising the profile of young people in the region, advocating to the state government and running an annual Youth Week of creative activities. In 1999, the South East Local Government Association withdrew funding.

At this time, Steve was 24 and keen to establish a youth council in Mount Gambier, so in the May 2000 local government elections, he stood for Mount

Gambier City Council to offer younger voters a direct voice to council. He believed a diversity of opinions would lead to better quality decisions on behalf of the wider community and promised to consult local and regional groups, business and particularly youth. Four candidates nominated for three positions.

'I have a philosophy that you only disappoint yourself if you don't try,' Steve said. 'I thought I might sneak into the third spot, but I got the most votes.'

He became the youngest person ever elected to the city council, catapulted there by 2302 primary votes. A change to postal voting brought many citizens to the ballot box in a 45 per cent return rate, the largest recorded in the council's history. Perhaps Steve had something to prove to himself.

'From my high school days of being isolated, I was determined to show what I could achieve in my life. I was no seagull.'

Steve was an independent who didn't like to be told what to say or do. From his early days on council, he listened to all sides and made up his own mind, often voting as a minority on contentious issues such as the deregulation of shopping hours in the city and the location of a skateboard park.

The following year, 2001, Steve attended a meeting of Rural Australians for Refugees (RAR), who were seeking to make Mount Gambier a refugee-friendly town. Against the advice of those who knew he planned to run for mayor in the future, he became involved.

'I feel passionately about the unfair way that people are detained, especially the children,' he said. 'Initially, RAR members thought we would be providing for one or two families. At short notice, we were asked to help a group of Afghan refugees on temporary protection visas who were to work at the Mt Schank abattoir. They had to bunk on the floor at the old jail; only two spoke some English. I packed their lunch that first day – probably the wrong food, but they accepted it – and helped them into rental housing and English classes at TAFE. Jaime, who was not in favour of asylum seekers, met these guys who had spent up to two years in Curtin and Woomera detention centres and heard their terrible stories. Her attitude softened as she learnt their backgrounds and how they had to leave their families behind in camps. They had qualifications at home that were not recognised here, so they took whatever jobs they could get. I was disappointed when the abattoir closed six months later and the guys moved on.'

Steve continues to support RAR and an initiative by a local farming family to bring Zimbabweans who fled the Mugabe regime to Mount Gambier.

In 2002 the mayor, who had held office for 19 years, died. Steve said to Jaime that he wanted to stand for mayor. The possibility of an out-of-term mayoral election just six months before the normal South Australian local government elections stirred strong emotions. In standing, the three mayoral hopefuls, including the acting mayor, were taking a considerable risk because the two who lost the election would have to forfeit their seats on council. Some people thought a mid-term election was a complete waste of council funds and that the acting mayor should be allowed to stay in the position. The acting mayor was quoted as saying, 'I think we are being inundated with people who should be the last people to stand', and instructed the other two contenders, including Steve Perryman, 'If you have aspirations of being mayor, leave it until after the general election'. Other people took the view that this was high-handed.

'I'm an all-or-nothing bloke,' said Steve. 'It was a bid worth making. I thought it was an opportunity for a new era in Mount Gambier. Sometimes people think it is their God-given right to be in office. I learnt at school and in the navy not to put yourself above anyone else. I can't stand it when people consider they are better than others. Jaime and I try to respect everyone.'

Steve and Jaime and their support team took a personal approach to campaigning – door-knocking, delivering flyers and talking to people about their concerns. Steve's platform was 'Vision and Progress'. Many citizens endorsed 'Steve for Mayor' publicly through the newspaper and embraced an opportunity for change, rather than a steady as she goes approach. Just before the election, the South Australian parliament changed the Local Government Act so that councillors who lost didn't have to forfeit their seats. Then, in December 2002, the postal ballot delivered Steve an early Christmas present. At the age of 27, he romped it in as the city's youngest mayor (and the youngest mayor in South Australian local government history), 1000 votes ahead of the acting mayor.

'I wasn't the youngest mayor in Australia, as was widely reported, but I was married to the youngest lady mayoress,' he claimed with a grin. 'I realised you didn't have to be extraordinary, just committed. We are ordinary people with a mortgage, jobs and children.'

Steve was immediately thrown into an issue that had been brewing for a while, the location of a skateboard park for young people. Neighbouring Grant District Council surrounded the city in a doughnut shape. The city council's favoured proposal was for the park to be on land administered by Grant District Council. The proposal had pitted the two councils against each other. Court action was pending and the Skateboard Working Group, made up of community members, was frustrated by delays on a decision and felt that their views went unheard. As a councillor, Steve had supported a minority proposal opposing the council majority. As the new mayor he found himself on the opposite side having to represent the resolutions of his council, which put him in the neighbouring council's firing line. He chose the path of diplomacy and tried to bring the sides together to resolve the issue.

'As mayor my personal view had to be put aside. I believe in listening and negotiating. Fight fire with water, I say.'

In the end two skate parks were built on either side of town, one on City of Mount Gambier–owned land, the other in Grant District Council area. A state grant was split between the projects; an additional Mount Gambier City Council contribution covered the extra expense of the second park.

'It took a fair bit of work for those of us who supported this proposal,' Steve said. 'Some councillors did not want a skate park at all while others thought one skate park was enough and building two was a waste of money. In the end it got up – you only need six votes to win. Both parks are popular and remain well used.'

Within six months of the previous election, elections were called in 2003 and Steve stood for mayor again. He urged voters to 'Stick with Steve'. He had set out to prove that he was capable of doing the mayor's job and to dispel the notion that a South Australian mayor had to be an elderly retired man in a comfortable financial situation. He wanted to motivate other young people to have a go. By the 2003 elections there were 19-, 25- and 30-year-olds nominating.

Steve cemented the mayoral position with a resounding win of 7372 votes over the other candidate's 1288. There were seven new councillors and no time to rest on any laurels.

'Council couldn't offer ground for industrial development because the city is hemmed in by Grant District Council,' said Steve. 'We wanted to have room to breathe. Mount Gambier Council sought boundary reform by resolving to move the city limits back two kilometres so it could plan for fifty to 100 years.'

It became a familiar tussle: a city wanting to expand, surrounded by a rural council keen to keep its land and favourable position bounding the urban area.

'Out of absolute frustration with lack of boundary reform our council passed a motion for amalgamation with Grant District Council,' Steve said. 'It was a unanimous vote. Although I don't vote as mayor, it was seen as a bold move on my part. Grant District Council saw it as a hostile takeover. They immediately ran a poll of their residents, which showed only 6 per cent of respondents in favour of a merger. Grant bashed us and we got bashed in the media. It was a difficult time for me as spokesperson for Mount Gambier City Council.'

The vehement reaction from Grant District Council particularly shocked the new members of Mount Gambier City Council.

'It knocked the wind out of us all for a while,' said Steve. 'In some ways it made us closer as we had to share public criticism. I learnt that if people get upset then you don't take it personally, but realise that comes with the territory. I don't try to be all things to all people now. If you're trying not to step on toes, then you're not doing your job properly. The priority has to be making decisions for the right reasons.'

Amalgamation is on the backburner, but Steve is convinced that merging of the two councils would be for the good of the greater number of people.

'In local government, you have to be patient because things happen so slowly.'

Despite early challenges, the highlights of public life more than balanced out the low points.

'Councillors are champions for different causes,' Steve said. 'I champion youth. In 2004 council employed a community services manager with a youth focus. She was able to attract funding for the local Youth Advisory Committee.'

This committee of sixty members has become a model for other areas. It takes on projects such as Youth Week and training young leaders. The Youth Advisory Committee secured an $80,000 grant to make a film on youth issues. Some members have been selected for the South Australian and national Youth Parliaments, where they can gain insight into politics and have a say to government.

'The most satisfying part about public life is recognition and genuine compliments for even the smallest things, such as a playground in which council has recently invested,' Steve said. 'We're proud of our city. In 2005, Mount Gambier won the national Tidy Towns award for the second time and has won the state award many times. It's not only about tidiness, but many fields of endeavour, such as community spirit, innovation and youth involvement. In 2004 we celebrated Mount Gambier's fiftieth anniversary of proclamation as a city and organised events that involved the whole community, not just the usual suspects. Here were politicians, mayors of the region and the like – and a diversity of people of different ages and backgrounds.'

Steve and Jaime demonstrate teamwork and the personal touch in their community, sometimes in a way more akin to their grandparents' generation. They respond to invitations to speak or open events with handwritten letters of thanks. Each year before Christmas, they host a free lunch for older and less fortunate community members. Father Christmas arrives with presents and the Perrymans bake cookies in Christmas shapes and box them as gifts.

'Last year we were up until midnight baking,' Steve said. 'We heard one person say, "I never thought I'd get a present from the mayor and lady mayoress". Another older lady, whose husband had recently died, was thrilled to be invited. "Otherwise I would have been alone for Christmas," she said.'

In April 2004, Jaime started the Mayoress' Family Fun Day. It came about after she had been to the local show and did the sums on what it would cost a family with two children for the day.

'It was around $180,' she said. 'I decided to do a free family day so there was equality for kids whether they came from the richest or poorest families. People who don't have money also want to do the best by their kids.'

She organised the day with a small, keen committee and found sponsorship. It was a day of games, food and camaraderie. That first year 10,000 people came along. In 2006 the committee raised $26,000 and another $80,000 of in-kind support for food, rides, prizes and the time put in by 100 volunteers.

'The sponsorship helps us provide food and drink at cost. In 2006, we promoted healthy living with nutritious food, energetic activities and prizes such as pushbikes, and golf, swimming or dance lessons. Our local talent sings and dances during the day. It goes down well.'

Jaime's lifestyle has altered dramatically since Steve joined council, not the least change being that she has had to adjust to being in the public eye. In the first year she struggled with the pressure and any disapproval of Steve as mayor; she cried at criticism. Steve took criticism calmly and would explain to her that it was not his or Jaime's problem, but the critic's. His ability to take stresses and pressures in his stride and remain himself in a position that can attract conflict is Steve's strength.

Jaime told how, when Steve was first elected, she pulled into the mayor's parking space at the council car park. Fred the gardener came up to her and said, 'Miss, you can't park in there.' Jaime tentatively explained who she was. He hastily apologised and over the years they became friends.

Steve and Jaime complement each other. Where he finds chitchat at functions a strain, Jaime is extroverted and enjoys circulating. After three years in the role of mayoress, she has become poised and capable. In this frenetic life, these former teenage sweethearts still talk through decisions, and cook, clean and rear their children together.

The day after my excursion on the boat with Steve, the wind came up and fishing was off. I asked Steve how he juggled his demanding life. Sleep seemed absent from the schedule.

'I pack a bag of council stuff and go to the office after we check out the sea at Port Mac, rather than returning home when the weather is too rough to go fishing,' said Steve. 'Some senior staff thought it was a bit dodgy in the early days. They'd say, "Who's that coming out of the mayor's office in white gumboots? Oh, it's the mayor." I'm tired for the six months until the cray season finishes. At times I nod off in meetings.'

Steve's family is involved in council activities whenever possible. When Steve hosts an event during the day, he brings his daughters. At meetings, he keeps toys at the office for the girls or they play computer games.

'People have got used to it,' he said. 'They knew I had a family when I was elected. Jaime came to a meeting not long after I became mayor and asked, "What do I do if Rori needs to be breastfed?" I said, "Just feed her under her blanket". Many people compliment us that we don't hide our kids.'

Mondays are family or rest time. It's the last-minute invitations that prove difficult – particularly 3 o'clock, the hour that Steve describes as 'neither your ear nor your arsehole' – after he has been fishing all morning and is snatching family time. But because it's seasonal, fishing fits in well with council work and family life.

'I choose to do the mayoral job,' said Steve, 'but the mayoral allowance puts South Australia among the lowest paid elected members in Australia. We are paid $29,500, up from $22,000 in 2003, and taxed at 50 per cent. No matter how big the council population, we still do the same duties. Mayors put in a tremendous amount of time and our families and businesses make sacrifices. I couldn't be in a public role without the support of my family. Jaime sacrifices the most.'

The January 2006 council meeting aired spirited and long-winded discussions. As chair, the mayor gave each councillor a chance to speak and carefully checked motions. Steve has a voice in debates through two subcommittees, which submit recommendations to full council.

His leadership favours participation, not autocratic control. He tries to build teamwork among councillors, staff and within the community. When people ask Steve, 'How do you get to be mayor when you're so young?' he says, 'Don't be afraid to succeed or fail. It's the same thing really.'

'If you don't reach your stated goal it's by not trying in the first place. I was young when elected mayor and people expected I might do something radical, but now they respect that I can do the job well – I hope. I think and speak broadly so my language isn't confusing. I'm never scared to ask questions. I don't have a good memory and don't know everything, so I take advice and criticism. In the end it's about building relationships.'

Steve put his hand up to chair the regional group of seven other mayors who make up the South East Local Government Association. It's a challenging role that led to him being a delegate and later elected as vice-president of the South Australia Local Government Association, which comprises sixty-eight councils. He was also appointed by the state government to chair the South Australia Marine Advisory Committee. This highly political position will work towards preserving unique South Australian ecosystems and establishing nineteen marine parks by 2010. Steve wonders how the professional fishermen will view the ambitious proposals for marine park expansion, which could affect access to fishing grounds along the coast for recreational and commercial interests.

One might assume that Steve Perryman, as he took on leadership positions at regional and state levels, was an ambitious person, but what he sought was to represent a wider range of people. The next South Australian local government elections were to be in November 2006 and Steve intended to stand.

'I'll run for mayor again so I can, hopefully, see out two terms. That would be eight and a half years in a public role. Then, who knows? People ask if I will go on with politics.' Like a true politician he answers, 'We'll make those decisions when the time comes.'

When next we spoke in October 2006, Jaime told me the election campaign was in full swing. Steve and one other contender were to fight it out for mayor. Again, it's an all-or-nothing battle. How will Steve go this time?

'He's pretty confident,' Jaime said, 'but I still stress for him. Negative remarks tear me apart. When I suggest we do something extra for the campaign, Steve says, "Jaime, there are only so many hours in a day".'

Six older, long-serving councillors were to retire, so only four of the ten current councillors were standing for re-election.

'The kids want to help this time,' said Jaime. 'Our car has the "Stick with Steve" slogan painted on the side in fluorescent green. I said, "Do I have to drive this car to school? Everyone will laugh at me." Steve just laughed. "Honey, it's OK". Baie and her friends are doing posters that say "Stick with Steve – like glue". We do things that don't cost much. People ring and ask to have signs displayed in their cars. We deliver 10,000 flyers around the city. People offer to help, which takes the pressure off. Steve has started fishing and still does mayoral duties. The fishing season began with a bang – $46 a kilo for crays.'

After three years of depressed international prices, the cray-fishing season ended as the best on record with an average of $40 per kilo compared to the previous year at $35 per kilo.

The 2006 Mount Gambier Mayoral elections were announced on 11 November: Steve Perryman received 86.3 per cent of the vote, a 2.3 per cent increase on the last local government election in May 2003. With the high turnover of councillors in the last two elections, Steve is now the only councillor remaining from the 2000 elections.

'I am now the old man of council!' said this 30-year-old mayor.

By October 2007 Steve can say that Mount Gambier City Council and Grant District Council have come together to negotiate the Greater Mount Gambier Master Plan to guide growth and development for the next twenty years and beyond. 'A milestone,' to use his words.

Steve believes there is a time to lead and a time to be led.

'People think because I'm the mayor I must be the boss on the *Aquatrice*, but I'm just the boy on the boat. Dad's the boss there.'

As I took my leave, I asked Steve about future plans and dreams.

'We're building a house and plan to be in it by Christmas 2007,' he said. 'I could stay fishing, but I could live without it. I might go to uni or run a business. It's open. Above all, I seek contentment. I want to stay married. The passion's still there, isn't it, Jaime?' He grinned at his wife, who ignored him. 'The treasured moments are with the kids. I could be the head of the United Nations, but if I lost my family in getting there I would be the emptiest man on the planet.'

Jaime Perryman with daughters Tulle, Baie and baby Rori, Mount Gambier, 2006

1 School captain Ellie Middleton with New South Wales Governor Marie Bashir, 2006. 2 Beck Byrne running the Houston Marathon, Texas, 2006. 3 Heath Francis and his Commonwealth Games Gold Medal, Melbourne, 2006. 4 Emily Murphy as Fantine in *Les Miserables*, Sydney, New South Wales, 2006 5 Mishares — Hebah, Hussein, Yasmin, Yusuf, Hajer and Mohammed — Shepparton, 2006. 6 Trevor Menmuir (*left*), coach of the Kimberley Spirits under 19s Aussie Rules team, winners Western Australia, 2004.

PART 3
Growing Resilience

Heath Francis taking off in the Men's 4 x 100 metres relay Athens Paralympics, 2004

13

Going for Gold

Heath Francis, Booral, New South Wales

It was a warm, still evening, perfect for breaking the world record in the 200 metres for Elite Athletes with a Disability – perfect, that is, if the competitors have a good start. At the 18th Commonwealth Games in Melbourne, on 23 March 2006, the first night of athletics was packed out. This race for arm amputees kicked off an exciting era in which Paralympic events are integrated into able-bodied games. The fastest qualifier was a sandy-haired Australian, Heath Francis, who was wearing his patriotic gold shoes. At 24 years of age, Heath has a streamlined body and sculpted sprinter's legs.

Everyone except the Indian in lane 8 made crouch starts. The starter raised the gun. The lane 8 runner wavered over the starting line, triggering the other seven men to bolt from their boxes. From lane 4, Heath raced down the track. Once, twice the gun blasted. A false start. Lane 8 was warned. They jogged back for another start. Lane 8 teetered over the line; again the others raced, again two blasts. At the Melbourne Cricket Ground, there is a collective groan from

85,000 spectators. The runners, now as toey as racehorses, returned. The race starter called, 'Ready, set …' Lane 8 wobbled, prompting an unusual appeal from the starter to the multitude: 'Quiet please, these men are nervous.'

At last, it looked like they were off – but no, a third bad start silenced the crowd. I held my breath for the fourth start and marvelled at how runners with only one arm, and how a powerful-looking Nigerian who has no arms, can run at speeds only seconds behind the best able-bodied men in the world.

Heath later told me that the starter called the first start a false start and the subsequent ones 'unsteadiness'.

'Otherwise the Indian would have been disqualified. This is unusual. I think the starter felt sorry for him and thought the crowd might boo him for disqualifying the wobbly Indian. It is a shame because we are athletes first and foremost.'

I met Margaret Francis, Heath's gently spoken, dark-haired mother, at a rural women's dinner in 2003. Margaret told me about the trials and triumphs of her younger son just at the time I was deciding to write a book about inspiring, young, rural Australians. Heath Francis sounded an ideal subject.

Six months after the dinner I met Heath in Canberra at the Australian Institute of Sport (AIS), our national incubator for great athletes such as Cathy Freeman, Michael Klim and Kerry Saxby. Here, a brick-red track striped with white lanes encircles an immaculate green lawn. Giant lights glinted on stalks above the track. The sight of these muscular men and women performing the rituals of disciplined training was intriguing. Some jogged, then burst into flight like startled cheetahs. Others ran around the track in dizzying circles, as if on a pivot arm. To one side of the track, a few athletes hopped, stepped and jumped into a sandpit, while beside them long-legged hurdlers skimmed low over bars. Behind, on the grandstand, another group warmed up – trotting up steps, extending legs along a rail or stretching prone on the concrete paths. From across the track, Heath ambled towards me. He grinned as he extended his left hand, dispelling my anxiety about how one greets a person with one arm. As we wove our way through athletes to the grandstand, Heath pointed out his training mates, two young men who are also arm amputees.

We adjourned to a quiet spot in the AIS café where his mother soon joined us. It was her first visit to the AIS. Heath hugged Margaret and took our drink orders. He stuck to water while we topped up our caffeine levels. Looking down from the walls were huge images of Australian athletes in action – a photographic honour roll of the AIS. Ordinary mortals pale into insignificance before these icons of inspiration, fitness and strength. Each one has their story of persistence and endurance to reach that point, just as Heath does.

Margaret and Kevin, Heath's father, married in 1973 after they had studied together at Hawkesbury Agricultural College. Margaret transferred to Tocal Agricultural College in the Hunter Valley and became its first woman graduate. Kevin's parents lived nearby on a farm where Margaret was able to stay while she studied. Kevin managed a large farm at Booral on the lower north coast of New South Wales, a rundown dairy farm with few fences, a handful of beef cattle and a small piggery. After Margaret's graduation, they managed the farm together and built up a colossal venture of 120 beef cattle, 90,000 broiler chooks, a stud of forty horses and a 100-sow piggery. Work was twenty-four hours, seven days a week over the following nine years. In that time, they had one holiday. As well as being a good business manager and farmer, Kevin, a big-hearted man, was quick to help others and a natural leader in the small, isolated community.

In 1980 their first child, Bryn, was born. When he was a year old, he contracted German measles, or rubella. Margaret was immediately tested for pregnancy and for rubella. Although she had been vaccinated against the virus, the blood test showed she had low immunity. Then, confirmation of her pregnancy came.

'We were happy, but worried about the next rubella test results. Kevin was so excited about being a father again, he couldn't help telling people,' Margaret said.

Five days later Kevin was carting a truckful of oats and had to roll start the vehicle. He parked across the slope of the hill with the handbrake on and the engine running while he stepped down to talk to a workman. The truck started to move, turning under the heavy load. As Kevin jumped onto a footrest above the wheel, his foot slipped. He fell under the wheels.

'I tried to resuscitate him,' said Margaret, 'but he had died instantly. Police, ambulance and friends arrived quickly. I went around our kitchen wiping benches, making tea for them. I couldn't keep still. He was only 30. I was 27 and suddenly a widow and a single mum. It was traumatic. A sea of people called for weeks, not wanting to leave me alone.'

The day after Kevin was killed Margaret was told that her results were inconclusive. She didn't have rubella, but it didn't mean the embryo hadn't been infected. Margaret knew that exposure to the rubella virus early in pregnancy could cause deafness, blindness and physical defects in the fetus. Because the virus could bypass her and attack the fetus, her baby had a one in 3000 chance of having a birth deformity. Health professionals advised her that one in nine babies were born with a problem of some sort, so Margaret decided to keep the growing embryo.

'From the moment Heath was conceived I didn't know whether he would be a normal healthy baby, but the decision was easy. How could I cope with losing the baby as well as having lost Kevin?'

Margaret was now the breadwinner and managing the farm. She was so busy juggling the demands of a 13-month-old son, making decisions and doing the farm work that Kevin would have done, she didn't have time to grieve.

Eight months later, Heath was born, ten days overdue. He hadn't contracted rubella *in utero* and was born without disabilities. He was an alert, blue-eyed baby, described by Margaret as 'an optimist from Day 1'.

'Workers' Compensation paid us for the loss of Kevin,' she said. 'Their reckoning of the price of a life in 1981 was $40,000, $20,000 of which was for the boys. It was held by WorkCover until they turned 18. I also received a monthly allowance for the boys until they left school starting at $40 per week and consumer price indexed. It was not enough to live on, so I had to work. I often wonder how I managed, but I did. Maybe it was because I loved being a parent, and had helpful friends and family. I also enjoyed running the farm.'

Heath took up the story. He enjoyed his childhood, he said, but there were dangers on the farm. At 5 o'clock on 3 December, 1988 the accident to change his life happened.

'One day my brother and I went yabbying in the creek. I was seven and Bryn was eight. The most exciting activity on the farm that day was the meat mincing in the farm butchery. We came back to watch. We were allowed in the room when they were cutting up meat if we stood back, but Mum would not let us in there during the band-sawing or mincing. That day, Bryn and I went in, despite knowing we shouldn't have been there. We both knew that Mum didn't want us in there, but she was busy packing meat with another woman and had her back to us. I dropped the meat in the mincer. The next thing my hand went down as well. I remember my hand going down. It happened so quickly. Then I remember people rushing around turning off the power. I was stuck in the mincer for the best part of an hour, maybe an hour and a half.'

'Four hours all up,' his mother said.

'Mum and Bryn were pretty frantic. It wasn't a great thing to have happened.'

The meat had been minced once through the machine. When Heath pushed the soft meat with his fingers it created a vaccum effect. Instantly, it sucked Heath's small arm down. An adult hand wouldn't fit, and nowadays a utensil is used to push the meat down, but then, Heath's hand was wrapped around the auger at the bottom of the mincer. All the tendons, blood vessels, nerves and bones in his hand were damaged and the bones in his forearm broken. Heath clearly remembers the mincer having to be cut from its moorings with his arm from the shoulder down still in it.

'I was flown attached to the mincer, by Westpac helicopter down to Royal

Newcastle hospital,' he said. Because there was no more room in the helicopter, Margaret had to travel to Newcastle in an ambulance. 'I had to wait about an hour and a half until Mum got there because she needed to sign the permission note in case the doctors had to amputate my hand. People were running around, but not near me. I didn't know what was going on. I was left alone in a cubicle and was pretty scared. It seemed like an eternity. The hand was still on my arm. There was no blood because my hand had been stuck in the mincer for so long that the blood flow had been cut off. I was in pain. After something so horrific you would think I would be screaming and yelling the house down, but I wasn't because I was in shock.'

'The helicopter crew later told me how brave Heath was,' said Margaret, 'They couldn't believe he was only seven and so stoic – no tears or screaming. He even looked out of the helicopter to enjoy the view.'

When she arrived at the hospital, her son was sitting all alone in the cubicle.

'I was appalled. I thought Heath would be in theatre by then; I didn't know they were waiting for me to sign papers to give permission for the operation. Amputation below the elbow was the only option.'

Heath was in theatre for a couple of hours. After the operation his mother joined him in the recovery room.

'I remember waking up groggy from the anaesthetic,' Heath said. 'It felt like my hand was still there.'

'I had decided to tell him about the amputation as soon as he awoke so it would slip into his consciousness,' Margaret said. 'It broke my heart when he asked, "But will it grow back?" He had to know that his arm wouldn't grow back again.'

Although Heath was able to move on fairly quickly, Margaret was devastated.

The day after Heath's accident, a journalist rang her at the hospital.

'He had heard I was a single parent and asked me if Heath was going to be taken away and put in care,' said Margaret. 'A wave of terror swept through me. I was so stunned I mumbled a few words. I can't remember what I actually said, but it must have been like, "Haven't we already been through enough? I am a widow and have been through a day of horror watching my son suffer a horrific accident. Maybe you need some compassion and empathy when asking questions at such a time" – and hung up. The journalist rang back later to apologise. He ended up writing a good story and thanking people on our behalf.'

On the day the drip came out, Heath bounced around the ward. He was home the next day and went to the school Christmas party that night. As soon as he arrived home, he began practising handball so he could challenge Bryn when he returned from school. Heath beat him left-handed and remained a worthy opponent.

'Life didn't seem so bad after I knew I could – or maybe he let me – win. It was really important to me to play handball. Even then the ability to play sport was so important, I didn't want the accident to change that.'

Heath missed only three days of school. A week after the accident he was at a swimming carnival and entered every event.

Margaret was striving to be the best parent she could be and to not cripple her heart and mind with guilt. She reflected on life being a matter of near misses.

'We take our lives in our hands so many times. Bryn was only a toddler when his father died. I'm not sure whether he understood the loss, but it must have had an impact. Bryn is a sensitive boy and the boys have a close relationship. He was so traumatised by Heath's accident, I arranged counselling for him. I knew I couldn't undo the damage. He suffered as much as Heath in some ways. The sibling can be overlooked when his brother needs special attention. Bryn wasn't jealous, but had to learn to cope.'

Heath continued. 'An accident is bad enough for the person concerned, but it can also be devastating for the family and the people around.'

Heath hated his first prosthesis, fitted soon after his accident. It was a claw with two fingers that opened and shut.

'It looked deformed,' he said. 'I had turned eight and going to school wearing this thing didn't help me, except when I played Ali Baba's brother in a school production of *Ali Baba and the Forty Thieves*. The brother was attacked by the forty thieves and had his hand damaged. I suggested to the teacher I could play this role quite well. When I was about 10, I walked past a shop window and suddenly saw my reflection. I thought, Whoa, who's that? I used to try and hide my arm. It irked me that people would only remember me for my disability.'

His mother said Heath was self-conscious at times, but rarely complained.

'Once or twice he said he could be a good cricketer if he had two hands. The occupational therapist told me not to fuss. I would turn my back so I wouldn't try and help him. I worried that his one arm had to do a lifetime and he might wear it out, but he managed incredibly well.'

At Booral Primary School near Stroud and later at Bulahdelah Central School, Heath had only two incidents when students made comments about his arm. Then, without the teachers telling them to, they apologised.

'When I hear people with cerebral palsy say how they were picked on at school,' said Heath, 'I think I was lucky to go to a small country school of seventy kids. It was the end of first grade when I lost my hand and the Christmas holidays came up a week later. My personality helped. I didn't let it affect me, so it became pretty much a non-issue. Apart from having one hand, I kept doing what I had done before – riding, swimming, playing tennis and soccer just like other boys, but left-handed. I even played the piano – atrociously. Only a doting parent would appreciate it.' He glanced at Margaret, who laughed. 'At high school I enjoyed athletics and played team sports on weekends – senior second division soccer for Gloucester while still a junior and A Grade cricket at Stroud. I was more of a bowler, never a great batsman because the prosthesis limited my shots.'

By the time he was 13, the doctor told Heath that the right side of his body was wasting through lack of exercise. The spine had curved in a C-shape and the lung was underdeveloped.

'I started weight training and running cross-country to strengthen that side. When I was 15, I made the state finals in the 400 metres for Combined High Schools athletics. I had to borrow some spikes because until then I had run in bare feet.'

It dawned on Heath that he wasn't at state level in any other sport, so maybe athletics warranted more effort.

'I think it was fate,' he said, 'because a few weeks later a colleague of the athletics head coach for the Australian Paralympics saw me run at a competition in Sydney. He was scouting for a runner in the Australian men's relay team for arm amputees and told me to get a coach. It was quite a learning curve. People think anyone can walk and run without being taught, but it takes a long time to develop good technique and change habits so you can go faster and not get injured. I had to learn what shoes to wear, how to warm up and how to run properly.'

Heath was just 16 when he was chosen to go to Hobart with the men's relay team for the 1998 Athletics Grand Prix series. At that competition he met runners like Cathy Freeman and Matt Shirvington. At the next Grand Prix series, held in Melbourne, he went to coaching sessions run by Michael Johnson and Carl Lewis and collected their autographs on his T-shirt. He was hooked.

But just as his athletic life was taking off, Heath's family life came under pressure. The owner of the house where they lived, and the farm Margaret had managed for twenty-five years, wanted to sell. Without notice, the family had no home and his mother had no job or income.

'I was devastated,' Margaret said. 'Our family had enormous emotional ties to that farm and it had been our living for a quarter of a century. The boys were still dependents. Bryn, as man of the house at 17, was particularly affected. He felt it was a betrayal and wanted to protect me. It was hard being a woman on my own.' She had to find alternative work quickly.

When Kevin was alive, they had bought two bush paddocks down the road. This was where the family now moved. There was no house on the 400 acres, so Margaret began to build and put in a road.

In 1995, Margaret had held a field day at the property she managed. 'Afterwards many people wanted to see the property and what I was doing with the cattle and other enterprises. One woman asked me to her farm for lunch and invited other farming women. We had such a good time that it became a regular event with a group of twelve women circulating to each property. When I needed an income, they encouraged and helped me begin as a consultant in whole-of-farm planning and education.'

She built the consultancy up into a good business that also includes farm safety and financial management.

When Heath was in Year 11, the Paralympic movement paid for him to go to the World Championships in Birmingham. For the first time he saw how talent, not disability, could define an athlete. On his return, in order to fit in his training with his Higher School Certificate study, Heath became highly disciplined.

'I realised how productive you could be and get more out of life.'

In 1999 in the lead-up to the Sydney Olympics, Heath won the Pierre de Coubertin national award for students who demonstrate excellence in sport. De Coubertin founded the modern Olympics. In 1999 and 2000, Heath was named Junior Male Paralympic Athlete of the Year, but the pinnacle of his teenage life was selection for the Sydney 2000 Paralympics.

Prior to the big event, Heath had been running a personal best of 49.93 seconds in the 400 metres. This PB, which gave him the drive and confidence to push towards the Paralympics, was just 0.82 seconds shy of Cathy Freeman's spectacular win a few months later in the individual 400 metres in the 2000 Olympics. Then, six weeks before the opening ceremony of the Games, Heath found he had stress fractures in both his feet: his left foot was severely injured. His doctor recommended six weeks in a cast, which would have meant he couldn't compete. Heath was determined not to go into a cast. Instead, he bought a $4000 ultrasound machine to speed up the healing and took painkillers to give himself an outside chance of being able to compete.

'I had only been running for three years with a coach, Louise Green. I didn't know how to run and you can make a lot of mistakes. I wasn't so attuned to my body at 18.'

As he couldn't bear weight on his left foot, he had to use crutches, a complicated and tiring business to manage with a prosthetic arm.

'Stress fractures are excruciating,' Heath said, 'When the bone is continually under stress, it is like bending a paperclip back and forth. It cracks and eventually breaks. The crack in my left foot was about one-third of the way through the navicular bone; the crack in my right foot was only a millimetre or two deep. You have to stop running and train in a pool or with weights. I don't think I've ever trained as hard. Twice a day I ran in the water at the local

Raymond Terrace pool to replicate running on the track. The pool was only half an hour from the farm, but after the training I was so exhausted that I would get halfway home and have to pull over for a snooze.'

Heath had only run once in the six weeks before the Paralympics. Right up until the Games, he wasn't sure whether he could run or whether he might break down in a race. When Heath walked out into the grand arena as a member of the Australian Paralympic team, there was too much happening for him to take it all in.

'There was this feeling of elation where you grin from ear to ear, but are not exactly sure why. I saw my family in the stands and thought, Here am I representing my country for the biggest sporting event after the Olympics.'

Three days into the Games, Heath ran his first race – the individual 400 metres – and won.

'On the television coverage, my face was like a stunned mullet. I thought: I've done it. It was incredible.'

His mother said the family couldn't believe what they were seeing when Heath won the gold medal.

'We were jubilant. We just screamed ourselves hoarse. Heath's lap of honour took a while as he stopped to kiss and hug all those people who had come to cheer him on. After the drug tests, the medal ceremony and the media interviews, the stadium was emptying. Then out came Heath and people appeared from nowhere. Everybody wanted to take his photo and get his autograph. A farm boy who arrived without fanfare was suddenly the centre of attention, a celebrity. Everyone wanted a bit of him, but he handled it well. He realised how important it was to others.'

Heath had only hoped to make the final of the 200 metres but ended up winning the silver medal. People assumed he would be disappointed with silver.

'It was a most satisfying medal because I wasn't expected to do well and it's great to say that you won the silver when you actually came second.'

The 4 x 100 metre relay was Heath's last event at the Sydney 2000 Paralympics. The team for which Heath ran the final leg was called the Four Missing Bits, or 4MBs. Two of them had lost legs and two were missing arms.

'The 4MBs work really well together because we're good mates and put relay training ahead of individual sessions,' he reflected. 'Athletics is normally such an individual sport. Tim Matthews, who was born without an arm, only one lung and no abdominal wall, ran the 4 x 400-metre relay in the Sydney Paralympics the day before his 100 metres final. He lost that final because he was still tired from the relay the night before. That's the sort of commitment we put in. Relays are great because they require four individuals to come together and get the baton around the track. More often than not the four fastest runners in a team won't win a relay because they don't work well together. Too many egos.'

The 4MBs won gold and broke world records in the 4 x 100 metre and 4 x 400 metre relays at the 2000 Paralympics. Heath was a triple gold medallist, as well as a silver medallist and world record holder.

He praised the ethos of the Australian Paralympic team in sharing the joys, supporting each other and not getting bigheaded.

'If someone annoys you, you just walk away. We've all come a long way, in dealing with our disabilities, I mean. That team camaraderie shows in our results.'

Athletes from some countries play mind games. They behave well when the cameras are rolling, but are different in the call room where athletes are checked before events.

'Some will try to intimidate you by staring you down,' Heath said, 'or making comments like, "You're looking fat". They flex their muscles so they look bigger. I've seen athletes fall apart under that kind of pressure. I like to keep quiet and focus.'

Sydney 2000 Paralympics produced a change in attitudes. People went home marvelling at the athletes' abilities, instead of their disabilities.

'Mums, dads and kids could afford to go,' Heath observed. 'They would see someone with a disability perform and say, "Gee, that would be difficult. How do they do that?" I'm not talking about myself here,' he added. 'I was lucky to compete because my disability is quite minor compared to many there. Sometimes I feel like an impostor. My jaw just drops when I see people with huge disabilities compete at such a high level. In Sydney there was a guy in a wheelchair with a prosthetic arm. You see athletes with severe cerebral palsy throwing the discus, which takes great strength. At my first World Championships, I saw quadriplegics doing the marathon. They had limited function in their arms and became so tired toward the finish that they had to push their chairs backwards using their triceps.'

The day our family went to the Paralympics was enthralling. Swimmers who had virtually no arms or legs were lifted into the pool and, using whatever limbs they had, churned along like whirling wheels through the water. In the wheelchair rugby, men with super-strong torsos wheeled after the ball, careered into each other's chairs and often tipped backwards. Then, there they lay, stranded on the floor like gasping fish until an official ran to right them. Off they zoomed to repeat the act. In the arena, young athletes ran, jumped and threw the discus with skill and strength. It was hard to believe they performed without a limb or lung, or were hampered by congenital conditions such as cerebral palsy or intellectual disabilities.

Heath's next hurdle was to deal with the inevitable slump after the high of the 2000 Paralympics. He had made a superhuman effort to recover from the stress fractures, and then ran, despite extreme pain. In the aftermath the stress fractures recurred and he spent six weeks on crutches. Training became difficult and, worst of all, his Uncle Jon (who was married to Margaret's sister) died. The whole family was affected. As they felt the full impact of Jon's death, belated grief for Kevin surfaced.

'Jon was like the dad I never had,' Heath said. 'When he died from leukaemia, I lost direction. I was just going through the motions at training.'

After six months, Heath's mother and his first coach, Louise Green, managed to get him to think about what he wanted from his life. In 2001 Heath began to study a full-time business–commerce double degree at Newcastle University. He was achieving high distinctions on a regular basis, living in a share-house, cooking and housekeeping and going home on weekends. Training had taken a back seat since the 2000 Paralympics. Heath's fortitude helped him through as he began to set athletic goals once more and prepare for the 2002 World Championships.

As a result of good performances at the World Championships, Heath won a prized scholarship to the AIS for 2003. Of the twenty-eight scholarships awarded each year, six were for elite athletes with a disability.

'It was a big move from Newcastle to Canberra, away from family and friends,' he said, 'but I wanted a wholesale change that would help me re-focus and opportunities to fulfil my athletic goals.'

In 2000 WorkCover had approached Heath to be an ambassador for its New South Wales Paralympian Sponsorship program and share his story with workplaces, schools and the corporate sector. He took the opportunity to alert rural people to the dangers of farming and the need for work safety to reduce accidents. The WorkCover presentation fees helped Heath put himself through university. After the Paralympics, he gave fifty presentations to schools, TAFE colleges, worksites, employer and employee groups, farmers' groups and even power stations, an astonishing number given that previously Heath hadn't talked about his accident at all.

'At the beginning I was scared to speak in public,' he said, 'but the presentations, which got me talking, were cathartic. Until I was in high school, I had dissociated myself. Now I can tell my story. I let audiences see how quickly and easily an accident can happen and harp on about how dangerous farms can be. I tell them how they need to keep the safety message ticking over in their heads, but also that there is life after a serious accident. People are able to relate to me. They come up afterwards and say, "That story sounds like what happened to my brother or father on the tractor or motorbike"– or whatever.'

Margaret Francis listened to her son's first presentation at a local school.

'His stress fractures had resurfaced and he was on crutches. Heath was doing up to three talks a day to chock-a-block gatherings. The kids were fascinated by him doing tasks such as tying shoelaces one-handed. When he was younger, the occupational therapist at Children's Hospital had given him tips. He would try her suggestions, and then say, "I think I can do it better this way".'

The kids always wanted to check out Heath's running arm. He showed them the silicon sleeve, made in Iceland, that goes underneath the prosthesis as an airtight seal. He rolled it over the elbow. It's a neat arrangement, which he can assemble with one hand.

'I tell them it's like fitting a condom. It has a ratchet inside where the prosthesis slides in. I screw it on tightly with a coin so it fits snugly on the arm. The weight of the prothesis is as close as it possibly can be to my forearm weight.'

He would remind audiences that farms rated as the most dangerous workplaces in Australia after mines. The statistics were telling for males, as adults and children, on farms: 135,000 rural enterprises produce commodities worth more than \$30 billion per annum, but that comes with a high cost in human injury and death. New South Wales hospital admissions due to farm injuries showed that 74.9 per cent were males and 16.3 per cent were children under the age of 15 years, mostly boys, according to the Australian Centre for Agricultural Health and Safety at Moree and Rural Industries Research and Development Corporation report *Injury on Farms in New South Wales: The facts*, published in 2005. In the decade from January 1990 to December 2000 in New South Wales alone, the Australian Bureau of Statistics recorded 1094 fatalities to farmers and farm workers, 94.5 per cent male – an average of 99 deaths per annum.

'As kids, we help out on the farm after school to make ends meet,' Heath said. 'What makes a farm different to other businesses is how many pieces of equipment can maim or even kill you. A farmer is expected to be an expert on, say, thirty pieces. The dangers are there 24/7 because the farm is also the home.'

In times of drought, such as eastern Australia has experienced over the last seven years, people work harder and longer hours, become more fatigued than they usually are, and so the risk of accidents with dangerous machinery increases. When farm families don't have the money, which is often the case during times of such severe drought, equipment doesn't get fixed or upgraded.

'Farmers are innovative with repairs,' Heath commented, 'which can make equipment more dangerous for the farmer, let alone for children. It's hard to regulate when most farmers don't employ people.'

When he goes to his friends' farms, Heath is tempted to lecture them about safety. One friend was running around a paddock barefoot and sliced his foot on a piece of iron, nearly cutting it off. Another had his clothing pulled into machinery: luckily, the fabric ripped before the friend was sucked in.

'Boys aged 16 to 25 years old are at the highest risk. We need to target that age group. Many are in their first jobs and are inexperienced, but they feel awkward asking anyone the proper way to do something. And, they think they are invincible. It's an awful mix. A vulnerable group is jackaroos whose work includes every activity in farming life. Getting the safety message across to them is difficult because they do jobs 'Dad's way'. Quoting statistics to them is a waste of breath. When they hear a WorkCover guy say that boys have double the number of injuries as girls, that 3000 adults had serious injuries in the workplace in 2003 and fifty of them between the ages of 18 and 25 lost their lives, they just go, "Yeah?" It means nothing to them, but seeing someone like me who is their own age and has had a serious injury, does make an impact.'

I visited Heath again at the AIS in September 2004. We met in the dining room. Around us athletes tucked into hearty meals and salads. In one corner sat the basketball players, tall and lean. At the next table were sturdy, thickset men – weightlifters and discus throwers. Heath and his friends were of slighter build, with bulging leg muscles – the runners and jumpers.

'My aim is to be the best runner I can be. The AIS gives me that chance and I love it. Everything is geared to training: top coaching, healthy food, good accommodation, sports medicine, massage and acupuncture, help with my prosthesis, travel to meets, even mentoring for uni assignments.'

These elite few are expected to work or study as well as train at their chosen sport so they can leave the AIS with a profession. Scholarships are renewed each year depending on performance, so the pressure is constant.

'Some athletes can get away with drinking and parties,' Heath said. 'My coach tells me, "Your athletic life is short. Life after athletics is long."'

When Heath first arrived at the AIS, he felt lonely. There were times when his friends would go partying and he was the only one home because he had a competition the following day. The friends he left behind in Newcastle were doing degrees, going out, having long-term relationships and pursuing careers. Some were even parents. Heath was leading a different life.

'When I went home to Booral, it made me realise how I missed out on thinking about and discussing anything other than race times and PBs. Friends said, "What you do is incredible", but for me that's normal. Running at a top level certainly does affect your life. I'm blessed to represent my country, but at times I miss the friendships.'

After lunch, we walked to the pool where Heath had a training session.

'Running becomes addictive, like drugs – not that I've tried any!' he hastened to add. 'There's an intrinsic high when you do well, but also a chemical reaction after training. Some say the 400 metres is the worst race. It makes you feel abominable. I think the 400 metre hurdles must be worse because you have to jump those sticks as well as run. After 300 metres the muscles stop processing oxygen and there's a build-up of lactic acid. Your muscles feel like they're on fire. You get headaches, your eyes go blurry and you can't see. You feel sick; some runners even throw up. I've vomited regularly in training, but not in a race. About half an hour after the race, you feel the euphoria of an endorphin rush. After winning the 4 x 400 metre relay, one of my mates said, "400 metre runners must have short-term memories or they wouldn't keep punishing themselves".'

Heath described a good 400 metre run as smooth. It doesn't expel energy or build too much lactic acid in the muscles so the body feels light.

In February 2004, Heath competed in the 400 metres at the Telstra A series meet in Canberra. It was an able-bodied race and he ran 48.88 seconds, which broke the Paralympic world record of 49.03 seconds.

'Running 400 metres in 48.88 seconds is quite fast,' was his understatement. 'I felt particularly satisfied that I could hold my own against the best able-bodied athletes in the world, but archaic rules for Paralympians say an official has to be present at the meet, or it's not recognised. My breaking the world record was a big deal for the AIS, but they couldn't understand why it wasn't recognised. In the long run I thought it was better that other competitors knew as little as possible about my times. The Paralympics are different from the Olympics because people can rock up and you haven't seen them run for two years since the World Champs or the previous Paralympics. I saw a potential advantage in no one knowing how fast I had run, so they'd underestimate me – hopefully.'

In the months before Athens Paralympics that were to be held in September 2004, Heath began to lose confidence and to question what he was doing, worrying instead of focusing on races. His coach at this time was Ukrainian Iryna Dvorskina, who told him, 'You're thinking too much'.

Heath pointed out a fit-looking woman in a tracksuit. 'She's a gem. There's no way I could run the times I do without her coaching. She has integrity, a strong, eastern European work ethic and calls a spade a spade. She is caring and able to convey knowledge. We also annoy the hell out of each other.'

Heath dived into the pool without his prosthesis and swam freestyle, completing one kilometre in 20 minutes. Even one-handed his stroke was smooth. Then we were off to the AIS track. He drove using a specially adapted lever on the left of the steering wheel. At the track Heath tied his shoelaces, anchoring the lace with his right upper arm while tying it with the left hand. It took dexterity. Heath needs three prosthetic hands to perform different activities. He uses a clamp hand for gym work to grip a weighted bar. Unlike athletes whose whole arm is missing, having part of an arm gives Heath an advantage because he can attach the prosthesis and exercise his biceps. An AIS staffer has improved his running arm by adding two thick rubber bands from the end of the prosthesis to his elbow, enabling the prosthesis to replicate the brachial radialis muscle and pull the arm up to a 90 degree running position.

While at the Athens Paralympics, Heath hit the headlines back home. After being fitted for uniforms, he walked out of the team management base, leaving the bag containing his most vital equipment, the running arm and spikes. He looked everywhere – in the dining room, the Lost and Found office, and then went to the Australian athletics team manager, by which time his cool demeanour was shaken. He checked all the Australian bags he saw – over 300, and they all looked the same. Finally, he opened a bag lying by itself in the team base. Persistence paid off. It was his. When he hopped on the bus with the bag, his waiting Australian team mates called out: 'Good job you haven't lost another arm.' Winning three silver and two bronze medals helped compensate for the stress of mislaying the $5000 prosthesis.

While in Athens, Heath got to know Christine Wolf, a tall, fair-haired German athlete. He had been training in Germany before the Games, but there they only exchanged hellos. At the Paralympics, they kept bumping into each other in the athletes' village and ended up spending much of the last few days together. After a flurry of emails, Christine joined Heath for a trip to Crete. He stayed with her family, near Stuttgart, for three weeks until Iryna insisted he return home for training.

Christine had fought cancer in the knee for five years. Eventually, when she was 15 and doctors had tried everything, even moving the ankle joint to became the knee joint and reversing the foot to be attached to the knee, Christine's leg had to be amputated above the knee. Without any previous sporting experience, she started to long jump successfully and in Athens won a silver medal.

Christine's running leg has a hydraulic mechanised knee. For walking, she uses a sophisticated computerised knee called a C-leg, which contains sensors on the foot that send messages to the knee to enable it to adjust gait and speed. She was the face of a campaign to advertise the C-leg for the manufacturer, OttoBock. When I met her at the Commonwealth Games, Christine walked with ease and grace over the long bridge and stairs to the Melbourne Cricket Ground. It was hard to tell that she had an artificial leg, until she went through a metal detector at the entrance and triggered the alarms.

'Her knee is amazing,' said Heath. 'She runs and jumps off a carbon fibre foot and mechanical knee. Prosthetics for legs have come on incredibly in the last decade. There is an athlete who is missing a leg from above the knee and has just run 12 seconds for 100 metres. Most men wouldn't be able to run 12 seconds. There are below-knee amputees running 11 seconds, 11 flat which is about one second outside what able-bodied Olympic champions can run. The foot, which moves up and down when you are walking, is a little easier to replicate mechanically than the hand.'

Christine came to Australia in February 2005 to see how her relationship with Heath would develop. She stayed, convinced that Australia was where she wanted to be.

'It's not an option for me to go to Germany,' said Heath. 'Christine has applied for Australian citizenship. She was blown away by the support and facilities at the AIS, but she feels it's not fair to use Australian facilities and not give something back. She has her own career as a qualified goldsmith and exhibited her jewellery for the first time in 2006. In leaving her family and country Christine showed great courage.'

Christine and Heath later broke up, but remained friends, sharing a strong commitment to their athletics team and paralympic goals. Since late 2006 Heath has been in a relationship with Peruvian swimmer, Valeria, whom he met at the AIS in 2003. She was 17 and on an International Olympic Committee scholarship to prepare for the Athens Olympics. After the Athens Olympics, Valeria had moved to the United States to study at the University of Michigan where she is on a full swimming scholarship. They stayed in touch via email and computer chat.

'In 2006 after the World Championships I decided to visit her in Michigan and we quickly decided we had more than just a friendship,' Heath said. Theirs is a long-distance relationship with hours spent on Skype each week talking to each other. 'While it's not ideal, modern technology and the fact that we both travel internationally and can tack on visits to see each other enables us to have a wonderful relationship.'

I kept in touch with Heath, but didn't see him again for 18 months until the 2006 Commonwealth Games. In that time he had graduated with a Bachelor of Commerce and was continuing with his business degree.

'I was too tired to study full-time after training. It's hard to excel at everything at once,' he said. 'If I'm doing well academically, training isn't so good; if training goes well, my studies suffer.'

As an athlete, Heath's life moves in a four-year cycle from one Paralympics to the next. Career-wise he is interested in current affairs and international diplomacy and is considering the Department of Foreign Affairs and Trade and studying international relations, if he stays in Canberra.

'When you are an athlete, you have to put your needs first, but I'm not a selfish person. When I retire from athletics, I don't want a career where I put myself first.'

Heath wants a balance between building a career and giving something back to the community. The Australian Paralympic Committee wants him to mentor young athletes with a disability. Post Athens, Heath thought he had peaked in his running, but discovered he had more in him.

'Sprinters mature as they build strength and become race smart,' he said. 'They peak between 26 and 28, so I'm aiming for Beijing Paralympics in 2008. I'll be 26 by then. I can see clearly to 2008 when my business degree will also be finished. After that it's very hazy.'

Back at the 2006 Commonwealth Games, Heath spent the day thinking about his 200-metre final race plan. Then he tried to switch off.

'I warmed up at Olympic Park. I was nervous in front of such a huge crowd. My goal was to put together the perfect race. I had run 22.8 seconds in the heat and hardly asked anything from my body. It was like I was jogging.'

It looked promising for a sensational final. His plan was to do a strong start, power to 80 metres, build to top speed using centrifugal force around the bend, hold that speed for 100 metres and accelerate over the last 20 metres.

'When it all comes together, you feel elated,' he said. It didn't work out that way though. In all, there were five of what the starter called 'non-starts' because of the Indian runner before the rattled runners finally got away cleanly.

'I ran a bad race,' Heath said afterwards. 'Bad starts happen, that's sport, but I tightened up. I thought I would go close to my PB of 21.95, or the world record of 21.83. I knew I could. Instead of being light-footed, I was stomping.'

Heath may have felt lead-footed, but to those watching he was flying. Around the bend, hot on his heels, came a Nigerian runner, who closed in at the finish. Heath leant over the line and won – gold! The Nigerian came second, but was disqualified for encroaching on Heath's lane. Another Nigerian, a runner with no arms, moved into third place. As Heath ran his victory lap, the crowd went wild. His gold medal glinted under the lights. He said that his legs were jelly and only adrenaline kept him jogging around the track once more.

A few weeks later, Athletics Australia named Heath the 2006 Athlete with a Disability.

The Commonwealth Games were a warm-up for the 2006 World Championships in Assen, The Netherlands. Heath's race schedule was heavy: the 100, 200 and 400 metres. He emailed results shortly after each race.

'Before getting down on the blocks for the 200 metre final, a Moroccan tapped me on the shoulder, pointed to himself and raised one finger. I didn't understand what he was doing at first and wished him luck.

'He tapped me on the shoulder again, pointed to himself and raised one finger. Finally, I understood that he was telling me he would come first.'

Heath chuckled and went back to concentrating on the race: he beat the Moroccan into second place and won gold. A day later, he fronted up for the 400 metres against the Athens Paralympic champion and world record holder from Brazil. Towards the end of the race, Heath tired. Yet he crossed the line in 49.4 seconds and 8 metres in front of the Brazilian.

Heath's final race was the 100 metres. Memories of the Commonwealth Games and the five false starts flooded back. Fortunately, there was only one false start.

'I was feeling lousy because of a cold. The final once again was between me, the Brazilian, the Moroccan and a young Russian who had no arms and was still able to run 11.4 seconds. I started tiring a little towards the end and felt my legs lose speed. Ten metres from the line, I heard the announcer call the Brazilian's name and saw him almost in line with me. For a second I thought he'd come over the top of me, but then I saw his face and realised that I was first to finish. I was ecstatic. I had won all three of the sprint titles.'

You might think an Aussie triple gold medallist in the World Championships would rate a mention in our sports-mad media, but not a word.

It was Heath's year, 2006. In Melbourne's Federation Square, the day after his Commonwealth Gold win, he couldn't keep the grin off his face. Young admirers clustered around for his autograph. It was baking hot, but Heath was good-natured and talked to everyone who asked him questions. I was taking photos of him holding his gold medal aloft in front of a sign proclaiming 'Champions' when three people came out of the building behind us and said their manager wanted to meet us. We followed them upstairs into a room crowded with people in suits who were sipping champagne. They started applauding Heath, handed us glasses of champagne and offered a plate of cakes. This was the Business Council of Australia, entertaining guests from around the world. Heath became their impromptu guest speaker. The manager congratulated him on his medal and asked how he lost his arm.

'Sorry to put you off your meatballs, but my accident happened like this ...' Heath went on to say. 'Even when you are careful, accidents can happen. You have to get on with living, not let trauma rule you. If I could go back and have my hand again I would, but at the same time the loss has opened doors. I have had opportunities I wouldn't have had with two hands. I can still do up to 95 per cent of what I could with both hands – and probably could do more if my mother would let me. If I want to drive the tractor at home, she is firm, "No, that is not going to happen".

Just as the young people outside had, the business leaders gave Heath a standing ovation and clamoured for his autograph. They too discerned the formidable drive and commitment of this man to move from personal tragedy to the top of his sport while still retaining his affability and down-to-earth humour.

Emily Murphy (*left*) and Ellie Middleton, Molong, NSW, 2006

14

You Be Famous, I'll Be Your Photographer!

Emily Murphy and Ellie Middleton, Molong,
New South Wales

This is the story of two girls who have been best friends since they were seven. Emily Murphy and Ellie Middleton are now 18 and live on opposite sides of Molong, a small town in central western New South Wales. Their lives ran together as children and separately as teenagers.

Molong is the centre of a productive mixed-farming area and close to the regional city of Orange. It sprawls across rolling hills, a pretty place of stone buildings and English trees. Like most country towns it has a strong community spirit built up through shared experiences of floods and droughts and shared interests in developing opportunities and facilities to cater for its diverse population. The young people tend to go to Orange or further afield for education, jobs and entertainment; the catchcry of 'There's nothing to do' can be heard here.

The district is widespread, so although I also live around Molong, I had never met either of these girls until 2006.

The Murphy farm, 20 kilometres west of the town, borders dense forest referred to as the Gumble scrub. Yapping dogs warned anyone for miles around of my arrival. Emily came out of the family's red-brick house, which overlooked undulating paddocks tinged with the green of emerging crops. She was small with a determined look to her jaw and a straight gaze. Her glossy brown hair was held back by a hot-pink bandanna.

Emily escorted me inside to the lounge room where a pianola and sheet music take pride of place. She didn't bother with dolls as a child, but spent her childhood in the Gumble scrub with her older brother and sister, Michael and Natalie, riding motorbikes and making cubby houses up the trees. She always had grazed knees. Emily wanted me to photograph her riding a four-wheel bike with her dogs as passengers. Sport was her forte: cricket, touch football and discus throwing. When in Year 6, she competed at local, regional and state levels of the New South Wales Catholic Schools cricket competition and was selected for the New South Wales Catholic Schools team in the National All Schools competition. Emily and her best friend, Ellie Middleton, were the only girls for most grades in their class of twelve at St Joseph's Primary School, so they just played soccer with the boys.

This little tomboy from the Gumble scrub also loved to sing.

'I used to sit in the back when we were in the car and sing along to the latest pop songs. My brother would tell me to be quiet. I liked Delta Goodrem, but wasn't into music in a big way at that stage.'

Ellie Middleton is a cheerful, blonde-headed girl with a broad Aussie accent. She lives on the Orange side of town at her family's two-storey house on a few acres called Polo Fields: there's not a polo field in sight.

Vicki, Ellie's mother, said, 'People used to play polo here. We had one old pony so we kept the name.'

When Ellie was seven, Vicki and Ellie's father, Tim, moved the family from Orange to set up a butchery in Molong. Ellie started school at St Joseph's and seemed to settle in well. Soon Vicki began to notice that when her daughter was reading a book, she would hold it to one side.

'What are you doing, Ellie?' she asked.

Vicki adjusted the book to the normal reading position, but the little girl couldn't read it.

'It's blurry,' she said.

Vicki and Tim immediately took her to an eye clinic in Orange. After a day of tests, three doctors remained baffled by her results. They identified pressure behind her eyes and referred Ellie on to a paediatrician for a CAT scan. Eventually, the specialist told Vicki and Tim that their seven-year-old daughter had a brain tumour. They were in shock.

'I remember Mum crying and Dad hugging Mum,' Ellie said. '"What's wrong Mum?" I asked her. Although I didn't understand much at that age, I thought it must be serious.'

The doctor told them to go home, pack and drive straight to Westmead Children's Hospital in Sydney. In hospital, Ellie had scans, needles stuck in her head, blood taken and regular magnetic resonance imaging (MRI). Vicki described the MRI machine as a scary tunnel that made a big noise. Fortunately, it didn't worry Ellie; she didn't cry or complain. She spent three weeks in Westmead and underwent an operation to insert a valve that would drain a build-up of fluid from her brain. She showed me the book her school friends made to cheer her up in hospital. A painted yellow sunflower adorns the cover. Inside, it is filled with photos of all the children and their messages: 'We miss you at the soccer training', and 'We need you back on the field'.

'We knew Ellie had a brain tumour,' said Emily, 'but we didn't really know what that was. We prayed for her. When she returned to school, she looked pale. She had a patch of hair shaved off and a scar on her head. It made Ellie and me closer because there were so few girls.'

Upon her return Ellie's classmates treated her with great respect: she had endured a major operation, had a large scar and she could still play soccer.

'My family didn't fuss about me, but as the youngest of five children, I was spoilt. Life went on as usual.'

Despite life appearing to continue as normal, Ellie's illness affected her family.

'I wanted to wrap her in cotton wool, to keep her to ourselves,' said Vicki. 'When she was really sick, I used to smoke to reduce the stress. She would say to me, "Stop smoking, Mum, or you'll die. I really need you."'

When they reached Year 7 Emily and Ellie went on to high school in Orange. Neither liked it. By Year 8, Ellie was refusing to go to school.

'I felt like a number, not a person, because it was so big,' she said. 'Nearly all the other girls wanted to look pretty for the boys. I thought, I'm not ready for this. I'm still not. I'm feral,' she laughed. 'I turned into a little shit. I would hide up the back of our farm so Mum couldn't find me to catch the bus. My mate, Em, was in a different class, but she stood by me through thick and thin.'

Ellie went into her shell. It was as if she were numb. She told her mother she would throw everything away, even her life, if she had to go to school.

'It was like a devil had switched on inside my head. I even ran away one day. I packed a wheelbarrow with my swag and a bag of clothes and took off up Yuranigh Road at the back of our place. I threw the wheelbarrow and swag over three fences and climbed over myself. I arrived at a friend's house and said, "How're you going?" They laugh about it now, but they rang Mum and said, "Ellie's here. We're really worried." Mum came and picked me up. She was frantic and pretty mad. She had been looking everywhere for me. Mum sent me to a counsellor because she was so worried. We discussed me changing schools, but I was scared and thought it would be the same anywhere else.'

Then Ellie began to complain of sore eyes. She looked sick. Her mother tried every cream and eye drop on the market. None of them worked. She became a hermit and only visited the neighbour whose place she had escaped to. Vicki said it was hell.

'Sometimes we would chase the school bus with Ellie still in her pyjamas. We tried everything – bribery, persuasion, yelling. She was like a blank screen, never yelling back, just sitting there. If her father said Ellie could stay home from school, I'd say she had to go. If I said she could stay home, he would want her to go. Her brothers Brad, Josh and Jake would tell her to pull herself together and go to school. She had no let-up from any of us. A doctor wanted to give her anti-depressants, but I thought that would make her more of a zombie. I was scared every single day. You never know how far you can push kids.'

Nobody suspected the tumour was causing Ellie's uncharacteristic behaviour. After six months of this turmoil, her parents moved her to Molong Central School. There the teachers helped her, her eyes cleared up and she began to enjoy school.

'I felt more comfortable because there were twenty-five students instead of 200 in my year. I no longer felt pressured to talk about boys and look pretty. They were my kind of kids,' she laughed.

For Emily Murphy, those early high school years involved three hours bus travel each day from Gumble to Orange and back. Every few weeks she stayed home for a day to catch up on sleep. She too found her classmates' preoccupation with boys, make-up and looking good galling. In Year 9 her parents, Robyn and Peter switched her to Loreto Normanhurst in Sydney to board.

'I looked forward to going away to school, but I didn't really know what was in store,' Emily said. 'It was hard to make friends at first because I was new and most girls had been together since Year 7. There were a lot of country girls. They were heavily into utes. Some were more like boys than most boys I knew. I tended to hold back and be quiet because I found it hard to relate to them. I really missed home and took everything to heart, so I copped some bitchy comments and bullying. My brother Michael told me to just be myself and not to worry about what other people thought.'

In 2003, when Emily and Ellie were in Year 9, Ellie was a bridesmaid for her sister Sarah's wedding. She had to walk down a rough garden track to the ceremony. It took immense concentration not to trip. She managed to stay upright, but the following day as they cleaned up the reception hall, Ellie toppled over on the concrete and gashed her forehead. Her parents took her to the doctor in Orange, who sent her on to Westmead Hospital. There she had a drainage shunt inserted in her head again.

'It's like a tap to drain the fluid from the brain into the stomach from where it can be excreted in my urine,' Ellie said. 'The shunt worked for a few months, but then I got sick again. For four days I lay at home in a darkened room and couldn't move because of the headaches.'

She was swallowing strong painkillers for some relief. One day she was so sick her mother rushed her to Orange Base Hospital, where the doctors immediately rang CareFlight. They loaded Ellie onto a stretcher and into the helicopter; she was surrounded by monitoring machines. There was just enough room for Vicki and the doctor. As they flew over the Blue Mountains to Westmead Ellie lapsed in and out of consciousness. On arrival, she was rushed to the emergency department for scans.

In the seven years since she had been diagnosed, the tumour had grown from the size of a 5-cent piece to the size of an orange and was now pressing on the middle of her brain. The dilemma was, if the doctors removed the tumour, Ellie would be blind and paralysed from the neck down.

'I couldn't lift my head off the pillow,' she recalled. 'The tumour had a cyst growing off it. I was scared then. I didn't want an operation.'

The consulting doctors recommended radical ray treatment and chemotherapy, but the neurosurgeon who was in charge didn't agree. Ellie had a operation, which lasted nine hours, to remove the cyst.

'The neurosurgeon told us the tumour had changed. He thought it was now malignant,' Vicki said. 'We were shattered. I didn't want to tell our other kids. My boys sensed the worst and didn't say much. They just cried, those big boys who are bricklayers and builders. We took it in turns to sit with Ellie in intensive care all through the night.'

When Emily Murphy was told about her friend's condition she wanted to go straight from boarding school to Westmead to be with her friend, but there was no immediate transport for her to be able to do that.

'My parents rang to say Ellie wasn't expected to pull through. She had fluid on her brain and the doctors were trying to drain it. I couldn't concentrate because I was so worried about her.'

Later that night, the neurosurgeon returned to tell the family that the cyst had been successfully removed and that the tumour wasn't malignant. Ellie had made it through the operation without nerve damage.

'After she came out of the anaesthetic, Ellie was the one patting me on the back while I sobbed,' Vicki said. 'We thought: If you are lucky enough to get out of hospital, you can count your blessings.'

Ellie's hospital room hardly had space left for her as teddy bears of all shapes and sizes began to arrive from well-wishers, some of whom she didn't know, but who admired her courage. At home, she showed me a bookcase stacked with the bears – big bears, small bears, pink, white and brown bears.

When she began to recover, Ellie's easygoing attitude returned.

'Westmead was great. I met the country singer, Shannon Noll, when he visited the hospital. There were kids far worse off than me, like little Sophie Delezio who was burnt over 85 per cent of her body when a car ran into her preschool. It made me think that you never give up on life.'

Emily was hugely relieved to know her friend Ellie was recovering and arranged to visit her during the school holidays.

Ellie had three more operations that year to adjust the shunt in her brain. Once the valves were adjusted the headaches caused by the tumour pressing on the brain began to abate.

'I have nuts and bolts in my head. Do you want to feel them?' I felt a knob behind her left ear, hidden under the blonde locks.

'The whole school supported me every time I went to hospital. Kids would ask me, "How many scars this time, Ellie?" Whenever I grew some hair, it would be shaved off. By the time my brother was married in November 2003, I was as bald as a badger. Now the shunt is right, it works like a miracle. I live each day as it comes.'

Ellie's doctors wonder whether her depression in Year 8 may have been connected with her severe illness, which became evident in Year 9.

Ellie has to be careful about what she takes on. In 2005, her fellow students were off on a Sport, Leisure and Recreation camp in the Blue Mountains.

'I almost didn't go,' she said, 'but my teacher, Mrs Adamthwaite, said she would look after me. I was a bit scared of abseiling because my head might get injured, but a TAFE teacher connected himself to me and down a 15 metre wall we went together. We had to do a capsize drill in a canoe. We tipped over into deep water. It was freezing cold and I couldn't haul myself back into the boat; nor could the boys who were trying to pull me in.'

Eventually, she tumbled in upside-down, ending up safe but with legs stuck in the air. Ellie also had a go at rock climbing.

'I barely made two metres up, if that, and called out to the teacher to get down low and take a photo of me, so it looked as if I was real high. There were heaps of wombats at Kangaroo Valley where we did the canoeing. One ran past as we were eating dinner around the campfire, grabbed some scraps and ran down a hole. We slept out in tents. I had the best time.'

When Emily began boarding at Loreto College, she joined a choir. The music teacher could hear a voice that stood out. She went around the room and listened. It was Emily's. The teacher tested her and told Robyn and Peter, her parents, that she had talent and should take lessons.

Her singing teacher, Lyndsey Gartside, noticed that Emily was unhappy at school because she was so homesick and missed her parents with whom she had a close relationship.

'She turned up for a lesson and I went through the routine. Emily was completely raw musically, but I thought, Wow, this girl's got a tremendous voice. She was ready to go. Some people have to work for years to get their voice to resonate, but hers was there. She had a talent for singing and was noticeably better than anybody else around her. It really inspired her to work hard at it and practise in her spare time.'

Lyndsey made a comparison with the famous Swedish soprano Birgit Nilsson, who lived on a farm and used to sing out over the valley. Nilsson had no aspirations to a professional career, but one day someone heard her and started her on the giddy path to stardom.

'Singing gave me purpose,' said Emily. 'I had found a niche, I had something to talk about and others respected me when they saw me performing on stage.'

The highlight of 2005 for Emily was a school music tour of France, Austria, Switzerland and Germany in the July holidays. The choir sang in La Madeleine, a huge church in Paris. Several hundred people walked in from the streets to listen.

'I sang solo and with the choir and orchestra. At an aged people's home in Vienna, which was more like a resort, I sang one of my favourites, "Oh, My Beloved Father". The old folks stood up and clapped me afterwards. Before the tour I had only made friends with boarders because their culture was not to hang around with day girls. I was judgemental, but when I travelled overseas with some day girls I had the opportunity to make friends with them. I began to realise that relationships are the most important thing in life.'

Emily's realisation about relationships was thrown into turmoil later that year when her mother left her father.

'I was down in the music rooms when my brother rang me,' Emily said. 'I broke down. Michael said to have a good cry and go back to the dorm and find someone to talk to. I didn't know who I could trust, but I have a close friend who had the same experience. She helped me by telling me her story. I wanted to go home straight away. I felt lost at school, but when I went home the house felt sad and empty with only Dad, Michael and me there [Natalie having moved out by then].'

'I quit choir, didn't have much enthusiasm for anything and put lots of things on hold, even singing. I stacked on the weight because I stopped doing sport.'

Emily's relationship with her mother became strained. Ellie was upset for her friend. She didn't know how Emily would cope by herself in Sydney and maybe not having anybody to talk to about it.

'I wrote and asked her if she was OK. When I saw her, Em wasn't her normal bubbly self. I said, "If you ever need someone to talk to, I'm always here". She thanked me, but we didn't talk about it again.'

Ellie told Emily not to close herself off, but to talk to her mother. She took her friend's advice and eventually Emily threw herself into singing again because it made her feel happier. She decided to audition for the musical *Les Miserables*, a production organised by St Ignatius College in Sydney. Girls from sixteen other schools were auditioning for the two leading roles.

'I was really nervous because I had to act as well as sing,' Emily said. 'I had no experience of acting. I needed a song to get into character for the audition, so I asked our drama teacher for help and she gave me a scene to practise. A fellow student showed me how she would do it.'

Emily landed the female lead of Fantine, the doomed factory worker who is hounded out of work for having an illegitimate daughter.

'In the beginning I was closed,' said Emily. 'I wouldn't move my arms or open up as a character. The drama teacher helped me to get into character by introducing us to the five-count approach where we have to feel the weight of the clothes on our skin, feel the floor where we are sitting or walking, take in the colour and form of our surroundings, feel the air on our skin and listen to the softest sound we can hear.'

It was a process that worked for Emily as she took on the character of Fantine.

'She was a wonderful part because she sings dramatic songs such as "I Dreamed a Dream". She dies in the sixth song. I had to walk in and fall down as I die while hallucinating that I'm talking to my child. Then Fantine returns as a ghost in the last song. I was so glad that I did it, despite the colossal workload.'

They rehearsed for seven months, towards the end three or four days a week from 4 o'clock in the afternoon to 10 at night and thirteen-hour days on Sundays. If other girls in the chorus were not driving to St Ignatius, it was a major undertaking for Emily, a boarder, to travel to rehearsals. She had to go by train, bus and taxi. In the last few weeks of rehearsals, she was so worn out she would fall asleep in class.

'I did no other work at all at school, but music is my main subject so all I was doing contributed to that.'

Emily enjoyed performing with boys who also loved to sing.

'I was used to boys who played football. I could never talk to them properly. Before I did *Les Mis*, I didn't know there were boys who were musical. We became great friends with no embarrassment at all because we were in the same boat.

'It taught me to be with other people and calmed my nerves. I became more open to other ideas. I made friends with ten boys and girls from different schools who all love singing and acting. We email each other every night and get together every weekend.'

Ellie has only heard her friend sing once, on a DVD.

'I don't listen to opera, but I thought: Geez, you're good Em! I had heard nothing like it before. I reckon if that's what she really wants to do she should go for it and keep trying.'

⁂

Ellie has been a member of Canteen, the cancer support group for teenagers, since she was 13. She was flown down to a camp in Sydney, but lasted one day before she wanted to leave.

'I don't like the city and being away from home. It wasn't anything to do with Canteen. It's just me,' she said with a rueful smile.

Vicki said her daughter can't bear to see other children so sick with cancer. On the kitchen table was a box of brightly coloured Canteen bandannas and pens that Ellie and Vicki sell every year to raise money for the charity.

Ellie is the first of her family to do Year 12, although the concentration of study drains her and the tumour affects her eyesight. At the end of 2005, she put her name forward for school captain for Molong Central School for the following year, but didn't tell her family.

'It was my last opportunity to give something back to the school. The teachers and students have been good to me and helped me out when I had troubles,' said Ellie.

After the election she said to her mother, 'Guess what? I'm school captain. Mum said, "You're joking?"' Ellie laughed.

Her art teacher, Chris Cowell always thought Ellie was the favourite.

'She has such amazing energy. Sometimes she gets a little stressed, but she works at being positive and smiling. She's resilient and tries hard all the time. We would not have a single problem if all the students did half as much as Ellie.'

Chris Cowell said Ellie was away sick for a long time.

'The other students respect her. They know she's been in and out of hospital. She doesn't talk about it and has to be asked if she is OK after she has check-ups. She just gives them the nod. Ellie is a special person. She's quite inspiring.'

Vicki said that being school captain has given Ellie confidence because she has to speak in assembly and organise events such as school sports. One of the perks of the role was an invitation to fly to Sydney to meet New South Wales Governor Professor Marie Bashir at Government House. The metal nuts and bolts in Ellie's head set off the alarms at Sydney airport.

March 2006 was the culmination of seven months rehearsal for Emily Murphy and 150 other singers, actors and orchestra members of *Les Miserables*. There were so many actors on stage at any one time that the school had to build an extra stage area. They performed to packed houses of 800 people over four nights. Every performance drew a standing ovation. Emily's portrayal of Fantine was described by the director as 'outstanding, perceptive and deeply engaging'.

'I love performing on stage,' Emily said, 'because of the buzz and all the people. The crowd adds 50 per cent to my performance. I work off the expressions of people in the front row. On the first night they were my family, friends and teachers. Everyone was staring at me when I sang a solo. It's a really good feeling. I was happy after the first night and couldn't wait for the second. There is a cue when I come back as a ghost. The stage is lit and smoke billows out. It worked perfectly on the first night, but on the second night there was so much noise backstage that the stage crew and I didn't hear the cue. So no smoke or lights came on. I had to start singing backstage as I tried to claw my way through the curtains. Some of the audience said it sounded as if I was coming down from heaven.'

For Emily's biggest fan, her father Peter, it was a real surprise to see his shy, quiet daughter come out on stage and act like a veteran. He thought his sister Joan was the only person in the family with a musical talent.

'I couldn't believe how Em sang,' Peter said. 'To see a little girl like her and this big voice that comes out of her mouth. She was on her own on stage, walking up a stairway singing and acting so well in the death scene. You could have heard a pin drop. It brought her out of her shell.'

Peter could see how she became a different person on the stage, a confident, enthralling performer who loved the wild applause for her solos.

'She is a pretty handy singer,' he said. 'Teachers say they walk past the singing rooms at Loreto and think they are hearing a CD playing. It's Em. If she were still in Orange, we mightn't know she could sing.'

A few weeks later, on Easter Thursday, I negotiated the labyrinthine tiled corridors beneath Sydney's historic town hall to join Emily and her parents for dinner at a seafood café. Everywhere people were rushing to catch trains for the Easter break. Emily was dressed in her blue and white checked school uniform; a badge which proclaimed 'senior' was pinned to her chest. Robyn sat beside her at the table; Peter sat opposite. Both parents spoke to Emily and to me, but not to each other. Peter later told me that his divorce from Robyn came through that day.

Emily, who had a slight cold, sipped water and tried to mentally prepare herself, as well as keep the conversation going at our table. She was about to face an audience of 3000 people inside the town hall in a solo performance for the 18th Loreto Music Festival. Any of these challenges – parental divorce, a solo performance before a packed house, having to strike high notes with a head cold – would reduce most teenagers to a quivering wreck: Emily looked composed.

'I'm not nervous until the last five minutes before I go on,' she said.

Sydney Town Hall dominates the square. Its steps were packed with eager parents and siblings, grannies and grandpas and students' friends. Inside, the grand pipe organ towered up to the ceiling. A bright sky-blue light shone above the organ. Emily's solo was her favourite aria, 'Ebben, N'Andro Lontana' from the opera *La Wally* by Catalini. It was first performed at La Scala in the Italian opera city of Milan in 1892 and tells a tale of love, deception, jealousy and murder. La Wally is the heroine of the piece who, with her lover, is eventually swept to her death by an avalanche. 'It's all good operatic stuff,' Emily's teacher Lyndsey commented.

'Ebben, N'Andro Lontana' is young soloist Emily's song of choice because it is powerful and open to interpretation. 'You can make it your own by adding ornamentation, depending on your emotion when you sing it.' The song makes her feel sad because the girl is lamenting having to leave her childhood home.

She prepared for a big performance such as this by getting into the mood five or ten minutes before she went on stage.

'I sit in a corner by myself and go through the song in my head with my eyes closed. I get into the character, add the facial expressions and relax so I'm calm to perform.'

On this night Emily worried about her voice because in rehearsal it started to crack on the high notes and she had already sung in two choirs before the solo.

'When you have a cold, it's hard to hold your breath for long.'

She had to change from her uniform into a silk dress, so she was rushed, but as Emily was announced, and then walked onto the stage, none of this was obvious. A tiny figure in a hot-pink, strapless silk dress, she was completely dwarfed by the stage and the massive pipe organ. But as soon as she opened her mouth to sing, it was clear that she had the measure of the vast space. Not at all intimidated, she began softly, soaring to a high F almost out of human range it seemed. The pure sound reached easily to the back rows. The power of it completely filled my ears. Her aunt told me that in the previous year Emily didn't use a microphone and was still able to reach the corners of the hall. At the end of her performance, the audience gave her rousing applause.

Later, I asked her how she could reach that high F natural so effortlessly.

'I have to prepare,' she said. 'I take a quick breath and smile with my eyes and cheeks, which lifts the soft palate in the throat. Then I have to pretend there's an apple in my mouth, so it will stay wide open for three beats.'

It sounds like hard work. Emily was puffing by the time she finished this aria. She had a drink and then took five minutes to relax again. As soon as she finished *La Wally*, her voice broke down.

Lyndsey, who is also a renowned singer, regards her pupil's voice range as exceptional. Emily can comfortably reach more than three octaves from top C, which is only five keys from the end of the piano, down to the C below middle C. Not many sopranos can reach those high notes without losing the low ones.

'I love high notes,' Emily said. 'I find them easy to reach. Going to the lowest register is what ruins my voice. High notes build a lot of pressure in your head. Your temples throb, your face goes red and your breathing is really heavy. I can't sing *La Wally* too often or I get a headache. You have to squeeze all your muscles – the stomach and thighs, everything – to get up there and hit the really high notes. I pretend the sound comes out the top of my head.'

Emily giggled as she remembered the strapless dress that she was afraid she might lose on the high F. She clenched her arms into her sides.

Singing is everything to Emily Murphy. Her teacher chooses her songs, but Emily is still learning how to read music so she has to learn songs by listening to CDs.

'Emily has a natural ability to let the music take over and speak for itself,' Lyndsey said. 'The rarity is the quality of her voice. It is such a beautiful instrument. She has the potential to be a professional singer, but it's a very competitive field. She will need skills other than a great voice. She needs to learn quickly, be a good musician, supremely confident and, in some ways, be ruthless. However, Emily is really committed and is developing those other qualities.'

While Emily pursued her music, Ellie was studying childcare at TAFE for the Higher School Certificate.

'I hope to go into a two-year diploma in childcare at TAFE and do a traineeship at Molong preschool. I also love photography. So I might do something in that.'

She was preparing major works in visual arts and photography. Lily, her niece, is a favourite subject for Ellie's special brand of black-and-white photos. She overlaid some photos with a colour, images such as the bright pink of a lily lying beside her niece, Lily. It creatively married her main interests – children and art.

'I don't want to go to uni or leave home for the big city life,' Ellie said. 'I like small country towns where everyone knows everyone else and sticks together. A teacher once told me that I should get out of my comfort zone. I said, "I don't want to. I like my comfort zone."'

Ellie was determined to enjoy life and beat her tumour.

'When I've been sick, I've thought: I can do this. God put this tumour in my head because I'm tough. My life's been a rollercoaster of being sick, then coming good, then being sick again. Now I'm good. The doctors aren't sure what will happen in future. They monitor the tumour's growth every six months. My friends and family have stuck by me. My guardian angels are my grandma, Theresa Nunn, and a friend who had cancer, Sally Mackenzie. Sally never gave up until one night she just passed away. I feel I can do anything with those two watching over me.'

I caught up with Emily when she came home for the holidays. She looked tired.

'Up late studying?' I hazarded a guess. She laughed. I'm way out. She was exhausted from a day at the picnic races with friends. Next question.

In 2007, after finishing secondary school Emily was accepted for her gap year at a small boarding school for girls called Towers Convent in southern England. She hoped the year overseas would be her opportunity to learn how to read music well and become familiar with different composers and operas.

'I'm so excited. I'll be a boarding supervisor, coach sporting teams and maybe do some music. I also want to learn Italian because it is lovely for arias. After I finish there, a friend and I will travel to the Austrian Alps for our first white Christmas.'

Emily's dream is to go to the Royal Academy of Music in London, where the standards are extremely high and entrance is difficult. Before then, she would like to study opera at the Sydney Conservatorium of Music.

'I can't go to the Con until I'm 21,' she said, 'although my teacher said my voice is ready now. In the future, I would love to be involved in an opera company such as the Bavarian Opera in Munich.'

Emily entered the Sydney City Eisteddfod. Singers who succeed in the Eisteddfod go on to compete for the prestigious Joan Sutherland Award. She has chosen songs so hard that she actually feels nervous. Emily hasn't mentioned it, but Peter tells me that she has notched up 74 out of 80 marks for singing in the Higher School Certificate.

Before the HSC exams Emily had felt happier over the last 12 months because there had been no tension or fighting at home.

'I don't talk to Mum much because it upsets me, but I feel a lot stronger. Before, I didn't stick up for myself. Now I'm not afraid to be myself, to be open and more independent. I've become more confident because I've gone through a lot. It's helped me when I'm on stage because I think that if I stuff up, it's not the end of the world. It's only one moment of your life. It's helped my acting too because I've experienced many emotions in my life.'

Emily said that Ellie, brother Michael, and Peter are high on the list of people who helped her through the tough times.

'I always listen to Dad, to his values of honesty and trust, of putting yourself in other people's shoes to understand how they feel. He said you always have to work for what you want. You can't sleep on the job or slacken off.'

As the HSC exams drew near, both girls received a boost. Ellie's teacher entered her photograph, 'On the Veranda', of her Lily with the pink lilies, in the Ilford School Photo and Digital Imaging Competition. Against competition from Year 12 students across Australia it won a certificate of merit.

Emily was nominated for the Encore Concert at Sydney Opera House in February 2007, an honour reserved for those select few Year 12 students who excel in their practical music exams. She had to prepare a video for the final selection of about twenty performers.

'I was surprised and so excited,' she said. 'I'll return from England if I'm selected. It is one of my dreams to sing in the Opera House.'

'You can become famous and I'll be your photographer,' Ellie suggested. By the end of 2006, she had landed the Molong preschool traineeship and began a four-day week in 2007; she does TAFE childcare by correspondence on the fifth day.

'I really love it,' Ellie said. 'I watch the other teachers and learn as I go, for instance, one TAFE assignment was about how to relate to kids. The teachers deal with misbehaviour by speaking positively, not negatively. "Please walk inside the building", they say, instead of "Don't run inside". My brother is getting married soon and his fiancée has asked me to take the photos. I don't know if I'm up to it, but she said she loved my photos of Lily.'

Despite their youth, these teenage girls showed a maturity and wisdom beyond their years. Emily was destined for great heights in her chosen career of opera singing. Ellie got on with life armed with her own brand of grit and courage. She didn't want to leave Molong because she felt happy there. Emily and Ellie's friendship has sustained them through the tough times and the good. They can just be themselves and enjoy each other's company.

Emily picked up Ellie for a day out together in Orange.

'We write to each other during the term and do something together every holiday. Em has just got her P-plates. I'd better wear my crash helmet.'

Emily Murphy's 2006 HSC artwork,
Imperceivable Emotion, which was used on
the cover of the Loreto Normanhurst Year 12
Awards ceremony booklet, 2006

Yasmin Mishare, Shepparton, Victoria, 2007

15

Our Second Country

Yasmin Mishare, Shepparton, Victoria

The path is long from Samawa to Shepparton, from a repressive regime in Iraq to the unknown territory of a new country and culture. It was raining hard on the wintry day I drove to meet Yasmin Mishare in Shepparton at the heart of Victoria's rich Goulburn Valley. At the suburban brick house the curtains were drawn and a mat, flanked by several pairs of shoes, lay at the door. I removed my shoes, as is the custom. A petite girl with large dark eyes opened the door. She wore green cargo pants, a white jumper and a knitted beanie. Yasmin saw my husband Bill, who was only dropping me off, hastily waved me inside and vanished. A few minutes later, she emerged wearing the traditional Muslim headscarf, or hijab. A strange man at the door had caught her unawares.

Yasmin was introduced to me by an Iraqi multicultural worker in Shepparton, Fatima al Qarakchy. When I phoned the 20-year-old student, my first question after the introductions was, 'Are you engaged or getting married soon?' Yasmin laughed and said, 'No'. This girl was different from many of her compatriots.

In 2003, I heard about the influx of Muslims to the Goulburn Valley, 160 kilometres north of Melbourne. Iraqis now number over 3000, or 10 per cent, of the population of Shepparton and nearby Cobram and have become the largest concentration of Muslims outside Sydney and Melbourne. The lives of Iraqi settlers in regional Australia have been shaped by their frightening experiences. They came to this country as refugees escaping persecution, not as immigrants who chose to leave their homeland. They are Shi'ia Muslims who fled President Saddam Hussein's brutal regime after the first Gulf War against American-led forces in 1991. US promises of safety for Shi'ias proved false after President George Bush senior signed a treaty with Hussein. Although Shi'ias formed 60 per cent of the population, Hussein's minority Sunni Muslim regime ruled through fear and intimidation. Sunnis and Shi'ias shared similar beliefs and worship, but, in the early years of Islam, parted ways over leadership: Sunnis believed that the best candidate could be elected successor to the Prophet Mohammed, whereas Shi'ias believed the leader had to be Mohammed's descendant.

Around 4000 BC, this same country, situated between the Tigris and Euphrates Rivers, was known as Mesopotamia and referred to as 'the cradle of civilisation'. It was the birthplace of Sumerian culture, predating the civilisations of Egypt, Greece and Rome by many thousands of years. Sumerians grew the first cereal crops on their fertile land and developed sophisticated irrigation systems. The earliest writing, cuneiform, a method of marking clay using chopped off reeds, evolved here. The Sumerians created accounting systems and calendars. They passed on complex agricultural techniques to subsequent generations. In modern times, the country has become a battlefield. Since the invasion of Iraq in 2003 by the American- and British-led 'coalition of the willing' forces, including Australia, Australian media have been saturated with horrific images depicting daily life in the capital Baghdad and around the country – destruction and, often, death caused by suicide bombers, snipers and car bombs, kidnappers beheading hostages, street fighting and neigh-bourhoods turned to rubble by US soldiers, tanks and bombs.

I became fascinated with these people in Shepparton, a community from a war-torn country trying to adapt to life in an Australian country town. I began to wonder how young people, particularly the women, coped.

Cutting Edge Youth Services in Shepparton works with refugees and suggested I talk with Mariam. She is a strict Shi'ia Muslim aged 15, who eloquently described her experiences to me in phone conversations and emails. Her life changed when she was a child of four. At that time, Saddam Hussein forced all men to join the army or risk imprisonment or death, so her father fled to Iran. He said to kill another Muslim was like killing your brother or sister. The rest of her family was soon forced to escape: they hid by day, and moved at night for six months until they too reached Iran and were reunited with her father. Mariam wrote of her experiences in *Stories from Home*, a Cutting Edge Youth Services publication in which young refugees told their stories about settling in the Goulburn Valley.

> **We left Iraq because it is dangerous, because people from our religious group [Shi'ias] are being persecuted by Saddam Hussein and if they stay their family is in great danger. Life is very hard if you are associated with our group. People are denied education, health treatment, employment and all the things you need to have a good life. People are murdered or they disappear. Their families are treated so badly that they would do anything, pay anyone, risk everything to escape. Imagine if that happened here. Would you wait for an embassy to come so you could stand in a queue, or would you gather your belongings and do everything possible to get your family to safety?**

Mariam lamented that she missed her country, her relatives and belonging in society. 'The way I look makes people stare. I may wear different clothes, but I am a person underneath. The difference between you and me is not that great.'

I never had the chance to meet Mariam because after finishing Year 12 she became engaged to an Iraqi boy. She had to obtain special permission to marry at 16, and after she did, she then moved to Melbourne to begin university. The community workers then introduced me to Hebah, an articulate 16-year-old who was emerging as a leader. Like Mariam, Hebah was a child when her father had to flee Iraq. He was involved in the failed uprising of southern Shi'ias against Saddam Hussein. Hebah and her family also became fugitives. They travelled from Iraq to Syria in the dead of night, hiding by day. After six traumatic years of separation, the family joined Hebah's father in Perth from where they journeyed on to the Goulburn Valley.

Hebah was the first Iraqi girl at her primary school. She wanted Australians to understand her culture and realise that Iraqis were normal people, not barbaric or terrorists.

'Some people really hate us,' she said when we met. 'They tell us to go back to Iraq, that Australia is not our country.'

Hebah became the first Iraqi student leader at her secondary college. As a teacher's aide at the local primary school, she also taught Iraqi children English and helped them to settle into school. But Hebah's most potent influence was through performance of her one-act play *Living in Between*, about being a settler in a strange land, and through fashion parades. At these women-only events, she and her friends showed the elegant, glamorous clothing and make-up of

Muslim women dressed up for weddings and parties. Hebah wanted to put the best things from her culture together with the best of Australian society. It complicated her daily life as she constantly tried to decide what those elements were. In 2005, after completing Year 12, Hebah also became engaged, married at 17 and moved away from the Goulburn Valley. She dreamt of being a lawyer. Maybe, like Mariam, getting married was her chance to go to university, which she couldn't do on her own.

A drive through Shepparton will reveal Arab women in hijabs side by side at traffic lights with teenagers in short skirts and midriff tops, men in shorts and thongs and the occasional farmer in riding boots and wide-brimmed hat. In this multicultural centre, you can see Aussie footballers in Mustafa's Café, an African face in La Porchetta Italian restaurant or an Asian family in Pizza Hut.

Yasmin lives on the southern side of Shepparton. She took me into the kitchen to meet her mother, Fatima, named after the Prophet Mohammed's daughter. The frame of her black hijab focused attention on her eyes – almost black in her olive face. Fatima sat crumbling bread at the table. I asked what she was making. As her mother doesn't speak much English Yasmin interpreted. She glanced at Fatima before telling me her mother has multiple sclerosis, MS, a progressive disorder of the nervous system that has affected her jaw and prevents chewing. Fatima dipped the torn bread into a dainty glass of sweet, black tea to soften it. Beside her was a packet of strong sedatives. It was pain that I saw in her dark eyes.

'Every day Mum has to inject herself for the MS,' said Yasmin. 'She was diagnosed in 2005. She still cooks, but my sisters and I clean the house and the boys tidy the yard.'

Yasmin, as the eldest daughter, is responsible for caring for her mother and keeping her company. Two days a week she attends TAFE in Shepparton to learn scientific laboratory techniques. Her father, Ali, runs a carwash business, her elder brother Ahmad, who is 19, studies information technology at TAFE and works part time at Target; the other five children go to school. Yasmin has two sisters – Hebah aged 18 and Hajer 16, as well as two other brothers, Yusuf, 11, and Mohammed, nine, who were all born in Iraq. Her youngest brother, Hussein, who is six, was born in Shepparton. The family is part of a close-knit community of Iraqis in the town.

'We also have Turkish, Italian, English and Australian friends,' Yasmin said.

We moved into the lounge room. Burnt-orange suede sofas stretched around in an L-shape to seat the family of nine. A large television set was tuned to an Arabic-language station. I asked where in Iraq Yasmin's family lived.

'Samawa,' she replied. 'It's a city of 250,000 people on the coast, 200 kilometres south of Baghdad. My dad owned a carwash business there. I remember date palms. Outside the city it was desert.'

Ali Mishare returned home from work after picking up the children from school. He is 41, a dark-haired man with a neat moustache. His brown eyes looked tired. Fatima has been sleeping poorly, he told me. The three younger boys gave me mischievous looks, quickly muttered polite 'hellos' and raced each other for the office. 'Computer addicts,' laughed Yasmin. 'They could play computer games forever.'

Hebah and Hajer removed their headscarves and joined us in the small lounge room. They had lively brown eyes and long, dark hair pinned in a twist on top of their heads. Yasmin brought in a tray of the sweet, black tea and chocolates.

Ali was the eldest of fourteen children. Ali's father had two wives, who lived in separate houses in Samawa. The girls told me that their grandfather's wives got on so well that people thought they were sisters, 'Although one was tall and skinny and the other short and fat,' Hajer laughed.

They showed me a photo of a tall, dignified man wearing a long white robe and a red and white checked headcloth, held in place by a black band. He farmed fat-tailed sheep in the desert outside the city, but paid a relative to tend the flock and only visited the farm every few weeks.

'It was a big family so we could help with the work,' Ali said. 'I worked for 20 years with my dad, but I didn't want to farm sheep. My father made money from sheep. He helped me to buy land and start a carwash business in Samawa. I did well.'

When the first Gulf War started in 1991, Yasmin was six and Hajer, the youngest child then, was two. Parents like Ali and Fatima were under pressure to keep up a façade for their children that Saddam Hussein was great because there were spies everywhere. Children could inadvertently betray their parents' sympathies.

'Even with your own family you had to be careful,' Ali explained. 'The walls had ears. Teachers would ask pupils if their parents said anything bad about the regime and if they said, "Yes", you were gone. People just disappeared.'

'Our school books – history, geography, even maths – showed photos of Saddam and told us he was the best role model,' Yasmin said. 'All the media said how good he was.'

'We didn't know what was going on,' Hebah said. 'We used to dance on Saddam's birthday.'

Saddam Hussein killed many Shi'ias in the south; he also killed Kurds in the north and some Sunnis. Ali's father knew of one site where Kurds had been brought south into the Samawa desert and shot or buried alive.

'My father was too scared to talk about what he knew,' said Ali. 'If you talked, it wasn't just you who would be threatened, but your wife and children too.'

According to a report for the Iraqi War Crimes Tribunal:

One grave alone of the 27 mass graves in this desert region contained 1500 corpses. All the victims at the Samawa site are thought to have been Kurds, brought there in mass transport operations. Based on partial probes, US investigators offered a rough population breakdown: only 27 per cent of the victims were adults, whereas 63 per cent were under 18 years old. 'Most were very small, and 10 were clearly infants', an investigator said. The few adult males uncovered there are thought to have been elderly men.

One day the security police commandeered Ali's car and made him drive them to the north.

'They would take you away for no reason. When I returned, I was angry – angry with my family, angry with anyone. My brother was suspected of being involved in the uprising against Saddam Hussein and jailed. There was no food in the jail, so I had to pay large bribes to the jailers who might pass on some of the food I took him. The toilet was in the corner and when they opened the hatch to pass in the food, the smell was terrible. Hundreds of men were crowded into one small room. You couldn't put a finger between them. We paid a big bribe and he was released three months later.'

In the first Gulf War, Saddam Hussein built bunkers in the industrial area near Ali's carwash. During an air raid, American planes dropped bombs and destroyed everything, including Ali's business. Looters stole whatever remained. There was no electricity to operate the carwash, so Ali was forced to make a decision.

'I had stayed in Samawa to look after my own family and thirteen brothers and sisters,' he said, 'but I had to leave or we all would have been killed. I went to a fortune teller with a friend – although I didn't really believe in it. He told me I would travel to Jordan and after that to a country far away. My father said to go ahead and find somewhere safe for my family. He and my brother would look after the family while I left for Jordan. I could only tell the children that I was going abroad to make money for them to live. It put a lot of pressure on my wife and parents.'

The Jordanian government allowed Iraqis to stay for seven months. Ali worked in a restaurant while he secretly organised for papers to leave the country. Just five days before the seven months was up, a forger handed him a passport that identified him as a Saudi businessman. Ali was in constant fear he would be apprehended and sent back to Iraq. Back in Samawa, Fatima was trying to raise funds for the family's escape. When she married Ali, he had given her gifts of jewellery – a gold belt with a large shield buckle, gold earrings, bracelets and necklaces. Gold was currency. It was time to cash them in. Fatima discreetly traded the gold for money and organised for it to be carried into Jordan in small amounts with taxi drivers whom they could trust. It was a dangerous task for the family and the drivers.

'There was no work, no certainty and no choice. Imagine – all your life is reduced to this.' Ali shaped a small square with four fingers.

Ali used the money to fly to Syria, then Egypt, and then Kenya as he tried to find a safe place for his family. At night in Nairobi, from the roof of his hotel he could see fighting in the street below. Ali felt vulnerable carrying their life's savings. He didn't know anybody and couldn't speak English.

'I was thinking, Why am I here in Kenya? I didn't know what to do or where to go. I was worried I might be jailed or killed for my money. Strange as it may seem, the fortune teller appeared to me in a dream and said I was far away from home, as he foresaw.'

Ali went to an airline office. 'The clerk asked me: "Do you want to go to Europe or Australia, or where?" Can I go to Australia? I asked. I didn't know anything about this country except that I remembered kangaroos from pictures in my old school books.'

The clerk told Ali that Australia was a good country and he would organise a visa.

'So he gave me a fake visa,' said Ali. 'He didn't know I already had a false passport. I bought a good suit and sewed the money into secret pockets in my suit. When I landed in Perth, I threw the passport in a rubbish bin and told the official I was a refugee. He said, "You look like a gentleman". When he heard my story, he said, "Don't worry, you're OK now". They sent me to Port Hedland detention centre. I could see from the plane that around it was a desert.'

Ali paused at this point of his story. Port Hedland was not as horrific as an Iraqi jail. He had food and a bed, but it was definitely a low point in his turbulent life. Ali thought he must have done something wrong for which he was being jailed. He shook his head.

'I didn't believe Australia would have a jail like this. We were inside a high fence that had razor wire curled around the top. I felt depressed and scared that I had lost everything.'

After paying for travel and bribes, he only had $100 left. Ali rang Fatima from Port Hedland to say he was in a jail with 500 men, women and children who had also escaped from persecution in China, Indonesia and Afghanistan, as well as Iraq. In 1999, six months passed, and then the Australian Government granted Ali permanent visas for himself and his family. He travelled to Perth where a fellow Iraqi told him about an Arabic-speaking community in Shepparton. Ali found his way there and stayed with a countryman while he looked for work. The productive Goulburn Valley reminded him of southern Iraq.

'Most Iraqis worked on farms,' he said. 'It was a hot summer and I started picking tomatoes. I had one set of clothes and no car.'

The bush flies made a big impression, swarming in his eyes and mouth as he worked. For six months Ali worked and slept, slept and worked for 12 hours a day, seven days a week until he had saved enough money for his family to come to Australia.

In the two long years Ali was away, his family lived with Ali's parents in Samawa. Fatima felt bereft, but the children continued at school thinking their father would return soon. Ali rang his brother as soon as he was released from Port Hedland. 'Please send my family to Jordan.' Yasmin was 13 and Mohammed was two by then. The adults had to discuss plans in whispers away from the house and the children.

'Even when we left home, we didn't know the truth about the regime,' Yasmin said. 'Mum told the Iraqi officials we were going to Jordan for a holiday and would return to Samawa. The day we left our home was the saddest day of my life. I cried so much. The taxi driver turned on a sad Iraqi song and I cried even more.'

'We didn't know why we were leaving Iraq,' Hajer agreed. 'It took two days to reach Jordan. We cried the whole way there.'

Ali's mother also travelled with them because she thought she would never see her family again. They left on Iraqi passports, but had to pay bribes to cross the border. Once there, they didn't know anyone except Ali's bachelor brother with whom they lived. As visitors they weren't allowed to go to school, so the children had nothing to do until they made Iraqi friends. Seven months later Ali flew from Australia to pick them up.

'We were so happy to see Dad,' Yasmin said. 'We all hugged him and my mum cooked a special dinner.'

At last Ali and Fatima could tell their family the truth about Saddam Hussein and why they had left Iraq.

'It's no good to lead a secretive life,' Ali said. 'I could finally feel normal, like a computer sent away and cleared of viruses!'

Stories from Home gives some idea of the scale of the exodus from Iraq:

Since the Gulf War in 1991, over 500,000 people have left their homes in Iraq. Some were directly involved in uprisings against the Saddam Hussein regime; others were threatened because of family connections, religious beliefs and political ideas, and were afraid for the safety of themselves and their families.

The reunited family arrived in Victoria in 2000, nine years after the first Gulf War disrupted their lives.

'My dad's friends were waiting at Melbourne airport,' Yasmin said. 'We planned to live in Melbourne, but because they lived in Shepparton they took us to stay with them until we could find a house. I liked Australia from the start and felt happy because we were all together. It was a beautiful country, so I didn't feel like a stranger.'

The first months in Shepparton were hard as Ali had no money left to rent a house. He received Centrelink payments at first, then went back to picking tomatoes.

'In Iraq my family had what they needed,' he said. 'Here we had to sleep on our jackets until some kind people gave us pillows, a bed and blankets, plates and food. I borrowed money from friends. The children said, "Why did we come here?"'

'At first,' Ali continued, 'the kids didn't know that I did big things for them and put myself in danger for their freedom. It was hard for them to understand.'

The Iraqi community helped each other financially, rather than going to a bank which would require interest on loans. An Iraqi community leader told the children, 'Tomorrow you go to school.'

'But we didn't go that first day,' Yasmin said. 'I was scared because I didn't know English.'

The following day she gathered the courage to go to McGuire College and was relieved to discover it was a multicultural school attended by other Iraqis. Yasmin was midway through Year 8.

'I didn't say anything and I couldn't understand anything either,' she said. 'I only knew "Hi" and "Bye" in English.' Although English was a compulsory second language from Year 5 in Iraq, Yasmin's schooling had been interrupted by war and the time in Jordan. McGuire College employed a teacher of English as a Second Language and Yasmin learnt quickly. She also studied Italian and spoke Arabic and English at home.

Hebah and Hajer went to a local primary school.

'I cried when I got home because I couldn't understand and didn't know what to say,' Hebah said. Twice a week she had classes in English as a Second Language and she soon made Australian friends who sat with her at lunchtime and taught her to read, write and spell because the teacher was too busy. Yasmin wasn't so lucky.

'There were some mean girls in my class. They would say, "Go back to your country", and call us rude names, like f****** bitch. I heard those words spoken in the corridor at school and thought, These are common words; they must not be too bad.'

Yasmin put up with the name calling for six months, then she decided to repeat those same words in English back at her tormentors.

'They were so surprised, their eyes opened wide – like this,' she demonstrated with a laugh. 'They didn't think I would know how to respond. The girls didn't say a word and walked away. The English teacher heard me, not them and said, "Yasmin, why do you swear?"'

By the end of the first year, Yasmin began to enjoy school because she could converse in English and had made friends with Australian girls who loved sport. Together they played competition basketball and squash.

'Some Iraqi parents are strict about their daughters playing sport,' she said. 'I don't know why because there is nothing wrong with it. Maybe they don't want their daughters to wear pants. I wore a loose T-shirt and long pants. Many Australians think Muslim girls don't play sport because of their religion, but Islam has nothing to do with sport. It's up to the family. Our family is open-minded.'

Australian neighbours helped them settle in. Some took the Mishare girls to English classes. Another helped Ali fix his 1977 car that broke down every morning. One night, during a storm that caused a power blackout, Ali had to shine the car lights through the house's front window to calm baby Hussein. A helpful neighbour heard the baby crying and gave the family a torch.

'When we came to Australia I met good people who helped me,' Yasmin said, 'and I also encountered people who were not nice, but I didn't really care about them. I only cared about the people who created a good image of Australian society in my eyes.'

Later that day I met Chris Hazelman, who managed the Ethnic Council of Shepparton and District. Chris was also mayor of the City of Greater Shepparton during the main influx of Iraqis from 1998 to 2003. If any rural region could accommodate different nationalities, it would be the Goulburn Valley. Many races have thrived since irrigation was introduced to the area in the late 1890s and their cultures have enriched the valley. Waves of people came for the seasonal fruit picking, which was hard, hot work but didn't require training or English – Europeans, Filipinos, Punjabis, Serbs, Croats, Bosnians, Pacific Islanders and, most recently, Congolese. By 2006, 22 per cent of the district were born overseas and comprised sixty language groups.

Muslim Albanians and Turks had already settled around Shepparton when the first Iraqis arrived in 1997. Families were followed in 1998–99 by men arriving without their families, like Ali Mishare. They had endured torture and starvation in Saddam Hussein's prisons or long separations from their families in the tough, barbed-wire camps of Iran or Saudi Arabia. When they were granted permanent visas, they sent word back to their families to come to

Australia. By late 1999 Australian Government policy had changed and temporary protection visas (TPVs) had been introduced. TPVs spelt great stress and an uncertain future for the holders because they didn't know if they could stay in Australia for more than three years. They lacked access to services available to the earlier refugees, such as 510 hours of English language classes, a healthcare card, childcare assistance and, most importantly, family reunion rights. According to Chris Hazelman, around 750 Iraqis held TPVs, which led to high stress levels in the community. Most have since been granted permanent visas, but some families on TPVs had to leave their children in Iraq until they obtained permanent residency. Chris Hazelman estimated that the region had 3000 permanent residents and additional transients during summer and the picking season. Local services tried to keep up with the influx of refugees in the provision of housing, education, interpreters and welfare support. It was crisis management.

The council, with Chris as mayor, set up the Iraqi Taskforce.

'We made it up as we went along and issues arose,' said Chris. 'Rural Australians are often conservative and these Iraqis had different customs. They came from a dry country, so they didn't waste water on lawns or cut them, which aggravated some locals. On one feast day, a crowd of Iraqis slaughtered thirteen sheep on a vacant lot. We had to find a bloke who could open a Halal butchery.'

Halal meat has to meet strict Muslim requirements: it must be meat of a vegetarian animal, which must be slaughtered by a Muslim butcher who recites the name of Allah as he faces Mecca, the holy city of Islam. No pig meat is permitted because it is considered unclean.

Local groups identified a problem that there was no appropriate doctor for Muslim women and lobbied for a female, Arabic-speaking doctor; there are now several at the hospital. Cultural practices created tensions. The women wouldn't swim at the aquatic centre because their beliefs forbade mixed bathing. Council battled for single-gender bathing and eventually obtained exemption from the Equal Opportunities Commission. The ruling caused a media stir. Now Muslim women can swim at the pool in the times set for women only. A problem also surfaced when Iraqi 15- and 16-year-olds were put into classes with 10-year-olds because of their English language levels. Many left school and joined the ranks of jobless and bored youth.

The year 2001 was a difficult one for Iraqi refugees and the Iraqi Taskforce. They couldn't have foreseen events that shook Australia and the world and hardened attitudes towards Muslim people. In the *Tampa* incident, boat people, many of whom were Afghan and Iraqi, were picked up by a Norwegian freighter, the *Tampa*, from a dilapidated vessel sinking off Australia's northwest coast. The federal government refused them landing on Australian soil at Christmas Island

and crack troops were sent to intercept these people seeking safe haven. Images of women and children flailing in the sea were used by politicians and the media to colour perceptions that people threw their own children overboard so they could get into the country. The alleged threat to national security from boat people desperate to escape Saddam Hussein's and the Taliban regimes dominated the 2001 federal election. Many asylum seekers were detained for long periods of time; later, some came to Shepparton where their husbands had settled.

Soon after the *Tampa* incident, the 9/11 terrorist attacks on the twin towers of New York's World Trade Center and the Pentagon occurred. Refugees in Shepparton who had previously felt safe, became nervous as some people identified them as being from a similar culture to that of the terrorists. Women wearing headscarves no longer appeared in the streets. Council set up community events to ease tensions and Iraqi leaders took steps to present the community in a positive light. However, Iraqi children could not hide from the taunts of their peers.

'September 11 was a shock to everyone,' Hebah Mishare recalled. 'Our community was scared because racism started and people said mean things. Dad told us that local people did not understand that we had escaped such violence ourselves. I was quiet at school. If someone called me names, I would tell the teacher, or my brother Ahmad would chase them. Now I just say I'm proud to be an Arab or ignore them and walk away.'

The Iraqi community bought land for a school and converted a factory into a mosque.

'Some locals claim it's a training ground for Osama bin Ladens,' Chris Hazelman said, 'even though the Turks did the same thing not long ago. They equate Islamic extremists overseas with this lot because they look the same. The suspicion of a different culture is fear of the unknown. When I was growing up here, Greek and Italian men would go into dark cafés and smoke, drink wine and talk. Strange garlicky smells would waft out and my mother would almost cross the street to escape. Those European boys I went to school with are now accountants and solicitors in town. The latest arrivals from the Congo were embraced by the local community. The Iraqis also helped them get established by sourcing a house for them, but noted that their own community hadn't received such a welcome.'

As Ethnic Communities Council manager, Chris also works with the Iraqi Embassy in Australia to clarify land ownership for people who fled Iraq with only a suitcase and their papers. Their property had been absorbed by Saddam Hussein's government.

'The ambassador was staggered to find such a large community here,' Chris said, 'but until Saddam Hussein was deposed in 2003, they hadn't wanted the

Iraqi government to know about them. The Iraqis here are industrious and well-educated people. The best we can do is to help them develop their potential.'

By 2004, Ali Mishare had saved enough money to buy a carwash in Shepparton. It was one of only a handful of Iraqi-owned businesses. His brother, who spoke good English, helped him to start.

'In the beginning I didn't know if I would be successful,' Ali said. 'I worked hard to make a decent life for my family. It's a good business and people know me now. They say, "Hello Ali". Other Iraqis ask me how to start a business and I lend them money.'

In 2005, after Yasmin finished her Year 12 exams, the Mishares returned to Samawa to see their family. Australian forces were stationed in the city. This area became the first where foreign forces handed back responsibility for security to the Iraqis. Ali found it was more peaceful than before they fled, but still not safe.

According to *BBC News* in November 2006, casualty figures of Iraqi civilians who have died in acts of war since the 2003 invasion are a controversial topic, with estimates ranging from 50,000 to 650,000 deaths. 'No official count has ever been made public. The head of the Baghdad central mortuary said that he was receiving up to sixty victims of violent death from insurgent violence and sectarian strife each day, at his facility alone.'

'In Samawa there was not much power and no gas,' Ali said. 'I couldn't run a business and there was no other work. I think we will stay in Shepparton and visit Iraq. It's a close community in Shepparton and I have good relationships with everyone.'

Yasmin noticed satellite dishes, mobile phones and news from the rest of the world were now available in their former city. 'We were sad when we had to leave our family in 2000, but we know we can travel back now Saddam Hussein is gone. We are getting used to Shepparton and have friends here.'

There was a knock at the door. It was Fatima al Qarakchy, who had introduced me to Yasmin. She wore a long robe and a hijab. With Fatima around, Yasmin visibly relaxed. Fatima had a broad grin and immediately began to tease me.

'Watch out for this woman, Yasmin,' she laughed, 'or you might end up married after an interview.'

Fatima al Qarakchy is in great demand. Like many Iraqis, she is highly trained. She taught microbiology in a university in Iraq, but Shepparton has no such work. Fatima has snatched an hour from one of her three part-time jobs – multicultural officer for Cutting Edge Youth Services and Arabic interpreter for Centrelink and Goulburn Valley hospital.

We adjourned to the kitchen to join Yasmin's mother who was cooking dinner. Enticing smells wafted from cooking pots filled with tomato sauce and onion, okra and lamb in fragrant herbed broth. We sat around a long wooden table and launched into a discussion about opportunities for young women such as Yasmin. After finishing Year 12, she had an offer from Swinburne University in Melbourne to study science.

'If Iraqi girls go to university away from home, we must have a male relative with us. So we have to get married or our family has to move with us,' she explained. 'I couldn't go to Melbourne by myself and my family couldn't uproot and come with me because my dad owns a business. We have also just bought a house and my sisters and brothers go to school here, so I had to refuse it. I decided to study for a diploma at TAFE instead.'

Yasmin was proud to be the first of her friends to go to TAFE. Others studied mainly English language at TAFE. She was the first Iraqi woman enrolled in her lab technician course and hoped it would give her a higher score to enter university in future.

'I will have more choice when I finish and might be able to study for a Bachelor of Applied Science. I did well in science and maths at school and want to diagnose disease.'

We turned to the subject of early marriages. Yasmin revealed she had had ten proposals.

'Ten?' This sounded like a record, but she thought nothing of it.

'We have a choice and I refused them all,' she said. 'Most of the men were from other countries. I want to know the person. I'm not going to force myself to marry someone unsuitable. It's good to make a family, but I have to choose the right person. His way of thinking has to be a bit like my way of thinking.'

Fatima al Qarakchy was quick to add that in their culture both sets of parents discuss a proposal first and then talk with the daughter. It is shameful for a girl to agree to marriage before the family sanctions it.

'We believe the parents have more experience than the girl. Even now in our culture, we won't allow a girl to contact a boy or to go out with boys.'

At McGuire College, Yasmin saw boys and girls kissing in the playground. 'I had only ever seen a kiss in films back in Iraq,' she said. 'We mix with boys at school, but are not allowed to have a boyfriend. We have a long engagement to get to know the boy and decide if we are right for each other before we marry. Most of the girls in Shepparton think about marrying young – I don't know why – and they don't continue study. Our family is very different from other Iraqis here because we have open-minded parents. My sisters and I want to be educated, get a job and then think about getting married.'

To build confidence and independence in other young women, Fatima al Qarakchy runs leadership programs.

'It doesn't matter what they wear or what religion they are, they can feel proud that they have a mind and can use it,' she said. 'If all the Arabic girls were involved in the leadership programs there would be eighty attending, not twenty-three, as there were this year. Some men still believe their daughters should go from home to school, school to home and have no other interests. Yasmin's father is strong in the Arabic tradition, but a modern man. He encourages his children to be involved in the wider community.'

Employment is the most pressing issue for girls and for the community. *Refugees and Regional Settlement*, a 2005 report written by Janet Taylor and Dayane Stanovic for the Brotherhood of St Lawrence, showed that, despite Iraqis moving to the Goulburn Valley largely for work, 60 to 70 per cent of the men were unemployed and relied on Centrelink for income. The lack of employment clearly distressed study respondents, who were often well-qualified teachers, nurses, engineers and scientists. Women were often isolated and jobless, even those who spoke good English. Of greatest concern to the refugees was that no second generation Iraqis in the 16 to 25 age range had full-time employment when the report was written.

'Yasmin has searched for work all year,' said Fatima. 'She is happy to do anything, but maybe it's too soon for a receptionist who wears a headscarf. Most Iraqis don't want to rely on payments from Centrelink, although they have to. If they don't attend appointments with Centrelink, they lose the unemployment benefits. They might attend for two or three years and are constantly referred to literacy and numeracy courses. When they do courses year after year and remain jobless, they lose faith in the Job Network. There is little incentive to pursue casual jobs because whatever they earn is subtracted from the Centrelink payments.'

Fatima was well placed to articulate issues for the Muslim community, especially for women in rural areas. In 2005, she was appointed for 12 months to the Victorian Women in Rural Communities Taskforce, set up to advise the government. Fatima believes women are the key to building relationships with the Iraqi community. Much falls on her shoulders, as women cannot relate to a male community worker. She was concerned about the women who speak little English, can't drive and are left isolated and possibly depressed in their homes.

'Through Cutting Edge we have coordinated social and recreational activities for women, such as excursions to Melbourne, family picnics, sewing classes, a walking group, a playgroup, crosscultural lunches and excursions.'

Fatima thought many Iraqis would leave the Goulburn Valley for better work and education opportunities, especially for the younger generation. She thought they would either move to the capital cities or wait for conditions to improve in Iraq and move back there. Some might relocate to an Arabic-speaking country such as the Arab Emirates on the Persian Gulf. The dilution of culture and language in the second generation was a real concern to older Iraqis.

'The dilemma of returning to Iraq lies with the next generation, like my daughter, who has learnt English and lives in Australia. Will the young people be able to adapt to Iraq, or will living in Australia damage their future there?'

'On the other hand,' Yasmin said, 'my younger brothers only know Australia. They speak English not Arabic, because Yusuf was only three when we came here, Mohammed two and Hussein was born here. When they communicate with Mum, they point to things. If they are fighting, she doesn't know whose fault it is. It's like they live in a separate world. They are real Aussies whereas our older brother, Ahmad, knows about Iraq and speaks Arabic as we girls do. My younger brothers have started Arabic classes.'

Fatima had to leave for her home to pray. She unfurled her green embroidered mat to show me and put a clay disc on the end.

'We pray five times a day facing the holy city of Mecca in Saudi Arabia. We have a special compass to find the right direction. The forehead rests on the disc or turba, so it doesn't touch unclean ground. As we pray, we read the Quran, our book of holy words.'

Schoolchildren, like Yasmin's brothers and sisters, pray when they come home. Ramadan, the holiest month of the year for Muslims and a time of worship and contemplation, is when this large Muslim community will fast from sunrise to sundown; in 2006 Ramadan began on 22 September and ended 32 days later on 23 October.

After Fatima al Qarakchy left, Yasmin's mother placed steaming plates of food on the kitchen table and motioned me to help myself. She urged me to take more rice, more meat and vegetables. Ahmad arrived home from TAFE. He had to rush to his part-time job at Target and so ate on the run. The lamb, tomato and okra tasted delicious on rice, but Fatima wasn't able to eat any because of the MS in her jaw. Ali had looked desolate as he had explained how their lives changed when his wife had become ill. Fatima, who could no longer go shopping or visit friends, was isolated at home.

'My wife went to a dentist and he removed many teeth, but it wasn't a dental problem,' he said. 'Multiple sclerosis is uncommon in the Middle East. The doctor said it is more prevalent in colder places such as southern, not northern, Australia. Fatima has had MRI scans in Melbourne to diagnose it. At first it was a shock, but we have to believe the doctors and live with it. My wife has been tied to me for 21 years and does everything for the family. I feel like I'm losing my best friend. I'm lucky to have three good girls to look after their mother. When I asked Yasmin, "Will you look after your mum?" she said, "My mother has looked after me for 20 years. I will do it."'

He had given his daughters the choice of doing what they want.

'Real Islam gives women freedom to do anything in their lives, except drinking alcohol and doing bad things,' Ali said. 'I understand that Yasmin wants to study.'

'My dream is to finish my studies,' Yasmin said. 'My fear is maybe something will happen that will make it hard for me. I like Shepparton, but I want to go to a bigger city because it's so quiet here. Melbourne has shops, lots of Iraqis, places to go, and life.'

Her siblings are also ambitious. Ahmad finished studying information technology at TAFE in 2006 and began work with his father at the carwash in 2007. Sixteen-year-old Hajer wants to study food technology, while Hebah plans to do a beauty course, then a Bachelor of Business Administration at the La Trobe University campus in Shepparton.

'Hebah loves make-up,' Yasmin said. 'Eventually, she wants to open a beauty salon in town for women only. She is persuading Hajer to learn massage therapy and work with her. In our culture we can dress up and wear make-up for parties and weddings – which are only with other women,' she quickly added. 'We don't wear make-up when we go to town.'

Family photos of weddings show the sisters, their eyes ringed in black, dressed in richly coloured evening clothes and elegant headscarves. Had I expected girls who wore black and no make-up, I would have had to revise my thinking. Yasmin took me to the room she shares with her sisters. There were rows of skirts and tops hanging up. Masses of hijabs in all the hues of the rainbow tumbled from the wardrobe.

'What colour do you think?' she asked as she prepared to don the hijab.

I chose a vivid burnt orange embossed with a leafy design. Yasmin emerged with glossy brown lipstick and black eyeliner. She demonstrated how she drapes the hijab over a small white cap that covers her hair, then sweeps it under the chin and pins it at the back. It may be a symbol of subservience to some people, but Yasmin didn't see it that way.

'Most people think it's our culture, but it's a religious thing. Hijab means covering. Islam desires the preservation of social and family peace. Hence, it asks women to cover themselves in their interactions with men to whom they are not related. Some people think we are forced to wear the hijab, but it's our choice. Some people say women in Islam don't have rights. Allah has given equal rights to men and women. He forbids either sex claiming supremacy over the other.'

Yasmin felt that wearing the hijab gave her identity and extra respect as a Muslim.

'I also feel protected and confident when I step out. I feel I am closer to Allah.'

The following morning was a Saturday. The family gathered in the lounge room so I could talk with them and take some family photos. They all have dark eyes, white teeth and fine complexions. The younger boys jockeyed each other for seats. The girls, in their long-skirted plumage and delicately draped green and pink headscarves, were like exotic birds. Their mother was dressed in a gold embroidered robe and black hijab. At a signal from her mother, Yasmin hurried away and returned with a woollen cloth. She shook out a fine, soft cape of green, red and black and draped it over my shoulders. It was perfect for winter. I was overwhelmed by the generosity of Fatima and her family.

Over the following weeks, Fatima's condition deteriorated. She had two trips to hospital with severe attacks, but didn't stay overnight because the family thought they would have to pay $1000. We had regular contact as I tried to enlist help from the MS Society and other services. Her neurologist in Melbourne changed Fatima's medication, which reduced the pain.

When Yasmin and I next spoke, in early October, it was the twelfth day of Ramadan. During the fast, older members of the family woke at three in the morning to pray and eat breakfast; they were not allowed to eat or drink during the daylight hours. Smoking and sexual relations are forbidden during fasting. At sunset, the exact time of which varies each evening as the days grow longer, the fast is broken after prayer.

'We eat special dishes of meats and sweets after sunset,' Yasmin said. 'When Ramadan ends, we celebrate for three days in the Feast of Fast Breaking, or *Id-al-Fitr*. We exchange gifts and get together with friends and family to pray and enjoy large meals.'

When I asked, with some trepidation, how her mother was faring, Yasmin became excited. Since visiting an Adelaide doctor who also practises complementary medicine, Fatima has been taking herbal medicines.

'She is eating, talking, going out again and looks way better,' Yasmin said.

I saw for myself in early 2007. Fatima looked happy and relaxed. She and Ali had just returned from Iraq and Saudi Arabia where they took part in the Hajj, an arduous, five-day pilgrimage to Mecca. There they joined 3,400,000 other Muslims. Sunnis and Shi'ias took the journey together amid rising concerns in the Islamic world about ongoing tension, violence and bloodshed between the two main sects of Islam in Iraq. Sectarian violence there has escalated into what many observers are openly describing as civil war.

Ali pushed Fatima in a wheelchair to prayer sites and to circle seven times around the sacred Kaaba at the Grand Mosque. He kept a close eye on her in this huge wave of humanity: at the 2005 Hajj more than 360 people were killed in a stampede during a ritual stoning of the devil.

While their parents were away in the Middle East, Yasmin, her sisters and Ahmad looked after the younger boys.

'Hebah, Hajer and I took turns cooking and cleaning,' said Yasmin, 'and Ahmad ran the carwash. Some days Hebah helped him in the office. Hussein was a little devil.'

While Ali and Fatima were away, the execution of Saddam Hussein on 31 December 2006 brought the Iraqi community out to celebrate – hugging, dancing and crying tears of joy. Many Iraqis who had been tortured in Saddam's jails or had family members murdered by the regime, flooded onto the streets of Shepparton.

Ali explained how coming to Australia has affected him.

'I previously thought I was right in my ideas and wouldn't tolerate other people's views. If someone upset me, such as in a car accident, I became aggressive. It was the constant pressure of war and the regime under which we lived. I often felt angry. Here, there is no pressure, no security police and it's safe. Even my friends in Iraq say how I've changed. I say to them, "You have a chance to improve the country now that the US has kicked Saddam Hussein out". I'm more open-minded and listen to others. I try to negotiate rather than fight.' Ali's wish is for Australians to get to know Iraqis and not judge them from media reports. Then, he reflected on how his family had changed. 'My children have become so easygoing, like Australians.' He sounded bemused by this development.

Hebah spoke up. 'Adults complicate life with stress and anger. Why make it so hard?'

By 2007 Yasmin wanted to change courses to graphic arts; she had been accepted at Shepparton TAFE. She loves photography and drawing and, while at home caring for her mother, had time to develop skills in digital design using the family computer. This new course thoroughly engaged her creative intelligence. Ali was also teaching his daughter to drive, so she could obtain her P-plates and get herself to classes. Yasmin enjoyed driving, but hadn't yet passed the tests.

The girls showed me what they love to do. Hebah, the make-up expert, painted flower designs on my hands in henna, a red vegetable dye. Hajer was the model as a dab of rouge, a touch of eye shadow, glossy lipstick, transformed her. It was adornment of an already lovely face, rather like painting a picture. Only family and women friends see this side of the girls on special occasions.

Yasmin casually asked my opinion of an exotic perfume nestled in a beautiful eastern casket that her mother brought from Mecca. When I sniffed the perfume and said it was lovely, she immediately gave it to me.

Fatima was cooking up a lamb feast for Ali and his male friends to celebrate the pilgrimage; she will celebrate with women friends during school holidays. A whole sheep cut into quarters, simmered in turmeric and onion broth in a huge pot in the garage. It will be ladled over rice and noodles. Fatima poked the meat with a large fork to test its readiness.

As I prepared to leave, Yasmin opened a letter and smiled. She had applied for ten different jobs and finally had an interview for a childcare position. Yasmin didn't get that job, but the following month succeeded in getting a weekend and public holiday job in a medical centre as a receptionist with an Iraqi doctor. At last – a breakthrough. She loves it.

Yasmin and her sisters want to study, have jobs, careers and to retain their Muslim observances and Iraqi culture. There are many hurdles for young women to overcome within the local community and their own culture, but there are also opportunities, especially for Arabic–English speakers in this rural area with its substantial Muslim population. Fatima al Qarakchy and their father show them the possibilities. Ali's determination to develop a business, despite his lack of money or English at the time, has inspired other Iraqis. Yasmin has a job at last. It is possible to imagine her as a graphic designer in the future, Hebah and Hajer running a beauty salon and Ahmad working with his father. The young boys, who have spent their lives in Australia, may have smoother paths to a career and acceptance. Women like Fatima, for whom change has been most dramatic, live for their families and instil the cultural traditions.

In the volatile world that is post 9/11, the mere words 'Muslim', 'hijab' and 'Iraq' can stir up resentment and drive a wedge between people. While the path from Samawa to Shepparton has been difficult for the Mishares, they are thankful to be somewhere safe. Yasmin said they view Australia as their second country.

'We can't live without Australia and we can't live without Iraq.'

Trevor Menmuir painting his didgeridoo, Kununurra, Western Australia, 2006

16

Kimberley Man

Trevor Menmuir, Kununurra, Western Australia

Trevor Menmuir is 35, a tall muscular man who stands as straight as the baobab trees that symbolise his Kimberley homeland. Trevor is East Kimberley manager of Garnduwa, the main Aboriginal sporting organisation in this remote region.

'I never had the father image in my life. In 1975, my dad was cutting cattle on the flat at Yeeda Station, out from Derby in the west Kimberley. The horse stumbled and fell. It rolled on him, crushing his head and spine. The Royal Flying Doctor Service flew him to a hospital in Perth. He was paralysed and has been cared for in nursing homes ever since. He knows me, but doesn't have much speech.'

Tom Wilson was 35 when he fell from the horse. Trevor was five years old, and Donna, his sister, six. Jean Menmuir, their mother, had separated from Tom just before the accident, but was pregnant with their third child. Jean and the children lived in a tin shed; she cooked and cleaned at Derby hospital to make ends meet.

As I flew into Kununurra that morning, a pall of black smoke flanked the town. Aboriginal communities had set fire to country to stimulate fresh shoots and attract game, as was their custom. Several fires were burning out of control. Smoke billowed from the Carr Boyd ranges between Kununurra and Lake Argyle. It hung in the gorges like grey ribbons threaded through the red ochre hills. Firefighters worked day and night to protect the fertile Ord Valley, where tropical fruit crops, melons, pumpkins and sugar cane flourished in an irrigated chequerboard of yellows and greens.

Trevor and I found a cool spot to lunch beside a water-lily pond surrounded by fragrant mangoes. The Scottish Menmuir surname, Trevor's light brown skin and his turned-up nose indicate his mixed heritage.

'My mum, Jean Menmuir, doesn't know much of her background,' Trevor said. Then, in a deliberate manner he pulled out a browning manila folder that contained a wad of documents and letters held together by a dog clip; he had to glean what he could from these archives. His maternal grandparents were Stolen Generation, part-Aboriginal children forcibly removed from their families and communities under government policies that operated from 1910 to 1970.

Jean's father, Alec Menmuir, was taken from Gogo Station near Fitzroy Crossing in 1921 and sent to a remote mission on the Forrest River northwest of Wyndham. At the same time, on Mt Anderson Station, between Fitzroy Crossing and Broome, Jean's mother Elsie was also taken away. Jean's parents met at Forrest River mission, now called Oombulgurri, and married in 1937.

Jean Menmuir's grandmother, Mary Ann Richardson, was known as Mary Ann Gogo after Gogo Station, where she and her five children lived. Four of the children were taken away and separated from each other. Mary Ann managed to save one child, Mona, from the authorities by rubbing charcoal on her so she looked like a full-blood Aborigine. That child was not found. One son, Bruce, was taken south to Swan Boys' Orphanage, despite obviously having a parent.

Mary Ann never recovered from the forcible removal of four of her children and never seeing them again. She developed leprosy and spent her final years in Derby leprosarium. In Trevor's possession is a letter from her file, dated 1946, from the Western Australian Inspector of Natives to the Western Australia Commissioner of Native Affairs. It said, '[Mary Ann Richardson] is somewhat anxious to know how her children are getting on and I think it would help the leprosy condition if her mind could be set at rest as far as these children are concerned'.

A National Inquiry into the Stolen Generation was conducted by the Human Rights and Equal Opportunity Commission in 1995. Its *Bringing Them Home* report, published in 1997 by the Human Rights and Equal Opportunity Commission, took evidence of attitudes towards children of mixed descent over that 60-year period.

[A] half-caste, who possesses few of the virtues and nearly all of the vices of whites, grows up to be a mischievous and very immoral subject ... it may appear to be a cruel thing to tear an Aborigine child from its mother, but it is necessary in some cases to be cruel to be kind.

Professor of Public Health (Mental Health) at the University of Queensland Ernest Hunter surveyed 600 Kimberley Aboriginal people in the late 1980s and found one in four elderly people and one in seven middle-aged people had been removed during childhood. A conservatively estimated 100,000 Aboriginal children across Australia, fathered by non-Indigenous men such as Trevor Menmuir's great-grandfather Scotty, were taken from their families. Dr Cecil Cook was appointed in 1927 as the Northern Territory's so-called Aboriginal chief protector. Cook supported biological assimilation to ensure that 'all native characteristics are eradicated. The problem of our half-castes will quickly be eliminated by the complete disappearance of the black race, and the swift submergence of their progeny in the white.' Chief protectors exercised powers to remove children at around four years of age and take them to missions and settlements. At the age of 14 they were sent to work. Young girls were left alone and vulnerable on sheep and cattle stations as unpaid labour, often to be abused and fall pregnant. They were then sent back to the missions to have their babies and suffered the same separation process as their own mothers had.

Bringing Them Home documented the impact of forcible removal in the poignant recollections of over 550 people. They spoke of broken hearts and depression, feelings of inferiority, difficulties in parenting in the absence of loving role models, loss of culture and identity, and substance abuse, violence and suicide. 'Subsequent generations continue to suffer the effects of parents and grandparents having been forcibly removed, institutionalised, denied contact with their Aboriginality, and in some cases traumatised and abused.'

Under an extension of official powers in 1918, all Indigenous females, regardless of age, came under the total control of the chief protector unless they were married and living with a husband of substantially European origin. Even then, they needed permission from the chief protector to marry. Trevor's father was not forcibly removed because his white father was married to an Aboriginal wife.

'Dad's father, Farmer Wilson, was a full-blood Irishman, who started Glen Hill Station where Argyle diamond mine now is,' Trevor said. 'His Aboriginal wife was born near Wave Hill Station in the Territory. They worked together on stations and the children were protected by their white father. They christened my dad Tom, and two other sons, Dick and Harry.'

Tom Wilson grew up to be a good stockman and a fighter.

'Dad fought in a boxing tent around the Top End and northern Queensland. Fighting was how Aboriginal fellas made a name for themselves back then.'

'It was hard for Mum,' Trevor said. 'She's real special to me. Mum dedicated herself to bringing up us kids.'

In the late 1980s, Tom was moved from Perth back to Derby nursing home, but by then Dick and Harry Wilson had become Trevor's role models. They were stockmen on stations around the Kimberley and the boy wanted to be like them. Every school holiday, from the age of 12, Trevor rode in stock camps with Dick, who was a head stockman, and Shirley, his wife, who was a camp cook.

Schoolwork came well down on Trevor's list of priorities. He could write his name and basic sentences, but couldn't spell. He felt ashamed to ask teachers for help in front of his classmates or to ask them to repeat words he hadn't heard or understood.

'Other kids would go "Uhrr" and it would hold up the class. Often I didn't understand the schoolwork so I would just switch off. I thought, Why would I need to read and write when I'm going to work on stations? I lost the hearing in my right ear a long time ago, which I only discovered when it was operated on recently. Maybe that also played a part in me not doing well at school.'

Trevor has a quality of silence, of listening attentively and concentrating before he speaks, which may hark back to this time. He enjoyed school because of the sport and his mates being there so he stayed until Year 10, but was largely illiterate when he left. He became a ringer and for six years was in a stock camp of ten men who mustered and branded cattle on stations around Derby and Fitzroy Crossing. They lived out bush for seven or eight months at a time.

'I liked it. We didn't get paid much – $10 a day for my first job in 1986 – but my mates and I would challenge each other about who could work the hardest, or break in the best horse.'

They learnt to be tough. Trevor was mustering on horseback at Meda Station near Derby when the girth on the saddle came undone, the horse bolted and the saddle slipped off.

'I fell off at full gallop. It knocked me out for a few seconds and scraped the skin off one side of my body. I rode back to camp. The contractor gave me painkillers and that was it.'

Rodeos brought the ringers into town. From Halls Creek in the east to Broome in the west Kimberley, they rode bucking bulls and horses.

'Somewhere at home I have a sash for bareback riding in a Turkey Creek rodeo,' Trevor recalled. 'Afterwards we would have a few beers, but I wasn't a big drinker. If I had a bad night, I'd be sick and not want to touch it again. Some of my mates made up for lost time when they came to town. They could drink beer for breakfast after a big night. A weekend in town was enough for us – too many people. We couldn't wait to get back to the bush.'

Trevor started working for fencing contractors, which brought him into town where he got involved in a relationship.

'My daughter Sapphire came along. She's 17 now. We have a close relationship. I also have two sons,' he said, 'Sapphire's brother, Kimberley, who is 14, and Joseph, who is 15. They live with their mothers. I was moving around on contract work so the relationships didn't last. That was my younger days.'

Trevor met his match in Lynette O'Meara. He worked for her brother-in-law, who was a contract fencer. He and Lynette attended Holy Rosary High School in Derby at the same time, though they had never said more than 'hello' to each other. Lynette was studying at university in Adelaide for a business diploma when her mother was diagnosed with cancer, so she returned to Derby to care for her. Her mother passed away and Lynette, the seventh in her family of ten children, stayed to look after her younger siblings.

Lynette started going out with Trevor in 1991. She knew about his daughter, but then discovered, before Trevor did, that he also had two sons.

'It was awkward,' she commented dryly. 'I saw a child who looked like a little Trevor. Trevor didn't know about these sons because the relationships had broken up and he had been moving around. I said, "Congratulations, you're a father again. Sort yourself out. I don't want to be in the middle of this."'

She urged him to go back to Sapphire and Kimberley's mother. Trevor made it clear that he would be responsible for his children, but wanted to stay with Lynette.

'Lynette's the lion tamer,' he laughed. 'She changed my life. I finished station work and got a job at Derby hospital as a handyman.'

They shared a devotion to family, a love of fishing and the skill and energy to play almost any sport. A common bond also arose from both of them having Stolen Generation grandparents. Lynette's paternal grandfather was an Irishman, Martin O'Meara. He married Topsy, who was taken from near Wyndham and sent to Beagle Bay Mission. Topsy became an accomplished midwife and delivered 'half of Broome'. Lynette knew little about her maternal grandfather, Martin Sibosado, who was born to Japanese parents and abandoned when he was seven. She heard from an aunt that the boy was taken in by the owner of a pearl lugger, Captain Gregory, who lived in Broome and had a son the same age. When he was 12, Martin was taken by welfare authorities to Beagle Bay Mission and later moved to Lombadina Mission, north of Broome. There he became a lay missionary at the age of 14 to protect himself from being detained during the Second World War when Australia was fighting the Japanese. The mission arranged Martin's marriage to Bertha Gidagor, a Bardi woman.

Trevor described Lynette as a beautiful blend of Asian and Aboriginal influences with her hazel, slightly slanted eyes, straight black hair and olive skin.

'She has a big smile and a very strong will.'

They married in 1995; their first child, young Trevor, was born that year and Chelsea in 1998.

'My other children spend holidays with us,' Trevor said.

Life in Derby meant the opportunity to get involved in sport. Trevor trained and competed in Australian Rules football, basketball, cricket or volleyball every week. Lynette was keen on netball, cricket and swimming and also trained and played each week. They came together in a family darts team with Trevor's mother, brother and cousins and played in that competition as well. Around the Menmuir home hang 180 darts competition medallions Trevor has won.

'It's not easy to get three darts into the triple twenty ring,' he said. This was his only reference to being a gifted sportsman. Lynette was more forthcoming.

'He's a natural,' she said. 'He played full forward in Aussie Rules and won leading goal kicker three years in a row. Trevor's years as a ringer made him super fit. Other footballers would train, but he would come into town untrained and dominate the best and fairest. He played many sports and represented the Kimberley in basketball in Darwin at the Arafura Games for Pacific nations.'

Trevor started coaching local children from Derby drop-in centre.

'He would knock off work and go straight to the oval to train the kids at footy,' said Lynette, who was a teacher's aide at Holy Rosary School at the time.

She and her sister Maureen, who coordinated the Aboriginal Sporting Association, helped him.

'Before the sporting association was set up, there wasn't a lot happening in Derby for Aboriginal and non-Aboriginal kids,' Trevor said.

The Menmuirs soon joined the group's committee. When a sports development job came up, Trevor applied and landed it. He went to Perth for training in basketball coaching, sports medicine and athletics, and began running school holiday programs and camps and took sixty young people to Broome for a basketball competition. It was the beginning of a focus on structured sport and recreational activities for Kimberley youth.

Trevor was excellent at organising such events but struggled with the paperwork. He couldn't read and write so Lynette helped him to write reports until Maureen suggested a literacy course at TAFE.

'Trevor lacked confidence,' Lynette said, 'but was determined to learn. He really pushed himself and gradually picked up spelling and reading.'

Trevor later marshalled eighty teenagers from across the Kimberley for a youth leadership summit. The traditional owners welcomed them and the Catholic bishop opened the two-day program. It was an unprecedented step for these shy kids from outback communities. They camped out on the May River near Derby and gathered the courage to discuss their thoughts about health, sport, education and employment in small groups with respected Aboriginal people.

'At night the kids played guitars around the fire,' Trevor said. 'Some Torres Strait Islanders cooked fish, beef, pork and chicken in a hangi [food cooked over hot coals in the ground]. On the final day, the kids sat in a big circle to talk. They really enjoyed the summit and wanted more camps and youth activities back in their communities.'

In 1997, Trevor was ready for a change. With no prior experience he applied for a job in Fitzroy Crossing as an Aboriginal police liaison officer. Even though he got the job, for eighteen months he worked without any training to cope with potentially difficult and dangerous situations.

'On my first night's work I went to a sudden death due to a heart attack. I often had to arrest people, or go to domestics. The same people kept offending. You needed common sense to do the job. It was lucky I had some and that people knew me from station work and sport.'

Trevor went on mounted patrol around town on his bay horse and foot patrol at sporting and community events. When the non-Aboriginal police were intimidated by an aggressive drunk at the Crossing Inn, they called on Trevor. He would try reasoning with the troublemaker to resolve the problem or remove them, but never had to use force to diffuse a situation.

'I was never attacked because people respected me. I didn't use my size or stand-over tactics to do the job.'

Geoff Davis, coordinator of Garnduwa in Fitzroy Crossing, became Trevor's mentor.

'The police would have been lost without him,' Geoff said. 'Trevor excelled as an Aboriginal police liaison officer because he knew how to deal with volatile situations, especially where alcohol was involved. Being a big, strong man helped. On the football field, Trevor would wander over and stand behind my shoulder if someone was attacking me about an umpiring decision. If they persisted, he would step forward and offer to sort it out. One young player was being hassled by a monster of a man, who kept it up after the game. Trevor walked into the middle of the bully's team and said, "What you're doing is unfair. If you want to pick on someone, pick on me." The big fellow fizzled.'

Young people presented special challenges for the 26-year-old novice policeman.

'I would see kids I coached in sport grow up and get on the booze. Then I would have to deal with them or arrest them. A cousin of mine from Bayulu community hanged himself after a domestic with his partner; he was only 19. Another boy found him. Two weeks later that boy, who was only 18, committed suicide.'

Lynette was also seeing the results of anger and violence in her work at the women's shelter so the Menmuirs decided to attend a suicide prevention course in Derby. The program, devised by Aboriginal psychologist Tracy Westerman, broke new ground and focused on depression and suicide in Indigenous communities from an Indigenous perspective. Unpublished 2003 data from the Western Australian coroner showed suicide rates among Aboriginal people in Western Australia had been close to zero in the 1980s; by 2000, the picture had changed dramatically and Aboriginal people had the highest incidence of suicide in the country. Rates in the Kimberley and around Kalgoorlie in the goldfields were at least 2.3 times the rate of non-Indigenous Western Australians – and climbing. Males were particularly at risk. Aboriginal men were committing suicide at a rate of 47.8 per 100,000 people, more than double the rate of non-Aboriginal men at 20.2 per 100,000. Suicide deaths accounted for 20 per cent of Aboriginal and 9 per cent of non-Aboriginal deaths in adolescents aged 13 to 23, according to *First Research Report: Patterns and trends in mortality of Western Australian infants, children and young people 1980–2002* (Telethon Institute of Child Health Research, 2006). Trevor and Lynette Menmuir could name more than 30 people they knew who had committed suicide.

The couple organised Tracy Westerman to run workshops in Fitzroy Crossing. They invited people from Bayulu community to come and meet her. Tracy's forums aimed to reduce the alarming suicide incidence by educating and empowering the whole community and individuals. Tracy's research showed specific cultural risk factors for Aboriginal people. Spiritual factors, payback, a transgression of Aboriginal law and other cultural factors could all play a part. This was in addition to the well-known triggers of poverty and lack of employment, relationship problems, substance abuse, sexual abuse and depression. The findings pointed to the cumulative effect of grief and trauma from forcible removal, disrupted communities and families, lack of traditional support networks and racism. Westerman also described an illness, similar to clinical depression, in which a person became 'sick for country' after being separated from traditional land or their place of Dreaming for an extended time.

Tracy Westerman's teachings had a powerful impact. The Bayulu forum participants learnt about the signs of depression and danger signs for suicide, such as low self-esteem through to constantly feeling sad and thinking about or planning suicide. The boy who found his friend dead had been a talkative person. Afterwards he lapsed into silence. His father wished he had known what signs to look for and how he could have supported his son. Tracy stressed the importance of friends and family watching out for each other when a person was identified as being high risk. One suicide could lead to subsequent deaths, as had happened at Bayulu.

Where suicide had been unthinkable two decades previously, it had now become a common solution to personal pain. A nine-year-old boy killed himself in 2005.

'I saw kids caught between the two worlds,' Trevor said, 'kids from a young age who were fending for themselves, exposed to drinking, physical and sexual abuse, drugs and self-harm, but not by choice. They didn't have the right guidance from parents because many parents hadn't had guidance themselves – and so the cycle continued. There were not enough good role models. Nearly every day we would hear about an incident of self-harm. If parents tried to discipline their children, the children would mention suicide and the parents wouldn't know what to do next. There was a time when the pub in Fitzroy Crossing was closed for several days due to flooding. Without alcohol, there was not one complaint to us as police officers, nor did we have to make any arrests.'

Geoff Davis told me in 2006 that there had been eleven suicides in Fitzroy Crossing, mainly of young men. The ramifications in a population of only 1800 are immense. If that depth of tragedy befell our district or any other town down south, the ripple effect would galvanise the media, politicians and the public to probe for causes and set up counselling and other services immediately.

Trevor's experience of suicide fuelled his dedication to building strength and resilience in young people.

In 1998, Trevor was finally sent to Perth for six weeks police training. As he found ways of combining youth activities with policing, community policing became his specialty. He was elected chairman of Fitzroy Valley Aboriginal Sports Association and represented it on the Kimberley-wide Aboriginal sporting association, Garnduwa.

'Trevor ran blue-light discos as drawcards for the town and isolated communities,' said Lynette. 'He would have ninety kids there. He'd also take the time to go to schools while he was out on police work. There, he would deliver drug and alcohol prevention programs and talk about sport.'

During this period, Lynette fell pregnant with their second child. When time for the birth drew near, Lynette was four hours away from Derby Hospital. Together with four-year-old Trevor she hitched a lift in a truck from Cadjebut mine to Derby. Trevor returned to Fitzroy Crossing to find his wife and son not there; when he learnt they had gone to the hospital, he went on to Derby, where he found that he had a healthy little daughter, Chelsea.

Soon after Chelsea's birth, Lynette had to take young Trevor to the health clinic.

'He was a skinny, sedentary child who didn't eat much and quickly tired,' she said. 'His heart would race as if he'd done a lot of sport.'

The visiting doctor examined him and picked up a heart murmur. When young Trevor was flown to Perth, the doctors discovered he had a hole in his heart and that he needed open heart surgery. He spent five days recovering in hospital.

'He's fine now and wants to be a footballer – like every boy,' Lynette said.

After five years in police liaison, it was the shiftwork, not the issues, that convinced Trevor to leave. His and Lynette's only contact had become when they passed each other in the hall as Trevor came home and she went to work. They were tired of it. Trevor accepted a job with Garnduwa. He also applied for the Aboriginal and Torres Strait Islander Commission (ATSIC) regional council, although he wasn't a political animal. He put his name forward because he wanted to be a voice for young people.

'There were eight candidates,' he said, 'some of whom told people not to vote for me because I had been with the police. I paid my $50 and didn't campaign because I didn't know what I could promise. I was voted in.'

The position gave him insight into the political process. Some councillors said nothing in ATSIC meetings until their own issue or community came up. Trevor had no community, so he spoke up for the small, isolated places that battled to survive and had no representative. Youth had no portfolio. Just as he was beginning to enjoy the ATSIC role, Trevor was promoted to head Garnduwa's East Kimberley team and the Menmuir family moved to Kununurra.

The East Kimberley was a problem for Garnduwa. There were no staff on the ground to boost Indigenous participation in sporting activities or to deliver the state programs in football, athletics and basketball. Trevor's tasks in 2002 were to develop and run programs, as well as to train coaches and umpires in communities and nurture the potential of young people. The name Garnduwa means 'big mob of people coming together'. A key part of Trevor's job was to bring the scattered communities together.

His team of six covered an area the size of Victoria, which included ten remote communities and sixteen schools. In any one month he could cover 1000 kilometres north on rough roads to visit Kalumburu, a former Spanish Benedictine mission on the coast, or drive south 800 kilometres into the Great Sandy Desert to Balgo, a community famous for its artists. He would spend a week at a time in each area. Trevor developed a calendar of sports for the schools and communities: basketball in Term 1, football in Term 2, athletics Term 3 and in fourth term, as the Wet approached, youth leadership camps. In each sport he searched for pathways for children with potential. A basketball player might be able to train in Perth or a footballer to compete in the state carnival. Young people selected at school level for regional athletics competition could qualify for the state All Schools Athletics, which gave them the opportunity to compete in the national All Schools competition.

'Children love to compete in any organised activity, whether it's marbles or basketball,' Trevor said. 'They jumped at the opportunity to play against another community. It wasn't hotly competitive, just good fun. In the desert communities, kids wore different-coloured tape around their wrists so they knew which team they were on. On one occasion I was able to give the kids real uniforms to play in and it really made their day.'

Sport was the great hope for Indigenous communities. One of Garnduwa's main funding bodies, the Indigenous Sports Program, had developed from the Royal Commission into Aboriginal Deaths in Custody. The commission emphasised the importance of access to sport and recreation to help discourage anti-social and criminal behaviours as well as build and sustain community cohesiveness. Trevor encountered huge barriers to community development and participation in remote areas. It was hard to get volunteers, even to fill paid positions for local sports coordinators. It was also a difficult task to change people's lifestyles and daily behaviour as adults and children were more likely to sit indoors watching television or amusing themselves with electronic game consoles than go outside to fish and hunt.

Garnduwa's aim of sports development officers such as Trevor delivering sport and recreation programs evolved into Garnduwa staff recruiting local Be Active officers.

'We wanted people to develop programs for their own communities and not sit down and expect us to do it for them,' said Trevor. 'In some communities, white people with welfare mentalities would say the Aboriginal people didn't have the skills to deliver programs; that set the local officers back.'

At times the arrival of someone in a community could turn things around. In Balgo, a new Aboriginal policeman, Lindsay Greatorex, took on co-ordination of programs and helped the Be Active officer develop the sporting prowess of Balgo people.

Trevor recalled a visit to Kalumburu in 2005 after a cyclone. Roads were blocked and the community couldn't get food supplies. Recreation activities for children dwindled because of the damage. They were bored and causing trouble. The Elders said the community needed more sports development for the kids, so Trevor flew in. He coached football, trained umpires, took on two men as Be Active officers and camped out with the children and their parents, hunting, fishing and making spears.

'The excitement in the week of the grand finals was intense. The whole community attended and each grand final was won by one point. The highlight was to see the old people play a half-time basketball shootout.'

Afterwards the community manager said, 'The Garnduwa holiday program saved us $125,000 in repairs, compared to previous years', and there were only minor incidents during the holidays.

One of the most insidious problems within communities was jealousy. If a young girl played sport, her boyfriend might feel jealous because she was outdoors and active or she became jealous when he played football and became the centre of attention. It took careful handling and involvement of all parties.

'They would fight and next thing they stopped playing sport,' Trevor said. 'We tried to teach kids about honesty in relationships. Some people don't want others to excel and become jealous of them. I know what it's all about from going to domestics when I was with the police.'

At high school level, many students didn't attend school regularly. Few Indigenous students were reaching Year 12. Through sport Garnduwa aimed to capture students before they left school and motivate them to stay, which would enable young people to be educated and lead healthy lifestyles rather than join the dole queue.

'When I talked with kids,' Trevor said, 'I would tell them what I had been through, not learning to read and write at school. I encouraged them to stay on.'

In areas where the Education Department was including regular sport and training in the curriculum, the absentee rates dropped. But some teachers were punishing Aboriginal students for misdemeanours in the classroom by stopping them from playing sport. Once they missed a regional carnival, they also missed opportunities to compete at the next level. Trevor thought that if students played up in the classroom, that's where they should be punished and questioned the teachers about it. They said it was school policy. By 2007 Trevor was working in Kununurra schools and planned to follow up this policy that not only discouraged Aboriginal kids' interest in schooling, but was also another blow to their fragile self-esteem.

Lynette was also recruited by Garnduwa. The two of them worked in tandem, at work and at home, sharing ideas and responsibilities. Garnduwa employed other husband–wife teams as program coordinators, which promoted teamwork and fitted in with the family focus in communities.

As well as working all over the Kimberley, the Menmuirs took in younger relatives to 'grow them up'.

'Trevor's nephew, Davin, started to mix with the wrong gang and miss school in Derby,' Lynette said. 'When he did attend he got into mischief so we took him on to give him family support and his mum a break by keeping him active with school, sports, fishing, hunting and responsibility for a few chores. He knew he couldn't get away with half the stuff he used to do and he made the choice to stay with us for that year. Another nephew, Michael, begged Trevor to have him as his parents were going to send him to Halls Creek District High, so we took him in too. He was in Year 9.

'My niece, Chantal, lived on a remote community called Bohemia Downs Station, 170 kilometres out of Halls Creek,' Lynette continued. 'She was entering Year 10, so she came and lived with us in Kununurra.'

In 2004 the Menmuirs had a full house – three teenagers attending Kununurra District High School, young Trevor in Year 5 and Chelsea in Year 1. Michael then won a football scholarship to Christchurch Boys' Grammar School in Perth and is in Year 11 and Davin is training to become a builder. Chantal went on to Clontarf College in Perth for Years 11 and 12 and graduated in 2006. Early in 2007, she trained in community program development and has since returned to live in Derby.

When I visited Trevor a year later, in September 2006, he was in the wars. His left arm was supported in a double sling, the shoulder muscle torn off in a football accident. His right foot, swathed in bandages after an operation, had to be propped on a chair, and his right ear was plugged from a separate operation to improve his hearing. He had handed coordination of the Garnduwa regional athletics carnival to Lynette. A whisper of spring preceded the Wet as the days began cool and quickly warmed up. The young athletes have to compete after dusk to escape the heat and humidity.

Since its establishment in 1991 Garnduwa has put sporting activities firmly on the calendar across the Kimberley and helped to build community spirit.

'It's not only about keeping people active,' Lynette had told me, 'but developing opportunities for training, coaching and umpiring. Trevor's really good at it. He is one of those blokes who never stop. It's like he's invincible.'

Trevor coached a boys' basketball team for three years and when they were 15 entered them in a senior competition.

'They won the grand final,' he said. 'It shows the work you've done with the kids. Parents come up to me and say, "My kid comes back and talks about basketball – or football or whatever sport they were doing – and how they really enjoy it". I used to focus on developing each kid's skills, but now I like to see them participate in team sports. It's also about encouraging kids on and off the field.'

Football has taken over from basketball as the most popular sport in the Kimberley. Every year since 2004, Claremont, a Perth Australian Rules club, in partnership with Kimberley nickel mining companies has offered four football scholarships. Garnduwa selects aspiring footballers from Kimberley communities. The kids they select go to Perth where they attend Christchurch Boys' Grammar School for Years 11 and 12. In Perth, they are coached by Claremont. It is their opportunity to train as footballers as well as get a good education and a career.

'Two boys finished Year 12 in 2005 and moved into Claremont House to play for the club,' Trevor said. 'It's the highest level they can go to in the state. They find work and pay minimal board. Garnduwa looks after them and supports their training.'

Every year, Garnduwa selects the Kimberley Spirits, an under 19s football team. In 2004, the Kimberley Spirits won the Western Australian B-grade competition in Perth. They made it into the A grade and were runners up in the grand final in 2005 and 2006. The same team won the premiership in the Northern Australian championships two years in a row.

Sport for girls has been harder to nurture. In a region where girls often don't pursue sport because of peer pressure – excelling might incur jealousy – Lynette is a good role model and understands the issues for young women.

'When I was in Fitzroy Crossing, I was getting fatter because there were no activities or structured sports for women,' she said. 'The lifestyle of hunting and fishing was really good, but my self-esteem had dropped. We women don't love ourselves enough, do we?'

She runs a Women in Sport program in the remote communities and coordinates a leadership camp to build the confidence and skills of girls.

For all Kimberley communities, the highlight of the sporting year is the Garnduwa Festival. Every October an intense week of football and basketball competition is capped off by nights of home-grown music and traditional dancing. Five thousand people converge on Fitzroy Crossing to camp out and enjoy the week-long action.

While policing in Fitzroy Crossing, Trevor promoted the idea that the Elders could keep law and order at the festival, an initiative that helped hand them back respect and authority. The group was called the Red Shirts.

'Drink, Play, No Way' is the festival's slogan. The Red Shirts search bags at the entrance and confiscate or pour out any alcohol they find. Their boss, a Fitzroy lawman, makes sure there is no humbug and that young kids know culture comes first.

'If they muck around, kids have to face those old people. They are more scared of them than they are of the police,' said Trevor.

The national head of the Indigenous Sports Program described Garnduwa Festival as special. 'There is no other such festival in Australia. There should be more because it raises kids' self-esteem through sport, but it also teaches them about culture.'

'The festival performs the role a corroboree used to for Aboriginal people,' said Geoff Davis. 'Sometimes Stolen Generation people find out where they came from and who their relatives are as they mingle at this event.'

The 2006 Garnduwa Festival saw Trevor coordinating fourteen football teams and sixty-five games over four days. At the time, he was living on painkillers and slept little as he waited for Kununurra hospital to schedule him for an ultrasound and an operation on his shoulder ligament. Fifteen months later, at the end of October 2007, Trevor's health problem was still unresolved, relegated to non-urgent by the health service – or so it seemed to Trevor.

'He was absolutely tireless, despite his shoulder giving him hell,' Geoff said. 'Trevor organised the program from 10 in the morning to 10 at night each day and kept the ten or fifteen support staff happy. It was 43 degrees outside, so games were kept to 30 minutes. It was an all-consuming job. For carnivals, he prepares two days before and is the last one to leave.'

The focus on sport in Balgo paid off. Its team won the A-grade football for the first time in 14 years.

'Aboriginal kids have a natural flair for sport,' Geoff said. 'They have excellent hand–eye coordination, balance and awareness of space, which gives them running, catching, throwing and hitting abilities.'

In his spare time Trevor goes fishing, makes and plays didgeridoos, carves boomerangs, boab nuts, coolamons and shields, or fashions spears, fighting sticks, clap sticks and woomeras. On one wall of the Menmuir house are displayed his carefully carved and painted instruments.

'I taught myself,' Trevor said, as he showed me a boomerang decorated in red and white ochre. 'I always wanted to carve artefacts. One day I made a spear out of jarrah wood. I learnt how from looking at photos in old books and museums and experimenting. When I showed an old lawman, he said, "You've made a traditional fighting spear. There's an old man down the road called Hitler who'll buy this." Hitler was brought up out bush; he was named by a whitefella.'

Trevor sells artefacts through the Waringarri Arts Centre in Kununurra and can't keep up with demand. When he worked for the police force at Fitzroy Crossing, other officers wanted to buy artefacts to take home when they went on leave.

'One bloke bought a didgeridoo off an old fella in a community. He said to me, "I'll pay you to do a design on this didge". I told him to get the name of the maker. He didn't do it, so I couldn't do a design because it was someone else's work.'

Trevor was finishing a didgeridoo. It was two metres long and had a fluid red grain. He left the bark on half of it. As we moved into the shady courtyard behind his house, young Trevor and Chelsea burst through the back door. School was out. They carefully held each end of the long, hollow log as Trevor transformed it into a musical instrument.

'I like to keep a design simple. It shows off the grain better,' he said as he crushed and mixed ochre. He applied red ochre to the smooth end and painted a band of yellow over it. Then he added a band of black paint and beside it another of white ochre.

'I don't do traditional designs because I don't have country and don't know the stories of my people – although I heard that my grandfather was strong in culture.'

The ochres dried quickly in the scorching sun. As I admired the striking combination of colour, grain and bark, Trevor asked whether I have much room in my luggage.

'Why do you ask?'

'This one's yours,' he said.

We yarned about the future as this big-hearted man packed away the ochres in separate jars. The Kimberley is where Trevor wants to remain. He and Lynette plan to retire one day to land owned by Lynette in the coastal haven of Gudumul near Lombadina.

'I'll only have fishing to worry about,' he laughed. 'Did I tell you about the day we were fishing below the dam wall at Kununurra? I left the family and climbed to a higher bank. I cast, and caught a big barra, but as I was hauling it in the fish got stuck on a ledge. Lynette said she could reach it. I said, "No", and bent over to grab the reel. Just then, a five metre croc jumped clean out of the water. Luckily the bank was too steep. He must have watched and waited until he thought I was within reach. I wouldn't have stood a chance. He was huge. The kids were playing when they heard the splash and jumped on top of the car.'

Trevor shuddered at what could have happened if Lynette or the children had followed him. They don't fish there anymore. Fishing and retirement will come after he has made a career of sport as a means of empowering youth. Trevor is proud of moving from working for the dole in his first job to becoming a leader in sports development, but wants the security of a permanent rather than a contract position. He aspires to regional management in the Department of Sport and Recreation, but thought he needed more training in personal development. Lynette was also on contract.

Two months later, both Menmuirs had been offered other jobs – Lynette a permanent position in the Western Australian Department of Indigenous Affairs with remote community development, Trevor a permanent job with the Clontarf Foundation in Kununurra. In 2000 at Clontarf Aboriginal College in Perth as the college was on the verge of closing due to student absenteeism, Fremantle Dockers AFL coach, Gerard Neesham, began a football program to keep students at school and to attract the drop-outs back. Six years on, the school has a waiting list.

'More Aboriginal kids are finishing school at Clontarf College than anywhere else in Western Australia. When our niece, Chantal, graduated in 2006 she was one of 21 students finishing Year 12 there,' Trevor said. 'The boys develop high self-esteem through improved school results and footy success. They have a future.'

The program began at Kununurra High School in February 2007. Students have their own space in a separate building with classrooms, a kitchen, their own common room, even a pool table. The program targets Indigenous boys at school and boys who have dropped out. There will also be a girls' program. On the first day for the boys who had dropped out, nobody turned up. On the second day there were three and by the end of the week, nine. After two months, forty boys were regularly attending Years 8 to 12.

'Getting out of bed and going to school is the biggest challenge they have to overcome,' said Trevor. 'When I went around houses door-knocking, I was amazed how many kids weren't at school.

'We do footy training three mornings a week and provide a healthy breakfast before they go to school. I help in the classroom too. Twenty-five kids turned up at six in the morning for training on the first day we had for those already at school. It was a huge turnout. The kids were so pumped up and happy. It's for high school kids, but a primary school boy showed up when we moved to the classroom. He was reluctant to join us, but one of his mates said, "Come and sit down". He doesn't have a stable home, but he is a real clever kid and finished the work quickly. This program would be good in all schools, I think.'

By mid-July, there were ninety boys in the program, half of them kids who had not been to school for more than a year. From Trevor's experience at school, he knows how quickly a child can slip backwards and lose confidence if not properly supported. He also knows the surge of self-esteem when you grasp concepts and feel accepted. Trevor's ability to really hear, understand the reasons behind kids' behaviour and quietly guide them in a positive direction makes him the ideal mentor for these teenagers.

Trevor's Garnduwa manager and mentor, Geoff Davis, describes the Menmuirs as a top team and excellent role models for modern Aboriginal kids.

'They started football, basketball and athletics programs for both adults and children in the East Kimberley,' he said. 'Trevor has Be Active officers in remote areas like Kalumburu and Balgo. He could hardly read and write and he skilled himself up. He communicates well. Trevor is sincere and humble. Both blackfellas and whites think he's the ant's pants. He's the best example I know of a contemporary Aboriginal man – hardworking, dedicated and he doesn't drink. Trevor has strong values and he knows how to empower people. He wants to be a good leader, but he already is. He just needs to believe it himself.'

Distilled in Trevor is the Kimberley history of Anglo-Saxon adventurers, the Stolen Generation and the insidious march of leprosy. In his own life, he has learnt the ways of Aboriginal stockmen, and enhanced the development of remote communities and youth potential through sport. He has found enduring pride, inspiration and a sense of place in his land – the Kimberley. Despite the legacy of his background and childhood, Trevor displays resilience. He chooses a positive stance, even on the impact of the Stolen Generation, which has left him without culture, country or stories.

'If I'd known more about my relatives,' he mused, 'maybe I would have pushed to go back to my country and develop one community. As I don't have ties to my background and don't know our culture, I grew up trying to develop myself and do the best for my family and, through my work, the best for everyone in the Kimberley.'

Beck Byrne after climbing 340 metre Devils Tower, Wyoming, USA, 2006

17

Run for Your Life

Rebecca Byrne (Carroll), Blue Mountains, New South Wales

When Rebecca Carroll resolved to lose five of her 55 kilograms and tone her shape, it was a common enough goal for a body-conscious 16-year-old. She hoped it would transform her from the outside-in into a vivacious, confident teenager, but the quick-witted girl who people knew and loved for her cheery smile, humour and zest for life, turned into an unpredictable stranger.

Beck is my daughter. She grew up on our farm in the undulating blue hills of central western New South Wales. A sociable child, her companions ranged from her brothers, Robbie and Duncan, to schoolfriends and a medley of feathered, furry and woolly creatures.

Beck's artistic nature emerged when she was young. She could be found pottering in the garden, picking bouquets or seated for hours at an old wooden desk drawing. She would chat and drink lemonade with her nana on the vine-shaded veranda overlooking our garden, or cling to her father Bill's broad back on the motorbike as they mustered sheep in the hills. We knew we had a sensitive child, one who suffered nightmares and needed security, familiar surroundings and encouragement. From an early age Beck cared deeply what people thought about her. At her local primary school she thrived in small classes with attentive teachers. Beck loved her group of mates, enjoyed schoolwork and felt accepted.

It was the 1970s. Our family was self-sufficient then: milk, meat, eggs, vegies and fruit. If we couldn't grow it, we didn't eat it. While saving money galvanised our efforts, it was more the sweet satisfaction of turning fresh earth, scattering seeds and picking the first tasty carrot or bean for veritable feasts straight from the garden. My good friend Jan Howe, a producer of ABC TV's *Play School*, admired our lifestyle and decided to film it to educate city kids about where their food was grown. Beck became a little television star, confident and at ease with the actors and twenty-five crew members.

Beck's issue with weight didn't arise until Years 5 and 6 when a couple of students teased her.

'"You're a fat loaf!" springs to mind,' Beck recalled. 'It doesn't sound bad, but it sank in deeply. I was always an overweight kid, but I didn't care about it until I was about 10. I played hockey on the weekends, but mostly my pursuits were more sedentary – drawing, hanging out with friends, watching television and cooking. I prepared many family meals to take the pressure off Mum and Dad, who worked hard on and off the farm.'

In 1990, we gave Beck a choice of local secondary schools or boarding. She opted for Canberra Church of England Girls' Grammar School, a school noted for its art, design and languages courses. It was a radical change for a girl who felt homesick when staying overnight at a friend's house only two kilometres away. Beck felt that boarding was the chance to grow up and become more independent. Robbie, her elder brother, was a boarder at nearby Canberra Grammar School and Beck's main support. Over those first months, as her heart-wrenching letters described how much she missed us and wanted to come home, we questioned the boarding school decision.

'I was a naïve and homesick little country girl,' Beck said. 'I think I cried every other night for about two years. Other girls had the same problem. You would always see someone with puffy eyes and flushed cheeks walking morosely along the corridors. Fortunately, the girls in our year group and the boarding house were like a family; we looked after each other. At night my friends would make me laugh until I forgot my woes. During the day I was so busy with school, sport and shenanigans that I didn't have time to feel homesick.'

Beck thrived in the competitive academic environment and discovered a love of team sports.

'I worked hard and did well at my subjects. We boarders fielded very sociable teams for softball, volleyball and basketball. I was more committed to hockey where I went from feeling like I made up the numbers to being a valued and active player. Mostly, my friends and I didn't take anything too seriously, including our many get fit, lose flab attempts. My mate Jane and I would egg each other on during brisk morning runs to Capital Hill or vigorous Cindy Crawford workouts, until I pulled a muscle doing one of Cindy's leg swings. It was more about feeling good than losing weight. If it wasn't fun, we packed it in pretty quickly.'

As Beck slowly adapted to her new life and grew a thicker skin, she became what we later saw described in eating disorders literature as a 'golden girl': good at everything she tried, but also a perfectionist who aimed for the top and was never certain whether she met her own high standards.

By Year 10 Beck was an athletic shape. She would race from one end of the hockey field to the other to score goals. Over the phone she sounded fine, telling us about the usual happenings: the good mark she had scored for an assignment or how they won or lost at hockey on the weekend. We didn't guess that our daughter was starting to have real self-esteem issues.

'I had never been part of the partying and hanging-out-with-guys crowd,' said Beck. 'I was having fun with my friends, sport and school. That was my comfort zone. The problem was that the social scene was becoming a big part of my friends' lives, so I started to feel like I was different. I was so afraid of being judged an idiot or boring by these sophisticated and socially adept teenagers that I couldn't relax and be myself. I wondered what was wrong with me. Why couldn't I be confident and cool like my friends? I began to dislike myself. As the Year 10 formal dance drew closer the pressures grew. It was the social event of our short lives, a kind of coming out – whatever that means!'

Beck had designed a stylish dress for the formal and worked up the courage to invite a good-looking boy. On the night, we parents dropped off our daughters; we weren't encouraged to hang around. These 16-year-old girls looked 26, made up like dolls with their hair curled and smiles firmly in place on glistening, ruby lips. Beck's friends were quick to compliment her on how wonderful and slim she looked. I thought she looked strained, but put it down to anxiety about the formal. Then, I overheard one mother telling Beck that she looked anorexic. This remark stopped me short. I took a really good look at our daughter. She certainly looked thinner, but anorexic – no, that couldn't be right.

'While we all ate dinner and my friends chatted and laughed with their partners,' Beck recalled, 'I kept thinking, Say something Beck, snap out of it. I was incredibly nervous and my sleeves dangled just low enough to rest in my gravy and roast beef. I couldn't speak, I couldn't dance and I felt like a total misfit.'

Beck believes that night in October 1993 was the breaking point for her self-esteem.

'I remember the next day vividly. My close friends and I went on a picnic to Yarralumla Park and sat on the grass with our racoon eyes, laughing and gossiping about the previous night. I was deep in my own thoughts, devising a plan to change myself. In my teenage mind I deduced that the girls who embodied everything that I craved – exuberance, social acceptability and confidence – shared some characteristics. To be like them, I needed to be slim and beautiful then everything in my life would magically fall into place.'

Looking back, Beck recognised that this was not brilliant logic, but she was desperate to feel better about herself.

'Then, by accident, I discovered the world's most successful diet. I would consume only a few mouthfuls of food each day. After a couple of weeks I found I wasn't hungry anymore and therefore didn't need to eat. It was a miraculous discovery for a young girl who had always struggled with her weight. I thought, If I don't need to eat, I'll never have weight problems again. I didn't think for a second about the possibility of any negative long-term effects. I was on a roll and felt strong, empowered and in control, not a feeling I'd give up easily.'

Her goal was to reach 50 kilos. She had a sense of purpose and after a few weeks of this extreme diet Beck lost focus on all else in her teenage life except losing weight. Friends noticed how quiet and introverted she had become. When they asked what was wrong, she would say she was fine. Girls were always on some kind of diet in the boarding house, so peers and staff didn't question her eating habits at dinner, which was the only meal girls and staff ate together.

'Voices became just hums in my ears. I still managed to pass subjects, but otherwise I was a zombie with a single thought: I have to keep going. My winner diet wasn't harming anyone and it made me quietly happy.'

When I drove Beck home for Christmas holidays, she looked thin and wan. During the 300 kilometre drive she suffered stomach cramps and tartly dismissed my enquiries into her health. My feeling of dread grew and I resolved to take Beck to our doctor immediately.

'Mum and Dad pulled the rug out from under me and my diet,' said Beck. 'I'd had so many weeks of my routine that now when it came time for me to eat, I couldn't. An invisible button had been pushed in my brain and the thought of eating made me physically ill.'

Beck had lost eight kilos in eight weeks and although Bill and I knew our daughter had a problem, she didn't. The change in her was dramatic. We always ate as a family, chatting and laughing at the day's stories. Now Beck shopped and cooked for herself, or disappeared into her room at meal times.

She was petrified that any food she put into her mouth would make her suddenly obese.

'It was crazy thinking, but all rational thought had deserted me,' Beck said. 'For every little mouthful I had I felt horrible. I started walking and eventually jogging for hours each day to ease my torment. It was the only way I could live with myself. My behaviour was becoming more extreme and I still didn't know I needed help. I really resented Mum and Dad for watching me and wanting me to join them for meals and making me feel like this.'

We didn't know much about eating disorders apart from seeing media images of emaciated dancers, gymnasts or models and reading about Princess Diana's saga of bulimia. The notion of not eating was alien to Bill, a farmer whose livelihood was growing food and who loved to cook and feed people. I loved fresh foods from the farm and had been working as a health promotion officer, so a healthy lifestyle was high on my agenda. We were puzzled and very alarmed to see our daughter, who had been brimming with life only months before, fade away before our eyes. The smiles and laughter vanished. She studied food labels obsessively, prepared but never touched delicious meals and pounded the back roads. A droll neighbour would call as he drove past her, 'Slow down, Rebecca, there's a speed limit around here!'

'Mum took me to our local doctor who gave me the pinch test. It was exactly the same test Dad did on lambs to see how much fat they were carrying. He was able to grab enough fat on my back between his thumb and forefinger to determine that I still had flesh on my body. He diagnosed anorexia nervosa and said that if I didn't start eating, I would risk being admitted to Bloomfield Psychiatric Hospital in Orange. I had no idea what anorexia nervosa was. I was just a teenager who, at a low point, hoped that a small amount of weight loss would bring me ultimate happiness.'

Beck and I fell silent at the doctor's description of some of the more extreme treatments for eating disorders: being strapped to a bed, force fed and not allowed to leave until the weight was back on. It sounded mediaeval and awful. I was determined she would not take that path. He also told us about a specialised eating disorder clinic in Sydney. It offered a supervised weight gain program, regular sessions with dieticians, psychologists and family therapy. Beck seemed to be going nowhere at home, so Bill and I decided we had no better alternative. The five-hour drive to Sydney was tense. Beck fretted and questioned me about what lay ahead while I feared she might jump ship as we travelled.

'That place was bloody awful,' Beck recalled, shaking her head. 'It was frightening being put into a special hospital where girls as young as 12 were depressed and suicidal. I looked at these waifs and they just reinforced my certainty that I didn't have a problem. Beside them I was large. If having to eat at home had been hard, this was an ongoing nightmare. After being woken at 6.30 in the morning, staff rounded us up and weighed us one by one like cattle. The weight was recorded and, gain or loss, there was pain. We had to gain a ridiculous 1.5 kilos each week or privileges, such as being allowed to leave the hospital, or join in the relaxation and stretching sessions, or receive visitors, were withheld. It's known as a "reward and punishment" system and it does not work. We had to eat our way to freedom – three huge meals a day in a tiny room with dozens of other terrified, tormented girls under the ever-watchful eyes of the staff. After meals we were herded back to our rooms to lie down and the bathrooms were patrolled until digestion time was over so girls wouldn't vomit in the toilets.'

Beck's weekly sessions with the resident psychologist left her cold.

'I might as well have been put in a room with a tape-recorded message asking if I had gained weight and how that made me feel. The so-called counselling session took about three minutes and I always left feeling like a number and a freak. It takes more than a few plates of food and the same two questions each week to help a terrified mind get through an eating disorder. I only had five kilos to gain to reach my base weight as determined by the clinic, but the eight weeks I spent there seemed like forever. It was not a place to make friends and I felt I was going crazy among other crazies. I saw emaciated young girls taken to hospital to be put on drips and monitored to save their lives. It was there that I learnt all about eating disorders from girls who were in much deeper trouble than I was.'

Beck kept her sanity with visits from the family and her childhood friend, Em, who lived close by. Her schoolfriends wrote letters full of love and encouragement saying how they missed her. We thought she would be in the clinic for a few weeks, learn how to eat again and come home. How naïve we were. Beck noticed the same girls going then returning; eventually, we all realised the clinic had a revolving door.

'Girls would put on weight and we would congratulate them on going home,' said Beck. 'Then two weeks later, when they had lost the weight, we would welcome them back. The only way I could go home was to endure the same hell, then figure out how to make myself feel better afterwards.'

By the beginning of Year 11 in 1994, Beck had regained weight and convinced us that she was well enough to return to school in Canberra. She was excited to be back with her mates. Only her close friends knew she had spent the Christmas holidays in an eating disorders clinic. I organised a team of people to support her – a dietician, a psychologist and the house matron – and had confidence Beck would see them every second day, as agreed. She had been back only five days when I received a call at work. "Rebecca hasn't been eating and has lost five kilos," the house matron told me. I didn't believe her at first. The weight she had taken two painstaking months to regain lost in as many days. I shut my door at work and wept. I hadn't cried like that since 1968 when my brother died.

We decided to take Beck to Narooma on the New South Wales south coast for the holiday she had missed over Christmas. We hoped her love of surf, sun and sand would help heal her. She was elated. Every day this tiny figure ran from headland to headland, picked at salads and retreated into her world. How could we maintain a normal family life? There's little doubt by then that we all suffered from the experience of anorexia, not just our daughter.

Beck resisted any moves to encourage her to eat. She would grab her thigh in disgust and say, 'Look at that. It's gross.' The poor leg was a shrivelled muscle and no fat, but she couldn't see that. The image we saw was not what she saw in the mirror. Her long, black hair lost its sheen and fell out in drifts. Her face became pinched and the bloom faded. Her periods stopped. As her fat layers diminished, Beck felt cold all the time; her body grew soft, downy hair to protect the kidneys and other organs. We would cuddle this unfamiliar creature and feel sharp bones, not soft flesh. Our strategies of surrounding our children with love, fun, friends and healthy food were no longer working for Beck.

By then we were realising that there was little good news on anorexia nervosa. People frightened us with dire tales of how eating disorders lasted for years, how marriages broke up with the trauma and how other family members left home or succumbed to depression. The real dangers for anorexics were depression and complications such as the shutdown of major organs. The statistics were frightening. Anorexia nervosa has the highest death rate of all mental conditions. Approximately 25 per cent of anorexia sufferers attempted suicide and about half of anorexia-related deaths resulted from suicide.

We didn't know what to do next so we drove home via the Sydney clinic to ask for advice. The staff warned us that Beck's life was at stake and that starvation, coupled with over-exercise, could affect her electrolyte levels and cause seizures or vital organ failure. They said Beck had to be readmitted to the clinic or they would wash their hands of her. At that stage we didn't know how detrimental its approach was and knew of no other options. Beck pleaded with us. She feared losing her freedom again and having no say over her life. She told us she had felt like Jack Nicholson in the movie *One Flew over the Cuckoo's Nest*, when he was given a lobotomy and all control was taken from him. She promised to try and get better. Bill and I couldn't agree on what to do. I was scared to bring Beck home in that state; he was adamant she couldn't stay at the clinic.

'I felt so frantic that I threatened to top myself if they insisted I stay,' said

Beck. 'I was incredibly low and the thought had often crossed my mind, but I never would have done it. Even then I knew I had so much to live for, especially the love of my family and friends.'

We took Beck's threat seriously, but we had not yet accepted the possibility of suicide or death associated with the condition or with our own daughter. We continually thought: It can't get any worse, and had been continually proved wrong. We had never seen our daughter so desperately unhappy and her threat persuaded me too not to leave her there. The clinic staff insisted that she should have tests in Molong hospital as soon as we arrived home. We drove straight to the hospital that same day.

It was 8 April 1994, the anniversary of my brother's death from cancer. I had an ominous feeling as Beck was admitted to hospital. She was 44 kilos, had dangerously low blood pressure and electrolyte levels and her heart rate was at an all-time low – 34 beats per minute. The local doctor, alarmed by Beck's vital signs and the responsibility unexpectedly landed on him, put Beck into intensive care. He told us she could die during the night and needed constant monitoring. Beck almost laughed at what she thought was his melodramatic reaction. She felt fine. What was all the fuss about? She slept soundly while I kept tiptoeing over to see if she was still breathing, as I had when she was a newborn baby. Her face looked untroubled. The nursing sisters later told me they thought I was far more likely to have a heart attack than Beck.

That endless night and countless others brought Bill and me face to face with fear and despair. Parents naturally ask: Where did we go wrong? What could we have done differently? We did too, but we were fighting an additional foe – Beck's denial. I kept wishing: If she would only put her formidable determination towards recovery. In some ways, dealing with cancer had seemed more clear-cut because my brother had had a fierce will to live. The following day the doctor allowed Beck to go home on condition she return for daily weigh-ins – with the now familiar stipulation of hospitalisation unless she gained a kilo a week.

We had read that approximately 1 in 100 adolescent girls developed anorexia nervosa and 5 in 100 had bulimia nervosa. Dieting was the worst risk factor for disordered eating. Naomi Wolf, in her famous book *The Beauty Myth*, documented the enormous pressures on Western women to conform to an ideal shape and notion of beauty. Her research showed that women spent much of their lives dieting, few were happy with their weight and shape and one-third of women in their teens and twenties worried more about weight than any other issue.

The literature of the 1990s listed potential causes for eating disorders, ranging from low self-esteem and poor body image to pervasive media and peer pressures to be thin, to mothers who constantly dieted, to sexual abuse, and so on. We trawled through the possible reasons for Beck's illness: maybe an unkind comment, her tendency to self-doubt, grief at the recent death of her beloved nana, our livelihood producing food, my busy off-farm job, a genetic predisposition to depression, or all of the above. But we were too late to change history. Whatever the original reasons, our daughter was now in the grip of overwhelming forces.

As we became less able to cope, Beck was oblivious, cocooned in her comfort zone at home. Rituals gave structure to her chaos. She continued to run impossible distances each day and at meal times would tell us she had eaten already, or cut food into small pieces and just push it around her plate. At times her self-loathing was terrifying. Where did it come from? It was as if a monkey sat on her shoulder whispering in her ear that food was her enemy, that she was fat and worthless. Beck called her strange habits self-preservation.

'If I didn't run, the voices inside my head would reach a crescendo, "You're disgusting. How can you live with yourself? Do something. I hate you." When I wasn't running, I felt like I was going mad. It was at those times, when I had no way to cope, that I was closest to doing something drastic.'

Duncan, Beck's younger brother, found living with his sister a torment when he came home from boarding school. He lapsed into silence.

'It was horrible to see her waste away. For a young bloke like me who grazed at the fridge all day I would think: Why don't you just eat? I remember fearing car trips because she would fidget until we'd stop so she could run. Dad would drive behind as she limped along, with Mum and me hoping she would be OK.'

Beck can now explain to the many people who said, 'Why can't she just eat and get better?' that anorexia doesn't work that way. 'When eating feels more self-destructive than not eating and life seems a living hell when you eat, but when you don't eat it is livable – not great, but livable – what would you choose? That's what is so scary about anorexia. Left to their own devices, sufferers will unwittingly starve themselves to death. Pushed too fast the other way into their greatest fear of eating and gaining weight, they may take the final step out of an unbearable existence. A person must have the chance to change their state of mind. This takes time, a heap of support and steady re-feeding.'

In June of 1994 as Beck complied with the daily weigh-in at Molong hospital, a nursing sister who was a family friend, hugged her and felt something hard at her waist. She lifted Beck's jumper and out came a book. Beck had been prepared to try anything to avoid hospitalisation. She had been doctoring her weight by strapping kitchen weights and books around her waist and ankles and drinking litres of water before standing on the scales. Once I knew that she wasn't improving as we had thought, but getting worse, I was forced to find alternatives. Bill was worrying constantly, not sleeping or eating well and looked very depressed. How could I cope with two such vulnerable people and continue to be the breadwinner? I thought. Although I spent my full-on working days as state coordinator of the NSW Rural Women's Network connecting rural women to assistance, I didn't know where to turn for our own situation.

Robbie returned home from a gap year teaching in England. He had a strong relationship with Beck and treated her with humour and gentleness.

'We had an indepth conversation,' he remembered. 'We seemed to communicate well and I thought I had really got through to her. Over the following days and weeks, I saw just how ineffectual our talk had been. It hadn't changed her thinking or behaviour at all. I had a feeling of powerlessness, that I hadn't even touched the sides.'

After living in the family turmoil for a few weeks, Robbie lost patience with his sister. 'He said he couldn't understand what was going on inside my head,' Beck said. 'All he could see was the fallout of my illness. "Can't you see what you're doing to Mum and Dad? You're being a selfish bitch, Becca!" I had never been called a bitch before and Robbie meant it. For the first time in nine months, blunt honesty caused a small snap in my brain.'

We gave Beck the choice of going to a place similar to the Sydney clinic, which she would surely refuse, or an Adelaide program that sounded promising. I told her that staying home was no longer an option because of her father's health.

'My wonderful mum tirelessly searched for ways to help me recover,' said Beck. 'She had heard of a program called Food Without Fear devised by Vonnie Coopman, a physiotherapist who had suffered from anorexia and bulimia nervosa for 13 years, yet recovered. I couldn't continue wrecking my family, so I agreed to try Adelaide. It was scary to leave home and go interstate to another hospital, but it seemed my best option.'

Food Without Fear ran at Blackwood Community Hospital in the Adelaide Hills. Vonnie had been through many reward and punishment programs herself and was unimpressed with their recovery records. She sought to provide an effective alternative through education and support. Food Without Fear had a huge waiting list and workload for Vonnie and her one assistant, Alice, so we were relieved when she said Beck could come over in July.

Just before we went to Adelaide, we visited a nearby farm.

'Why are we here? Is it another counsellor?' Beck asked suspiciously.

'It's a surprise.' I replied.

The farmer emerged carrying a basket. Inside it were five kittens, eyes still unopened – two fluffy and jet-black, two snowy white and a short-haired tabby.

'Ohhh,' said Beck. She peered into their little faces for ages searching for I don't know what. Finally, she chose a small, black kitten she called Toby that became her constant companion when she returned from Adelaide.

'It was lovely to have a little friend who followed me around. As far as Toby knew I wasn't fat or skinny, weird or crazy. To him I was just great.'

We arrived in Adelaide. Before doing the program the person had to accept that he or she had a problem and want to get better. Vonnie gave each person control and responsibility for their recovery, but could see Beck was half-hearted about accepting that she had a problem and the challenge to get better. She convinced our daughter that her lifestyle of compulsive exercising, not eating and worrying about food all day and night wasn't normal.

'You can go on doing that, but you'll be miserable and you may not survive,' Vonnie said. At last Beck started listening to someone.

My understanding boss, the director-general of New South Wales Agriculture, gave me leave to be in Adelaide with Beck for as long as it took and my capable colleagues ran the Rural Women's Network in my absence. I stayed for a month with Bronnie and Don Plowman, our Adelaide friends who had first told us about Food Without Fear. Kind people supported Bill at home.

Vonnie was our salvation. She explained that the causes of anorexia could be as simple as someone teasing Beck when she was younger, but that there was little point in looking backwards. The priority was to re-feed a starved body and mind. She taught Beck that food was not the enemy but an essential building block for sustaining life. To demonstrate this lesson, her patients were re-introduced to eating voluntarily, using a diet of controlled portions from the five food groups. Vonnie showed Beck how all foods, even cake, peanut butter or a Mars bar, no matter how scary they might be, fitted into these food groups and that keeping a balance and control of the portions made eating safe.

To my initial dismay, the first stage of learning how to eat normally was actually learning how to lose weight safely. The greatest fear of an eating-disordered person is that if they eat, they will get fat. If they are able to eat – in Beck's case ten times the amount she had been eating at home – and yet lose weight, slowly the fear of food subsides. As a starving mind and body is nourished, physical and mental strength slowly return along with logic and a will to live. Renewed strength helps a person persevere with recovery, agonising though it may be. Teaching someone how to lose weight safely gives that person a safety net, so that they will avoid the trap of an eating disorder in future. It was an ingenious and incredibly logical approach.

Vonnie only allowed her patients to follow the weight loss program until they felt less fear of food. They then moved on to maintaining weight and, when ready, to gaining weight. Through the whole process, Vonnie gave constant support, education and reassurance as well as the crucial element of empathy.

'Everything Vonnie said was practical and believable,' Beck recalled. 'I knew she understood what I was going through. I also knew that she was right and it was only downhill from here if I didn't try to get better.'

On Day 1, I discreetly observed from the corner of my eye while Beck faced up to her first meal in Blackwood hospital. She had chosen a minute piece of quiche from the menu, a scary meal for her because of its pastry. After consuming what seemed little more than fresh air for nine months, Beck panicked. She was like a matador edging towards the inoffensive quiche, which was to her mind the bull ready to attack. I looked away and crossed my fingers out of her sight as she chewed and swallowed it. It stayed down and I imagined the zillions of Beck's cells breathing a collective sigh of relief – at last, some food. It is almost impossible to convey to anyone who eats normally what that small mouthful signified for an anorexic and her hopeful mother.

'Vonnie challenged me to choose something different from the hospital menu each day, apart from brown bread or fruit and vegetables. I ate more in four weeks than I'd eaten for months and actually lost weight. It was bizarre. Vonnie had given me a safe weight loss strategy if I ever needed it, but more importantly, she had taught me how to eat again. Every bite I took I was frightened, but I was in control of my recovery and sometimes, somewhere in my rejuvenating brain, I felt proud of my courage.'

Blackwood hospital was a nurturing environment and Beck's room was near the maternity ward, a life-affirming place. She had the freedom to walk in the gardens and receive visitors. The warnings were also visible. A 35-year-old woman who had a long-running eating disorder ran the hospital kiosk. She was exceedingly thin and looked twice her age. Beck got to know her.

'She was a lovely lady. We became friends and would chat when I bought a sweet food to challenge my daily plan. I really felt for her. For 20 years she had suffered from anorexia. If I was stuck in this vicious cycle of self-destruction after less than a year, imagine 20 years of that hell. Vonnie later told me that my friend passed away when she was 37. She had so much more living to do.'

Vonnie explained the long-term effects of eating disorders: osteoporosis due to lack of calcium, inability to fall pregnant if she didn't menstruate, tooth and nail weakness, hair loss – the list grew. We had to trust in Vonnie as Beck's weight dropped to 40 kilos. Every afternoon she walked me off my feet, but we talked as we walked and an occasional smile escaped her lips. We stocked up on postcards, a simple way of breaking her long silence with family and friends.

Her malnourished brain couldn't remember or concentrate much so she made lists, endless lists strewn around and rarely looked at once made – what to do, who to write to, but mostly, what to eat. Although eating seemed to be the focus, any progress was really about regaining normality, feeling happier and making decisions again.

'I didn't feel imprisoned or forced against my will, as I had been in the Sydney clinic. To cope with my stress, I would often sneak out of the hospital grounds to run in the hills. I wasn't supposed to because I was weak and vulnerable. I could have had seizures while exercising due to electrolyte imbalances. The threats seemed unreal to me because I felt normal and running helped me through each day.'

After four weeks, we returned home optimistic that Beck was on the road to recovery. I persuaded her to try a TAFE design course for a day a week in Orange. The teachers understood Beck's lack of concentration and let her go at her own pace. She designed a tennis umpire's throne, a 44-gallon drum wrapped in corrugated iron. Beck painstakingly cut the backrest into points with tin snips, but was too weak to pop-rivet the iron onto the drum. She sat on the drum crying with frustration while her silver-haired dad tried to cheer her up as he did it for her.

'Most days Beck and I did stock work together while Marg was at work in Orange,' Bill said. 'I enjoyed her company. But then she would go running. One day I found a set of clothes and sandshoes folded neatly beside a dam. I ran around the edge in a panic looking for footprints. I had never felt so worried in my life. Eventually, Beck showed up. She had changed her work clothes at the dam to go for a run.'

Bill only told me about this 12 years later as I was writing Beck's story. We kept our constant worries to ourselves at the time. At home Beck ate as she had in Adelaide – at first small portions of a variety of foods in strict accordance with what Vonnie had taught her. Then, as her skeletal body got into the swing of being fed and tried to make up for lost time, it was as if an alien had invaded her brain and body. Vonnie had warned Beck that she would have 'cupboard attacks' where she would eat anything she could find.

'I didn't believe her. I still thought that I could control my body. It was the most frightening thing to have your head saying, "No, no more food", and your hands reaching for something. I ate food from the freezer, stale stuff, any carbohydrates any time of the day and in the middle of the night. Mum's cupboards didn't have anything tasty in them, lucky for me. Once she brought home a custard Danish, which used to be my favourite. I had a small sliver and put the rest away. A few minutes later I cut another slice. I couldn't stand myself for being so gluttonous, so I threw the rest in the chook bin. Soon I retrieved it from the scraps. I had become a starving animal diving for food in the garbage bin. The second time I threw it out, I buried it under sloppy scraps so I couldn't get at it. My behaviour horrified me. I called Vonnie in tears to ask if I was crazy.'

Beck wanted to get better at her own pace and was terrified that she would not be able to control her eating again.

'What if my weight ballooned with all this uncontrolled eating? Vonnie talked me through it over the phone as if she'd heard it all a million times. She said, "This is good, Rebecca. This is all normal. You are right on track. I know how awful it feels. You just have to persevere. It will end." Then she used an analogy that I will never forget. "Imagine you're in a burning house. The flames are high and surround you. You have two choices – you can either run through the flames and get burnt, or you can stay inside and burn down with the house." I understood. I could go through the pain to have a life outside the hell I was in, or I could let anorexia consume me and ruin my life. Burns can heal, I thought. I've come too far to turn back now. I want my life back.'

Running through the flames was the hardest thing Beck had to do. Every mouthful she took created a huge battle in her mind.

'I was completely out of control – crying all the time, feeling like I was going nuts, running for miles in the paddocks and screaming. A couple of really manic times I felt like bashing my poor, crazy brains out on the bathroom wall after a meal. Fortunately, I had enough sense to know that would really hurt and achieve nothing, except possibly brain damage. My family and friends stuck by me and I was constantly shown love and support without pressure or judgement. Without that support, I don't know what I would have done. Thank heavens I had the freedom to escape to our deserted paddocks and be crazy in private – not be labelled a nut.'

Those three months after we returned from Adelaide were hell. Every day we could see a battle between good and evil being waged deep inside Beck; losing her iron control of eating plunged her into despair. We feared for her sanity and life. Bill and I could only try to keep her safe as she struggled with her demons. One sunny morning when Beck's weight had dropped to 37 kilos, she went berserk. It was as if that weight marked the red danger line on a machine. Beck raced like a terrified animal first one way then another and took off across the paddocks. I was afraid she would jump into a dam. I shadowed her from one paddock away so she wouldn't be frightened into hiding. It was hard to keep up and difficult to see her through the trees, but eventually she ran out of steam. I approached carefully, hugged this tiny, agonised girl who once had been the same size as me and somehow we got home. Once she calmed down, I rang Vonnie. She was not at home. It was a Sunday. Then I rang every counsellor I knew. Nobody was home. Then Vonnie called back that night and her voice soothed us. She suggested to Beck that she return to Adelaide immediately.

It was December and my father by then was at a critical stage with Alzheimer's disease and also needed constant attention. We were in a bind – Beck in South Australia, my dad in Orange, Bill in better spirits but dealing with drought and two sons at home who had been paid scant attention for a year. Our Adelaide friends became Beck's supports for a month while she was in Blackwood Community Hospital. She missed home, but the hospital routine of three meals a day and no cupboards to attack felt like a godsend.

'When I was alone I thought about the people I loved and how much I had to live for,' Beck said. 'The only emotion I had had for so long was fear and my only thoughts were about food and exercise. I hadn't been interacting with people or nature. I wanted to get back to the land of the living, to have excitement, expectations and ambitions for the future. As I became healthier, the fear began to slowly subside.'

This second visit to Adelaide began the long haul back to eating normally without thinking about it and without weight being the sole focus. We were fortunate to find the Food Without Fear program that helped our daughter recover relatively quickly. Many anorexics don't ever recover. As food fed Beck's brain and body, running was becoming a pastime rather than a compulsion. One day she entered an eight kilometre fun run in Orange and was astonished to be the second woman home.

'I suddenly discovered I was a half-decent runner. Finishing the fun run gave me a boost of self-confidence. The endorphins released through running, which had helped me to cope throughout the past year, now made me feel happy.'

After missing a year's school through anorexia, Beck went into Year 11 at James Sheahan High School in Orange. It was a brave step. She was so thin she had no bottom to sit on the hard classroom seats, was as restless as a prowling tiger and struggled to concentrate. What worried me most was how she would cope interacting with her peers after a long period of isolation.

'I wanted to be a regular teenager and have fun again. I had been introverted for so long that I took my time making new friends. It was comforting to know that nobody there knew me and I could start afresh. I felt quietly strong and composed, like I'd never felt before. I still looked scrawny and some boys called me Fruit Bat. Why? I asked one boy. "I dunno," he said, "just 'cos you eat a lot of fruit." Strangely enough, it didn't matter to me what I was called. By coming through my eating disorder I had found inner strength and a whole new side to my character. Soon I made good friends, got into the academic and social swing of things and even snagged a nice boyfriend. I was eating well again and running, bike riding or swimming every day. I started feeling fitter, stronger and more confident than I had in my whole life.'

Beck entered triathlons and cross-country races. The exhilaration of pushing herself and crossing the finish line far outweighed the pre-race jitters.

'I was always surprised when I did well. I qualified for the New South Wales Cross-country Championships in 1996. I was so nervous I nearly missed the start when visiting the loo for the thirteenth time that hour. The starter gun went and elbows dug me in the ribs as the pushy girls muscled to the front of the pack. I was behind on the flat, but hills were my forte. I managed to catch up and pass people. As I crossed the finish line in fifth place, an official called out that I was second reserve for the Nationals. I was flabbergasted. How could this girl who had once been a couch potato and later so ill be selected to represent New South Wales at the National All Schools Cross-country Championships?'

Sadly, the Nationals clashed with Higher School Certificate trial exams so Beck couldn't go, but she was showing a talent for endurance, maybe that was what had helped her survive anorexia. Year 12 was a milestone in her return to being a normal teenager. A friend from Molong, Belinda Crich, nominated her for Young Australian of the Year for our region. The nomination extolled Beck's courage in overcoming a debilitating illness to become a successful young sportswoman.

'Receiving that Australia Day award was one of the proudest moments of my life,' she said. 'I was truly touched by the gesture of my running mate Belinda, and felt so honoured.'

Beck became a role model for younger students and encouraged girls to take up sport. After being at school for only a year, she collected an armful of awards at speech night and her peers elected her as house captain. They admired her strengths and sporting prowess, but Beck doubted her leadership ability and almost declined the role. Every week she would quail at having to speak in front of hundreds of students, but she managed well.

'People who know me often have more faith in me than I do. Maybe I'm a better leader when I don't know I'm leading.'

Eating disorders remain an enigma. Anorexia was treated successfully back in 1874 by Sir William Gull, who discovered that 'self-starving adolescent girls were not only emaciated, but also restless and hypothermic'. Considering their poor physical condition, the restlessness surprised him, especially in that it was hard to control and seemed 'agreeable'. He reduced his patients' physical activity and supplied external heat during treatment. Gull concluded that the origin of eating disorders was the brain, rather than the gastrointestinal tract, and named the disorder anorexia nervosa. Swedish founders of the renowned

Mandometer program Cecilia Bergh and Per Sodersten noted in an article in the British medical journal, *The Lancet*, in 1998:

Today the outcome seems to have worsened since Gull's time. Anorexia nervosa is one of the most serious health problems facing teenage girls. Thus, patients have less than a 50 per cent chance of recovery within 10 years and a 6.6 to 15 per cent risk of dying 10 to 20 years after the onset of the disorder.

Bergh and Sodersten found that eating disorders are not the result of mental disorders, but of self-starvation which *causes* depression, anxiety and suicidal inclinations. They postulate that self-starvation is initially rewarding. 'The stress of physical activity with reduced food intake activates the reward mechanisms in the brain', through release of dopamine. Then the brain continues to associate the two activities as pleasurable. After having been unsuccessfully treated by other programs beforehand, 75 per cent of Bergh and Sodersten's patients recovered and a further 15 per cent made significant progress.

Disordered eating relapses are common. The test of whether Beck really had recovered or would snowball back into anorexia came all too soon as she encountered 'the farm from Hell' in 1997 after she finished school. She was accepted for an international agricultural exchange to Switzerland. On a mere 20 hectares, this Swiss-German family grew fruit and vegetables, pigs, 7000 chickens and five hectares of Christmas trees. Beck arrived there expecting to help in the house and on the farm and to learn about Swiss culture, as the program had promoted.

'My host family had unfortunately mistaken the word "host" for "hostile". I worked from six in the morning until six at night every day, with one Sunday off a fortnight and was paid less than $3 an hour for hard physical work. I was yelled at in Swiss-German for either not working fast enough or for not instantly understanding orders. Kind neighbours and lovely Polish friends who worked on the farm for a few months, communicated in broken German and kept me going.'

Beck felt helpless halfway across the world trying to grapple with abusive treatment, living in close quarters with this family and learning a new language. After bad days, no matter how tired she felt, Beck would run around the lake. On the 22 kilometre runs she saw the Switzerland she had imagined: steep hills, lush farming land, quaint villages, pretty houses with red geranium window gardens and cows wandering the hillsides softly jingling their bells.

'I always arrived back exhausted but happier. Workers weren't allowed any food apart from the three 20-minute meals. Being a slow eater, I was always hungry and lost over 10 kilos. When I was really hungry, I would borrow an old bike with no gears and ride the 10 kilometres over hills into the capital, Bern, to buy bread. On Sundays I would call home and cry to Mum and Dad, who pestered the host organisation to resolve my situation. I was 20, on my first overseas trip and I didn't want this horrible family to ruin it, but I felt trapped and isolated. I had to tell myself that I'd come through harder things. I said to Dad once, "I'm not going to let the bastards beat me".'

We were extremely worried about Beck and frustrated that the organisation seemed unable to act, but at that point she needed to decide for herself whether to stay or leave the farm and not have us take control away from her.

'In retrospect, I should have left,' said Beck. 'The experience left me with a stutter and nightmares for six months afterwards. Mum surprised me by flying over a week after I left the farm to travel with me for a great fortnight around Germany, the Czech Republic and Italy. It made the whole trip worthwhile, although my nightmares and sleep talk in German disturbed her a bit.'

After those harrowing years when she learnt that whole health means nurturing body, spirit and mind, Beck decided to move to Sydney and study Naturopathy at the Australasian College of Natural Therapies. At her housewarming party, with the help of some Dutch courage, Beck met Scott Byrne, a medical science student at Sydney University and a close friend of one of her housemates. She quickly fell in love with his considerate and romantic nature, sense of humour, open mind and dark good looks.

'I can be myself with Scott. I know he loves me for everything I am, foibles and all, as I do him. He has never judged me. He is the most thoughtful person I know and he goes out of his way to make me happy.'

Scott brought out the confidence and fun in Beck.

'From the earliest moment I knew that we made a fantastic team,' he said. 'Becca is an extremely strong person, physically, which she prides herself on, and mentally. She makes me laugh with her quick wit and has an insightful mind – although she may not agree. Which is another of her endearing qualities – modesty.'

Beck had completed three out of four years of naturopathy when she realised that advising other people on their health was too stressful and might put her own health at risk. She decided to change direction and Scott suggested horticulture. A friend told Beck about apprenticeships at the Sydney Royal Botanic Gardens with horticultural study at Ryde TAFE. When the positions were advertised, she applied and won a coveted spot in a job made for her. It was a daily dose of fresh air, nature, physical work and stimulating learning.

In 2002, Scott and Beck married in our autumn garden. Family and friends who helped her over the good and traumatic years gathered to celebrate. As the couple exchanged vows, a gust of wind shook the huge deodar pine overhead and anointed them with a cloud of green pollen. A sudden storm caused power failures all around, but skirted us. Beck draped her white train over one shoulder and, armed with a shovel, planted a eucalypt for the occasion while her horticultural mates contributed helpful hints: 'Dig a bigger hole. The tree's pot-bound. Clip its roots.'

In 2004, Beck graduated from Ryde TAFE and wrapped up her apprenticeship. Scott, by then having finished his doctorate, won a fellowship to Houston, Texas, for two years of research. Skin cancer research captivated his interest at an early age and still holds his passion.

'Cancer can affect anyone at any time for no apparent reason. We need to conquer this disease and I think I can make a contribution to this effort. I find the mechanisms behind tumour growth fascinating. Science is about making new discoveries. To me, there is nothing more exciting than finding out something that no one else knows and then sharing that information with others.'

A new life in Houston provided the chance for Beck to blossom in new directions. In a huge American city built around the black gold that is oil and the car, she joined a non-profit organisation, Urban Harvest, that taught urban communities how to conserve and replenish, rather than consume. Volunteers such as Beck helped the Dominican Sisters grow organic fruit and vegetables to feed the city's poor and homeless people. Through Urban Harvest, she also began studying permaculture.

'My teachers laughed at me for coming from the home of permaculture to study in Texas. Permaculture's focus on designing and implementing systems to make our lifestyles more sustainable made so much sense to me. I realised that this was the direction I wanted to take in both my life and career. A friend at the gardens asked me to help her redesign her front yard. That led to several other jobs where I designed and installed a shady forest floor garden, a native cottage garden, an oriental garden and two permaculture gardens. I had gone from being an apprentice to being my own boss and one-woman landscaping crew.'

Her next challenge was to fulfil a long-term ambition to run a marathon. Beck signed up for the 2006 Houston Marathon. The city has few parks or footpaths and traffic is thick, so Beck trained along the bayous, fingerlike channels that drain into the Gulf of Mexico. She ran up to 100 kilometres a week for months. On those lonely three-hour runs, when she felt like packing it in, Beck would remember the non-refundable US$80 entry fee she had paid and was loathe to forfeit. On 15 January, Beck rose early to warm up and psych up for the 42.2 kilometre course.

'I felt calm, maybe because it seemed too long to be a race, or maybe because I was so relieved that I wouldn't have to train any more. Thousands of Houstonians who lined the streets called out encouragement for us and every so often, I'd spot a green and gold banner that said "Go Becca". Beneath it were my Aussie cheer squad of Scott and my old primary-school mate, Em. The amazing crowd support really lifted me.'

Over the last ten kilometres Beck could only do tiny steps as her whole body ached. Her mentor, Janice, who ran eight of the last ten kilometres with her, urged, 'Go your hardest in the last k, pass three women and lots of men – and smile as you cross the line.'

'When I saw the finish line, I finally found second, even third gear and barrelled toward it. I forgot to smile, but felt absolutely exhilarated when I crossed that line. Running the marathon renewed my faith that I can do anything if I put my mind to it.'

Beck finished in three hours, forty-nine minutes and came in 1161st of the more than 5000 runners.

After her marathon high, Beck looked for the next mental and physical challenge. She convinced Scott that they could climb Devils Tower, a 340 metre monolith that juts up from the red hills of Wyoming. Bill and I were travelling across Wyoming with Beck and Scott. With an expert guide they learnt the rudiments on a climbing wall while it was snowing outside and next morning took off to the Tower. The two novice climbers clambered over boulders behind their guide until they reached the base of their climb. From there, vertical grey columns towered into the sky. We could hardly watch as, attached to each other by ropes, they searched at full stretch for tiny handholds or ledges for a foothold. The moment they clambered over the top after three and a half unrelenting hours was more than a pinnacle of climbing: they had overcome their fears and prevailed as a team. On top they signed a leather-covered scroll stored in an iron canister. Beck wrote: 'I can't believe I've done this. I've only ever climbed a tree before. What a crazy thing for a couple of Aussies with vertigo to attempt, especially on our first rock climb!'

'I need to push my boundaries every once in a while. With each test you learn more about what you are made of. The exhilaration I feel when I harness my energy and determination and rise to a challenge is hard to beat. My mind opens up to all the potential in our beautiful world and within myself.'

Scott said, 'Beck has become more confident in her own abilities over these last few years. She has conquered many of her fears, including heights. She knows when to quit, as with the naturopathy, which was hard for a perfectionist, and she accepts that she can't do everything. She is the perfect partner – loving, giving and unselfish.'

The life one hopes for one's children can so easily be shattered. We were among the lucky parents to find help in time. The slide into the black hole of anorexia nervosa looked almost impossible to reverse, but there is effective treatment and recovery is possible. To hear our beloved daughter laugh, to see her joy in life with Scott and know that she is happy and healthy is as good as it gets for us.

'My experiences have taught me that I have enough courage, strength and persistence to get through anything. I just put on my joggers, take a deep breath and run up life's hills,' Beck says.

Back home in Australia, she and Scott are making a life together in the Blue Mountains of New South Wales. Beck plans to have a thriving permaculture garden and an energy efficient home in time for the arrival of their first child, which is due on 11 November, 2007.

And so, the cycle of life continues.

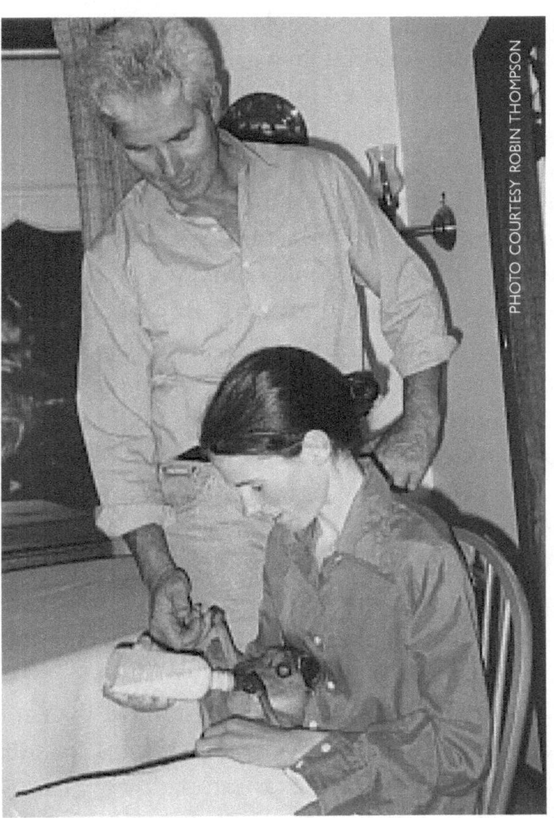

Beck Carroll when anorexic, feeding a baby roo, and her father, Bill Carroll, Orange, New South Wales, 1994

Acknowledgements

A book of personal stories and photographs such as *Reinventing the Bush* can only be completed with the help and encouragement of many people. For his patience, love and good cooking, Bill Carroll, my husband, deserves several medals. Bill drove many thousands of kilometres with me to visit the people I interviewed who were scattered across the country, from outback Queensland to the Territory, the Kimberley and back through South Australia, Tasmania and Victoria. I shamelessly enlisted the aid of my wonderful family – Robbie Carroll for legal advice, Beck Byrne, our daughter, whose sharp eye shone on editing, son-in-law Scott Byrne, for computing advice, and Dunc Carroll, Kim Harper, ThiThi Lam and my sister, Sahni Hamilton, for reading the stories. Thank you all.

To my youthful storytellers who have stuck by me over years of interviews and being photographed in your vigorous and ever-changing lives, you give the inspiration, honesty and zest to these tales. Your collective experiences, wisdom and humour will hold hope for many other young people around the country and shed light on youth for those to whom it is in the past. Thanks also to the partners, parents and friends of my storytellers for your generosity and friendship, and to my friends across Australia who cheered me on with a meal, a drink or a bed.

People always ask how I found such good subjects. The answer is – with help. I am grateful to all of you who recommended people: Alex Dowling, Annette Wylie, Elaine Reeves, Cathy McGowan, Jill Jordan, Geoff Davis, Dr Rod Mitchell, Marg Francis, Jan Richardson, Jeanette Long, Nic Kentish, Tim Fischer, Joe Ross, Fatima al Qarakchy and Robbie Carroll.

In the writing stage, my friend and talented writer, Susan Temby, tirelessly edited stories, encouraged me and kept reminding me that good writing is digging for meaning and expressing it clearly and simply. Thanks to graphic designer Peter Murphy for his great job in preparing the photos, and to Julie Evans and Robbie Scott for resurrecting my ailing computer.

Film Australia provided initial funding for researching a documentary in 2003, which enabled me to make my first trip, with filmmaker Dave Roberts, to start interviewing some of the people who are in this book.

Wherever possible I have attributed sources within the stories. However, I want to acknowledge the many people whose contribution has enhanced this book: poetry by Glen Sheppard and James Fitzpatrick; artwork by Em Murphy; subject photos of subjects by their family members, friends and professional photographers; additional perpectives from videos – *Message from Moree* produced by Judy Rymer and *Rainmaker*, a Canadian documentary; statistical material from the Commonwealth of Australia Bureau of Statistics; and, in particular, insightful interviews with families and mentors of my subjects. Thank you all.

On a sad note, I had asked our friend and local Independent member for the federal seat of Calare, Peter Andren, who was a great champion for rural Australia, to write the Foreword. However, Peter was struggling with pancreatic cancer and died on 3 November 2007.

My publisher, ABC Books, has striven to produce a high-quality book of interest to all Australians. Thank you so much to manager Stuart Neal, managing editor Helen Littleton, and the production and design teams. Thanks, too, to copy editor Sandra Goldbloom Zurbo.

To all those on the marketing end – where would we be if a book didn't sell? Thanks to the ABC, book launchers and a team of enthusiastic promoters for your two bob's worth.

Last, to the readers – I hope that, in these stories, you find ideas, insight and inspiration.